CITY
OF
LAST
CHANCES

Contents

Factions of the City of Ilmar

Allorwen – from the nation of Allor
Armigers – the aristocratic families of Ilmar
Divinati – from the nation of the Divinates
Gownhall – the Ilmari university
Herons – resistance faction of the riverfolk
Indwellers – the people of the Anchorwood
Lodges – criminal gangs
Loruthi – from the nation of Lor
Ravens – resistance faction of the Armiger families
Shrikes – murderers for the resistance
Siblingries – workers' organisations
Vultures – resistance faction of the Ilmar streets

Factions of the Palleseen Occupation

Temporary Commission of Ends and Means – the ruling body of Pallesand
Palleseen Sway – the occupied territories as a whole
Perfecture – an individual occupied territory
School of Correct Erudition (Archivists) – responsible for learning and magic
School of Correct Appreciation (Invigilators) – responsible for art and the judiciary
School of Correct Exchange (Brokers) – responsible for trade
School of Correct Conduct (Monitors) – responsible for military and enforcement
School of Correct Speech (Inquirers) – responsible for religion, language and espionage

Dramatis Personae

Aullaime – Allorwen conjurer with the Siblingries
Benno – Vulture thug
Blackmane – Allorwen pawnbroker
Fellow-Monitor Brockelsby – Correct Conduct
Carelia – one half of the Bitter Sisters, Vulture leader
Cheryn – Vulture thug
Sage-Invigilator Culvern – Perfector of Ilmar, Correct Appreciation
Dorae – Allorwen antiques dealer
Dostritsyn – ruin-diver
Mother Ellaime – Allorwen landlady
Emlar – student
Ergice – Vulture thug
Companion-Monitor Estern – Correct Conduct
Evene – the other half of the Bitter Sisters, Vulture leader
Fleance – Heron gambler
Fyon – Shrike murderer
Archivist Gadders – Correct Erudition
God – divine entity
Maestra Gowdi – Gownhall master
Grymme – ruin-diver
Mother Guame – Allorwen brothel-keeper
Fellow-Inquirer Hegelsy – Correct Speech
Hellgram – bouncer at the Anchorage, foreigner
Hervenya – student
Hoyst – hangman
Jem – Divinati bartender at the Anchorage
Kosha – priest, Yasnic's master, dead
Langrice – keeper of the Anchorage

Lemya – student
Petric Lesselkin – Siblingry scrapherd
Meraqui – ruin-diver
Companion-Archivist Nasely – Correct Erudition
Nihilostes – priestess of the divine scorpionfly
Fellow-Broker Nisbet – Correct Exchange
Sage-Archivist Ochelby – Correct Erudition
Father Orvechin – Siblingry leader
Orvost, the Divine Bull – divine entity
Maestro Ivarn Ostravar – Gownhall master
Maestro Porvilleau – Allorwen Gownhall master
Archivist Riechy – Correct Erudition
Ruslav – Vulture thug
Statlos Shrievsby – officer, Correct Conduct
Sachemel Sirovar – former head of the family, dead
Shantrov Sirovar – Armiger and student
Vidsya Sirovar – Armiger and Raven
Fellow-Invigilator Temsel – Correct Appreciation
Tobriant – Allorwen furniture maker
Johanger Tulmueric – Loruthi merchant
Maestro Vorkovin – Gownhall master
Yasnic – priest
Zenotheus, Scorpionfly God of Chaos – divine entity

Yasnic's Relationship with God

Yasnic the priest. Thin and not young, though not quite old. Half lost in clothes tailored for a larger man in the voluminous Ilmari style. Face hollow, hair greying before it should, thinning, creeping back from his temples like an army that, seeing its opposition is time, no longer has the will to fight…

That morning, God was complaining again. Yasnic lay crunched up in bed, knees almost to his chin and his feet twined together. Trying to tell from the way the light filtered in through the filthy window whether the frost was just on the outside, or on the inside again. He could have put a hand out to touch the panes and check. He could have put a foot out and kicked out at God. Or the far wall. It was, he decided, a blessing. A small room held his body heat longer. If he'd been able to afford anything larger, then he'd have needed a hearth and to buy wood or coal, or even magical tablethi, to heat the place.

"It's cold," God said. "It's so cold." The divine presence was curled up on His shelf like an emaciated cat, and about the same size. He had shrunk since the night before, and perhaps that, too, was a blessing. Sometimes Yasnic could do with a little less God in his life, and here he was this morning, and God was smaller by at least a quarter. He gave thanks, his knee-jerk reaction ingrained from long years of good upbringing from Kosha, the previous priest of God. Back when Ilmar had been a more tolerant place, and old Kosha and Yasnic and God had lived in three rooms above a tanner's and had meat at least once a twelveday.

Not a twelveday, he reminded himself. The School of Correct Exchange was levying fines and making arrests for people using the old calendar, he'd heard. He had to start thinking in terms of a seven-day week, except then he couldn't look back on the way things had been and quantify the time properly. How often had they had meat, back when he'd been a boy learning at Kosha's knee? What was seven into twelve or twelve into seven or however it might work? His mathematics weren't good enough to work it out. And so, obscurely, it felt as though a swathe of his memories was locked away by the new ordnances. Also, he'd just given thanks to God that he had less God in his life, and God, the recipient of those thanks, was right there and staring at him accusingly.

"I need a blanket," said God. "It's only the beginning of winter, and it's so cold."

God looked all skin and bones. He wore rags. It was only a season since Yasnic had sacrificed a good shirt to God, but the diminished state of the faith – meaning Yasnic – tended to mean anything God got His hands on didn't last. A blanket would go the same way.

"I only have one blanket," Yasnic told God.

"Get another one." God stared at His sole priest from His place on the shelf up by the low ceiling. His spidery hands were gripping the edge, His nose and wisps of beard projecting over them. His skin was wrinkled and greyish, hollowed until the shape of His bones could be seen quite clearly. "In the old days I had robes of fur and velvet, and my acolytes burned sandalwood—"

"Yes, yes, I know." Yasnic cut God off. "I only have this blanket." He lifted the threadbare covering and regretted it instantly, the chill of the morning taking up residence in a bed with room only for one. "I suppose I'm getting up now," he added pettily.

"Please," said God. Yasnic stopped halfway through forcing numb feet into his overtrousers. God looked in a bad way, he had to admit. It was easy just to think that God was being selfish. God had, after all, been very used to people doing what He said and giving Him all good things, back in the day. Back in a day long before Yasnic, last priest of God, had come along. Their religion had been dying for over a century, ever since the big Mahanic Temple had been raised. And yes, Mahanism had actively spoken against other religions, but more, they'd just... expanded to fill all the available faith. People went where the social capital was. And now, under the Occupation, there really were people purging religions. Making arrests for Incorrect Speech. *Just as well it's only me and God*, Yasnic thought. *Easier to go unnoticed.*

"Ask the woman," God said. "Ask her for another blanket. I'm cold."

"Mother Ellaime will not give us another blanket," Yasnic said. In fact, their landlady would more likely want to ask about last twelved—last week's rent. And that was another thing, of course. Since the Occupation, everything had to be paid sooner, because of the weeks. And he couldn't quite make the maths work, but it seemed he was paying more each day of the seven than he had each day of the twelve. And it wasn't as though being the sole surviving holy man of God actually brought in much. There were few perks and no regular take-home wage. And, under the Occupation, begging meant risking arrest for Incorrect Exchange.

"I'll see what I can do." Clothes on, he shambled out of the room and went down for tea. One thing Mother Ellaime did provide her boarders with was a constantly churning samovar by the fire, and both fire and tea were just about enough to set up Yasnic for a day's scrounging.

God hadn't been with him on the stairs but was sitting beside the samovar down in the common room. Yasnic took down a cup from its hook and filled it with dark green, steaming liquid. He wanted to avoid Mother Ellaime's notice as he jostled elbows with his fellow boarders to get space at the single table. God was there, though. God was hunched cross-legged on the tin plate Yasnic's neighbour had eaten porridge off.

"Ask her," God insisted.

"I won't do it," murmured Yasnic. His neighbour, the big man named Ruslav who never seemed to have a job but always seemed to have money, stared at him. He couldn't see God sitting in the remains of his porridge. He probably thought Yasnic wanted to lick his plate clean. Jealously, he pulled it closer to himself, making God scrabble for balance. Yasnic winced, aware that everyone was looking at him now, even the student girl who'd turned up a tw—two weeks ago, and whom he dreaded talking to. She was very clever, and Gownhall people loved to argue metaphysics. He was afraid he'd listen to her tortuous logic too much and then look around for God, only to find God wasn't there anymore. And he was afraid of what he might feel, if that were ever the case.

"Ask," God insisted peevishly. "I command it."

"Mother," Yasnic said. "I don't suppose I could beg another blanket from you?" Loud enough to carry to the old woman. Aware that his quiet words were expanding to fill the room. Feeling the student's judging eyes on him. Feeling ashamed. And it wasn't even a useful shame, the sort that earned you credit with God or, in this case, got you a blanket, because Mother Ellaime was already shaking her head. And if there was a little more money, there might be another blanket. And likely that would mean someone at the table, who had a little less money, would be missing a blanket, because it was a closed blanket economy here at Mother Ellaime's boarding house. And if it had just been Yasnic, he would have accepted the lack of a blanket and known that he was making someone else's life better, and tried to warm himself with that. But it was God, and God was old and petty and selfish, but God was also cold, and Yasnic had given himself into God's service. And so he begged Mother Ellaime, with the whole table listening archly to every word. With Ruslav, who probably had two blankets or even three, snickering in his ear. God was cold, and God didn't have anyone else. And it was all for nothing because there wasn't another blanket to be had, not without money he didn't possess.

When darkness and the cold at last drove him back to the boarding house that night, he still didn't possess the money. He'd tried to find work, because he could translate two dead languages, he could teach, he could sing, and even though he was a priest, he could also lift and carry and scrub. Nobody wanted him to do any of those things, or at least not if it meant giving him any money. He mostly begged, but nobody wanted to give him money for that, either.

The common room seemed swelteringly hot as he came in, the fire banked profligately high, so that he was loosening his collars immediately and shrugging out of his shapeless, too-big coat. God was waiting for him by the samovar. Even smaller, of a size to fit into the teacup Yasnic reached down. He found barely half a cup left in the urn. The discovery felt like a blow. It had never happened before. Mother Ellaime treated her tea-making responsibilities with considerably more fervour than he treated his duty to God, and that was with God actually sharing a room with him.

"Ah…" Hearing his own voice, thin and cracked.

The room was oddly quiet. He hadn't actually registered its contents, save for God – whom he could always see clearly – and the samovar, which he had found by long familiarity and the smell of roasting tea. He had the sense of more people than usual present, and a peculiarly pregnant silence as of all of them staring at him. He rubbed at his eyes and squinted, mole-like.

The front room of Mother Ellaime's boarding house was filled with Palleseen soldiers. Or, if not filled, they had all the seats around the single table, and they had all the tea.

The old woman herself was waiting on them. She'd pulled her shawl close around her to hide the little beaded choker she had about her neck. Not because they might steal it – though they might, glossing the act with the word 'confiscate'. But because it would tell them she wasn't native Ilmari, and though the Occupiers weren't exactly kind towards the locals, they could be a great deal worse if you were from over the border in Allor.

On the far side of the room, the student girl was holding her cup to her chin in both hands, staring at its contents furiously, as though she was divining an angry future there. Mother Ellaime's other lodgers had already made themselves scarce.

With the exception of the student, everyone was staring at him. The soldiers had definitely made the place their own. There were boots up on the table beside the peaked caps they'd taken off. Their long batons were propped carelessly against table-edge and chair-back. One had slid off onto the floor, utterly unregarded. The gold of its tableth gleamed, drawing the eye. *Death*, it said. *I bring death*. The crooked characters of sorcery glittered on its little face: the whispered word that would have it discharge its burden of magic with lethal effect.

The soldiers' uniforms were familiar from every street corner since the war ended and the Occupation began: the boots, the brass buttons, the uncomfortably close cut of everything, like the Palleseen preferred. Half were in the charcoal of the Occupiers. The rest wore paler grey. Locals. Because there weren't many walks of life prospering in Ilmar right now, but 'collaborator' certainly was. The Palleseen wanted the Ilmari to police themselves, they said, under Correct principles of law and thought. Three years under the boot and it was already working very well. And perhaps a few of those men in the pale grey were shifty about meeting Yasnic's gaze, but he knew any residual shame in them would curdle soon enough. An extra kick at a beggar, another neighbour reported to the Schools. Once you wore that uniform, it was easier to embrace it than to live a life divided against itself.

"I just wanted tea," he told them.

One of them stood, their officer, the Statlos. His face was bleak. "Again, please," he said. Except he said the words in Pel.

"Forgive me, Statlos," Yasnic said quietly, in the same tongue. "Tea. Just tea." And it was easy, Pel. It had been designed that way by all the clever men over on the Pallesand Archipelago. A new language, new thought, new correctness. Forward to perfection! Except somehow, an Ilmari speaking Pel always sounded different to the Occupiers. Cruder, subservient, no matter how they worked on the words.

"You heard your honoured guest," said their Statlos to Mother Ellaime. "Get the man some tea."

The look the old woman shot Yasnic as she hunched over to the samovar told him just how little she'd needed her day to get any worse. He tried to help her bring fresh water over, but she wouldn't let him.

"Why are they here?" he whispered.

"Something at the Anchorwood. In case of trouble," she said. Speaking Maric, her Allorwen accent came and went.

The student girl was sidling close. Yasnic winced and tried to find a smile from somewhere. "Good evening, my child," he tried. She was perhaps eight years younger than he was, though he felt there was at least twenty years between them in ground-down experience and misery. She looked fresh-minted and sharp-edged.

"Excuse me, rasophore." She eyed him. "You are a priest, Mother said?"

Yasnic grimaced. "I'm not of the Temple." Aware that he had just admitted something that would get him arrested if any of the soldiers had heard. "No 'robe-bearer', I'm sorry."

"I no longer go to Temple," she said. The hushed words came out hard as spat stones. The Mahanic Temple, spiritual guide of Ilmar and the rest of occupied Telmark, had survived the Occupation despite the Palleseen's well-known loathing of religion. The established priesthood had made accommodations. Their sermons echoed the Occupiers' Correct Thought. It hadn't sat well with a lot of people, but to Yasnic – constantly strung between the tenets of his faith and his hungry belly – it was forgivable. Perhaps not to this girl though.

"Will you bless an endeavour?" she asked him flatly.

Yasnic exchanged glances with God. In that moment, the girl seemed to have enough fire in her to go and murder half the Occupiers' Perfecture. "I… don't really…"

"Tonight is very important," she told him. "To me and to a friend. A friend who can buy me another blanket, after I give you mine."

He coloured. She had been listening that morning, then. And here he was, known as a priest who couldn't afford bedclothes. "I…" He sought out God, standing indignantly by the samovar.

"She's not of the faith," God told him. "I won't." Little fists on hips, beard stuck out pugnaciously.

"If you could perhaps… make an allowance this once. Because it is so cold and will only get colder." Aware that the girl was looking where he was looking and seeing nothing.

"It doesn't work like that." There was a whining tone to God's voice, as though He too was bitter at the strictures of the universe. "Bring me the faithful, priest. Or convert her here and now. But to unbelievers, nothing. You know how it is."

And Yasnic, last believer in God, did know. And God's commandments also forbade a priest helping *himself*, because that would be selfishness and not virtue. And so God's power, whatever that was actually worth, ventured forth not at all, and the girl would get no blessing, and he would get no blanket.

Unless I lie. And he lifted a hand, three fingers together for benediction, the fourth crooked so he could flick away evil. And there should be holy water, but the last of *that* had gone to the Occupiers and their insatiable thirst for anything with power in it. And the girl straightened, her facing lighting up. She didn't believe in God, but she believed in him.

"I can't, I'm sorry," he told her. "For myself, Yasnic, I give you every blessing I can in your endeavour. But for God, I cannot give you His blessing. He is... particular."

And it was a miserable thing, but somehow, she seemed to take it positively, and she went to her room – one of the ground-floor ones that was bigger and had its own fireplace – and came back with a blanket, a moth-eaten piece with some embroidery still on it, better than his own.

"I haven't earned this," he told her. "It wasn't a proper blessing." But she thrust it into his hands anyway, with a little smile of pity. And he saw she thought he was mad. Mad but honest. Apparently, that was enough to get you a blanket these days. "Please tell me you're not going to do something violent."

She blinked at him. He had the sense that she was actually flattered he'd believed it of her. "It's an art exhibition," she said, as though embarrassed it wasn't slitting the throat of the Perfector.

The Statlos of the soldiers was staring at the pair of them. Yasnic knew the man was about to take the blanket, purely because he could.

Even as he thought it, there came a shrill whistling echoing distantly over the rooftops. The familiar signal of a Palleseen patrol calling for reinforcements. The soldiers were jumping to their feet, batons to hand. Chairs were kicked backwards. Two cups, slapped down carelessly at the table-edge, toppled towards the floor. The student girl caught one, but the other shattered. Mother Ellaime stared at it sadly. The soldiers were gone in a flurry of uniforms, leaving the door flapping on its hinges.

They heard shouting a little later, and the faint rattle of batons being discharged, but Mother Ellaime had barred the door by then, and nobody felt like going to see what it was about.

Instead, Yasnic went out into the little yard at the back of Mother Ellaime's boarding house. It was where the woman hung washing out, a space small enough he could have lain down and put his head against one fence while the soles of his feet touched the far one. There he made a tiny fire from scrapings of tinder, just enough to catch one corner of the blanket. He'd thought of trading it with his own threadbare covering and burning that instead, but that would be putting himself before God. He let the embroidered blanket burn, thinking of the work skilled hands had put into it, a generation or more back. And here he was, turning it to ash. But that was how you sacrificed to God. And back in the day, it had been great valuables, rich meals, prayers written on fancy paper in gold ink. But now, it was an old blanket because God was cold.

Soon after, the news burned down the street like a wildfire. The Sage-Archivist of the School of Correct Erudition, second most powerful man in the Perfecture's hierarchy, had been killed in the Anchorwood, just two streets away.

The Final Moments of
Sage-Archivist Ochelby

The Sage-Archivist. A dignified old man, prosperous without being fleshy, because the Palleseen valued moderation in all things save ideology. Someone people felt they could confide in, so that when their doors were kicked in and they were taken off for re-education it always came as a surprise. A dagger of ambition in the sheath of a generous uncle with a pocket full of sweets.

Sage-Archivist Ochelby had a kindly face. It crinkled in pleasant, paternal ways when he was conducting the more demanding tasks his position required. Such as deconstructing primitive magical belief systems – a task that often involved deconstructing primitive magicians. He had, in his career, taken action that might be seen as distasteful – certainly to foreigners, perhaps even to some of his fellow Palleseen. Sometimes those acts had been to bring the perfection of Pallesand to the untidiness of the outside world. Sometimes they had more to do with his own career in the School of Correct Erudition, and that was regretful. Personal ambition was imperfect, after all. The hierarchy of talent should admit none of it. And yet, he had undercut rivals, stamped down promising subordinates, denied applications, curried favour and played favourites. And this was, he concluded, simply a sign of how much work there was to do, in bringing perfection. He worked tirelessly for a world in which a flawed vessel such as he could not use such underhand tactics to prosper. But until then...

Back home, the real power was held by the Temporary Commission of Ends and Means. Everyone knew the days of the Commission were numbered. That was, in fact, the first axiom of the Commission, recited whenever it was in session. The same perfectly formulated words had been used when the Commission first convened several centuries ago, affirming its own transient nature and its willingness to disband the moment lasting perfection had been brought to the rest of the world. Until then, the Commission ruled, and Sage-Archivist Ochelby had his eye on a seat there. But those seats were filled by the backsides of ambitious oldsters just like him, and they'd stamp him down, ruining his career just as he'd ruined the careers of all his own underlings who had been just a bit too capable. Ochelby needed a triumph to distinguish himself, and it was that desire which had brought him here to Ilmar. Here, in fact, to this little stand of trees on the outskirts of one of the meanest districts of the city, and the hostelry that stood by them. A placard above the door displayed only the symbol of an anchor. Ochelby tutted. An establishment run according to principles of Correct Exchange would have man-high boards setting out tariffs, regulations, prices and permits, so that any prospective patrons might enter properly informed. And it would be so, in time. Perfection would come to the city of Ilmar. He wasn't here to enforce ordnances. That was menial work not befitting the second most senior academic of the Ilmari Perfecture. He made a mental note to remind his secretary to send a memo to the Brokers about it. It was always a joy to further the perfection of the world by adding to another School's workload.

His secretary was standing with the soldiers, looking at that little stand of trees. She was barely out of the phalanstery. He preferred to surround himself with youth. His preference for assistants and personal staff of twenty years at most had attracted some attempts at censure from those who suspected him of improper use of resources. That kindly, crinkly face of his was exactly the countenance of a man who used his position to sleep with his subordinates. In truth, Ochelby's tastes were more exotic. He had slaked them earlier, as a little personal celebration before embarking on tonight's grand voyage of discovery. Another flavour of imperfection in his nature. Another stain of wrongness that he and his peers would eventually steam out of the fabric of the world, leaving it all starched and neatly folded. But until then, he would indulge his little peccadillos. And Ilmar was well-supplied for those of his particular kink. There was a discreet establishment that knew him, whose bawd was a skilled conjurer and knew to keep her mouth shut.

Not lechery, then, but merely caution that meant his secretary was twenty years old and so wide-eyed he wondered the orbs didn't just pop from her head. A steady parade of disposable youngsters meant he didn't have to watch his back. He'd trade innocence for capability any day. He'd had quite enough intradepartmental skirmishes to get this far. He wasn't interested in any underling using him as a rung on their own ladder.

This one was Companion-Archivist Nasely, unless that had been the last one. She was staring at the trees and shaking her head.

"I don't understand, magister," she told him. "You can see right through to the other side. There can't be more than twenty trees there."

"You don't understand because it is not wholly understood," he told her, in his best crinkly-faced kindly tones. "You see through the trees now because the moon isn't up yet. We have a little time. Let us patronise the establishment."

There were a good number of patrons already there, but most of them left soon after Ochelby and his escort moved in. Twenty armed Palleseen soldiers took up more room than mere physical presence might suggest, especially in the minds of a conquered people. Ochelby considered detaining and questioning them, just to pass the time. It was more than likely many had something to hide. Winkling it out of them might be an amusing way to wait for moonrise. After all, people came to the Anchorage – came to Ilmar as a whole, in fact – because they thought there was an escape here. And sometimes, if the moon was right, and if they possessed the proper key, a door might be found. Outside these walls, within that little grove.

The Anchorage was an old building, wood-built, predating anything else nearby. It wasn't in the local style which preferred brick and tile, plain walls with coloured borders. The central taproom rose to a peaked space defined by the slope of the eaves. The visible beams and ceiling had been carved with knotted, irregular vines like grasping hands. Twin rows of pillars in a similar style turned what should have been a pleasantly open space into something secluded and shadowed. The place was full of little tables half hidden from each other, alcoves and cubbyholes, odd little balconies and spyholes. Little brass trinkets, bones and wooden carvings hung in looping strings across the space above without discernible pattern. Undisciplined, Ochelby felt. He'd already seen one unimaginative Fellow-Monitor's request to tear it down. And eventually, they would tear it down. But first, it would give up its secrets to the School of Correct Erudition. As would the grove beyond. As would what was beyond the grove. To perfect the world, one must first understand it, after all. Should such understanding bring with it personal power and status fit to catapult a humble Sage-Archivist to the Commission, then Ochelby was willing to make the appropriate sacrifices. Perhaps literally. Another advantage of access to a constant train of young secretaries without any important departmental connections.

"Magister."

The solid-built woman stood at the end of a couple of levelled batons, but if the weapons concerned her, she gave no sign of it. She wore those messily loose Maric clothes: blouse, skirt and apron. Her headscarf was about her throat like a neckerchief. Or perhaps it was just a neckerchief. More uncertainty and imperfection. Her hair was dark, shot with grey, face flat and the colour of tanned leather – like most of the locals. They had met before: she'd been his guest then, a routine interrogation. The proprietor of the Anchorage should have been a mine of lore about the Wood, but she'd proved as dull and ignorant as most of the locals. Langrice, her name was. A sly woman, his notes said. An opportunist.

He gifted her with a smile, nodding permission for his escort to accept the mulled cider that a tall, bony outlander was proffering them. The small woman behind the bar wasn't local either – one of the Divinati, from the look of her. Native Ilmari wouldn't work here, Langrice had said.

"Your man there," he said. "I don't recognise the look."

Her eyes flicked to her employee. "He came through the grove, magister."

It wasn't often Ochelby was surprised, but there it was. "Not an Indweller, surely?"

"Magister, no. A traveller. Lost. Searching."

"And what wonders is your man there searching for, that he must serve drinks and mop floors?" Ochelby wrinkled his nose. *Undisciplined, all of it. Everything out of its correct place.*

"His wife, magister."

Ochelby had his escort bring the man over. Tall, hollow, a warrior's height and long bones. Wearing Maric clothes awkwardly, standing awkwardly. Ochelby sniffed. *I should take him in.* Honestly, he should take up everyone at the Anchorage. Half of them might be magicians ripe for interrogation or decanting, half might be trying to slip out of the Perfecture, if they could only put together the necessaries for safe-conduct. Ochelby patted his satchel at the thought, feeling the reassuring jut of the little bundle. Even a Sage-Archivist could not be lax with his precautions.

Most of the patrons at the Anchorage were probably just the regular sort of criminals; none of these groups was mutually exclusive. He let the rabble cower and fear and sneak away, and judged that his mere presence here was sufficient contribution towards universal discipline and perfection.

Then the Indwellers arrived.

They came masked, faces hidden behind curved plates of wood painted with stripes of white and green, violet and orange. No eyeholes, no mouth, just a jagged blankness. They came robed and cloaked, their bodies strung across with cords from which dangled charms and bird legs and little skulls. They carried staves. They came from the trees, that little stand of trees out there.

Everyone in the taproom went silent the moment they appeared. Here was a superstitious dread that predated Ilmar-the-city, that came from when these lands had merely been river winding through forest at a mountain's foot. Even Ochelby, who had tried to cut all such foolishness out of his heart decades before, felt it.

The lead Indweller struck his – her? – staff on the sawdust and boards of the floor. Langrice gestured, and a mug of mulled cider made its way hand-to-hand from the small woman at the bar to the lanky wife-hunting foreigner to Langrice's grasp. She proffered it, and it was accepted, an ancient exchange. When the Indweller pushed that mask half up to drink, Ochelby flinched despite himself.

The mouth and chin beneath were painted with jagged patterns, lightning-bolt puzzle pieces of black and white, red and tan. He still couldn't see the eyes or discern the gender, or anything about them. His inability to categorise the figure felt like a wound in the world. He was grateful when the Indweller's mask fell back into place.

"Who goes?" A soft voice, quiet and unknowable. Ochelby sensed a little twitch from two or three across the bar, who would have been leaping up and begging their chance to leave Ilmar this secret way. And perhaps they had the means and protections to let them do it. Or perhaps they were just desperate enough to risk the crossing anyway, reckless enough to doubt the stories.

"I and my retinue shall travel with you," he announced. "No others." He faced up to that mask, choosing two white slashes and fixing on them as if they were eyes. *Order out of chaos*. The chaos regarded him for a moment, and then the thin shoulders beneath the mantle shrugged.

"No others?" The Indweller spread wide arms, lifted the tip of their staff to jangle at the ornaments suspended above that echoed the strings of charms across their own torso. The desperation of the other would-be travellers was like a scent in the air. But there would have to be another time for them. Ochelby would have no fugitives as travelling companions. This was to be a formal embassy from Pallesand to distant lands.

Distant lands. That was the truth that had filtered out of Ilmar and across the sea to the Commission. *There are yet realms of power we have no foothold in. Someone must meet with the lords of these places, give them our greetings and spy them out so that we might bring perfection to them.* And partly, that was the dream, and partly, it was that any distant place reached through a sometimes-open path through a magical world must surely be magical. Which meant power, to be taken and decanted for a thousand mundane uses, the little learnings that made Pallesand supreme. Ochelby was travelling with fine words and diplomatic credentials; he would be laying the trail for an army.

He and his retinue left the Anchorage with the Indwellers, his soldiers marching along suspiciously, clutching their batons. *There will have to be a more regular way to make this crossing*, Ochelby knew. Perfection could not be made to rely on this capering band of mummers for every trip. He would take readings and measurements as they travelled, and soon enough, the Indwellers could be done away with, along with all the ridiculous traditions the Ilmari held to. Up to and including Langrice and the Anchorage. The Perfecture would build an austere set of offices here, with a barracks and a properly indexed library, and one more piece of unruliness would yield to order's crusade.

"Do you see clear through the trees now?" he asked Companion-Archivist Nasely.

She did not. Nobody could. The dark between the trees went on forever.

When the time came to step within that darkness, he waited for the hesitation in himself. That primal fear he'd be ashamed to admit, and that no man of his station and rationality should own to. When it failed to light on him, he was pleased. He had his rituals, in the face of the unknown. He had completed the last of the paperwork on his desk that morning, and then he had gone quietly to Mother Guame's circle house and stoked his fires by indulging his particular lusts. Those acts that bolstered his sense of control over the cosmos, be it never so wild and mutinous. No more gratifying lover than one bound to your will by pentacle and arcane word, after all. He smiled at the memory and rallied his people.

"Tell me of Scrymisa," he demanded of one of the Indwellers, once they were within the trees. Once their progress had taken them far enough into that dense and trackless tangle of trunks and canopy that any pretence of occupying the same landscape as Ilmar was gone. Head in this direction from the city, and you'd be halfway up a mountain by now. Their progress had taken them mostly downhill if Ochelby was any judge. Downhill, into warmer climes, too. Not balmy by any means, but he was sweating under the fine robes he'd brought, and the soldiers plainly wanted to doff their half-capes and loosen their collars. *It would be undisciplined*, he decided. He forbad it. All around them the air hung with moisture, fuzzed to mist between the trees. *And so we do need guides, at least for now.* Except he had a curious sense of *back*, the one direction this gloomy wood permitted. He could have turned and walked out. The one thing he wasn't was *lost*. He could not account for it, but the idiosyncrasy would yield to appropriate study. One more topic to assign to an underling when he returned.

He'd aimed his question at the Indweller he thought had been talking at the Anchorage. The woman, he decided. She struck him more as a woman and, once he had made that decision, the conclusion seemed so obvious he wondered how he could have questioned it. *All things in their properly catalogued place. The perfect world has no room for uncertainties and edge cases.*

"I know of no such place," she said.

"The Ilmari know the name," he prompted. "A city."

"The Emerald Shore City? That is one place." Her mask tilted quizzically. Around them, the other Indwellers stopped. There was a tree here that had lost hold on the earth and was leaning perilously against its neighbours, bound to them by moss-bearded vines and lianas. *Messy.* The Indwellers – or someone – had chipped a shelf in the slanting trunk, and there was a handful of little objects there – wooden vials and bowls and the like, crawling with insects that they brushed away gently. They burned something ash-like in the bowls, poured something blood-like into the containers. One had a leather pouch of orange-red pigment at their belt and daubed it in random-seeming marks that began to fade almost instantly. Ochelby wrinkled his nose at it all.

"Scrymisa is the name wayfarers give your city, yes. What do you call it?" Dealing with primitive minds called for great patience, but he could be a patient man until he held sufficient leverage to turn the tables.

"It is not our city. We do not go there," the Indweller told him. Which accorded with at least one theory: these savages were not even connected to the places they could lead one to. Scrymisa, so said those travellers who had returned from it, was a place of wonder and power, dazzling and wealthy, hedonistic and corrupt. And if those last two adjectives marked the place in need of perfection, the first four meant that an expedition to occupy and perfect it would be profoundly beneficial to those commanding the mission. Ochelby licked his lips at the thought.

Scrymisa, the beautiful, might exist in the same world as Ilmar, separated by vast distances that the Anchorwood bridged. Or else, it might be in some otherland, reachable via no other means. Scrymisa and the other places the Wood led to, source of a hundred potent curios, the least of which would make its finder's fortune. *Yes*, he knew, *we will go there. Now we have Ilmar, we will untangle the laws and axioms behind these woods. We will cut trees and lay trails and do away with the need for these ridiculous guides. We will come to Scrymisa and bring them the gift of perfection.* And he, by then, would be on the Temporary Commission and would enjoy his status there for the rest of his days. In his wake, he'd leave the Ilmari's superstitions severed on the floor. They'd curse him as the destroyer of all they held dear. Their grandchildren would praise his name as the man who brought them reason and order.

Then the beasts came.

This much, at least, he was prepared for. His soldiers shrank back around him, levelling their batons, but he waved them down archly. This, more than needing guides, was why none crossed recklessly into the Anchorwood. Hungry things hunted there.

They were not quite as they'd been described to him, but then, everyone described them slightly differently. They were tall, flattened, a great deal like fish. Great goggling eyes like plates, pale flanks striped with dark bars. Mackerel things walking on lizard legs with jaws enough to gulp down three of his soldiers in a single lunge. Their teeth were not the needles of fish but jagged bone wedges like the interlocking gears of a living machine. Their tails were those of crocodiles. Their glassy gaze was detached and clinical.

He reached into his satchel that he carried with him always. Within it were his papers, that would tell any citizen of Pallesand how senior he was in the hierarchy of the

Schools. Within it, also, was that special identification the Anchorwood demanded, if you were to avoid the attention of its ravenous guardians. Ilmar was crammed with fugitives and malcontents seeking escape through the Anchorwood, but most would live out their meagre store of days without stepping into the trees. Because these little bundles of sticks and feathers, carven wood and precious metals, they were so rare. Their manufacture was the skilled work of a dozen artisans and enchanters. Their components were ruinously expensive or hard to find. The shadow-markets of Ilmar swarmed with fakes. He had not been willing to trust anything his agents and servants in the city had tracked down for him. Instead, he had sent the exacting specifications home to the Archipelago, and there, scholars and smiths and a handful of immigrant experts had created proper and rational credentials. A warding bundle without question, fit to turn aside the monsters of the Anchorwood and give the Sage-Archivist, bringer of unasked-for perfection, safe passage.

The nearest beast took a jerky-quick step towards him, that narrow jaw hanging open and then further open again, and nothing but teeth all the way down inside. Ochelby stared down those dead eyes, or tried to. The thing couldn't even look straight ahead with its weirdly flattened body. He brought out the ward and presented it boldly.

The monster took one more step, its body flexing sidelong down its length, ending with a flail of that armoured, ridge-crowned tail.

"Magister..." Nasely said in a hoarse whisper.

He held in his hand a straw doll. *Not* a bundle of carefully selected and crafted implements wrapped in ritual declamations denying the beasts of the Anchorwood the right to feast on him and his followers. A straw doll, that had felt just like a warding bundle when he reached for it. Reached for it in the satchel that was never not at his side, and never not securely buckled.

Save for when he'd had breeches about his knees and his

robes pooled on the floor behind him, at Mother Guame's. And there, he realised, he had seen this doll. Just a piece of worthless occult dressing, hung on the wall with the other invocations of magicianly grandeur the tired circle house had so little claim to. On the wall when he entered. In his satchel when he left. And the ward, gone.

"Kill it!" he snapped. The Indwellers were just standing back, he saw. The beasts ignored them. They needed no wards. They were of the Wood. "Help us!" he demanded, but they did not seem to hear.

Half his men fired their batons, the tablethi in their sockets flaring briefly with discharged power, bolts of pale magic lashing across the hides of the beasts. They left char but no scar. The monsters gurgled and shook themselves and did not care. One lurched forwards, almost lazily, and snapped up the closest soldier, clamping him in jaws that scissored through uniform and flesh, throwing him up in the air and then gulping him down. A bolt struck it in the fish-belly skin of its throat and was turned aside, no more than light and false fire.

"Kill them all!" Ochelby insisted. He wrestled a baton from one of his men and levelled it at the closest Indweller. "Help us!" They were melting away, he saw. He wasn't even sure how many there had been, but it was fewer and fewer.

He shot her. The one he'd been speaking to. The bolt pierced her chest and flung her back, and she lay still, mask tumbling from her slack face. It achieved nothing. The beasts weren't theirs to control or call off. Then the hungering jaws were among his people, closing on him. He looked for his secretary, because if he could thrust her in front of him, he'd win himself a moment's more life.

She was running. She was already half lost in the trees, heading down that inexplicable thread that led *back*. He howled at her to return, to help him, to take his place. As his escort died, he staggered in her wake, robes snagging, open satchel flapping at his groin.

One of the beasts was momentarily beside him, shouldering him over almost incidentally. It paused, watching him scrabble at the trees for purchase. That huge eye was his whole world.

It made a sound like deep, liquid chuckling.

"Go after her!" he ordered it. "Look, there she goes! She's escaping you! Take her, not me!"

It knocked him down again, an almost playful twitch of its neckless head. He struck at it with the baton, seeing the golden tableth spring from its mounting, becoming lost in the tangle of fern and dead wood. He broke the empty baton across its snout. It did not care.

He cursed it. From his earliest childhood, he called up ancient curses from the rich old Palleseen language that had no equivalents in modern Pel. Words his great-grandmother refused to stop using, that the Commission had taken her away for.

It did not care. It turned its head sideways suddenly, the twist of the movement rippling down the whole of its body. Those merciless jaws gaped. Ochelby screamed, and then the sound died with him as the beast bit down.

A Game of Chaq

Langrice, keeper of the Anchorage: a woman apart, uncanny by association. The thought of what lies beyond her doorstep means respectable Ilmari turn their noses up. You kept strange company, if you kept the lights burning at the Anchorage. Reserved, lean-faced, hardened by time. There had been suitors once, before she chose her profession. Now, none would dare.

The year before, when he'd had her in his interrogation room within the Donjon, the Sage-Archivist had finished his interview by asking, "Given the office you have taken on, you've been strangely cooperative. There is more value in that stand of trees out there than in the whole rest of your city. And yet you've not tried to barter with me or wheedle some concession for your people."

Langrice had shrugged. "Magister." Speaking Pel easily because running the Anchorage meant you needed to be good with languages. "No Ilmari will work for me. It's bad luck. Only the desperate will even come buy a drink from me. Or those who need to leave Ilmar the least convenient way." She'd shaken her head ruefully, as though she'd give up the Anchorage and its trade in a moment if only there was someone else. "They won't even take my money from my hands. I have to send my staff to market, or else pay some middleman. So why, exactly, would I not work with you Palleseen?"

Which interview had been at least one cobble on the road

that led to him striding out with his escort now, following the trailing hems of the Indwellers into the Wood. Hellgram stood at the window and watched, signalling her when the Palleseen had entered the trees.

Langrice went to the hidden door, the one an inconvenient number of people knew about, but not – apparently – the Sage-Archivist.

"They're gone," she called in. "Except for…" Over at the window Hellgram held up two fingers. "Couple of sentries left at the trees, looks like. I'll send Jem out with something warm for them, compliments of the house. Anyone who wants out can get out under cover of that."

The door she'd opened had been just a part of the ornately carved and garlanded wall to the unwary eye. The room within was windowless, and they'd doused the lamps so that no glimmer would creep out and betray them. Now Ruslav was up on a chair with a sparking taper, lighting the collection of purple-and-red-shaded hanging lanterns. The other players sat around the table, eyeing Langrice as if not entirely convinced she hadn't prepared an ambush out in the taproom. She hadn't been lying to the Sage-Archivist about how the Ilmari saw her and this place. She *had* lied about why they might come here. Some came here to play chaq for peculiar stakes.

"Right," she announced to the room. "Let's get back to important business."

Once every twelveday or so, she hosted the Game. Chaq, that ancient clash of tiles and symbols of obscure origin. Some regulars, some who turned up at her door begging for a seat. Generally, she let them in. Her usual crowd liked fresh sheep to fleece. Only if they had the appropriate stake, though. And although there was coin about the table – the old stuff you couldn't spend any more and the Occupiers' tacky little tokens – that wasn't what people came to her table for.

She resumed her seat, trusting to Hellgram to sound the alarm if it looked as though more Palleseen were on their way.

Blackmane, the last game's winner, set up. Everyone dumped coin on the table, because you always started cheap and worked upwards. Langrice racked up her first set of little ivory tiles, skimming the paired icons on them, deciding which she'd play face-up, and which face-down.

Blackmane set down a thumb-sized vessel of dark green stone with gold ornament. "Eroic salve. Vintage Divinates manufacture." His Allorwen accent gave his voice a rough huskiness. He was a big man, one of the great wave of refugees who'd come out of the Palleseen conquest of Allor – the one nobody in Ilmar had seen as anything to be worried about. A lot of those Allorwen had been trying to get out, but most had failed and ended up lodged in the underside of Ilmar like stones in a shoe, trading on the mystique of their traditions. Blackmane's sorcery made him something of a big man in their circles, Langrice understood, but what won him a place at her table was his pawnbroker business. He always had something interesting to stake.

The man after him was Ostravar, the academic from the Gownhall, very much slumming it but also very much too comfortably off to care. He had some crumbly old papers some other academic was probably going to miss if his luck turned. Then came thin, snickering Vidsya Sirovar, who had yet another piece of her family's inheritance to lose, because she never learned and never cared, so long as Langrice let her play. Some day, a Sirovar scion was going to kick in the Anchorage's doors for a reckoning, but until then, Langrice would continue to profit from the dwindling fortunes of the old aristocracy.

Next to her, obviously rattled by the interruption, was a newcomer. He was in off the river, from his clothes, and, though he'd not been at the table before, she'd seen him around. Fleance, his name was, though Blackmane had taken to calling him Flea. And he was jumpy, for sure. Narrow-shouldered and twitching with every tile that clacked down. He'd shown her the device sewn on the inner lining of his coat, as part of his bid to get in the Game. A heron, meaning he was part of that branch of the resistance that moved things up and down river without the Pals seeing. Probably he could get his hands on all sorts, on his travels. Langrice was all for the resistance. It was a rare night her cellars didn't have some weapons or supplies or even people hidden in them, to keep one faction or other sweet. Not exactly rampant patriotism on her part. More that they'd come break her chairs if she ever told them 'no'.

Another couple, going round the table, stakes down and tiles rattling as they built their forts one piece at a time. The first was 'Fish' Cheryn, a resistance woman with another bird badge hidden under her collar. Back before the Occupation, the royal line of Telmark had boasted a phoenix rising from a river as its heraldry, and the unmourned Duke of Ilmar had two fighting hawks on his shield. The squabbling resistance factions had picked the birds that best fit them, and it said a lot about how the fight was going that this gambler's little handmade crest was a vulture: all corpses and waiting. Beside her was Tulmueric, that smooth-talking Loruthi merchant, with his laugh and his sweet-smelling pipe, who turned up whenever he was in town because Langrice had let him into her bed once.

Then Ruslav, street thug and bravo. Some days a patriotic resistance fighter, other times he'd shake you down for pennies. His turn to play, and his tile-fort a tactical shambles, under assault from Tulmueric and Langrice herself. He'd staked a gilded timepiece, gold sun and silver moon motionless. Exactly the thing that you'd need to sell to someone like Blackmane for two coins because its original owner would know it on sight. But then, the Lodge families employed a lot of fools dipping pockets or fishing through windows, and trusted to the upright militia and the Occupiers to weed out the worst and teach wisdom to the rest.

"Ruslav," Langrice prompted him. The look he gave his tiles suggested he had no idea what was on them, but it was all swagger and style when you got two rungs up the ladder of

Ilmar's criminal Lodges. You never let people see you weak. And these days the Lodges had fingers everywhere, given half Ilmar's trade was technically illegal under one Palleseen ordnance or other.

"Screw you all," he said and brought out three gold rings. One had an empty socket instead of a stone, and one looked more brass than anything. Langrice met Blackmane's eyes, but it suited both of them for the stakes to go up. Everyone dipped into satchels and bags and inside pockets; everyone's stake was assessed and topped up with coin if found wanting. Langrice sized up the little Heron, Fleance. He had an impassive face slapped on, but his nerves were clawing visibly all around the edges of it. He put down a hookah of sandalwood and crystal – that was tourist nonsense down in Lor but would likely fetch some sort of price in Ilmar. Tulmueric cackled and jogged Ostravar's elbow, making a louche suggestion. Cheryn pushed her chair back and squinted as though that would change how the tiles sat. Langrice met Blackmane's eyes again. The faces at this table were different every twelveday, save that his was almost always among them. This was the furthest he willingly stuck his neck out of the Allorwen quarter. They knew each other. And sometimes four hands were better than two at a shearing. When Fleance had been whining to get in on the Game, she'd had a sense that, if you picked the little Heron up and shook him, something valuable might fall out of his coat.

Steering a game of chaq was hard, but between them, they made sure Fleance wasn't driven from the table by the sharp practice of the others. She and Blackmane coordinated their attacks on Ostravar and Tulmueric so that, at the close, the riverman would end the game happy while having lost enough to want to get it back. Ruslav was their inadvertent stalking horse, playing wild and badly, his mind on other things. She saw some twisting decision go back and forth over his face as he lost the game and his stake, and wasn't surprised when he stood and made his excuses. The lost timepiece and a handful of tin-tack coin were beneath his notice. If she didn't know him for an unconscionable bruiser, she'd have said he was nervous.

"Got somewhere to be?" she needled.

Ruslav couldn't even muster a glower. She knew the hangdog look from her usual clientele of wastrel thugs. They all liked to pretend they were sophisticates-about-town when they had the coin. He was about to go and sing ballads under some young unfortunate's window.

In his absence, Fleance's talk expanded to fill the space. He was nervous but thought he was playing well, so now he was boasting. He might have talked about the river and where he'd been, which could have been halfway interesting. What was novel to the Ilmari was debased currency to him, though. Instead, he was spilling too much about his business in-city. Clumsy hints at important people he knew, resistance linen he shouldn't be airing. And he was stacking up what looked like a good fortress of tiles, save that she and Blackmane were both positioned to bring it down, if they did the unthinkable and worked together. What were the odds?

He'd laid out two or three pieces of tat by now, barely valuable enough to pass muster as stake save that Langrice and Blackmane had given the nod and the others wouldn't go against the two of them. She still had that whiff of something special in the man's pockets and she wanted to see it. The game was well advanced, and Fleance's brow glittered with sweat as the haul on the table built up just like the tiles. He hadn't realised that the first game of a night was only a palate cleanser. His new stake was just a box of circle chalk, a good set but not exactly vast value. Blackmane leaned forwards ponderously. A flourish of his fingers had the lamp wicks dancing higher.

"That's from Mother Guame's," he murmured.

"It was a gift," Fleance said tightly. He put on a defiantly cocky air. "On account of my performance there."

And the tricks at Mother Guame's weren't exactly in a position to give gifts to their johns, Langrice well knew. And the whole conjuration-bawdy-house business had arisen out of some sacred cultural thing Blackmane's people had brought from Allor, which Ilmar had degraded into vice just as it did with everything. The big Allorwen met her eyes and then looked sidelong at Fleance. It was, he was saying, time to get the shears out.

They let the Game run for a few rounds, each player slapping their tiles down in quick succession, nobody wanting to hold things up. Ostravar was doing well but without solid foundations, Tulmueric already turtling, trying to hold on to what he'd built rather than attacking. Vidsya Sirovar's erratic play had stabilised into something dogged and narrow, even though she'd not stopped drinking since the Game began. Langrice and Blackmane had, between them, an executioner's stand ready to muscle in on Fleance. She let her left eye twitch and wander a moment, the old signal.

Blackmane brought out a brass-bound tusk a foot long and clunked it down on the table. Langrice almost rolled her eyes: she'd seen the damn thing at four previous games. It might as well be his lucky piece because he'd never lost it yet. In his low, accented voice he told them all, "From the last of the Knife-Bearers, the cats that thought like men. Once the property of our dear dead Duke. Previously to be found stabbed through the heart of his uncle, in circumstances mysterious." She could almost recite the pedigree with him by now. "Utterly unique, in provenance and substance, and fat with blood and power, my friends. Now ante up."

Tulmueric weighed his losses and flicked his fortress into disarray. "Too rich," he complained. Cheryn followed suit. Ostravar the Gownhall maestro tried to offer services instead of goods: a sponsorship for any three people who could at least read and write. That went against the table rules, and in the end, he wouldn't quit and dumped a pouch of old money and most of a mechanical monkey on the table. It was missing an arm, which interfered with its intended task of playing the tiny guitar it was holding. He put the pot right with a tableth, the gold lozenges that were standard magic fuel among the Occupiers. You could always find a ready market for them.

Vidsya sighed and took off her signet ring, reciting lineages and virtue against poisoning. There was a folded fan, too, and probably that had its own storied past. Langrice was watching Fleance, though. He was in deep. They'd plucked away all the tat he'd been willing to part with. It lay on the table with his money and everyone else's goods. A fortune. He could buy a new boat and hire a crew, become a big man in the Herons. And his tile-fort was steady, or it must look so to him. She saw his lips twitch, greed and panic fighting over them.

"We're waiting," she told him.

"My boat," he said.

She clamped down with, "If you can't put it on the table, it's no stake." And she doubted the boat was his to wager, but the lawful ownership of a lot that had crossed her table was a matter of debate.

"No, but…" he said, eyes flicking as though trying to escape his head. "I'll split the pot. If someone will lend me. Advance me. I'm good, here. I'm good."

And it would be hilarious, she considered, if he actually *won*. There were face-down tiles she could only guess at. He might be able to hold them all off and sweep the table.

But she didn't think so. She'd read each twitch of him. He didn't have a grand surprise to pull out, or else he was a master at faking nerves.

And nobody would lend him a thing. Ostravar and Vidsya just pinned him with their gazes.

"No, but…" he said again.

Blackmane shifted in his chair, making the feet grind on the floor. He hadn't forgotten that ritual chalk and where it came from. Probably he had some extra reasons, now, for turning the Heron out of doors with nothing in his pockets save regrets.

She watched Fleance reach into his coat. The tension was almost sexual. Even though they weren't in on the hustle, the rest of the table had picked up that something was going on. Tulmueric and Cheryn, refilling their cups from the row of bottles at the corner table, were staring hungrily over. Everyone was watching.

Fleance's look was trapped, defiant. He set down on the table a neatly wrapped bundle of black-lacquered sticks tied about with ribbon and tape that bore a host of minute Pel characters. It was barely five inches long, but it was beautiful. And Langrice had seen plenty of the things in her time – nobody more – but never one like this. Never one so finished and perfect, so finely crafted and neatly lettered. A warding bundle, but not the sort of thing that got faked and resold and passed from hand to desperate hand in the hope it would keep some fugitive safe from the beasts of the Wood.

Far later than it should have, her mind set the immaculately crafted thing and Sage-Archivist Ochelby side by side and found them a perfect match. But he had *already* gone into the Wood and so...

"Oh," she said, for once entirely wrong-footed by events. And then the ground shuddered, the whole of the Anchorage seeming to flex around them. Outside, a woman was screaming, and she heard the shouts of the Palleseen sentries, their shrill whistles, the crackle of baton-fire.

Everyone spilled out into the taproom together, most of them halfway to the door by instinct. Wanting *out* before any soldiers came *in*. Hellgram was at the window, signalling them to stop. She heard a high, terrified voice shrieking that the Sage-Archivist was dead. An answering whistle from somewhere further into the city. Always a damnable patrol close by when you didn't want it.

Hellgram spat something filthy in the language only he spoke. Langrice reached the window in time to see a woman – one of Ochelby's retinue – running off down the street, headed north where she really shouldn't be going. Only after that did she see what the sentries had been shooting at. Somehow, the mottle and stripe of its flanks had slipped her gaze from it. Huge as it was, she'd overlooked it entirely. One of the beasts had come out of the Wood.

She'd never seen one with her own eyes before. Descriptions and tall tales and shaky pictures, certainly. Not this. It loped with a sinuous flex of its fish-like body. There was blood in its jaws and a tattered uniform jacket was snagged on those dagger teeth. It took one of the sentries and shook him into loose joints, then cast him aside. It had other prey in its nose and wouldn't be distracted. It was off after the Palleseen woman, claws tearing up the stones of the road.

"That's never happened," Langrice said, trying to convince herself, and then, "The Pals will be all over this place if one of their big men is dead."

"Game adjourned." Blackmane was already striding towards the door with a face like thunder. The others were scrabbling their goods back into pockets and bags. Vidsya was under the table chasing her signet ring.

A high wail of despair then, to mix with the shouting from outside. "Where is it? Where's it gone?" Fleance, scattering tiles and loose coins from the table as though his treasure might be hidden beneath them somehow. The bundle. Ochelby's bundle, that so neatly explained why the man's assistant had just fled the Anchorwood pursued by a beast. *The Sage-Archivist of the School of Correct Erudition is dead.* The second most powerful man in the Perfecture.

There will be blood on the streets. There will be fires and necks in nooses. And all through this, Fleance was wailing, trying to bar everyone's way to the door. "One of you took it! One of you took it!" And he was right, of course. Someone had possessed the presence of mind to make a grab for the priceless piece of passportery that guaranteed safe passage to better shores, not just for a solitary wayfarer but the whole bristling escort Ochelby had just led to their doom.

Blackmane – three times Fleance's bulk – shoved the man

aside. If the Pals arrived and found an Allorwen on hand, then arrest was just about the best he could hope for. It wasn't as though he hadn't been arrested before, but that hadn't been linked to a dead Palleseen grandee. His usual evasions and string-pulling wouldn't suffice for that. The rest were scrambling after him, Ostravar and Tulmueric, Cheryn and a tottering Vidsya Sirovar. All of them piling out and running away, while the surviving sentry was shooting at the tail of the galloping monster. And there were whistles and shouts as more soldiers ran in to assist. The word would be running on winged feet all the way to the Donjon. There would be Pal Inquirers prying into everything before dawn broke.

And doubtless, everyone from the Game would be replaying the last moments at the table thinking about who'd been in arm's reach of Fleance's ritual ward. Any of them. It could have been any of them.

Fleance turned on her, the last possible target for his grief. "You're responsible!" he shouted. "I need it! The Allorwen thief took it! You have to go get it off him!" He struck at her as though it was her fault, but Hellgram caught his wrist and slung him away, spilling him across the open doorway.

"Go before the Pals get here," she told him.

"You don't understand," he said. "I need it. I have to take it to… I can't. I can't not. You don't." He was crying. "They'll," he got out. "They'll. To me. You don't. Understand."

But Hellgram was a long-limbed, raw-boned son of a bitch, and unnatural with it. When he loomed, Fleance shrank away. Hellgram drove the man out of doors by mere presence, then bolted the portal after.

Nobody is getting any sleep tonight, Langrice knew. She and Hellgram and Jem would be answering questions, and probably at least one of them would get the sort of inquiry that came with a beating attached. And the Pals would learn nothing new, but that wouldn't stop it hurting.

Ruslav in Love Again

Ruslav the soldier. Not a veteran of any actual fighting, but the Lodge families had stolen the word for their own use, as they'd stolen so much else. A big man, heavy-jawed, thick-waisted. Scars of use on his knuckles. The beard cut close to chin and cheeks. The brows teased out and darkened. A little lead under his eyes to give his gaze that penetrating quality. His clothes are of the bright colours and extravagant cuts of the street bravo who always has money and never holds on to it, the barbed rakishness of the made men of Ilmar.

He'd heard the talk from his fellow soldiers, as they'd sat drinking and waiting at the Aunties' pleasure. Or that time the day before when him, Benno and Ergice, they'd had to chastise Sergyen the chandler, who'd been talking to the wrong people about what was in his cellars. And that had been awkward, because Sergyen had either fled the city or already been at the bottom of the river, depending on who you believed, and the Bitter Sisters had been expecting results. In the end, Ruslav and the others had lucked out, though. Some nobody they'd run into had looked a bit like Sergyen in a bad light, especially after he'd lost at cards and had his face carved up for him. And probably the Bitter Sisters weren't fooled, but so long as the real Sergyen stayed gone or dead, it would still serve as a lesson to the next snitch. And they'd gone through all of that, and he'd even held the knife, but it had been sloppy work. His mind had been elsewhere.

Ruslav's in love again, they'd said, half jeering and half envious. So he'd quit their dull-as-arses company and come to Langrice's Game instead, to win or lose his stake outside of that kind of side-eyeing. Except his mind was full of that slow, sweet sense he had when the Pursuit was just starting. He played badly, not even badly enough to amuse himself. He couldn't concentrate.

The object of his ardour had come to Mother Ellaime's just a half-month ago. One more student at the Gownhall, because there were parents, out in wider Telmark, who'd still send their kids to the pit that was Ilmar city just to read books and get talked down to by lecherous old men in long coats. Send and spend, too. The Gownhall squeezed the pennies out of its students and spent it on big dinners and books. Most of the students Ruslav had ever known were dirt poor for anything else. More than a few had ended up in trouble with the Lodges over small-time grifts and swindles as they'd tried to improve their lot. More than a few had ended up taking Lodge coin themselves. Sometimes a good hand with a pen and a familiarity with old books produced a good forger. And every year, a new crop of them kept turning up, despite the Occupation and everything else. True, some of them were just the second or third children of Armigine Hill, the little wart of money where the old aristocracy still clung on in the shadow of the Pals. The Old Duke might be gone – Ruslav spat at the thought, *good riddance!* – but plenty of his by-blows and distant relatives were doing just fine after coming to accommodations with the Occupiers, and a trickle of their progeny still oozed its way under the doors of the Gownhall. The rest, though – like this girl of his – they were children of merchants and artisans and anyone else who had a fistful of coin they didn't need for food, and the delusion that sending their girl or boy to the Gownhall would in some way open doors.

Her name was Lemya. She was fresh out of the provinces. She was, Ruslav could tell, one of those who *believed* in things. She'd already spent a night in the cells because some idiot students had refused to leave some idiot place when the Turncoats had told them to. Not even Occupier patrols, just the locals in their uniforms that were literally a pale imitation of the Pals'. Ruslav knew about that, because he'd been in the cell across the way after being too slow to get out of a punch-up. He'd heard her and her idiot friends arguing about morals and ethics and other things you couldn't eat or stab someone with. He heard that she was being evicted from the little garret she rented because of the arrest, and he'd had a suggestion about that. Hence her ending up in the slightly smaller room Mother Ellaime had going. And at the breakfast table, she met his eyes boldly enough over her tea, and Ruslav had to confess to himself that he was in love again. It was time for the Pursuit.

That was how it went. There were old stories about it from when the Armiger families had been more about charging around in heavy mail and less sitting in rich houses and owning things. The idea had been passed down over the generations like cast-off clothes. Those below aped those above, in fashion, in talk, in pastime, in amours. It was what made life sweet. And the peasants had no time for it, and the merchants and makers were too practical, but when you were a Lodge soldier, you could indulge in life's pleasures.

It was not about the sex. Or rather, eventually it would be about the sex. At the end of the long trail there would be, he hoped, a moment of consummation when all the waiting and the agonising and the delicious thrill of wooing collapsed down into those rude physical motions and exchanges. Good moments, but after that, it would be ended. There would be someone else by then. The exquisite anticipation would be done with.

Until then, he planned his campaign. She wasn't on the hook yet, not by any means. He must woo her a hundred little ways. He must let her obstinacy whet his ardour. And she, ideally, would place obstacles in his way. There would be watchers to be evaded, difficult liaisons, choices where his duty to the Lodge and his private longings clashed. He loved the Pursuit, far more than he actually loved any of the objects of his affections. The weird cocktail of desire, helplessness, strength, weakness – the *purity* of seeking to serve she who disdained him. There were powders and philtres that would enslave you with a single sniff or taste that didn't give the same high as a good romantic Pursuit. And in the end, it didn't matter if the woman rejected him entire, if there was no union. Sometimes that was even better. He could always slip a coin to a working girl or go to a circle house and have something conjured up in the image of his heart's desire. The longing was all. *Ruslav's in love again*, and when they whispered it, they envied him.

Right now, Lemya was doing some student thing. She'd said at the breakfast table there was some *art* business. She made art. Of course she did, and that was right and proper as an object of his passion. She and some other students were having a bunch of her pictures put up. They were going to sell them, and the money would go to… some cause. He hadn't really paid attention to the details, too busy focusing inwards on making sure he got the yearning right. Probably some cause that would get her arrested again, because she was all on fire with outrage about every damn thing the Pals did, just like half the students seemed to be. And he'd been ready to turn up later and hand over coin for the daubs she hadn't sold, as part of the wooing. Admire the work – he hoped it was actually *good*, or that might dampen his fires a bit. He bought art, just like he wore good clothes and drank wine. Lodge soldiers were supposed to put a velvet glove on over their fists, or what was the money *for*? Only, sitting there at the Game, he'd thought about her in some attic with her dullard friends, lumping boxes about, getting into arguments, raising a sweat, her hair writhing out of its bun to hang like tangled writing down her cheek. And he'd lost his stake, and decided it was only right and proper he should be there to help Lemya. That seemed to accord with the principles of the Pursuit that a rake of Ilmar held dear.

She'd mentioned an address, some garret, hard up against the river, where you could just about see the towers of the Gownhall if you squinted and used your imagination. He set off through the streets, already feeling that anticipation. He loved being in love. He'd done it a hundred times. He gave it perhaps a twelveday before she either yielded to his attentions or very definitively made it clear she wasn't going to, at which point, he'd go find someone else to be in love with. Or else she'd end up in the gutter like him. It happened. Often it happened *because* of him. The quarry of his Pursuit ending up within the orbit of his Aunts, becoming just another tool of the Lodge. And that was the death of romance, as far as he was concerned. He needed the object of his affections to have a certain purity and detachment, or at least, he needed to kid himself about it. They had to be *better* than he was, or why else adore them? You couldn't do that with someone from *work*.

There were four students unloading a wagon outside the joint, two to a crate. He just muscled up and hoisted one on his shoulder, enjoying their dismay. They thought he was robbing them, and they didn't dare complain. He leered at them, pasty little insects that they were, and said, "Up the stairs, am I right?" Savouring the sweat of their relief as he turned his coat from thug to friend.

Bookworms, he thought derisively. And possibly, she was mooning after one or the other of them, and that wasn't right. She was too good for weeds like that.

Up at the top of the house was a single room defined by the slope of the roof, so that only a homunculus could have stood upright at the edges. A shortage of straight wall meant they'd had to dangle boards from the eaves to fix the paintings to, so that the whole exhibition swayed gently in the draft from the open door down below. The lanterns they'd hooked up swayed, too, and for a moment, Ruslav felt oddly off-balance, as though he'd found a wild place or the view from a ship's rail here in the heart of the city.

And there she was: Lemya. Sitting at a desk that was just two of the emptied crates upended. She had a little casket, paper and ink, and a stack of coin. A couple of women were standing there with pinched-lemon faces, discussing the nearest daub. So apparently, the business was already underway, even though they were still setting up. Lemya was talking animatedly, and he watched her face light up with all the wonder and the drama, the inner life she had squeezed onto the canvas, that they were so ambivalent about.

Deserves better, and he considered just going over and looming, putting the two women in their place. Who were they anyway? Probably just relatives of some student comrade of hers, coerced to come to this mean place and look at the art, but not willing to part with their pennies. He decided it would be gauche of him, though. He'd keep an eye, in case she ended up in need of a defence he could leap to, but right now, he'd go look at her pictures. He'd prepare some lavish praise, perhaps collar one of the students and exact a couple of educated-sounding comments he could recite to her. If she was the object of his Pursuit, he was honour-bound to admire her work, after all. Even though he didn't really get painting. It was all stuffy-looking rich people and bowls of fruit and the countryside.

The garret was a terrible place for art, he decided. Probably the day would be better, the sun streaming in over the river and lighting up all these gloomy canvases. No telling if the owner would let them stay that long, though.

Ruslav unhooked a lantern and brought it close to the nearest board, where three scenes were hung for his delectation.

A little while later, he heard the Gownhall clock tolling dolorously from across the city and shook himself, unsure precisely how long he'd been there. His eyes flicked about the room – around the same number of people present, but different ones. If a rival had found him there, in that moment, they could have put a knife in his kidneys and he'd not have known it until he hit the ground. And then only because, from down there, he couldn't see the canvases anymore.

They were landscape scenes. He hated landscape scenes. Any peasant could look out of their barn and see a landscape. Except these were no landscapes anyone ever saw. They were vast, even though the canvases were small. Great brooding forests bristled. Ruinous walls and castles loured from clifftops, lit by a half-obscured moon. Chasms choked with barbed brambles. On a lonely road, there might be a rider, a lone traveller with a lantern, armour and mount gleaming with unlikely fire. At the edge of his radiance, perhaps, a beast: bear or wolf or some chimeric blend of creatures, eyes alive with reflected light. They were so real. They were somehow all the more real for being utterly unreal. Were they locations beyond the Anchorwood? Had Lemya travelled through that place and come back with these sights in her head? Ruslav looked on each image in turn and felt as though they were open doorways, and he could hear the lonely wind howl. *A terrible beauty*, his heart whispered to him. And he knew he wanted to go there. To walk the dreadful roads. To stare from the eye-socket windows of those crumbling edifices. To ride the white horse and do battle with monsters.

When he turned his eyes to Lemya again – she was taking money from some ignorant townsman who couldn't possibly appreciate the masterwork he was buying – she seemed to glow in his sight. She seemed to be lit by the hallucinatory moon that glowered down in her paintings. He approached her almost timorously. Not the manufactured abjectness he'd been working up to, but something he'd never felt before. All the games of the Pursuit were gone from him.

She looked up, smiled brightly, just as if she was a regular person. "Ruslav!"

He wanted to kneel before her, but that would have just been part of the Pursuit game, and his head was full of chasms and ruins. It would have been empty exhibitionism – that was all his love had ever been. He was full of something he'd never experienced before, a sickness that had come in through the eyes. Now he tried to expel it through the mouth, but all the words he'd ever relied on were just vacant platitudes.

"I like," he said, "the pictures."

She nodded enthusiastically. "I know." Leaning into him, so that he felt his breath catch at the closeness. Not of *her*, but of the talent within.

"You have," he said, "a gift." Each word dropping like a stone. She blinked. "I have…? Oh! Oh, no. I'm on later. For the morning crowd." A self-effacing grin. "My poems. I'm reading some poems. For the cause. For money. Hopefully, there'll be money."

His turn to blink. "Your pictures," he said.

"Not mine, I'm just taking the money." She looked down at the open casket in front of her, which had a bare scatter of pennies in it. "For what that's worth. Shantrov is the artist."

And she jerked a thumb over her shoulder towards one corner of the room. A mouldering couch that had probably been up in this garret for a generation. Its stuffing leaked, and at its fringes, the moths had built dense cities for their wormy offspring to grow and learn in. Half reclining on it, a sketch board propped on one knee, was a slender youth with short, dark hair and long features. Almost comically long, really. The kind of look the Armiger families got after too many cousins had married each other. As if warned by the burning intensity of Ruslav's gaze, he looked up, one eyebrow crooking quizzically. If he was alarmed to find a street bravo at the exhibition, he didn't show it. His look contained a cool and distant interest.

Ruslav felt himself colour. He wanted to argue with Lemya. He wanted to explain to her that she was mistaken, somehow. Obviously, she was the artist. Let this vapid boy be the poet;

he looked the type. The paintings had lanced through Ruslav, because they were brutal and fierce and terrifying, and that spoke to something in his soul. No wonder the comfortable townies were reluctant to part with their pennies. These were daubs for a thug, for a monster of a man. For a hero. The art saw through all the fine clothes and affected manners to the creature Ruslav knew himself to be, the dog he kept chained until it was time to unleash it. He was seen. And surely, it was Lemya who'd seen him. Yet it wasn't, and 'Shantrov' was still looking at him with that weighing stare.

He made some sound, some attempt at explanation or apology. He stumbled from the room, feeling within him exactly that agonising roil of emotions he'd always pretended to feel in the Pursuit, but never known.

Outside, Benno found him, looking strained. Benno always looked strained. He had a small head, but his eyes looked like they'd come from a face three sizes larger, popping out angrily, plotting their escape. He was shorter and less rakish than Ruslav, and hated him, and usually ended up working with him. And now he was showing a lot of yellow teeth which meant he'd been given a stick to beat his fellow soldier with.

"You were at the Game," he said. "The Anchorage Game. That's where you were."

Ruslav welcomed the man. Benno was small and mean and mundane, and he could deal with that. He could shove back the gut-churn of indigestible feelings and focus on this squit of a creature. Normally he'd just have snarled. Right now, he backed Benno into a wall and half choked the man with his own collar.

"What business is it of anyone's? Nobody told me to go, and nobody told me to leave. It's my own time."

"Not anymore," Benno choked around his collar. "All kind of turds started dropping after you left." And he told just what had gone on, what Fleance the Heron had pulled out as stake, and what had happened next.

Ruslav let him go by the end of it. And obviously, he couldn't be blamed. He wasn't to know. Nobody would expect a sixth sense to tell him to stay in the Game because a priceless treasure was going to show up. Something that his Aunts, the Bitter Sisters, would most certainly want to get a hold of. Except he knew he'd get blamed somehow. Bad luck was still a hanging offence in most of Ilmar. Among the Lodges most of all.

"What, then?" he growled.

"We're after Blackmane, the pawnbroker," Benno said, adjusting his coat and flicking away imagined dust. "They reckon he walked off with it. The skinny bastard who brought it was making enough noise about losing it, and you know how those Allorwen are. We need to catch him at his shop before he can sell it to anyone. The Aunties've got a hunger on them for it."

Ruslav didn't like heading into Mirror Allor at night. Not that it was all Allorwen exiles there, but it was where the refugees had built their little power base. The native Ilmari in the quarter worked for them or had trades that were useful to them, or else complained bitterly about them to anyone who'd listen. And the Allorwen held out, even under the Occupation that hated them, because of all the trades they were masters of. The delights of the circle houses, the fortune-tellers, the scholars of the occult. Sellers of charms and trinkets and potions that actually worked some of the time – if you could pick out the real magicians among the fakes. And it wasn't as though his Aunts didn't have their hooks in the quarter, but the Allorwen had their own family businesses to push back. It was fraught. Two Lodge soldiers just turning up on their turf. It could turn ugly.

It was already ugly when they arrived. Not local trouble; worse than that. Benno and Ruslav turned the corner of the narrow street where Blackmane's shop stood, and there it was, lanterns on and door open, and inside were Palleseen soldiers turning over the contents.

Blackmane's New Collar

A bear of a man, a gravity to him more than merely physical. Heavy furs and layered clothes, and charms and talismans interleaved between them, half on show, glinting from collar and cuff. Just a reminder that he has more than just his fists to defend him. A mop of dark hair streaked with distinct arrows of white, the forked beard likewise. The very picture of a dangerous backstreet sorcerer.

"You've put some weight on," tutted Hoyst. "Blackmane, my friend, I worry that you're not taking care of yourself. That rich food. Your poor straining belt."

"I thank you for your concern," Blackmane growled. The smaller man fussed around him, fastidious as a tailor.

"Might I interest you in a shave? You have quite let your beard go. Why, last time you were so gracious as to accept our hospitality you were trim, sieur. As painstakingly barbered as one could wish. And now from your chin to the hollow of your throat is quite the snarl of untended undergrowth. It is unsightly. I would love to have one of my trusties attend to it. You are about to make a significant public appearance, after all. One must look one's best for the audience."

"And the charge for such a service?" Blackmane asked. He would have liked to glower, but Hoyst was up on a box behind him. He'd be looking over his selection of collars, choosing the most apposite.

"Three pennies, sieur. I have had to raise our rates for these little kindnesses, but for you, Blackmane, I will tender the old price. For old time's sake. Since you have patronised us so often. It is now... your fifth visit to the establishment?"

Blackmane grunted.

"Fifth and, I suspect, last," Hoyst said, with every indication of regret. "But all things pass, and there's only so many times the papers can come through at the last moment, eh? And now... I have a fine selection here, sieur. I know you Allorwen have delicate skin. I recall you had quite the rash from last time, and I am, as you know, averse to causing any of my clients discomfort. So I have Loruthi silk here, rather than the traditional hemp. Most comfortable. Luxurious, one might say. And what is more important, as we grow into our last days, sieur, than a little comfort? Why, you and I, we have grown old together, have we not? I will miss you, sieur. I will be most regretful when you finally accept our full range of services."

Blackmane stared straight ahead and fought down the fury. There were half a dozen of Hoyst's 'trusties' nearby, men of so little moral character and material resource that they would not only end up committed to the Donjon, but would then become the familiars of a man like Hoyst. Plus, two Palleseen soldiers, truncheons to hand and doubtless more than ready to brandish them. Blackmane had a black eye and loose tooth already from when they'd taken him in. No need to give them any more excuse.

"Doubtless," he said, with ponderous dignity, "you have a list of prices."

"Indeed, I have. Two pennies for the finer weave of hemp. Three for flax – suitable for an artisan, let us say, but not a respectable pillar of the community such as yourself. Your silk is the man, for you. The product, so they say, of a monstrous great insect down Loruthi ways, that weaves the unbreakable strands to catch prey – and catch men and women too. Only the most intrepid Loruthi hunters dare brave the misty forests where these beasts lair, for who is to say which hanging whiteness is the fog and which the webs? And yet, brave they do, and their ships carry the inestimable cargo all the way up our rivers here to Ilmar. And to me, sieur. I place a most particular order with them each time the boats come to dock. And from me, my hands, sieur, to your neck. For nine pennies, sieur, let me fit you with a collar of silk. It will not chafe your skin, I guarantee. It will be a comfort befitting your station and quality, to the very end. And you may step from the scales now, sieur. The weighing is done."

Hoyst was an innovator. Before him, the hangmen of Ilmar had just trusted to their ropes, and men had dangled and choked, or else they'd had their heads pulled clean off, and some, worst of all – from the perspective of the executioner – had even lived. Hoyst provided a bespoke service, his ropes precisely tailored to his clients. Since he took the post, some six years before the Occupation, nobody had needed to face the drop twice, nor made a mockery of the judicial process by way of a death too protracted or spectacular.

"Nine pennies," Blackmane said, "is a lot for a cravat I'll only wear the once."

Hoyst laughed with genuine mirth. "Oh no, sieur," he said. "Think of it as paying nine pennies for a garment that will last the rest of your life. Looked at from that perspective it's a bargain and a half, is it not?"

His name wasn't even Blackmane. That was the Ilmari mangling of it. In the language of Allor, the word meant *Of the White Manor* and precisely located him in seniority and magical affinity. But although the Maric and Allorwen tongues were closely related, somehow the word for white in one had become a word for black in the other, and when he'd fled across the border, he'd ended up saddled with a ridiculously foreboding moniker. But he'd had less grey in his hair then, and a little brooding menace had fended off a lot of the local jeers and snubs. Nobody loved the Allorwen refugees back then, and nobody had started loving them since. And if love was off the menu, then a little fear went a long way.

Back when he'd earned his name, he'd been wealthy and respected among his own people. A sorcerer and scholar, conjurer, natural philosopher, priest of Allor's godless religions, because in his tradition, you couldn't be one of those things without becoming all the others. A man who was consulted on matters of significance, asked to intercede with fate, to bless, to curse. And because nothing of the Allorwen magical traditions counted as Correct Erudition in the Pallesand book, he'd most definitely have been taken by the soldiers had he not fled. Most of his peers had been, and they'd either worked their skills in chains under the hard hand of Pal overseers or had never been heard of again. The Pals wouldn't stand for sorcery that didn't fit their view of perfection, and they flat-out hated anything approaching faith. The very culture of Allor had been an offence to them.

And the people of the city of Ilmar, and the wider nation of Telmark, had... well, not cheered them on exactly, but they'd not raised much of a complaint. They hadn't been over-fond of their neighbours' ways. Blackmane was more than aware, since fleeing here, of the locals' view of his countrymen. Witches and warlocks, poisoners, child-cursers, potion-brewers. In over a decade, since crossing the border, he'd watched that twisted view of his people become more and more true, because if the Ilmari reduced your art to love potions and curses and the venal conjuring of the circle houses, then that was all they offered you money for. Even sorcerers needed to eat. In those ten years and more, a whole trade had grown up in the Allorwen quarter, like a bitter reflection of how life had been. All their traditions grown depraved and base from contact with the appetites of the Ilmari. But if life gave you only one way to put bread on the table – and perhaps help out the next boatload of Allorwen who'd got out from under the yoke – then you took it. You made accommodations. You became less than you were.

Then the Palleseen had come to Telmark and brought the Marics, too, within their Sway. There was really only one place left to run, after the Pals came to Ilmar. The Anchorwood. Blackmane had seen a trickle of his countryfolk into the trees over the last three years. Each clutching the ritual wards that were harder and harder to find, both because of the expense and because they were lost within a welter of fakes. And just last night, the most magnificent example of the breed he'd ever seen had been within arm's reach in the hands of that wretched little Heron, and—

Hoyst broke him from his reverie. "Blackmane, I am afraid your audience is ready for your grand performance, sieur. You must select from the wardrobe."

"The hemp," Blackmane growled. "The roughest hog-bristle hemp you have. But I will have the shave. Let my corpse show the rope burn."

They'd taken him as he crossed into Mirror Allor, the Allorwen quarter. Sometimes in the past, they'd tried to ambush him at the shop, but there'd always be someone to tip him a warning before he returned to it. They'd learned, or rather, the man who'd set them on him had learned. The Pals, in Blackmane's experience, weren't good at learning to do things differently. They relied on making the world fit the way they did things. And if he'd been at his best, then perhaps he could have evaded them – a little gloss of sorcery and a good knowledge of the streets around the river. But his head had been full of the events of the night, and they'd been all around him with truncheons and batons, and that had been that.

Because the Palleseen liked their paperwork, there had been a clerk from the School of Correct Appreciation to inform him what he was charged with the moment they hauled him into the Donjon. Improper conjuration, malign sorcery, receiving stolen goods and the rest. And none of it necessarily untrue, save that they didn't actually know the details of the various times he'd done those things. They were simply the standard list of accusations levelled at an Allorwen, plus an additional list thrown at any accused criminal with a mercantile concern. He'd spent the last few hours before dawn in a cell, and now here he was before Hoyst, being measured for a necktie.

He squinted as they led him out into the Donjon yard. They'd opened the main gates, and there was a respectable crowd. He knew plenty of resistance sympathisers who'd say the audience were collaborators who'd shown up just to curry favour with the Occupation. Blackmane had a longer memory. He'd been here before, just like Hoyst said. He was that rarest of things for the executioner, a repeat customer. The crowds had turned out just as avidly when the hangings had been at the order of the Old Duke. People just liked a little kicking and dangling to start their day right. The only difference now was the uniform of the soldiers and the details of the charges.

Hoyst and his trusties were up on the scaffold now, stringing the nooses. Nine of them this morning, a good catch. Each one precisely calibrated for its tenant-to-be. Blackmane was in a line, now. Placed fussily in order so that Hoyst's craft could be properly executed. Watched keenly by the soldiers, both the Pals and their Turncoats. There were some thieves up for the dangle, he saw – some of his acquaintance, even. There was a woman who'd killed the man who'd beaten her each night. Two down from Blackmane was a lean girl with a hard face and a wing tattoo right there in plain view. They called themselves Shrikes. The other resistance factions despaired of them. *You can't just stick knives into the Occupiers and hope to achieve anything.* From where Blackmane was standing, he reckoned it was no more futile than anything else the Ilmari resistance did.

He'd read a penny ballad of a hanging once. The camaraderie

that had sprung spontaneously up between those about to get their necks stretched. All nonsense. He'd been here more than most. He felt nothing for the other wretches, and if they spared him a look, it was one of despite, as though they wanted to demand that Allorwen criminals should be hanged at some other, less prestigious, place.

The ballad had ended with the snap of the trap and a completed execution. Where the writer had obtained their revelation from was a mystery.

A soldier jabbed him in the back with a baton-end, and he stepped up to the scaffolding, taking his place between the Shrike and a petty thief whose name he could probably recall with effort but reckoned that – given their circumstances – it wasn't worth it. He made an imposing figure. The crowd's eye was very much on him. He heard his name whispered from mouth to ear. Or not his name. Just the Maric bastardisation of it. The foreigner, the sorcerer. A special treat for afficionados of the noose.

Hoyst was coming down the line, followed by a trustie carrying a four-legged stool. Hoyst was a little man. It was one of his common jokes to say that he bore the world no ill will for it. After all, was his chosen profession not setting others on high?

The man hopped up behind the Shrike, murmured something to her. She snarled and spat at him; he made a grand piece of theatre about avoiding the spittle. The crowd loved it. That, in Blackmane's considerable experience, was one of the most vexing things about being executed by Hoyst. The man's interminable sense of drama.

Then it was his lips at Blackmane's ear, and even with the stool, he was on tiptoe, as though he was the one dangling at the bight of the rope for a moment.

"I hear no patter of feet, sieur. Can it be that today your booking with us shall not be cancelled at last? You know, I have held a place here open for you since that first time." Fitting the coarse hemp of the noose about Blackmane's freshly barbered throat. It itched. *Should have gone for the silk.*

"There are those in my quarter," Blackmane murmured conversationally, "who shall find my body and lift my spirit from it. They shall decant it into a blade and whisper the names of all my enemies to its freshly honed edge. And within the year, its steel shall have found every one of their hearts." And most of that was impossible, or at least would put a conjurer to more trouble than anyone would go to. But it was the sort of thing to give an ignorant Ilmari nightmares.

Hoyst just laughed politely. "Why, Blackmane, you may be sure that I have several scholars and the School of Correct Erudition bidding on who should have your corpse, the better to decant your residual power for themselves. As a dealer in exotic goods, you must surely recognise that, to their profession, you are a collector's item?"

The noose was tightened to the very point of discomfort, and Hoyst moved on.

There was very little more to it but to close his eyes. Another thing the accounts of hangings leaned long on was the witty speeches of the condemned, but that was for solitary executions of significant villains, and even then, the Palleseen had put a stop to it. If a man was for the drop, they had no interest in listening to anything he had to say. Dead was dead, and residual animation was a resource to extract for their tablethi, just as they might render down a sacred relic or a long-dead sorcerer's bones. They did not believe in rewards or afterlives or next worlds, and they could show you seventeen pages of equations to prove their worldview. And if that didn't suffice, they had soldiers to arrest you and willing collaborators like Hoyst to prepare the noose. It was a persuasive system, all in all.

When the Old Duke would hang a clutch of criminals, he'd keep a drummer and a bugler, the one to strike a brisk tattoo and the other to sound the signal for the traps to open. The Palleseen had abandoned the practice, although Blackmane recalled that the corkscrew mind of their Perfector had brought it back just once, when they'd dangled the Duke's own bulk at the end of a rope. Which had carried its own consequences, as it happened, but who was to know?

Blackmane had known. He hadn't felt it was in his interest to warn the Palleseen leadership, though.

The baton struck up, just the butt of a soldier's weapon striking against the planks of the scaffold. No drum, no bugle. Five solid strikes and then the trapdoors. And that was the first.

The second.

The third. He felt it through the soles of his feet.

They didn't quite push melodrama to its utmost, in the end. The cry to halt came after the third beat. Still, from Blackmane's point of view, they'd left it late. That was the problem with the Palleseen. Unlike Hoyst, they didn't know what to do with showmanship and had no sense of timing. It would be terrible to end up executed, just because some Pal messenger had tripped over his entry.

The soldier had paused, baton raised for the fourth strike. A clerk was bustling over, a local wearing the uncomfortably tight Pal clothes: narrow jacket and pinned cuffs and a collar near as onerous as the one Blackmane was wearing. For a ruinous moment, he thought it would be a call for someone else, a last joke at the expense of his dwindling stock of optimism. But no. Blackmane was to be let down. A pardon had come at the last moment. Just like the last four times.

The disappointment of the crowd was palpable. He knew better than to feed it. He could snarl and spit at them now, from his elevated position on the scaffold. He was a man with a reputation both physical and sorcerous. They'd not come at him with their frustrations. There would be Allorwen men and women and children who'd suffer down the line, though. Any angry flame he lit here would burn one of his compatriots sooner or later. So, he made a show of humility and hung his head. The trustie came and severed the rope so that he could step down.

The noose was his, after all. Hoyst would never dream of re-using the rope. He ran a bespoke and personal service.

The hangman was there to greet him, of course. No frustration, just the man's perpetual sunny disposition.

"Never fear, Blackmane," he said, as though speaking to a child who'd missed a treat. "We shall have you as our guest again, and perhaps next time to stay. Something I shall look forward to. You are, of course, a businessman, and I trust you to always make good on an outstanding contract in the fullness of time."

And there was a moment between them then: the huge Allorwen pawnbroker and sorcerer, the diminutive Maric executioner. They really had been here, severed noose and all, both before and after the Palleseen had taken Ilmar. No kind of relationship that Blackmane would have chosen to include in his life; not one he could entirely disown, either.

"One day he'll tire of you," Hoyst whispered cloyingly. "And you'll be mine."

If he opened his mouth to reply, Blackmane reckoned the despair would drown him. Instead, he just stomped off, limping slightly because they'd kicked his bad knee when they'd taken him.

And then the voice, calling. "Halt that man, Statlos."

The long-established script of this drama, played out between Blackmane and Hoyst and the other man, went awry. This was the point when he, penitent Blackmane, slunk home and brooded over all the vengeance he couldn't have, because this sort of theatre was the price of being an Allorwen who reached any kind of status and power. Instead of which there were soldiers standing in his way, and crisp clicking footfalls from behind. The sound of the little metal plates that prominent members of the Occupation Perfecture had in the heels of their shoes, so every step sounded like the tick of a clock.

He stopped. He turned, the bear at bay. The man striding towards him was narrow and neat. A civilian administrator's tight shirt and jacket, breeches and stockings, a velvet cloak over it against the morning chill. A sash with precisely spaced awards for Correct Scholarship, badges of rank within the Perfecture. A plain black rod, neither of office nor used for walking, but carried like a threat. His face was hollow-cheeked, high-browed; his lips fell naturally into a disapproving purse, as though he was perpetually about to pass some mild remonstrance on the moral habits of his peers. *Tsk, tsk!* Blackmane knew him by sight and under no circumstances wanted to know him by conversation. This was Fellow-Inquirer Hegelsy, senior academic of the School of Correct Speech. Master of the Occupiers' spies and informants, persecutor of the faithful. Anybody's faithful. The man who, rumour said, was just desperate to bring a couple of hundred soldiers into Mirror Allor to root out any evidence that they were preserving the ways of their homeland. One day, his rivals within the Perfecture would let him, and that would be the end of Blackmane's enclave of compatriots in the city.

The soldiers drew him out of earshot of the crowd, although Blackmane could feel plenty of eyes follow him. Hegelsy was tall for a Palleseen. He only had to look up slightly to fix Blackmane with his gaze.

"You are aware that one of my esteemed colleagues was murdered last night, Probationary Citizen Blackmane." Leaning into Blackmane's shadow, that wry face of his making it seem as though he was about to tell a ribald joke and then be scandalised by his own temerity. Pronouncing the awkward title with relish, because it put the bigger man in his place, and if the Pals couldn't take pleasure from putting things in their place, then what was perfection for?

"Someone died," Blackmane said. "I heard. Magister."

"Murdered," said Hegelsy. "His protection stolen. We are investigating. I am told you have seen the item. Perhaps only seen. It was not on you when you were taken. A missed opportunity for a man of your trade. You surprise me."

"Magister, I am a dealer in goods of many kinds. People come to my shop. I offer fair prices."

Hegelsy's face twisted a little further. "Perhaps it shall come to you. You will ensure it comes to us, along with the identity of the seller. This is how you shall gather favour with us. And you and your kin shall find they need our favour. Lest the weight of our disfavour cause discomfort in the near future. As my people investigate how the poor Sage-Archivist, who sought only to expand the range of human knowledge, was so villainously betrayed." All spoken quite pleasantly, as though over a steaming cup at the tea gardens, save for odd words that came out larded with venom. "I have seen you on the scaffold more than once, Probationary Citizen Blackmane. And that is disorderly. Some destinations are only to be visited a single time, and not returned from. I may need to investigate. At this moment, I am interested in the identity of your fellows at the table, though."

"I didn't know them," Blackmane said automatically. "You play with who's there." A lie, and he wasn't sure why. He had no friends among them, surely. Save that to sell someone to the Pals was a betrayal he wouldn't wish on his enemy's dog.

The baton of the soldier on the scaffold had started again, and Blackmane – and the crowd – tensed for the fifth beat. Hoyst had his own count and his own sense of humour, though, and affected to believe that they'd just picked up where they left off. On the second beat he had the levers thrown, before anyone was ready, least of all the wretches still on the platform. Blackmane heard the staccato crash-snap – trapdoor and neck like an old joke and its punchline. He tried to keep his face impassive, but something must have shown, because Hegelsy visibly fed off it.

"Yes," the Fellow-Inquirer said. "Next time, we'll have none of this last-minute reversal. Suitable only for stories. And, even those, we discourage. I look forward to hearing from you, Probationary Citizen Blackmane."

★ ★ ★

It was a long walk from the Donjon back to Mirror Allor; not long enough to take the edge off his foul mood. He knew what he'd find, back at the shop. What this whole rigmarole had been in aid of. Save that, now, the Fellow-Inquirer was involved, and that meek-seeming title hid a world of brutality. None of the Schools of Correct Thought endeared themselves to anyone. Exchange meant taxes and fines for the wrong paperwork or currency; Conduct was the police and soldiers, obedience to the 'perfection' of the Palleseen social structure; Erudition meant appropriation and exploitation of anything magical, the stamping ground of the late Sage-Archivist. Correct Appreciation had its nose in every form of artistic expression and ran the judiciary, Hoyst's current employers. And then there was the School of Correct Speech, the Inquirers. Inquisitors into faith and religion, enforcers of the Pel language, furthering understanding of the creed of perfection. Spies, fishers of rumours, the people who came for you before you'd even done something. In short, the police of the mind. Of whom Hegelsy was the ranking member within Ilmar, a man of whom even his fellows were wary. Whose eye Blackmane could comfortably have avoided for all his days, which gaze was now most definitely upon him. It wasn't as though the School of Correct Speech needed much of an excuse to vanish away an Allorwen merchant-magician.

Too close. And given that these visits to the scaffold were becoming increasingly frequent, he'd had his eye on some insurance to get himself free if the next noose turned out to be tighter than he could wriggle from. If Correct Speech was involved, he would need to pursue that particular little relic, for all he'd have to put up half the real gems of his stock in exchange. There was no treasure more precious than a man's unstretched neck, after all.

The early morning streets grew busier as he neared the river.

At the Donjon end, it was just Pal traffic: last night's patrols returning with whichever unfortunates they'd taken up. Clerks and officials hurrying to their desks to stamp more papers, secure in the comfortable distance between the neat little movements of their manicured hands and the lives they were impacting. Some late gawpers coming for Hoyst's second performance. Blackmane shouldered through them, hunched inwards, feeling their angry looks glance off his fur cloak.

In the Hammer Districts by the river, the air roared with factory work: the seething host of people, the clattering machines; the metallic tang of magic rendered down for sheer mechanical power. The bellow of demons, slaved to the wheels and mills and looms. Enough of his own people here that he got a few respectful nods, and nobody jostled him too much with their sacks and crates. You wanted someone with some sorcerous education to wrangle the demons, and half the time that meant an Allorwen. And the Pals spoke out against magicians, but they were more than happy to make use of the sweat from demon brows, if it made their precious economy run smoothly.

He crossed the river on the Portbridge alongside the little Divinate Enclave that sat across Jowley Street from Mirror Allor. The Divinati he saw peered at him suspiciously, but then they looked at everyone suspiciously. He knew them. They were never as self-sufficient as they liked to pretend, and they'd come to their fellow immigrants before they'd trust the locals, let alone the Pals. They liked to put on their show of uncracked unity, peace and order, and it certainly had the Occupiers fooled, who held them in a weird kind of awe and left them alone. Behind closed doors, they were all factions and rivalries, and crippling self-esteem issues, just like everyone else.

And home, and of course, the shop door was open and the contents in disarray. There were a couple of Allor women loitering in the street to make sure that no mere opportunist made matters worse, but the real damage had already been done by official hands. The squad of Palleseen soldiers had gone through his stock, and they'd done it without much care for his careful systems and arrangements. He'd be all morning putting it back in its proper place, and only then could he be certain what had been taken. From past experience, though, he could trust the note.

It sat on his counter: a neatly written little slip in an elegant but overwrought hand, all unnecessary loops and flourishes. The writing of a man who had plenty of leisure time.

To my good friend Of the White Manor, it ran. *Please find herewith my note of hand for the following goods received with thanks. One ornate writing desk, Orcoba period, inspirational literary imp bound within; one mirror of brass, former property of Count Jodorev 'the doubting' of Rosvof, allegedly enchanted so as to show the gazer as they appear to an individual uppermost in their thoughts; one wand, bone, carven with scenes of Loruthi hunting walrus, unknown provenance and potence. You have my personal and professional word that these items shall be held secure for study within the senior lecturers' rooms of the Gownhall and not, as might otherwise have occurred, be sold on for processing into raw magic. In such ways, our mutual past is preserved. With thanks, your fellow illuminate, the Maestro Ivarn Ostravar.*

Blackmane righted the overstuffed and oft-patched armchair behind the counter and planted his bulk in it. He never knew when Ivarn Ostravar would take a sudden interest in his stock in trade. Items of curious provenance and power were constantly passing through his hands. Every impoverished Ilmari with an heirloom knew Blackmane would take it off your hands for ready cash, to be displayed in his shop until you had the wherewithal to buy it back. Or until your time ran out, and it was sold into other hands. Often to the factories or the Pals, like Ivarn had written, because if there were no other takers for a piece then rendering down for magic was the fate of

anything with a drachm of puissance to it. The learned men of
the Gownhall, though – having already made their détente with
the Occupiers – complained that such a fate was unfitting for
irreplaceable relics of Ilmari history. Or at least those relics they
felt would look pleasing displayed in their common rooms and
museum. Most simply trawled the pawnbrokers and antiques
dealers of Mirror Allor and the surrounding streets, paying as
little as they could for whatever interested them. Blackmane's
old acquaintance Ivarn, though, had tight purse strings and
other arrangements. Before the Occupation, it had been the
Ducal Guard he'd been in with, but since the Pals had taken
up residence, he'd been quick to come to terms with some of
the Monitors of the School of Correct Conduct. It had been
Palleseen soldiers kicking their way through his shop, but they'd
made their visit at the prompting of an Ilmari academic, and
it would be to the Gownhall that Blackmane's vanished goods
would go. And Blackmane had a buyer lined up for the mirror,
a very important one, and he'd have to go risk his hide and eat
the humble meal before them soon enough, to explain why he
couldn't make good on his side of the deal. The Bitter Sisters
weren't going to be pleased.

And there would be other items missing as well. The soldiers
would have pocketed their share of trinkets and eye-catching
nonsense. But anything both pocketable and truly valuable was
hidden in the box beneath the floorboards under his desk. His
real loss was to Ivarn's predations. Blackmane was left wrestling
with the fact that the man had known all these wheels were
turning when he'd sat across from Blackmane at the Anchorage's
chaq table. And Blackmane, in turn, could have given the
maestro's name to Fellow-Inquirer Hegelsy already, and had
some pre-emptive revenge, but the thought of shopping even
Ivarn to the Pals had always rankled with him. Even though
he'd been standing on Hoyst's platform with a fresh shave and a
coarse noose for no other reason than Ivarn wanted him out of
the way to turn his shop over. Ivarn loved the idea of playing a

game against an Allor sorcerer that he simply couldn't lose. He doubtless laughed genially as he wrote his note and imagined Blackmane somehow taking the near-execution and the loss of business in the same humorous vein.

By that time, one of the boys had arrived. A young Allorwen sprout of no more than eleven years, shuffling from foot to foot, wearing a shapeless smock that fell past his knees.

"Report," Blackmane said.

"Pals are all over, searching for someone. Some little riverman, they say," the boy told him obediently. "Going over every boat on the river, and a clot of them still at the Anchorage. Plus, there's some woman of theirs gone missing. They say she went…" The boy swallowed. "There. The place." And it was tiresome having superstitious spies because *the place* could mean the Anchorwood itself or half a dozen other taboo regions, but Blackmane had seen the direction Ochelby's secretary had run off in. The one place in Ilmar the Occupiers were terrified of. "What more?"

"They came into the Mirror and raided Mother Guame's," the boy said, scowling down at his feet. "Took her away."

The circle house that the Sage-Archivist had whiled away his last hours of pleasure at, before he'd gone and got himself killed in the Anchorwood. A fixture here in Mirror Allor, where the one reliable way to get coin from the Ilmari was to offer them services their regular whorehouses couldn't provide. And so, because Sage-Archivist Ochelby had been an old lecher with specific demands, Mother Guame was in the cells. Blackmane could feel the frustrated anger building in him, no way to let it out.

He opened one of the desk's hidden compartments. "Take this to the Donjon jailers," he said, handing over a leather purse. "Tell them, it's to provide for Mother Guame. Food, blankets, books, whatever she needs." Because they made you pay for everything. He was already scribbling a note, his own handwriting spiky and dense like venomous insects crowded onto the paper. "Take this to Mother Isildor." Because there would be more incursions into Mirror Allor and the community would have to come together to weather them.

Unless there was some way of deflecting the attention.

"I want all eyes out for a skinny little riverman, the same as the Pals are looking for," he told the boy. "Every beggar, every factory-hand of ours, every ear in every room. He calls himself Fleance. He's with the Herons. It won't just be us and the Pals looking for him either. We want to track him down first. And."

He bit down on that 'and', but the boy was still looking at him expectantly. He'd have memorised everything, Blackmane knew. Mirror Allor's children lived half on the street and ended up caught between the wheels of the mills or the machinations of greater powers just like every other poor child, but they were schooled. A little reading, a little reckoning, a little sorcery for those with the knack. The boy before him was probably a year off getting arrested and hanged for stealing a pastry from a distance with ghostly hands.

"And," Blackmane said.

"Mesne-Lord?" the boy asked. The ghostly echo of the position he'd have held if the Pals had never come to Allor and imposed their brutal perfection. A man who stood between the human and the occult, rather than the shabby dealer in desperation and stolen goods he'd become.

He clenched his eyes shut for a moment, because it wasn't fit the boy see tears there.

"And I have another message. Get one of the older boys to take it. A clerk's assistant or someone who won't just get turned away or taken up if they're found on an official doorstep." He was writing now, blocky letters for maximum legibility. *For the attention of the Fellow-Inquirer Hegelsy*. Hating himself. Knowing he was setting wheels in motion he couldn't predict or control. Remembering the noose about his throat that dawn, and Hoyst's gleeful chatter. Unable to prevent himself pushing back this once, in this small way that fate had dealt him.

He finished his message, taking extra care that the names he'd set down there were clear and unambiguous. The Maestro Ivarn Ostravar of the Gownhall and Statlos Shrievsby.

The Old Songs

Lemya, come from the provinces on a scholarship to study at the Gownhall, Ilmar's ivory tower. A lanky, graceless young woman, dun hair cut short because that was how the factory women wore theirs, dyed black because she'd heard, a twelveday gone, that was how the Raven faction wore it, though that had turned out just to be someone's joke. On fire with a drive to do something, to pledge herself to anyone. Sometimes sitting too close to her was like being burned.

There were soldiers outside the Anchorage. Not barring the door but standing a way off, towards the clutch of trees. Some were sitting, smoking, or eating the little rolled bread things the Pals used for rations. The rest, about half, stood with batons in hand. One flicked a suspicious look at the group of students approaching the inn. The others had eyes only for the Wood.

Still, people had been arrested for drawing a single suspicious look, Lemya decided. Her fellows weren't helping, either. Most of them were visibly skulking past the patrol, as suspicious as anybody could possibly look. Then Shantrov cracked a joke and laughed uproariously at his own wit, and abruptly, half the soldiers were glancing over. And probably they'd just see a group of Maric youths, and spot the students' ribbons at their belts – the ones they were all supposed to wear everywhere in the city, by Pal statute. Lemya had kept hers off, and Shantrov too, but a few of her fellows lacked her conviction and had allowed themselves to be slaves to the ordnances. *I don't see what's wrong about it*, dull Emlar had complained, and she'd told him, *The Pals tell you to do it. That makes it wrong.* And he'd taken the powder-blue ribbon off reluctantly but, like magic, it was back at his belt now.

Shantrov was eyeballing the soldiers. He made direct contact especially with the Turncoats, the locals under uniform. Staring back at them, as though he could make them immolate from shame. He was, in short, drawing too much attention. She yanked on his arm, then saw a familiar figure sitting beside the Anchorage door. A narrow man in layers of ragged clothes, a tin bowl out optimistically for alms. The boarder at Mother Ellaime's who had the chill little attic room. The priest.

She guided her fellows over and got them inside, hoping there weren't more soldiers enjoying Langrice's hospitality. When she cast her shadow over the begging figure, though, he started, and she realised he'd been half dozing in the wan sunlight, wrist balanced on knee and hand somehow retaining the bowl.

He squinted at her. "I know you."

"How's the blanket?"

An odd look came to him. "I... gave it to someone who needed it more."

He'd sold it, then. Possibly he'd hustled her out of it, though the actual sequence of events suggested not. That arguably still meant he'd needed a blanket, even if just as collateral. She'd still done a good deed. And his benediction had certainly worked. "The exhibition went beautifully," she said, crouching down by him. "The one you blessed me about."

"Oh." He looked embarrassed. "I'm sure it wasn't..."

"Shantrov sold a dozen paintings. And then I performed some of my poems. Everyone loved them." Every one of the eleven people in the audience, but she chose to believe they carried the words away with them to light fires all over the city. Her forbidden words. Her illegal poetry. Outside the strictures of the School of Correct Appreciation. Had anyone there been an informer, why, the Invigilators might already be hunting her!

"Oh, that's…" He mustered a weak smile. "That's good."

He didn't seem to understand the magnitude of her transgression. His faint praise felt like her father, when he'd not really grasped important things either. Abruptly, she felt a need to convince him. He was a Maric. He was a priest of something forbidden himself. He should be a kindred spirit. "Come inside," she told him. "Have a drink."

"It seems early…" He squinted again. "A drink?"

"My friend Shantrov is about to buy drinks for whoever is around the table. If you're there, you'll get one."

"I can't really…" But she was already reaching down to help him to his feet. He was no taller than she was, and not as old as she'd thought. Not quite thirty, surely. "Yasnic, isn't it?" and, by the time he'd nodded, he was inside with her, heading over to where Shantrov was waving jovially.

"Who's your friend?" sullen Emlar wanted to know.

"This is Yasnic," she explained. "He's a priest."

And of course, *that* went down badly. Plenty of bleak looks. Hervenya, who carried a six-inch knife everywhere and wanted to be a Shrike, growled, "A *priest?* Are you crazy?"

Yasnic tried to back out then, but Lemya had his sleeve. "Not a *Temple* priest." Aware he was shaking his head frantically. "Some old faith."

They reconsidered, in light of that, and Hervenya hooked a stool from another table and pushed it towards Yasnic.

"The Temple," she told the man, "sold us out. The Temple licks the boots of the Occupiers. Any enemy of the Temple is a friend to the people."

"I don't like to have enemies," Yasnic mumbled, but he was seated then, and Shantrov was hollering for the Divinati woman to bring them full jugs and empty beakers. "Beer, woman! Good Maric beer!"

Yasnic winced, looking as though he wanted to shrink to

nothing inside his clothes. "You people are mad. There are three Palleseen soldiers over there."

And he was right. They were attending to their own steins, but they had batons leaning against their chairs. Probably the officer of the patrol outside and his favourites. But they had their collars turned up in the universal sign of people minding their own business, and they weren't staring. Inside the Anchorage was bad ground to start a fight. Everyone knew it.

"Over there," Lemya told Yasnic, pointing at another table, "is Father Orvechin and half a dozen of the Millwright Siblingry." Indicating a big bald man with an angry grey beard and his big angry friends. "And that table there is… Hervy, what do you say?"

Hervenya eyed them. "Birds for sure," she said.

"Ravens," Shantrov insisted. "Sterling fellows." Meaning his preferred stripe of the resistance, followers of the Armiger families who'd survived the conquest. Lemya didn't contradict him – of all of her friends, Shantrov was deepest in with the resistance. His family, the Sirovars, were well-known sympathisers, funding the fight behind closed doors. She thought the mob of probably-resistance-fighters looked too rough to be noble retainers, though. If they had bird badges sewn into their seams or cuffs, probably it was a vulture rather than something more noble. *And yet the Vultures still play their part*, she told herself virtuously.

"Our point," insisted Shantrov to the priest, "is that the Pals won't start a thing here. It would be like throwing a lit candle into a flour mill." The drinks had arrived by then, and Lemya watched as the priest tried to hide spilling a little libation onto the tabletop. *An offering.* She wondered at the superstition of it, though when she looked back the pool had entirely disappeared.

Her fellows segued straight into an argument about the curriculum, and the ideological value of boycotting those classes forced to be taught in Pel, as against the risk to their final awards.

Because the Palleseen had mandated their ugly language for all the truly essential subjects. And poetry, of course, was among them, even though you literally couldn't convey Maric poetry in the language of the Occupiers, with its rigidity and restricted vocabulary. Hence her daring, last night: declaiming banned words in a banned language.

Yasnic looked on as Shantrov slapped down a fistful of coin, a wager over some point she'd missed. And of course, Shantrov had money. His family didn't let him go threadbare. Shantrov's coin had bought her a replacement blanket, after she'd given hers to the priest. And that all seemed perfectly reasonable when she looked at each stage of the sequence, but a whiff of the wrong clung to the whole of it.

"You're all mad," the priest whispered.

"You're the priest of some god nobody ever heard of," she told him, then regretted it, but he didn't seem to have taken offence. "What god, anyway? Where is your church?" Things he probably wouldn't want to tell her, given he barely knew her. But he shrugged.

"Just God," he said. "The Healer. Mender of all wounds, the Great Curate, Sickness's Bane. You know."

She didn't know, and it sounded important enough that she should have. He smiled at her expression.

"Even before the Temple started cracking down, there weren't many of us," he said. "Don't feel bad." Embarrassed for her being embarrassed.

"That sounds a useful god to have, though," she tried.

"Oh, no. Quite useless. A burden, really." And he shot a weirdly combative look at the tabletop, as though he had a longstanding dispute with the furniture. "He won't help anyone. Or just the faithful. Those who keep His commandments."

"And that's…?"

"That's me," Yasnic said. "I'm the last. It's why I couldn't bless you. I'm sorry. I let you believe I could. I can't give you the blanket back. It's… There are a lot of rules, and He's very strict about them. I can't heal anyone who hasn't sworn themselves to His rules."

"Must be handy if you cut yourself or stub your toe," she said brightly.

He blinked. "Oh, I can't heal myself. That would be selfish." Ducking away from her incredulity. "There are a lot of rules. God is very strict." Another baleful look at the stained wood. "I shouldn't really be drinking. But that's a minor rule. I'll fast, or something, to make up for it. Fasting is easy, after all."

"Could you heal someone if they converted?" she asked, because she was a student and her mind tended to pry at things like that.

"Oh, yes. But you wouldn't want to. It's very onerous. Not as much as for a priest, but still. A pain, honestly. That's why I came here. Or... long ago we used to come to see if people had been hurt, Kosha and me, in case anyone would like to... But they never did, or it never lasted, and now..." A tiny laugh. "I suppose we just come to look at people in pain. Which doesn't sound very holy, really."

"We?"

"Me. I. God and I. We." A twisted look, as though begging for her understanding. "He's all I've got, too."

Hervenya had gone over to the alleged resistance fighters and was bothering them. Lemya caught a hint of a word. The girl was talking too loud about some Pal business or other. They were trying to ignore her, hunching, until at last, one of them just took her aside and gave her a few words that were plainly a threat or at least some hard advice. Hervenya was strutting when she came back, though, pretending she'd been recognised for her patriotic fervour.

"You know Ruslav, don't you?" Lemya said to Yasnic, out of the side of her mouth. It was why she'd seized on him, after all, though just getting the man some free beer was surely a good deed.

He nodded warily.

"He likes art much?"

"Not that I'm aware of. But these... men of the street. They have odd tastes. Sophistications. Who knows what he wants? I really don't know him well." And then, drawing himself up. "If you're... Has he... been improper? I can speak..." Already wincing at the thought. "Speak to him. If you want. If it would help." His voice so quiet she couldn't imagine it would help.

"I don't know what he's been. Odd." Thinking of the way the man had turned up swaggering, lost the swagger by the time he'd studied Shantrov's daubs, and then... reacted. Very oddly. Left before the poetry, which was a shame.

"He's with the resistance, isn't he," she said. "A fighter?"

"A soldier," he corrected, a city distinction she didn't know how to parse. Was that a yes or a no? And she'd observed the big man when she first took a room at Mother Ellaime's and, soon after, warily noted he'd taken an interest in her. But last night at the exhibition, after he'd had a look at the pictures, his face had been practically on fire with something. Inspiration. And Shantrov had claimed his work was all 'a depiction of the shackling of the Maric Soul under the Tread of the Occupiers'. And if Ruslav was a fighter for the resistance...

But then he'd suddenly left – even left behind the painting he'd bought, which she'd pushed under his door the next day. She didn't know what to make of it, save that Ruslav had suddenly become a more interesting man on a number of levels.

There was more drink by then – their third at least, and all on Shantrov's tab. That was when Hervenya started singing. She had a raw, flat voice, but she wasn't carrying the burden for long because – she told Lemya – it was one of the old factory songs you used to hear out of the riverside mills back before the Occupation. Half the other students knew it, because it had done a tour of the common rooms earlier in the year. An example of honest working Ilmari culture that the students were so desperate to emulate. Lemya glanced over to the Palleseen soldiers. They were watching carefully, but didn't have their batons to hand. Like she'd boasted to Yasnic, they weren't about to start anything. Not even at this display of Incorrect Thought.

Let them see that we students don't fear them.

From across the room, she heard a bass rumble joining in the chorus, and saw that a handful of Father Orvechin's people had joined in – the very ones who used to sing the song back when the mills turned for Maric owners and not the Occupiers. She felt a sudden thrill of *being present*, at feeling herself standing at the very fulcrum of events. Imagined the song spreading out through the city. *What if this is the moment it all touches off?* And she was up on the table without a thought, startling her fellows, almost treading on Yasnic's fingers. Her head was full of words, one of the pieces she'd conned for the previous night. *City of Last Chances*, after one of Ilmar's age-old nicknames. Here, turned from the hard luck story of those who ended up on the streets to a prediction that on those same streets the fire of revolution would be lit. And all in Maric, of course, because you couldn't say true poetry in Pel. The very language fought you over any attempt at beauty or art. To speak her heart had become a crime, and one she entered into willingly. And the song was still going on, and she wasn't honestly sure how much of what she declaimed was actually heard. And Yasnic was tugging at the cuff of her trousers, more and more urgently, and then the song came to a broken halt and the three soldiers were at their table, batons in hand. And she, on the table, arms outstretched, had their full attention.

Shantrov stood, and he was about to try some variant of *Do you know who I am?* because even though the Armiger families were greatly reduced, the Sirovars still had a lot of influence. Yasnic was on his feet too, she saw. He was babbling excuses for her, taking on himself a culpability that, of everyone there, he certainly hadn't earned. Letting his extra years make him a target. And if they found out he was a priest of some tinpot little religion, that was enough to have him in the Donjon cells at the pleasure of the School of Correct Speech.

I will go, she decided. *I will take it on myself.* She wouldn't let anyone else steal this from her. She would be the spark. From her cell, she would hear the roar of revolution as they stormed the Donjon gates.

Her reverie lasted around half a second before the newcomer entered, and everything went quiet.

A wood-masked figure in furs and green robes. And it was daylight, and surely the stand of trees out there was just a copse you could see the far side through. The Indwellers *never* came to Ilmar save when the moon was right, and the Wood had opened its gates.

Whatever the soldiers had been about to dish out – arrests, beatings or just some harsh words – they had other business immediately. And more soldiers were coming in, the whole patrol from outside.

"What's going on?" Suddenly, being on the table seemed ridiculous. She didn't want to be arrested at all. It was something in the way all those uniformed men bore themselves. The way their batons were half aimed at that solitary figure. It approached a table, and the two women there got up and left, even jostling the soldiers as they went. The Indweller stood there quite calmly, their back to the batons. Langrice's man, Hellgram, hurried over with an earthenware mug of tea, then skittered out of the way.

"What's happened?" Emlar asked for all of them.

"You didn't hear?" Yasnic said, and was abruptly the shrinking centre of attention. "One of the Palleseen. Their Sage-Archivist. He went into the Wood. He was killed."

Lemya stared at him. Of course, she had been busy with the exhibition, raising funds for the cause (save for that coin already gone on drinks). But how could she have missed such a thing? The whole uprising could have started right then and there, and she'd have been absent! Except there didn't seem to be an uprising going on, and Father Orvechin's people were sliding out of the door, as were the group she'd identified as resistance fighters, as was everyone. And Hellgram's long-boned frame was at their table, bending low, murmuring that they should go now. The taproom of the Anchorage wasn't a healthy place to be.

She was the last out, and she paused in the doorway. She couldn't not. The scene had a hook in her she couldn't get loose from. The patrol was standing in a crescent around the table the Indweller had chosen. Langrice and her woman, Jem, were behind the bar, and Hellgram right in front of it, all pointedly not part of what was going on.

The Indweller stood and turned quite calmly. Lemya heard their voice, very clear despite the mouthless mask.

"The folk of Pallesand have shed the blood of the Wood." A voice shorn of identifiers, reciting the Pel words as though it had learned them by rote. "They are barred from the trees on pain of death. Let it be known among all your kin. You are forbidden our ways until restitution is made."

Even the Indwellers hate them! But her usual knee-jerk patriotism wouldn't quite cover what was going on. There were great stone blocks of meaning shunting about the City of Last Chances, and she didn't understand them.

The Indweller walked forwards, and the soldiers parted with a ripple of superstitious fear. Lemya shrank back, retreating out of the doorway as the robed figure approached, their staff-end thudding on the floor.

"Look out," she croaked. Their didn't seem to hear her. Or else their knew and was resigned. She'd seen at least some of the soldiers levelling their batons.

"Look out!" she managed with more force. The mask seemed to fix on her, trying to communicate something in a language she didn't know.

By then the patrol's Statlos had recovered from his surprise and barked an order. For a moment, his soldiers hesitated, but ingrained obedience beat out superstitious dread and two of them laid hands on the Indweller. Lemya waited for the explosion, the magic, the lash of that staff to beat them away. They took the staff from the figure's unresisting fingers, and there was no thunderbolt, nor did some corrosive venom leap from their flesh to theirs. The Statlos stalked forwards, half furious, half frightened at his own boldness. He ripped the wooden mask away with a convulsive jerk. Beneath was a face, just a face, foreign, painted, dark hair hacked short. The Indweller stared dully at nothing.

"Get this thing to the Donjon." Hoarse, not believing his own daring. The Pals had *arrested* the Anchorwood's emissary. At Lemya's back, the patrons of the Anchorage murmured. Traditions older than the city of Ilmar were being defied right before their faces.

"We have to get to the Gownhall," Lemya decided. "We have to tell people." The Occupiers were at war with the Indwellers. What that actually meant, she didn't know. Other than the curious traditions of the Anchorage, it wasn't as though the Indwellers went abroad into the city or actually *did* anything. They guided people through the Wood when the moon was right. Guided them to the strange places the Wood led to. The Anchorwood predated the city, had been here when *all* of this had been just trees. It had always been a perilous escape for those who could get their hands on the wherewithal to cross. The fact had been as much of an irritant to the Old Duke as it was to his Palleseen successors.

It must all mean something, Lemya decided. It must advance the cause, somehow. It was more weight on the scale that would inevitably swing to revolution. What if the Indwellers came through with their beasts and helped drive the Pals out…?

One thing was certain, she would have to tell her mentor all about it. Ivarn Ostravar would want to know.

Shantrov had boasted that he'd already missed two classes that morning, because he had an enviable confidence that could survive anything. Lemya had missed one, but it was Literate Form, conducted in Pel and worthlessly formulaic, where the same lessons were trotted out by a bored lecturer each week, trying to bludgeon Palleseen Correctness into unwilling students. She didn't care about leaving an empty chair there. It was in itself an act of rebellion. She did clear the Gownhall gates in time to reach the special supervisory session with Maestro Ostravar, leaving her fellows to gossip about what they'd seen.

Ivarn Ostravar was a tall, lean man, face pale like a statue's. He had a hooked nose and a long jaw, and kept himself meticulously shaved. He wore the long-sleeved robes of a Gownhall maestro with impeccable dignity and invited his favourites to extracurricular sessions, where they could discuss historical Ilmari literature and culture in his private rooms. The glory of the ancient Maric language, the great epics of noble Ilmari princes, the battles, the romances. She loved to hear him talk about it. His face lit with ancient fires, his strong voice lifting with the beautiful rhythms of the old sagas as he talked through how stress and alliteration carried and complemented the themes and emotional through-lines. He had a wonderfully precise way of speaking, neither florid nor pedantic. A man who loved his subject, and who grew a love of it in his listeners. A patriot, Lemya knew. A man who had made himself a custodian of all that the Occupiers were trying to wipe out. One of the Gownhall's inner circle who had staved off a complete takeover by the Palleseen, so the institution remained at least halfway free for young dreamers like Lemya.

She arrived early enough to beard him as he entered, even as her classmates were shambling in, unshaven, hungover, rubbing sleep out of their eyes though it was closing on noon. Lemya, of course, hadn't even gone to bed, but sleep had been kicked past lunchtime by the news she had to impart.

And here was the maestro, looking somewhat grey around the eyes himself, and she was already whispering her news to him. The Sage-Archivist was dead! The Indwellers were at war! Desperate to earn his surprised gratitude at the news. What she got was even more gratifying. Ivarn leaned in and smiled, in that enigmatic way he had. "Oh, I know, dear child," he confirmed. "You're not the only one who was abroad last night. And how did the exhibition go, by the way?" Leaving her with a maelstrom of emotions to master as she sat down. Because Ivarn was way ahead of her, of course. How could she think he'd be far from the centre of things? While she'd been reciting her little compositions, he'd been a part of great events. And he cared enough to ask after her own meagre efforts. Yet, in the *how did the exhibition go?* there'd been amusement, even a little contempt that it was *all* she could do for Ilmar. She'd been so proud of her daring, speaking banned lines in a little garret for an audience of less than a dozen. And here was Ivarn, witness to the turning points of modern history. She felt simultaneously put in her place and even more determined to impress him.

"Now," he addressed the class. "Where were we? You'll forgive me. Some of us have had urgent business keep us up most of the night. You students would know nothing of that, of course…" Another of those smiles. Laughing with them. Laughing at them. "I'm sure one of you was about to explain the significance of the middle quarto structure of *The Ford of Rovescu* to me, in such a way as to make plain you've not in any way wasted the previous week of study time in debauchery—"

And then the soldiers came in.

There had been shouting beforehand, Lemya registered. At least one of the Gownhall porters crying a warning. She'd been so absorbed in Ivarn's words she hadn't heard, and perhaps so had he. And here they were, a dozen charcoal-grey uniforms pushing into his little study, filling it out, backing the students against the wall. A writ thrust right into Ivarn's face, and then hands on him, hauling him forwards, even though he wasn't resisting. "A mistake," he was insisting. "Let me speak to the Sage-Invigilator. This will all be smoothed over."

The Statlos of the soldiers yanked on his arm hard enough that he stumbled. "You give yourself airs, old man." Lemya felt a jolt inside her. They'd come for him at last. They'd recognised

– as she'd always recognised – that he was the very heart of Ilmar, its history and proud culture. And if she stood by now, there was nothing she stood for at all.

The soldiers had Ivarn out of the room and down the hall, heading the quickest way for the gates. Or the quickest way *they* knew. As a student, she already had a dozen shortcuts across the Gownhall's maze of rooms and stairs and passageways. Simplicity to get ahead of them. And she was shouting, thrusting her head through the door of every class and common room. *Maestro Ostravar is arrested! The Pals are trampling our rights and freedoms!* Leaving chaos in her wake as students leaped up from their writing. As other maestros abandoned their teaching to see what was going on.

When the soldiers marched Ivarn out into the courtyard of the Gownhall there was already a crowd there. By that time Lemya had gone from herald of the flood to just one more eddy in it, outstripped by her own words. And nobody knew what to do, she saw. The soldiers had halted, Ivarn a dignified stiletto shape sheathed in their midst. The students were looking down on them from balconies and the walkways of the courtyard walls, and a fair number were between them and the gates. And there were maestros, some of whom were reconsidering, shuffling back into the crowd or loitering in doorways. A brace of them went forwards to make demands, though. Lemya saw the fox-russet curls of Maestra Gowdi, who taught theories of magical exchange, and the blue-tattooed baldness of Maestro Vorkovin, who had been in the army before he'd retired to teach music and the sword. They were talking, and the soldiers' Statlos was making demands, and Ivarn had his hands raised to say something. Lemya couldn't hear a word through the buzz of the crowd, and she was up on a balcony anyway, too far from the centre of things as always. Then the soldiers were pushing forwards. Gowdi got out of their way in a flurry of robes, but they had to give Vorkovin a shove before he'd do the same, knocking the man down. The sight of it had the students incensed, shouting personal insults and the slogans of Armiger families. The Pals just trudged across the courtyard, shoulders hunched against it. All the noise, none of it to any effect.

Lemya felt a sudden clutch of *destiny* at her heart. *If not now, then when? When it's too late, and they've taken everything from us?* In that instant, she grasped the closest thing: a stone vase of wilting flowers. And she threw it from the balcony with all her strength.

It missed everyone. Possibly for the best, as it came down just as close to the students as the Pals. And the soldiers were at the gates, already exiting. When it was too late, though, everyone else was copying her. There were stones and books, even pens and inkwells in the air, clattering on the cobbles or against the gates themselves. And still, there was no answer from the soldiers, just that steady retreat until they were out on the street and marching their prisoner off. And *then*, the students down below swarmed after them, crammed the gateway like ants at the entrance to their nest, catcalling and jeering after the unconcerned patrol as though it was a great victory.

And it *was* a great victory, Lemya decided. They'd defied the Palleseen, and the enemy had retreated. The students had thrown the Pals out of the Gownhall. That was what everyone around her was suddenly saying. The word spilled out onto the street and into the city. She'd wanted to light a fire, and now there *was* a fire lit, but it was mad and directionless, already guttering. It needed a leader, a true patriot whom everyone would listen to. And the only man she would cast in that role had just been led off to the Donjon.

Shantrov was at her shoulder abruptly. He had his sword in hand, the one he almost never carried but was allowed to, by the agreements negotiated between the Armiger families and the Pals. He almost cut someone's ear off as he brandished it.

"We need to get into the Donjon," she shouted over the hubbub.

His eyes gleamed. "I can do that!"

Parliament of Fowls

Vidsya Sirovar: slender, elegantly dressed. A cat person, both in that she loved the animals, and that she had something of their quality. Not a straight line to her – sit her in a chair, and she'd pool at a louche angle. Constantly seeming drunk and careless. Too young to be important or to take anything seriously, though in truth, she was forty now and some of that youth was applied at the mirror each morning. A public rake and clown, coasting by on Armiger money and family sway. In private: a player, like steel wire. The beak of the Raven.

When Vidsya's aunt used to call a gathering, they'd come. Even the ones who hated her family. But Aunt Sachemel had been old, and had died last winter. The Sirovar clan weren't the only ones robbed of a leader. When people had gathered clandestinely to talk about opposing the Occupiers, Sachemel had spoken for the Ravens. Now that loose and squabbling affiliation of old families was rudderless, but Vidsya was doing her best… in between reminding the Occupiers and half the rest of the city of how spineless and hedonistic she was. Which she was, she admitted to herself. In another life, she'd just have given herself over to it and stopped resisting her natural inclinations. Right now, she had the family to think of. And so here she was, and instead of playing the genial hostess to the resistance, she was someone else's guest.

She hated the Vultures. They weren't resistance. They were

the criminal Lodges by another name. They didn't have the city's interests at heart. Come the time when Ilmar took up arms and drove the Palleseen out, she and her peers would absolutely need to make sure that the banners being waved had ravens on them or, better still, the arms of the old families. Right now, the Vultures had their claws too deep in the city. Partly because there was a growing mob of the poor and dispossessed who'd fallen for the Vulture lie of speaking for the common man. Partly because Ilmar's criminals had only prospered after the Pals had made half of everything illegal.

But she had to live with the city the way it was, which meant cutting deals with the Pals sometimes, and when the Bitter Sisters called, putting on her best face and going.

Carelia and Evene were their names. They hated the Pals and they hated each other, and that was about as much common ground as Vidsya shared with them. And that mutual loathing was a blessing. It meant they spent half their people's efforts undermining each other, rather than shouldering out the other resistance factions.

Right now, they were having a little disagreement, and it meant somebody was going to get killed.

They made their lair in a cellar below one of the mills, where the rattle of the machines and the bellow of chained demons would cover any sound. They called it the Fort. Their throne room was circular, seats around the outside like it was a fighting den, and a covered pit in the centre. Vidsya made very sure to stay back from that pit. She'd seen into it before, and she suspected she was about to do so again, and it wasn't a pretty sight. The Bitter Sisters ruled their mob of thugs and desperadoes by fear. Object lessons were learned by observers, because the actual subjects didn't live to mend their ways.

The Bitter Sisters sat side by side in carved chairs that had patently belonged to someone of better breeding. Their people filled a block of seats or just squatted on the floor on either side, all except for the man up before them. Their twin glower had his heels to the very edge of the hatch.

Carelia wore wine-red; Evene wore piss-yellow. Probably it was meant to be 'old bone', but that was how Vidsya characterised it. Their clothes were of identical cut. They sported mirrored jewellery, matching style, opposing material. Their hair was dark, cut off the shoulder. They were ten years' Vidsya's senior, and it had just made them hard, not old.

The subject of their ire – or of Evene's ire, since the man was Carelia's – had overstepped himself. He'd made a private arrangement to stir things up and enrich his boss, and it had gone spectacularly wrong. Vidsya, in fact, was in a uniquely privileged position to know just how wrong it had gone. She was watching the trial of the man who'd put that wretch Fleance up to his little theft.

"We've had a half-dozen of ours taken up," Evene was saying. "Two safe houses broken, all the proceeds from the gaming ring on Oroyeltnin Crescent taken. The Pals are everywhere across the city looking for this thing, or anyone who knows anything about it. And your Heron's disappeared with the goods."

"It was worth it," the man insisted stubbornly.

"We decide if it was worth it," Carelia spat, and with that, he knew he'd been cut off. Evene wanted to stick the knife into their mutual loathing, and Carelia wasn't going to defend her man. He'd screwed up that badly. "You, Heron! Where's your prick got to?"

It wasn't just Vidsya's Ravens who'd been peremptorily summoned. The other major resistance houses were represented too. A lean, twitchy man with a carved-up face was probably a Shrike, although what other freelance murderers he spoke for was anybody's guess. Then there were a handful of riverfolk, on behalf of the smugglers and boat people who served as the Ilmari resistance's links to wider Telmark. Their leader was a lean old boy in a grey coat, fingerless gloves and a russet scarf about his neck, even in this muggy underground space.

"Fleance got himself in trouble," he pronounced.

"We *heard*," Evene agreed. "So this priceless whatnot he stole for Useless here ended up on a fucking gaming table or something. And then he legged off with it. So you've got him belowdecks on a barge or what?"

"We do not. It was when things kicked off at the Anchorwood. We think he… We don't know if he even had it when he ran but… some say he went into the Reproach with the Pal woman and the beast."

A thoughtful silence at that, enough to dampen even the Bitter Sisters' ire. You had to be desperate to enter the Reproach. Most Ilmari were just happy that the Reproach couldn't come to them. There was a radius of eight streets from those ruined districts where only the most desperate lived. Because it leaked out, they said. Vidsya shuddered.

"Busy place right now, the Reproach," Carelia mused. "You, Useless." And Fleance's accomplice was abruptly back in focus again. "You've fucked over a lot of people stirring up the Pals like this. And you don't even have the goods."

Vidsya saw him bristle for a moment. Stirring up the Pals was what the resistance was supposed to be doing, he was about to say. Except she agreed with the Sisters on this point. No point just flailing around in random acts of resistance. When the uprising came, it would be carefully planned. *And at our direction.*

"So, you get to go after him and grab it back," Evene added. It was amazing how the two of them could talk in lockstep like that and still make it plain they hated each other. "Now it's out there, we'd better have it."

"Go into the Reproach," Useless echoed.

"You'd better," Carelia agreed, and then someone was winching the doors of the pit open, and the man had his heels out over thin air.

Not just thin air. Over the thing in the pit. A current of revulsion went through the room, all those hardened street thugs who thought hiding a bird badge in your coat made you a revolutionary.

In the cellars and storehouses by the river there were rats, and there were things that caught them down in the damp dark. Centipede things that were like mats of spindly legs arching out from a flat body. They moved quick and skittery enough to give a spider nightmares. Light a lantern suddenly, and you'd see a score of them in a mad scramble for the dark.

The thing in the pit was like that, but as long as five men end to end. The confines of its prison forced it to coil over and around itself, a thicket of limbs clutching the pit's sides and covering every inch of space down there, so Vidsya could barely follow the twisted knot of its body. As the light from above struck it, the whole carpet of chitinous flesh shuddered, and then one end of it was questing upwards, jointed mouthparts gaping like a spread hand. It humped itself three quarters of the way up the pit's sheer side before sliding back down in a flurry of legs. It was always hungry. They kept it half-starved. Vidsya had seen it fed, the clawed fingers of its head kneading and injecting and then pulling apart the venom-softened flesh.

"The Reproach," Evene said. "Go find the Heron's boy and what he took. Bring it back. Him too if you can. It's hungry. You don't want it hungry, do you?"

And that was Useless screwed either way, Vidsya reckoned. She wondered if she could get to him, offer him sanctuary in exchange for any dirt he had on the Sisters. Except, that sort of thing got out, and the Ravens weren't ready to go talon to talon with the Vultures right now.

That was when one of the Sisters' people burst in, shouting about news from the Gownhall. Except the bang of the door was such that Useless jumped with shock and went straight down into the pit, and that usurped everyone's attention.

The thing in the pit, the centipede-demon. It had come from the Wood, they said. Or else, it had been the last triumph of a conjurer who'd gone from over-ambitious to dead very swiftly. How the Sisters had ended up with it penned down here, Vidsya had no idea. Evene had said it was hungry. Vidsya thought it was angry. Certainly, it tore into Useless with a blind rage, those crooked fingers driving their curved fangs into him over and over, mauling his body even as that ghastly mass of limbs closed on him like jaws. It was a while before order was restored and the news could be heard.

And the Sisters had put out their call to talk resistance business, not for this circus. Everyone knew the second most senior Pal had got himself killed, and that was an opportunity. The better informed knew that now the Pals were in some kind of feud with the Indwellers of the Wood, and that was maybe an opportunity too, though nobody liked the Indwellers much either. But even as the great and the good of the resistance factions gathered, events had been marching on without them. The Pals had marched into the Gownhall to arrest Ivarn Ostravar, and the students had gone mad over it.

Vidsya wriggled from the clutch of the Sisters' hospitality as quickly as she could after that. She needed to work out her own response and get the other Raven families on side. The rest could talk and talk, but it was clear that, until Carelia and Evene got behind closed doors and had their own little slap-fight, there wasn't going to be a unified Vulture response, let alone anything else.

She dictated three letters, each with a smart-dressed messenger to carry it to one of her blood kin or relatives-by-marriage in this house or that across the Armiger district. It was their great advantage that the respectable old families all lived close enough for easy communication, while the Vultures were strung out across the Gutter Districts, hopelessly factional and splintered. And then a servant coughed discreetly at her door and announced that cousin Shantrov and another student had come calling.

The Sirovar family was a sprawling one. They had cadet branches everywhere, junior members sacrificed by marriage to middle-class factory owners or the respectable professions, even enough spares to scatter like grain into the soil of the Gownhall to see what would grow. Vidsya had been one such herself, in her day. And she had entertained her own stock of ideas and ideals in that time, and then further time had mostly dashed them out with a bucket of cold reality. And now she, and her aunts and her cousins, were committed to managing the family and ensuring its prosperity and, most of all, survival in these hard times.

Shantrov was still at that ideal stage, also very much at the drinking and revelling stage. She had several bills on her desk that were his accounts from taverns and tailors. She had been waiting for the first serious gambling debt to slide itself under the townhouse door, or perhaps a complaint from a brothel or the son of some middling merchant. Not to mention the brawling. He'd yet to fight a serious duel, but it seemed inevitable that his expensive sword lessons would be put to the test sooner or later. Vidsya, who had a long scar along her ribs from fifteen years before, hoped he was less of a fool than she'd been at his age.

With him was some student girl, a mix of bravado and nerves that immediately placed her in terms of upbringing and politics, to Vidsya's practised eye. Her name was Lemya, apparently.

"Well, you're not going to believe what we saw this morning, cousin," Shantrov drawled. He was looking ragged, a man who hadn't seen his bed in more than a day and a night. He took the seat Vidsya indicated, and one of the servants brought him a tonic. The girl stood awkwardly, shifting from foot to foot, exploding with words and simultaneously too cowed to say anything.

So Vidsya listened to Shantrov tell her all the things she already knew about the situation at the Gownhall, and of course not tell her how things were now, because they'd left to come here the moment Maestro Ostravar had been hustled out of the gates. She nodded sagely and pretended it was all news. She knew Shantrov when he was gearing up to ask the family for a favour. In fact, the two of them had been in this position enough times before that he choked on it, in the end. He'd begged money enough, or got himself into minor scrapes enough, or just missed classes enough, that now he had something serious he needed help with, he couldn't quite make himself ask.

The girl, Lemya, spoke into his silence. "Ivarn Ostravar is in the Donjon right now."

Vidsya nodded, waiting for it.

"He's a hero, Aunt." That old term of respect, not quite proper for their respective stations, but the girl was trying at least. "He's a champion of Ilmar. He's lit fires in every student's breast about our heroes, our history. All the things the Occupiers want stamped out." And there was certainly fire enough in her, barely held back. She didn't want to be in this well-furnished townhouse study. She wanted to be out on the streets with a bird flag shouting to the mob. And if Ostravar had accomplished anything in his academic career, it was making sure people like this sat attentively in his classes rather than ending up in the Donjon themselves, or on deportation barges out of the city.

"I know you have... channels. People in place. From before the Occupation," Shantrov said.

"What are you asking?" Vidsya enquired coolly.

What Shantrov might have said was lost when Lemya exploded, "We have to get him out! They'll execute him! He's done so much for the cause. We need to do this for him!"

Vidsya was amazed the phrase 'the cause' hadn't come up before now in the conversation. She let a servant serve tea then, three fragile little cups and a better blend than the girl had likely ever tasted, for all it would go unappreciated. Time to think. Ivarn Ostravar had got himself locked up. She was a little surprised, because he was an old fox and played the tightrope game with the Palleseen just as carefully as the Sirovar family did. The Ostravars weren't really Armiger material anymore, but they were a deep root running through Ilmari history. The man was a survivor. And yes, he was radicalising the students in his quiet way. But he was wise enough to be a patriot behind closed doors or in ways that wouldn't come kicking in his door at past midnight. How he'd ended up marched out of the Gownhall was an ugly mystery Vidsya didn't like.

Ivarn knew a lot, and some of what he knew could damage the family. Damage the Ravens, certainly, because Ivarn was one of those people who moved in a lot of different circles. She trusted to his discretion, up until he was under sufficient pressure that being discreet wouldn't help him.

If we let him stew. She could push things with the Pals, certainly. How much of an overboiling pot was the Gownhall right now? There were students in every drinking den within ten streets of the place who were singing the old songs and talking a good fight. What if this was it? For a moment, she permitted herself to imagine Ivarn's arrest as the updraft that would lift the Raven. The restoration of the old families, the banners taken out of storage to flutter in the wind as the Occupiers were driven out. It wasn't the time, though. She and her fellows had been planning the revolution for a long while. If this pack of children actually *did* it, then where did it leave everyone? Firstly, the Pals would come down on the Gownhall district with an iron fist, and finally burn what men like Ostravar had managed to preserve for so long. Or worse, if it did become a general uprising, the Bitter Sisters and their Vulture faction were far better placed to profit from it. They had that grassroots support among the desperate that the Ravens were still clutching for. Another year, another five years, and everyone would flock back to the old banners. They'd remember the stories of noble princes and heroes, and perhaps they'd forget some of the excesses of the Old Duke... It wasn't time for the grand gesture.

"I can get you into the Donjon," she said. "But with papers, not with force. I have people who will do this for me. You can enter quite legitimately to speak with Ivarn. He will advise you on what he needs and what you should do. You want to do your duty to Ilmar? Then do this." Lemya's hangdog expression needled her, if only because she might once have worn it herself. "This is how things are done," she said, knowing that Ostravar would talk them out of any foolishness. The old shyster would already have his exit planned. She trusted his shrewdness. He'd put a lid on this student situation, and then she and the Raven faction could get back to what was important – namely outmanoeuvring their rivals so they'd be on top when the real fight came along.

Maestro in Durance

A man used to being the fulcrum of events, the pivot of things,
rather than one swinging end. A choice of words that struck Ivarn
as unfortunate, after they marched him in past the gallows. Always
composed, even in the solders' midst. Always dignified, whether
playing elder statesman of the Gownhall or slapping down the chaq
tiles in the Anchorage's backroom. Or sending Palleseen soldiers to
haul off his competitors so he could reappropriate objects of cultural
value from the grubby hands of pawnbrokers. Ivarn Ostravar, the
fox caught by hounds.

Even when they slung him in one of the low cells, the underground ones, he didn't let it daunt him. He'd guessed at what might have gone on within the Perfecture by then. Some bright young spark straight off the boat had decided to make their mark. Ivarn's name had crossed their neat little desk, and they hadn't known enough about how things worked here in Ilmar. They just needed to be informed of the arrangements in place, regarding the freedoms of the Gownhall and the comfortable ruts the Occupation had worn into Ilmari society over the last three years. Ivarn would wangle himself an audience with the Sage-Invigilator, and it would all get straightened out. Whoever was being over-keen would get a talking to, and probably Ivarn would receive some public but minor reprimand. And that would help him, in the long term. That he'd been taken to the Donjon and then fined – the Gownhall would pay – or had some property confiscated – he could always haggle for it later – or even just been held in these cells for a few nights. It would add to his reputation among the student body, give him more leverage with the birds, garner more respect. There would come a day when the shackles of the Occupation loosened, and until then, he would preserve himself and the Gownhall and the traditions of Ilmari scholarship, and to be honest, they were all three the same in his head.

A little privation, therefore, was to be endured, just like the heroes of old. He fortified himself with a few classical quotes on the subject as he peered into the neighbouring cells. The Old Duke hadn't felt that his meanest prisoners were owed any privacy, so there was nothing but a lattice of bars between Ivarn and his neighbours. He saw a one-handed thug who must be a Lodge man taken up for violence or larceny and doubtless destined for the noose. Next door was a couple who looked like rivermen, and he wondered if they'd been grabbed for regular smuggling or customs evasion, or if they were associates of the man who had been at Langrice's table. The Palleseen must be going mad trying to track that one down, right about now. Ivarn permitted himself a chuckle.

In the cell beside them was a broad woman of middle years, heavy-featured and wearing cast-offs that had gone through more than one pair of hands, darned and re-tailored, before ending up with their current owner. A low woman putting on airs but not exhibiting herself, and there were a couple of charms about her neck that looked Allorwen, so...

He made the connection, and the woman was abruptly a lot more interesting. *Mother Guame, is it? Yes, it's Mother Guame.* And he wouldn't want to be in her shoes for anything, right now. As a good Maric patriot, Ivarn was expected to disdain circle houses like Guame's establishment. It was a particularly insidious foreign vice the refugees from Allor had brought with them, so said the angrier voices about the city. Illegal before the Occupation and just as illegal now, save that there had always been those in power for whom such places were convenient, either to extort money from, or because they had a weakness for the vice. Ivarn was aware that more than one of his fellows at the Gownhall had dabbled, and it was something of a rite of passage for the students... The Palleseen weren't immune to the temptation, certainly. He understood they even preferred their people to go to such places over a Maric brothel where they might get entangled with women connected with the resistance. As many of them were. Ivarn himself was a pragmatist. The circle houses were a part of the landscape, and there was a whole unexplored area of study in how the sacred traditions of free Allor had been twisted into such practices. *I could write a paper...*

That the Sage-Archivist had been parted from his protective magics at the Sage of the circle houses had been Ivarn's guess. The man's proclivities had been an ill-kept secret at the best of times. Mother Guame had obviously ended up at the very heart of the Pals' angry wasp's nest of a response to what had happened. Probably she'd be up on the gallows soon enough; probably three or four different Pal officers would rake her over the coals first. Ivarn watched her sitting on the board bench her cell afforded. She met his gaze once and then looked away. No demons to come to her aid now. And it wasn't as though that art had helped the Allorwen much when the Palleseen army had marched in.

His contact came along soon after: Statlos Shrievsby, strutting up to the bars in his slightly dishevelled uniform, cap under his arm. Tall and narrow chested, the close-fitting Pal clothes straining around his waist showed just how a posting in Ilmar agreed with him. Ivarn had done his best to make sure it had. He and Shrievsby had done each other plenty of favours since the Occupation started. Most recently, of course, locking up Blackmane and rifling his shop so that Ivarn could recover Ilmari antiquities that deserved better.

"What have you let yourself in for, Ivarn?" Shrievsby asked, leaning against the bars and passing his gaze over the other prisoners. "Normally, you at least get yourself a room with a view."

"Why don't you tell me?" Ivarn replied in careful Pel.

Shrievsby smirked. His business associate's predicament was plainly cause for amusement. "Nothing to do with me, old man. You been teaching from the wrong books?"

"Nothing that should have clipped any noses here. So how about you go find out just who has my name on their desk, and grease some wheels. I want to be back at the Gownhall before any of my peers can raid my study."

Shrievsby raised an eyebrow, pointedly loitering still.

Ivarn rolled his eyes. "Haven't I lined your pockets enough?"

"Pocket lining is expensive, maestro." The title, inserted into Pel, came out like slang, devoid of respect. "My squad have plenty of pockets. It's the cut of the uniform."

Ostravar leaned close so Mother Guame wouldn't catch the next words. "You know what you brought to my rooms from Blackmane's place. Do you think I don't have ready buyers for the goods? Good Armiger families who'll make a donation to keep our relics out of the wrong hands, hmm? And you know that money trickles downwards." And he wanted to say *Like the clear concourse of streams combining*, as in the old saga, except it didn't work in Pel. The artificial language sucked the beauty out of anything you translated into it.

"Downwards, is it?" Shrievsby complained, but mildly. "Well, all right, old man. I imagine you'll be out in a day or two, greased meat that you are, but I'll go give things a squeeze, so you pop sooner. Just so's you remember who's your friend."

"Yes, yes." And then the Statlos was sloping off away from the cells, and Ivarn found Mother Guame's eyes on him. She hadn't heard anything incriminating, he was sure, but the simple fact of Ivarn Ostravar chatting so casually to one of the Occupiers might tarnish his reputation a little. Even though everyone did it, behind closed doors.

"There are," he said loftily, "sympathisers, even in dark places such as this."

She wasn't much impressed by that, but the other prisoners seemed to accept it, perhaps because it gave them hope for their own cases. Which hope was sadly misplaced. And probably, if they swung or got sent downriver, it would be for actual everyday *crimes* anyway, nothing to do with Ilmari liberation. He couldn't help everyone. He needed to preserve his own liberties for the days ahead when he'd be able to make use of them.

Then there were soldiers shouldering in, a grim squad of Palleseen, and everyone went still, waiting. Even Ivarn felt a little clutch of the fear at his throat, thinking, *Has there been a mistake? Is it me?* But they came for Mother Guame instead. Slammed her barred door open, hauled her out, marched her away. And she didn't come back. He never saw her in that place again. But that was what happened when you were an Allorwen and came to the attention of the Pals.

A dull wait later, one of the jailers appeared. The man was Maric, a 'trustie' as they called them. A former prisoner brought in for minor wrongs who'd been useful enough to keep on. Several of the breed, menials at the bottom rung of the Occupiers' Perfecture, were on Ivarn's sporadic payroll, though sadly, none of them working prison duty right now.

"Visitors, maestro," the man – or possibly woman – said. Poor light and a starveling-thin frame made it hard to tell. "You want them?"

"Visitors who?" he asked.

"Your students. Two of them. Want an assignment to work on while you're here, y'think?"

"You overestimate both the duration of my future here and the speed with which any of my students actually work," he said. "By all means, though, let them come." He would likely be down here for another day or so. It would be useful to ask them to bring him a few luxuries: pen and ink and paper, some books.

Perhaps a few preventative elixirs. He didn't fancy catching anything nasty. And he could show them his magnificent sangfroid in the face of incarceration.

The trustie was almost knocked down on the way out by Shrievsby's hurried return, long legs poling him over to Ivarn's cell.

"Where is it?" he demanded. Gone was the sly, louche and, above all, corruptible man with whom Ivarn had done such business. His face was purple in the low light, as though his tight collar was strangling him. He gripped the bars as if he was the one caught. "What did you do with it?"

"Shrievsby, calm yourself." Ivarn was trying to calm *him*self. This was thoroughly out of character.

"You old bastard, what did you *do*?" Shrievsby demanded, heedless of who overhead. "They know you've got it."

"Got what?"

"Don't act the innocent with me. The *thing*." A superstitious eyeroll around, afraid to even specify what he meant. "The Sage-Archivist's thing. The reason he's dead. They say it turned up where you were, and you walked off with it. It's in your rooms? Tell me where. If I can turn it up, then I can still fix this." Gabbling the words out, spittle spraying. Holding to the bars as though a tide was coming to sweep him away.

Ah, that. Ivarn had a moment of thinking how to play things. Admission, denial, misdirection. "I don't know what you mean," he said flatly. Not exactly convincing but it set the battlelines between them well enough.

"They *know*," Shrievsby hissed. "They know about you and me and everything, and they know you've got *it*. You want to hear who's on your case, old man? It's the Fellow-Inquirer, Hegelsy. You're his special project. And me, and *me*!"

Right then, Ivarn didn't much care about his co-conspirator. *Hegelsy*. The Inquirers. Correct Speech. He felt suddenly ten years older and very cold. "Get me out of here," he said flatly.

"What?" Shrievsby demanded.

"Out of here. Whatever way. I'll pay. Not the… the thing. Not that. But anything else."

But the Statlos was shaking his head. "They're sending me," he whispered desperately, "into the *Reproach*. After the Sage-Archivist's stupid assistant. It's a suicide detail. They're killing me the worst way, you old bastard, and it's all your fault. Tell me where the *thing* is. I will have men turn your goddamn rooms over. I will smash every damn thing and burn every book until I find it, I swear." His long face was suddenly brutally ugly, the very portrait of the Occupation.

Ivarn felt the last threads between them part. So much for that. "You'll never find it," he said simply.

Shrievsby snarled, fumbled for his knife, thought better of it, then turned and stalked away.

When the two students turned up, all of that magnificent sang-froid he had been indulging wasn't exactly *restored*, but he could put up a tattered mask of it for them. A little strain at the edges was to be expected, after all. Probably they'd think he'd already had a bout with the Inquirers and was being stoic about it. Whatever worked to keep them on the hook. A moment ago, a visit from students was a useful way to apply leverage to the Gownhall. Now it was life and death. This pair of naïfs was all he had.

The Sirovar boy, he saw – one of the hedonist crowd who made a lot of noise and coasted on family influence – plus the worryingly intense girl who always stared at him so fixedly in class. Given Ivarn's experience of the student body overall, it was disturbing to find one who actually *did* look like she was paying attention. Exactly the sort to go and do something catastrophically stupid while waving a flag, and a moment ago that would have made her a liability. Right *now*, though…

"Listen to me." He hunched close to the bars. His eyes kept straying past them to Mother Guame's empty cell, that had gone from a cause for philosophical reflection to a grim portent of his own fate. *The School of Correct Speech. The one branch of the Perfecture you don't want to take notice of you.* "Have you pen, paper?"

The girl had. He flattened the crumpled page against the wall and wrote in hurried, characters. "I need you to do something for me. Take a message. Make sure a thing is done."

"We'll do it," the girl said, confirming his opinion of her as someone not long for this turbulent world, given she had no idea what *it* was.

"No. Just make sure it's done. Arranged, by the man I'm sending you to. You know Blackmane the pawnbroker?"

Baffled looks between them. "Maestro?"

"I need something fished from a very dangerous place. Some*one.*" Because what he needed now was leverage. Leverage over the whole of the Perfecture. He needed to have control of something they wanted. And while there was *one* thing they very obviously wanted a great deal, he wouldn't be handing *that* over to anyone any time soon. But Shrievsby had let slip what else the Occupiers were trying to get back.

"A Pal woman. I need Blackmane to have her found and taken somewhere safe." *Because where she is right now is about the least safe place in all Ilmar.*

"Blackmane, maestro?" Sirovar asked, baffled and contemptuous.

"Because it's the Reproach," Ivarn told them, flat-out, seeing their reactions. Seeing the girl flinch but square her shoulders. *And she would go, the idiot. She's lucky I'm not asking her.* "The ruin-divers, more than half of them are Allorwen. They say their trinkets protect them." Of all Ilmar's gutter professions the ruin-divers' trade had the wildest swing between potential gain and brevity of lifespan. Two successful trips could set you up for five years, and your family too. One successful trip was more than half of them ever got. "Blackmane's a big man in Mirror Allor. He knows people." *And he'll do what I tell him.* He was scribbling the bait now. The hook he'd catch Blackmane on for long enough to extort this service from the man. *Burning bridges now.* First Shrievsby and now this, but if it was a choice between that and the Inquiry, then he'd burn every bridge on the river if need be.

"We won't fail you, maestro," the girl assured him. He'd have preferred more reliable messengers, in all honesty, but as with chaq, he'd play the tiles he was given.

Mother Guame's Interrogation

Back when she'd been younger, in Allor, she'd been a votaress. What the Ilmari would call a priestess, save Allor didn't have the great ossified hierarchy of the Mahanic Temple. Now she wasn't so young, and she wasn't so holy. A big woman, solid enough that sometimes, when a customer got ugly with her people, she didn't even call for the bouncer. Cunning enough that she could slap down a recalcitrant demon, if one of her girls got the sigils wrong. The inheritor of centuries of magical tradition, and there she was turning sorcerous tricks for Ilmari Armigers and sweating Pals.

And here she is beneath the Donjon, when even that debasement hadn't been enough.

They'd already had her before the School of Correct Conduct. Bound to a frame while a clerk snapped questions at her in Pel too fast for her to follow half the time. A pair of their Monitors – the thugs who were more police than soldier, though the distinction was a fine one – had beaten her across the bare back and shoulders with their batons. They'd accused her of conjuration and being a corrupting influence. She'd mumbled that she just ran a house of hospitality: tea and sympathetic ears. They'd shown her the ritual chalk, the tomes, the fetishes. She'd said it was all just decoration and set dressing. People went to an Allorwen establishment, they expected the trappings of mysticism. And all this had been entirely standard, not even the first time. Mother Guame had enjoyed similar hospitality from the Occupiers on three separate occasions, and before that, there had been visits from the Ducal Guard. It had always come down to *How much can we shake you down for?* And she'd paid, always more than she could afford, because she had no choice. Some official felt their purse was too light, and so someone like her would go hungry. The way of the world.

Then the questions had turned. That little rat of a Heron. Fleance, his name had been. Not even a client, just delivering supplies off the river. Ointments and powders, dried claws and bones and organs from magical beasts, water from certain springs. The accoutrements of her trade that were so hard to get hold of. And he'd loitered around, as they always did. Gawking at the girls, trying to catch a glimpse of the demons. She couldn't afford to alienate the close-knit boat clans. And there was always something missing, when one of them had been and gone. She'd learned to leave out occult-looking tat for the very purpose. Except this time, the weasel had either got very lucky or been after something special.

The thing that got her through *that* part of the investigation was the Pals' own curious prudishness. The one thing they absolutely would not say, nor let her say, was that their sainted Sage-Archivist Ochelby had been in her house. Had been her client. Had, when he needed to exercise the withered tool between his legs, not wanted to soil it with anything so mundane or prone to complications as a human woman. And, as they couldn't admit to *that*, she and the Monitors had negotiated a curiously roundabout conversation, with the occasional blow, about the little Heron thief. And then they'd thrown her back into the cells while they went to raise welts on the back of whoever's turn it was next. She'd watched the Gownhall maestro brought in and known that *he* wouldn't be on the rack or feel the baton crack against his shoulder blades. He'd leave here with his skin unbruised and complain bitterly to his compatriots over brandy about the brutality of the Pal regime.

Then they came for her again. She was already thinking through the consequences, if this was *it*. She had nothing to do with the theft, after all. And while she was absolutely a criminal under Occupier and Ilmari law, that had always been the case and had never been quite enough to sink her before. A great man was dead, though, and in her experience, the first thing those in power wanted to see was the sacrifice of the lowly. A scapegoat at the gallows, just to remind everyone of why you didn't get above yourself.

They marched her twice as far this time, and she reckoned that was a bad sign. Out of habit, she felt for the little string of charms about her neck, but it wasn't as though protection from stomach cramps or grief-lung was going to help, and the few that deadened physical pain had been wrung dry already. She was thrust into a windowless room where the cold lamplight shone on a trim Pal woman – a few years short of Mother Guame's age – sitting at a desk. The room was low-ceilinged but large. Enough to leave the prisoner feeling like a child at the scholomance again, shrunk to insignificance by the grand halls of learning that the Pals had later torn down.

She braced herself for the same questions, fresh beatings, or worse. This woman wasn't Correct Conduct but Appreciation, one of the Invigilators. Justice was one of the arts, to the Pals. The same people who ruled on what you might put in a book or on a stage held trials and handed down sentences. All with the same sense of disapproval of anything that didn't belong in the perfection they claimed to be bringing to the world.

The guards retreated to the back of the room, leaving her even more isolated. Just a slump-shouldered old woman far from home, here between the teeth of her enemies.

"So, tell me…" The woman's voice, clipped Pel words like stones, came to her more as echoes from the walls.

"I didn't know him," Mother Guame said. "The riverman. He was just delivering. I didn't know he'd taken anything. He wasn't one of mine." Not her kin, not her girls, not her community. "I told your people which boat he was off." Nothing they hadn't already known. "I said—"

"Tell me," the Invigilator interrupted, "about your *practices*." A shudder in the words. The prurient Palleseen confronted with the degenerate superstitions of the foreigner.

Something shifted in Mother Guame then. Something she'd not looked for, down here in the darkness.

"The conjuration," she said hoarsely, "of demons."

"That vile trade." The Invigilator leaned forwards over her desk. "And the sordid purpose to which you put it. Or do you deny it now?"

And of course she'd been denying it. She'd not given the Monitors the satisfaction, though they beat her. All just mundane hospitality. No magic here, that would be in contravention of Correct Thought. Not the least sniff of sulphur, and the magic circles on her floors mere decoration.

Right now, she looked her questioner in the eye.

"Invigilator..."

"Fellow-Invigilator Temsel," the woman told her. A decent position directly under the Perfector, the ailing Sage-Invigilator himself. Temsel was a woman of substance staring at Mother Guame with a curious hunger. With a hungry curiosity.

"I confess," Guame said flatly. "Such things have gone on in my house. I myself have set the sigils and called up beasts of alluring guise, to serve the lusts of my clients. I am guilty of it. It is all true."

"A most wicked business," said Temsel softly. A little arrow of a tongue darted out to touch her lips, and Mother Guame knew she was saved.

"I repent," she said. "I recant my primitive Allorwen ways, Fellow-Invigilator. I would welcome the chance to help you save others from the corruption of my trade. But to do so, I would have to demonstrate how such things were done. In private perhaps. For you. For your better education."

And there was that knife-edge moment when she might

be wrong, and Temsel's attitude feigned in order to draw just such a confession. But in truth, when had the Pals ever needed anything so concrete just to have a hanging?

"For my better education," Temsel echoed. A very proper and buttoned-up Palleseen woman come to this foreign city, hearing such stories about what went on. Plenty of her compatriots had passed through the doors of the circle houses in the past. Either she'd never dared to go with them, or they'd not trusted or liked her enough to make the offer. But here was a conjurer, tame and in Temsel's power. And perhaps she was unlucky in love, or recently jilted, or just trapped within the cage of her position and role and unable to navigate the maze of human interaction. Or maybe she just wanted a liaison with a thing that could be called up and commanded and sent back without complication or recourse. But whatever moved her, Mother Guame could supply her needs.

Mosaic: City of Last Chances

To pull out from within any one head, then: Ilmar. Third greatest of the Maric cities, after the capital of Teleomarn where a mad king paces endlessly under the house arrest of the Occupiers, and the beautiful city of Mahastar, centre of the Mahanic Temple faith and favoured posting for the most self-indulgent Palleseen officials. Ilmar, most recently dubbed City of Bad Decisions after the Occupiers stepped up the scale of the Old Duke's hangings. Before that, the locals used to call it the City of Last Chances, after all those who came seeking an escape they never quite managed to find. Because the Anchorwood keeps its secrets, and always has done. The Wood, which gave the place its first name, long before someone set stone and stone and named it Ilmar. The Wood, the hole in the world, the Indwellers, the last house and its long succession of keepers. The Port to Nowhere.

Half told, Mother Guame's story trails away. Our attention splits. Three separate sets of travellers leave the Donjon of Ilmar, heading west across the city. Towards the Gownhall; towards Mirror Allor and the seedy little shop that Blackmane keeps; towards the blasted ruin of a district the locals call the Reproach and the Occupiers prefer not to reference at all.

A pair of students, Lemya and Shantrov, bearing the words of imprisoned Ivarn Ostravar. A squad of Palleseen soldiers led by Statlos Shrievsby, Ivarn's erstwhile accomplice, now acting out his own death sentence. The solitary Mother Guame, released after turning magic tricks for Fellow-Invigilator Temsel. Released, with one more string tied about her neck. Not one of Hoyst's made-to-measure nooses but one more member of the Occupation who'll be turning up at her door to use Mother Guame's services without paying. She already has an impressive list of officials and Statloi from the Perfecture who know they can have one of her girls call up something to their specifications, to sport with. Some ashamed of their predilections, others just after a liaison without strings, consequences or emotional demands. And there's the other list: the high-ranking Lodge crooks who take their pleasures in lieu of protection money, the patriotic members of the resistance who need a reason to overlook her trade's very existence. All the big sticks of the city who come to rap on her door and make demands she can't say *no* to. Better they come for that reason than any other. Her contracts and agreements with the Infernal Realms are many and ironclad. There are always more demons. Just as there are always more Pals and Marics to decry the practice, and lie with them anyway behind closed doors.

She sees Shrievsby and his men commandeering a patrol-wagon and riding it off through the clutter of streets around the Donjon. She gets to walk. They shook her down for her coin when they took her in, and half the Draymen won't take you if you look too Allorwen. And she's not young; her legs and feet and back won't thank her, but she's short of options. Lemya and Shantrov are ahead of her too by then, because Shantrov spotted the coach of a distant cousin and talked them into offering a ride as far as the Gownhall. No further, though. Certainly not as far as the river or even – shudder – across it to the Gutter Districts. All very well for a roistering student like Shantrov, but *one* would *not*, don't you know, wish to be *seen*.

They leave Mother Guame stomping along in their dust, winding her way from the Donjon onto what used to be the Ducal Parade, leading from the palace all the way past the Gownhall, but which is now Liberation Way. Mother Guame, who has few fond memories of the last Duke of Ilmar, finds the name grimly ironic. Over the three years of the Occupation, she's seen the tarnished name of the Old Duke desperately polished up by a succession of would-be rabble-rousers among the Marics, and none of them has yet been able to buff it to a shine. Not a good man, the Old Duke. Half the resistance fighters opposing the Pals had been opposing *him* just a few years before. She sheds no tears. The man still casts a shadow, as the Perfector himself knows more than most.

After twenty minutes of dogged trudge, a cart slows beside her. The driver, coming back with two apprentices in the otherwise empty bed, has been making deliveries to Armigine Hill. Deliveries of what? Clinking, rattling deliveries. An open secret, that the best of the Allorwen alchemists sell their cures and restoratives, prophylactics and potency-enhancers up the Hill. The little district with the big houses that gets to look down on the Donjon as if it stands between them and the moral turpitude of the rest of the city. The thing hitched to the front of the wagon wears cloth from neck to tail and a chamfron over its forehead, and is in the shape of a horse, mostly. But Allorwen are forbidden from owning horses. One of a scatter of forbiddances that have outlived any original rationale but have never been repealed, because they don't inconvenience anybody known to the law-makers. A demon steed, such as ancient heroes might have commanded to fly to cloud castles or tilt against giants, now used as a beast of burden for a peddler of impotence cures.

The driver knows her, because Mirror Allor's a close-knit place, and despite her fall from votaress to bawd, she's still one of their community's old bones. That's her weight taken off her aching feet and a lift down Liberation Way to the river.

She can look towards the overwrought spires of the Ducal Palace, where the Perfecture now stamp their laws and hold their departmental meetings under the racked gaze of the Sage-Invigilator. She imagines the place seething like a colony of ants as the occupants react to Ochelby's death, and all the other chaos last night seems to have unleashed on the city. Like any good conjurer, like any ageing woman, she doesn't trust chaos. So little of what it brings is ever good to those at the bottom of the pile. Looking back and right is her view of the high ground and the Armigine, hazed by the smoke of the day. Back and left shows her more spires, the gilded ring-topped beauties of the Mahanic Temple, bells ringing to call the faithful to their reductive, restricting prayers. All the things these Marics must and must not do, to be faithful. And the Occupiers will bring it all down one day with their relentless rationalism. But so long as the priests keep telling their flock to obey and go in peace, the Temple remains at the foot of the list of things for the doctrine of Correct Thought to correct.

The congregation has been shrinking ever since the Occupation, Mother Guame knows. A lot of people don't want to just *obey*, and they spit on the priests who beg them to. The city's rife with native and foreign cults promising more and spreading disorder, or just with angry men and women who, in their need to oppose the Occupiers, have found a common atheism with them.

Foolishness, Mother Guame knows, and it will end badly for her and for everyone.

Liberation Way is mostly lined with half the same shopfronts and stalls it hosted back when it had another name. The newcomers have mostly jostled into the shells left by those artisans and merchants found in breach of Correct Thought in the first wave of the Occupiers' purges. After which, everybody started treating their rules a lot more seriously. The occasional blackened scar of a burned-out front Mother Guame sees is where some trader went too far the other way, became too comfortable with the way things are. The Pals burn books but not buildings. That's the resistance's job.

The birds of the resistance do not fly proud over the city. They skulk in cellars and backrooms, and the concealed smuggling holds of boats. But if they could, if they could soar away from that labouring demon-cart, they'd set the wind and the tall houses of the Armigine at their back and look towards the river. They'd see that those prosperous stalls (the unburnt ones) are a gloss, the prices and wares and quality leaching away while the desperate hunt for cloth to suit their purse. A warren of markets and courtyards and drinking dens and gambling parlours reach out into the heart of the city like a fungus. And all this for the well-to-do middle classes, the landlords and the clerks, the suppliers and the masters of their trades. Those who were established before the Occupation and have come to accommodations since.

And by then, the cart is approaching Gownhall Square – more spires, but these are black, stone as old as the Temple but seldom cleaned and never decorated by ancient rule. The heart of Maric learning, and there are angry clumps of students blocking half the street. There are Pal soldiers keeping a watchful eye. Anger in the air. The driver guides his cart cautiously around them, the demon balking and snorting yellow from beneath the white metal of its mask. No way forwards for a bulky wagon down this road, and the driver just hunkers down, preferring to wait for them to disperse rather than risk his livelihood to the back streets. A dozen carts and carriages ahead of him have made the same call. Mother Guame disembarks, careful of her old back, her old legs. The students stare and shuffle at the clutch of charms at her neck and the cut of her skirt, but there are a few Allorwen among them. They're a more cosmopolitan crowd than your average Ilmari. More than a few have pressed coin into the hand of Mother Guame's girls for a conjuration. A dare, a rite of passage, a recurring vice. So she weaves through them and stomps on, heading for the Portbridge by foot. Outstripping Lemya and Shantrov, who have stopped to stare. Outstripping Statlos Shrievsby, who's inside the Gownhall, making things worse.

The Gownhall is directly along his fastest route from the Donjon to where he's going. He has one chance only, to buy his way out of his doom. He's marched most of his men through the doors, trooped them up to Ivarn Ostravar's rooms. Not the first time he's made the visit, though previously it was to share a brandy and a pipe. To divide the spoils, take his cut of whatever goods his men delivered for the academic's pleasure. They had a good run of it, the pair of them. Shrievsby feels no guilt over that. There's scarcely an officer or official of his acquaintance who hasn't found some way of screwing satisfaction out of the people they're set over. Why else join the army and go overseas?

Except now it's gone sour. He doesn't understand how. Someone's put his name in the ear of Fellow-Invigilator Hegelsy. And perhaps Hegelsy *is* that one incorruptible man. Or more likely, he's one of the many who cover their own indiscretions by rooting out the vices of others. Hegelsy knows about Shrievsby's little side hustle for Ivarn, and this is his response. *Sent to the Reproach.*

He's aware of the growing discontent of the students and staff behind him as he storms through the dark stone corridors of the Gownhall. He's knocked down four porters and one elderly maestro who tried to delay him. He doesn't have the *time* for niceties. He's walking a cheese-wire rope strung between Hegelsy and the Reproach.

He is ruthless with Ivarn's property. He is exactly the brutish monster the educated Ilmari characterise the invader as. He tears down paintings looking for alcoves. He rips open books looking for spaces cut into their pages. He slits the seams of Ivarn's spare robes. He goes at the scholar's antique desk of black-lacquered wood with an axe, hacking it into splinters, finding three separate hidden compartments but none containing the ward. Sage-Archivist Ochelby's bloody *ward.* The priceless protection manufactured by Pallesand's greatest artisans for the specific purpose of getting their ambassador through the Wood, so they could have their foothold in one more imperfect place. And the old fool went and lost it, and now here's Shrievsby and his people tearing apart Ivarn's rooms until there's nothing whole, no place anything larger than a finger could be. And no ward. Wherever the old man hid it, it's proof against the Statlos's desperate attempts. And without it…

Standing amid the ruin, Shrievsby lets out a cry of despair. It leaves him defeated. He's out of time and options. He wants to throw a match into the splinters and torn pages, but that seems pointless now. Ivarn has outsmarted him, and the fact that the academic will get *his* soon enough is no consolation. Shrievsby has orders and no further excuse to delay them. And if he goes now, he might just get in and out before nightfall.

He marches his men out, collects the two on the gate. They head for the river, and the Portbridge. We'll catch up with them later.

Lemya and Shantrov see them exit the Gownhall and go. Spilling out after them comes the word of what they've done. The comprehensive vengeance enacted on poor Maestro Ostravar's chambers. Not only has the man been arrested, but his books, his art, his very desk has been smashed, methodically and without exception, and then the vandals just left. Didn't even take anything. A perfect encapsulation of the contempt the Occupiers hold for the occupied.

The embers already glowing at the heart of the student body flare and burn. And Lemya wants to stay there and be a part of the arguing and singing and swearing of oaths. But she's been given a mission by Ivarn himself. The pair of them extricate themselves from the words and emotions of their fellows and head on foot towards the Portbridge.

That bird again, never still. Circling south of them through air heavy with mill-smoke, coursing back along the river's churn. To the west, the mercantile docks, with a hundred strung ferries coursing back and forth to feed goods to the hungry money of eastern Ilmar. On the south-eastern bank, the Hammer Districts' factories and mills and foundries. People came here because of the Wood, but they built here because of the mountains and their metal. The air of the Hammer Districts is like brimstone and sandpaper in the throat and lungs. The men and women who work here day and night are hard and rough and a law unto themselves. In the old days, the Ducal Guard had plenty of standoffs with the workers' Siblingries over conditions and pay and who had to kneel to whom. The Pals have a heavier iron fist than ever the Duke did, but even their patrols tread carefully. The workers lost more often than they won against the Duke, even more so against the Pals, but there's always another surge of anger gathering in the cellars or the unlicensed taprooms. But in the end, even though the Herons can smuggle in many things, they can't bring in bulk shipments of food in ways the Pals won't see, and the workers need to eat. The factories are hungry too: fingers, toes, arms, children. And demons. The factories guzzle demons. The leading lights of the workers' Siblingries are conjurers fit to make Mother Guame take notes, though the specifics of their contracts with the Kings Below are quite different.

Look towards the river and it's not that the buildings get smaller as the people get poorer. Larger, in fact. On the far side of that silver knife that bisects Ilmar, they lean three-, four-storeyed, slumped against each other like drunkards lurching home. The Gutter Districts. Our bird can't see how each tottering edifice is subdivided inside, hovel on hovel, piled slant-walled like a careless child's bricks. Stretching off south and away to the tapering outskirts and the first farms. And north, though to the north the tenements become more ruinous, less inhabited, until there is a ring of derelict shells no landlord could ever milk rent from. And beyond that, like a hole in the collective vision and memory of Ilmar that nobody can look straight at: the Reproach.

But before that, right on the far side of the Portbridge, the enclaves. To the north, the Divinate, where the inhabitants desperately try to keep up a regulated and orderly existence that amazes even the perfection-seeking Palleseen – and fail, but at least they try. To the south, the ramshackle darkness of Mirror Allor, with borders that ebb and flow with each wave of arrests or influx of refugees. The district of circle houses and quacksalvers, fortune-tellers, curse-mongers and just *people*, perhaps three quarters of them Allorwen, trying to live and eat and escape the notice of the patrols. And buried in there, like a hook in the jaw of a pike, Blackmane's shop where we'll pick up the story of Mother Guame.

But first…

The Reproach of Statlos Shrievsby

The Palleseen Sway — their term for the grand outreach effort that had conquered Allor and Telmark and other lands besides — was always expressed as a great service to the world. A world bitterly at odds with itself, beset by superstition and ignorance, divided in countless ways: language, currency, laws, understanding. The Temporary Commission of Ends and Means, having brought perfection to their own islands, understood that their achievements could not stand so long as a tide of foreign chaos lapped against their shores. They had a duty. A crusade. They could perfect the world and improve the lives of all. For this universal and noble aim, it relied on tools such as Statlos Shrievsby.

Half his squad were gone.

Shrievsby and the survivors had holed up in a house that at least boasted four walls and an intact roof. Half the Reproach had less. The walls crawled with black mould up from the river. The cobbles of the streets rocked in filthy water like stale bread in soup. Some houses had fallen in on themselves. Others had slumped out into the street to stretch out their disarticulated bricks like the bodies of drunkards. The decay seemed accelerated beyond reason, even for how long this district had crumbled here, abandoned. Or not abandoned. People lived in the Reproach. Although not exactly people, or perhaps not exactly lived.

He heard the voices pass by outside. The high, tittering

laughter, the good-natured whoops, as though it was just parlour games they were at. Calling each to each with their elaborate titles. Shrievsby's remaining followers pulled closer to him, as though it would help. The raucous din of it passed by.

Some came here from outside. Fugitives so desperate they had nowhere else, just this place where nobody would be mad enough to follow. Shrievsby wasn't mad. He just feared the certain vengeance of Correct Speech more than the very probable doom of the Reproach. His men had thought likewise, and now half weren't with him anymore. Though not dead. Not most of them.

Gone native.

"We need to move on, Statlos," said Murredy. The man's pasty face was strained. "The others aren't coming."

Shrievsby hadn't ever thought they were. He'd come in here because there were still shutters on the windows, and he couldn't be seen from outside. Be seen by *them*, nor *see* them. And his squad were waiting for him to give them orders and he didn't have any. The Reproach wasn't even very large, but it was overgrown and ruinous. And worse.

When they'd fled down the last street, he'd looked back and seen buildings and avenues that weren't even the ones he'd passed. The place was changing around him.

"We'll…" he started, and then there was a rattle and a clatter of stones, and someone was scrabbling their way into their hidey-hole.

They snatched up their batons. Shrievsby had his to the shoulder, tableth in place, ready to speak the word to discharge it. The others were even more jittery. It took Murredy's hiss to stop them just shooting the newcomer en masse the moment she turned up. It was Plummel, her uniform torn open at the collar and ripped down one sleeve, eyes wide.

"Statlos." She flinched back from the batons pointed her way. "Statlos, is that you?" Squinting into the dark.

Shrievsby's throat was dry, but he forced words into it. "Report, soldier."

"I've seen her, Statlos. The Sage-Archivist's assistant. Companion-Archivist Nasely."

"You've what?" And the roof here was whole, but he felt like a ray of sunshine had broken in nonetheless. "You're sure it was her?"

Plummel nodded rapidly. "Saw her in a window. Holed up on a top floor. Woman in Archivist robes, who else is it going to be?"

"Go poke your head out," he told Murredy. The man looked mutinous for a moment but, with Plummel's news, Shrievsby's authority held. Murredy went from window to window, peering out gingerly. Not frightened of what might see him, but of what he might see. *It comes in through the eyes, they say.* Though, as the Perfecture wouldn't officially admit to the Reproach's existence, nobody really knew.

"Clear, Statlos," he confirmed.

"Then we go," Shrievsby confirmed. "Fast and quiet, all of you. Plummel, lead."

Still plenty of daylight sky, when they crept out. Two hours until dusk, at the very least. That was the dreadful thing. The evils of Ilmar needed darkness to hide in: the sorcerers and the thieves and the bird-badge insurgents. Not so the things of the Reproach. The day that shone on their streets was as much the enemy as was the night.

Plummel led them with reckless abandon, leaping over piles of rubble, stumbling on the loose cobbles, blundering from leaning walls. She kicked through the thickets of weeds that sprouted everywhere. The fingers of crooked trees that had grown out from walls, or thrust up where the streets let them, snagged at her torn uniform and her hair. And then she was up the slope of a tumbled wall, crouching there with her knees up by her ears and her baton askew, looking back at them, signalling urgently. And by then, Shrievsby understood something was wrong, was lagging back, but his people outstripped him and he didn't dare raise his voice to call them back.

Murredy was first up the rubble, staring over the other side. "Where?" Shrievsby heard him demand. "Which building's she in, Plummel?"

"What sayest the varlet?" came a new voice. A scarecrow figure was strutting out of a weed-choked side street, face cracked almost open by the width of its smile. A handful of others skulked behind him, and the corners of Shrievsby's eyes were registering movement from all over. Stick-thin men and women creeping out of holes or clambering from the rotten sockets of lost windows. He'd swear they almost seemed to seep from between the stones.

Just men. Just women. Beggarly-thin and wearing the least of rags. All elbows and knees, and hardly a weapon between them. A stick here, cradled like a sceptre in the crook of an arm barely thicker. A cobblestone held like a regal orb. One had a sword, true, but it was an ancient bar of rust that looked heavier than the starveling rake who bore it, surely looted from a tomb.

"My Lady Ironyar," the scarecrow called to Plummel, "what babble call'st they?" Speaking not Pel, not even the regular street-Maric Shrievsby could hold a conversation in. Speaking an antique Maric full of strange stresses and suffixes, a whole ghost lexicon of qualifiers and genders nobody used any more.

And Plummel's head swivelled to bless the newcomer with a delighted smile. "Why I beknow me not, my good Count Dirovesnic," she declaimed, in that same idiolect. "Some pet name he hath for me, prithee. But look who I hath brought!"

Shrievsby was backing off now. Most of his people were. Murredy had half scrabbled, half fallen off the rubble, trying to put as much distance as he could between himself and Plummel. The scarecrow's eyes found him despite it all, and that gaunt face lit with a hollow delight, like a candle set aflame within a gourd.

"Why, my good Lord Ystrovir! You come to join our revels! Right glad we are to have your company!"

Shrievsby shot him. A word spat to his baton and the gold tableth set within it flared incandescent with spent power. A bolt of fire lanced from the weapon and struck the scarecrow man in the brittle cage of his ribs, sending him somersaulting backwards, brains dashed out against the heaped stones even if the fire hadn't killed him. For a moment, in the echo of that, all else was silent. Step by careful step his surviving squad were pulling back to him, their own weapons levelled. He sensed a dreadful hope in them. A terrible, false hope. Maybe the mystique of this place was lies. Maybe a charged baton would suffice. Shrievsby slipped a fresh tableth into the weapon's slot, hands finding their way without his eyes leaving the enemy.

Plummel hadn't come back to them. Had she still been his when she'd come to the squad in their hiding place, or had she been lost already and lured them out? Or had she somehow been *both*, Plummel enough to know what words to speak, and yet, and yet…

Murredy wasn't coming back either. He stood halfway down the fall of tumbled stones that had been someone's house once, someone's life. Stopped where he'd halted at the shot. And now he turned to look at Shrievsby, and on his face was such a look of recognition and joy.

"Why, my good Lord Ystrovir!" he cried to Shrievsby. "You come to join our revels! Right glad we are to have your company!" Murredy's voice but the same intonation as the dead man, the same antique Maric words. His face, with another man's expression gripping it in bony fingers. And more movement now, shuffling at alleys and windows. The gaunt and the starving, and some of them half-naked, so he could count every rib and sore and untended wound. Others had clad themselves in age-rotted finery looted from what had once been the houses of the great. At the back, a circle of them were dancing on stick legs with stilt-walker elegance. Some ancient capering of approaches and demure backsteps, bows and hand-kissing, enacted by men and women surely just a step this side of the grave, or else a step beyond.

Murredy strode forwards with perilous dignity, his baton like a walking stick, its true use forgotten.

"Thou art come right readily," he addressed Shrievsby. "The Count of Osboryat and all his court have bless'd us with their presence and the minstrels e'en now strike up."

Shrievsby heard the music, faint on the air. Warped strings and rot-clogged pipes, and drums that echoed forever. Then something else arrived that should have struck more terror into him but brought a weird release instead. Forcing its bulk along a narrow gap between two leaning buildings came the beast from the Anchorwood. And Shrievsby had assumed it had returned there, or else dissolved away like a demon whose contract is done. Yet here it was, fish-faced, scale-flanked, tearing up the decaying cobbles with its claws. It made a sound, partly screaming, partly like strained metal, and tore right through the dancers and the thick of the emaciated court. Shrievsby saw at least two of them trampled down, smashed to ruin by the thing's bulk and speed. Then it had Murredy in its teeth with a snap. The man made no attempt to avoid it. None of them had reacted to the monster at all. It did not exist for them.

And they barely seemed to exist for it. It shook Murredy and then let his limp form fly, all the way up, until his ragdoll corpse lodged in the broken rafters of a roof. It pawed at another body, but whatever had infected the damned of the Reproach had left them unfit fare for the beast.

It lunged past, and the hideous trap of those jaws closed on the closest soldier, and *that* was sustenance for the monster. It crunched and ground at him, shredding flesh and uniform, and cracking bones, and its vast plate eyes rolled with pleasure.

Shrievsby staggered back. His people were running, and no two of them together. He tried to call them, but his voice was thin as a reed.

The beast looked up. For a dreadful moment, he thought he

had its attention, because those eyes saw everything on both sides of it. Some other scent had hooked it, though. It snorted and growled and then was off again, flexing sinuously down its length as it got into its loping stride. Its armoured tail flicked another of the ragamuffin men away like a toy. It passed from his sight between the buildings in heartbeats, and then he heard a high scream. A real voice, not one of these puppet jesters.

Nasely, he realised. The Sage-Archivist's assistant. The woman he'd been sent to find. The monster was still hunting her. Somehow she was uneaten, and still in her right mind. Because none of the vacantly grinning marionettes around him had a scream left in them.

He ran. He ran after the beast, because if he could snatch Nasely from its jaws, that was his ticket out. That was the thread he could follow back to a normal life. He hadn't ever been a courageous man, but desperation gave him wings.

And he was heading into stranger quarters now. The path the beast had smashed through the Reproach was overshadowed by taller walls, and more solid. He was running into the very heart of the place, practically riding on the monster's tail. The stones were dark here, set square and not riven through with weeds and sprouting trees, and when the beast reached a bridge he'd thought was fallen in, the arch was whole, capped at its apex by winged statues that still showed a gilded gleam.

And all around was other movement, the frantic spider-scurry of the starveling men and women. Those luckless Ilmari who'd been drawn here or fled here or come hunting their fortunes, and never left. He saw them clad in mismatched finery like children in the cast-offs of their grandparents. Tall caps and flowing capes with bright linings, wide-sleeved tunics and many-layered gowns. They ran like rats, and yet he saw them dance and pirouette, genuflect and wheel.

Then he broke into open ground and stopped, staring. Ahead was a palace. The Duke's own – now the seat of the Palleseen

Perfecture – paled in comparison. The walls were set with murals of turquoise and gold and chalcedony, miraculously complete. The roof lifted into fantastical spires and onion-domes, capped with spread-winged ospreys and condors, meticulously covered in gleaming gold leaf. There were statues of bears holding halberds either side of doors of brass-studded, carven wood.

Impossible. But here it was, and he could almost hear the vaults, the treasures, the tapestries and wonders within, calling to him. And the beast had stopped, snarling and pacing. And up there, through the window of one narrow tower: a pale face, a *Palleseen* face. Nasely.

The monster stared up, cavernous maw agape, and then loped away with a rattle of scales, hunting for a way in. Shrievsby stepped out into the square, walking along a rank of robed statues whose gilt stone swords crossed above his head. There was snow falling, he saw, from a sky that had surely been clear. The woman above leaned out from her window like a princess in an old story.

"Statlos?" Her thin and ragged voice. "Did they send you for me? Can you get me out of here?" Speaking the hard, flat words of Pel and not the florid arabesques of antique Maric, but shot through with hope.

He could feel them all behind him, the revellers. They were capering and skittering down every street, their eyes mad with visions. Shrievsby opened his mouth, extending a hand to Nasely up above.

"Why," he called, "what bless'd visage do I see regards me? It is the Lady of Tresov or I mistake me!" Mouth pulling into a wide smile. "Come down, O lady, for I fain would dance."

And her face contorted into horror, retreating from the window to find a new hiding place. But in his eyes, she was smiling, and the minstrels played the overture of the next dance, and every note was beauty.

The Pawnbroker

*Mirror Allor was never much like the nation it was named for.
Pushed to the very edge of the Gutter Districts, where the smoke of
the factories thickened the air. Factories that had needs the Allorwen
could supply. Nobody negotiated a labour contract with the infernal
quite like an Allorwen. Fleeing Allor had been a privilege. It took
money or influence or friends. Those who escaped were the mystics
and sorcerers, the upper echelons of Allor society, ending up as gutter
magicians, pox doctors and brothel-keepers. And artisans, crafters,
makers of sacred objects. Skilled professionals denied legitimate
opportunity to practise their trades. And everyone who had fled
brought what goods they could, which soon had to be sold for food
and rent and bribes. And so, along with all the second-hand magic,
Mirror Allor was where goods could be bought and sold for ready
money and no questions; half of Ilmar's treasures passed through
there among the host of skilfully crafted forgeries.*

And so we return to Mother Guame.

She pushed her way into Blackmane's shop to see him dealing
with a customer. The selling kind. A shifty Maric youth in
poor, shapeless clothes, perhaps a very junior Lodge soldier,
more likely not even that yet, just a street vandal who thought
he'd struck lucky.

Blackmane was hunched behind his desk, his bristling fur
mantle making him look like a beast in its lair. He had a glass to
his eye and was looking at most of a wooden statue of a leaping

cat. Dark wood, the glint of a gem in one eye socket, the tail and rear legs ragged with splinters. Blackmane's eyes flicked once to Guame, then returned to their prey. He sighed theatrically.

"If you'd only brought me all of it," he said. "But look, you've—*some* previous *owner* has murdered the poor beast. Plus gouged out its left eye. What am I supposed to do with this? A paperweight?" He placed it on his desk in such a way that it fell over onto its side. "Not even that."

"It's magic," the youth insisted.

"Is it, now?"

"I got it – the man who sold it to me said it was from the little temple on Crab Way. The old Loruthi one to the leopard god, that the Pals shut down. It's magic."

"It's nothing. Seven pence. And that only because it still has one eye that might fetch something."

"Look, they said I'd get thirteen pence for it. They said… No, that was it. Thirteen pence, *White Manor*."

Blackmane stood. Not even a sudden movement, but abruptly he seemed to fill that end of the shop and loom over the youth besides. "Five pence," he rumbled.

"What? You said—"

"You do not know enough to come here and *White Manor* me. You do not have it in your veins or your past to earn that. You do not get to empty my purse just because you parrot a word and think yourself wise. Five pence if you leave now. Three if you stay and waste my life with your arguing."

Guame saw the youth's hands clench and unclench, but Blackmane scared him. The whole of Mirror Allor scared him. The windows garlanded with paper charms to ward off sickness, the bright painted banners to seal in luck. He probably thought there was a demon behind every door, contracted to devour the souls of thieves. It was a convenient thing for potential thieves to believe.

He went off with his five pence and a scowl. Blackmane came out from behind his desk, cat statuette forgotten, and took her left hand, opening it palm up and pressing his fingertips there. The old greeting of sorcerers, that life in Ilmar had debased to just the way Allorwen of any stripe acknowledged each other. As though they were all magicians now, just like the Marics said.

"What did it cost you to get out?" he asked.

"The usual," she said, and put a precise distance between them. Because they both wielded influence among their people, but they were neither of them entirely trusted by their fellow Allorwen, nor by each other. They were both too much in the company of outsiders. And while there was a certain sanctity to Mother Guame's trade, Blackmane dealt in stolen goods and pilfered relics. He associated with criminals from within the quarter and without. Beyond the pale, or at least with one foot either side of its boundary line. And he saw that doubt in her eyes and looked away, but said nothing that might dispel it.

"It's good," he said. "Good." Hand reaching for the broken cat, in which Mother Guame could sense some dregs of latent power. It could be burned, and the ash used for ritual chalk, or else its power decanted into a gem – these days, more likely just a glass bead. Even as the Pals melted down pillaged magic into their little tablethi that gave life to their engines and weapons.

He wanted to ask her, she could see. Ask the same questions the Pals had, about the events of the previous night. Or else ask how much she'd told them.

The door rattled on its hinges, though. Two new visitors – more Maric youth come to gawp or buy cheaply enchanted tat or sell their grandmothers' heirlooms for beer money. A better dressed clientele than the vandal who'd just left. Students, if she was any judge. A girl with that wide-eyed, defensive look a lot of Marics got in Mirror Allor. A boy a little older with a better tailor and the long face of an Armiger scion. Mother Guame backed away, letting the shelves and drawers and hanging taxidermy of the shop half eclipse her. Blackmane regarded the newcomers without love.

"Yes?" he asked them. "What does the Gownhall want with

my humble establishment?" Not welcoming. Students weren't good customers. The dares and flippancy that brought them to Mother Guame's tended to take the form of stolen stock and pranks in Blackmane's trade.

The girl spoke. "We're here from Maestro Ostravar." Blackmane went still. His face still polite, nothing overtly hostile, but Mother Guame knew the calm that came before knives, even if this girl didn't.

"And what," Blackmane's voice rolled rich in his throat, "does Maestro Ostravar want with me?"

"Your help, maestro." For a moment, Guame had thought the girl would repeat the vandal's error with the title. Labelling Blackmane as if he were a Maric schoolmaster was a worse joke, in a way, though at least not in poor taste.

"Help." Blackmane echoed incredulously, but she was thrusting a crumpled paper at him. He took it and retreated back behind the desk, his glower pinning them where they stood. Mother Guame followed him, though. She didn't trust the Gownhall bringing its business into the quarter, and she didn't trust Blackmane either. And though he scowled, he knew her well enough to show her what the man had written.

To my erstwhile gaming companion Blackmane, it ran, in fine handwriting cramped by circumstance. *I find myself in durance vile and under personal threat, and must needs have something to offer my persecutors. It would greatly please me if that leverage were to be placed within my power to call upon. In this case, it has come to my notice that there is one adrift within the Reproach whose return to the Perfecture would carry considerable weight. Namely, the survivor of the late Sage-Archivist's battalion whom we witnessed exiting, pursued. Or else our hapless companion of the table who suffered such a loss, though none seem to know if he is in the ruins or not. Either or both might suffice to allow me to keep the current wolf from my throat. I am aware our friendship is of a complex and transactional nature, oft strewn with sharp stones. So it is that I induce you with this. The thing we both witnessed and coveted. I cede my title in it to you, should you accomplish this trifle for my benefit. Failing which, when I am asked the hard questions, I would greatly regret should my answers have a hair of the black dog to them. Your respectful peer in chance and scholarship. I.*

Mother Guame's eyes narrowed to slits. "What have you done?" She eyed the two students who were keeping a politic distance, their gaze straying to the intermingled tat and wonder displayed about the little cave of a shop.

"I? Ask rather what has been done to me," growled Blackmane, but he saw she wouldn't let him go at that, and his shoulders slumped beneath the furs. "I had a moment of weakness and indulged my vindictive nature. Which has indirectly led to this."

She was able to parse that easily enough. Blackmane and Ostravar's rivalry, and the latter's occasional predations upon the former, were well known about Mirror Allor. Scowled and muttered about, but it was hardly the only such barbed relationship one of her neighbours was snarled in. Become prominent enough in the community, and someone from outside would mark it. Mother Guame had her own list of scavengers who took advantage of her, after all. And you didn't strike back, not unless you were absolutely sure you could get away with it. Apparently, Blackmane had overstepped.

"He doesn't know, though?" Voice low so the students wouldn't catch it.

"Or he has nowhere else to turn."

"This... 'thing' he mentions..."

"You know what."

The reason she'd been Ivarn's near cellmate in the Donjon. And Ostravar...

"He has it?"

"He was there," Blackmane admitted. "And if he gave it to them straight, they'd take him up for the death of the

Sage-Archivist, most likely. If he gives it to me, perhaps he thinks he could just take it back again." He stared down at the paper, pinned beneath his heavy hand to the desktop. "I notice you haven't asked about the Reproach."

"If you think I don't know where half your stock comes from," she told him, with a curl of the lip.

"Not half. Only a little." A hurt look, as though she'd impugned his establishment. And then he was shambling past her, a bear too big for the cramped spaces of his own den. An act, she knew. Making himself the clumsy clown, so the students forgot he was dangerous. Belying the bumble, his hands had four little cups and a flask in them when he reached the desk's far side. Wordlessly, he poured out a little blood-red spirit into each.

"To the ongoing health of my good friend Ivarn Ostravar," he said, and that meant they had to drink, of course. And that fourth cup was for her, binding her into the covenant. A little contract, to seal her to silence over what he was about. She sighed and took it up.

"You seem ragged, my students," Blackmane rumbled. "Long nights for all of us. We've been back and forth across the city, we four, last night and this morning. Go get what rest you can, I advise you."

"But—" the girl started. He put his cup down with a definitive clunk that cut her off.

"Three nights' time. Come to the Anchorage."

"No, no," the girl tried. "Ivarn—"

"Will have to endure," Blackmane said. "Will have to use those words of his to dance his interlocutors along. Three nights' time. Get the word to him. Let him know Blackmane accepts his bargain, but the ruin-divers I have pull with don't convene until then. Come to the Anchorage, and you'll see me do my part."

"But these people, the ones the maestro needs, they'll—"

"Already be lost," Blackmane said with finality. "Some skinny thief and a Palleseen clerk? They will be wearing the phantom velvet already, and three days will mean nothing."

Mother Guame saw the girl twitch another couple of times, trying to construct counter-arguments. Blackmane just stood there: intimidating, impassive. A foreigner in a foreigner's quarter.

"Well, do we even have to be there then?" the boy student demanded abruptly. "Can't you just—" But his friend elbowed him in the ribs and shut him up.

"We will be there," she confirmed. "So we can tell the maestro we saw the deal done, the instructions given." And more, Guame saw. She meant more, that she wouldn't tell her friend because he'd talk her out of it. *Ah, youth. Stupid youth.*

The Face of Perfection

Fellow-Inquirer Hegelsy. Last seen calling Blackmane back at the hangman's yard, so that, soon thereafter, a couple of names found their way to his desk. Ostravar, Shrievsby, collaborators who'd rooked Blackmane one time too many. One in chains now, the other lost. Hegelsy always gets what he wants out of the city. Find the fracture and the friction, apply pressure against the wound until results run red out of the cracks.

An audience with the Sage-Invigilator was never a pleasure. At the man's door, Hegelsy almost had second thoughts. He liked to think he had a delicate stomach. He certainly had a keen nose. It served him for wines and cheeses and the flower-flavoured clear candies he indulged in. And the secrets of others. He could smell fear, he liked to think, separate the reek of guilt from that of an unwashed body.

So he hesitated, because Sage-Invigilator Culvern stank. A thick rope of it oiled its way even past the timbers of the door. The man lathered on perfumes and oils each morning, bathed and had his servants scrub his flesh, and still he stank. Hegelsy could pick out the sourness of it past any amount of rosewater and lavender-petal and oil of jacinth.

He needed the authority, though. If his promised promotion had come through – if they'd finally make him Sage-Inquirer – then he'd be able to take the appropriate actions himself, as a man only one step below the city's senior official. A Fellow had limits, though.

If I was a Sage, I might not even need to bother. But it seemed unlikely his personal ambition would stop at the rank. There was always a Professorship back home, on the Temporary Commission. He needed to prove to his superiors within the School of Correct Speech that he was worthy of the honour. Extra badges and ribbons for his coat and sash, to establish he was suitably learned in the scholarly study of rooting out superstition and ingratitude.

He rapped, and a sound came from within that he interpreted as permission. He had a pouch of herbs drawn up to his chin, in any other circumstance enough to water his eyes. It wouldn't last, he knew. He needed to make his case swiftly and get out.

The Sage-Invigilator's servants parted for him. They went masked, leather snouts like gargantuan shrews. *Looking exactly like the sort of cultists Correct Speech is supposed to root out,* Hegelsy thought. None of this was putting on the proper show for the natives. It was a circus. About time Culvern was called home to account for his poor choices. Except back home, they'd doubtless heard what had happened to the man and didn't want him anywhere near.

He was in his bath. He was often in his bath when Hegelsy visited his private chambers in the Ducal Palace. One more reason Hegelsy preferred to work out of the Donjon. The water in the bronze tub was murky and greenish. Where it lapped against Culvern's skin it carried away a greasy scum that spread out from his body like spilled oil. The man's torso, above the water, was spotted with fist-sized pustules as though something had laid its eggs in him. His skin tone was greenish-pale, week-dead fish bellies. One side of his jaw was pushed out, half closing the eye above it.

"What?" he rasped.

"The matter of the Gownhall," Hegelsy pronounced carefully, the herbs right beneath his nose now, and none of it enough to ward off the sheer rotting stench of the man. "I sent a missive. With utmost urgency."

Culvern's eyes rolled. "I have," he said, "many matters requiring my attention, Fellow-Inquirer."

He had been tall, straight and strong, Hegelsy remembered, when they'd marched into Ilmar at the head of an army. He'd masterminded the street-fighting and bearded the Duke in his palace, then broken down those doors and hauled the man out to face Palleseen justice. Culvern back then had been a man to be respected. Not this man.

"*Utmost* urgency," Hegelsy repeated. "Two days ago. Sage-Invigilator—"

Culvern let out a groan and sank a handful of inches lower in the bath. The air about him seemed to ripple, and one of his sores opened like a red mouth. "What do you *want*, Hegelsy." An unforgivable liberty, to refer to his inferior by name as though they were peers or friends. Hegelsy felt the familiarity as though the man had reached out and smeared pus over him with ungloved hands. His gorge rose at the thought, and he fought it down.

"I require *signatures*," he hissed, through clenched teeth, trying to screw his very nose up to keep out the sour reek of decay. "To deputise sufficient Correct Conduct soldiers. I am concerned by the hotbed of lassitude and inappropriate talk that the Gownhall has become."

"We have arrangements," Culvern told him, eyes screwed up in pain. "With the Gownhall. There are benefits…"

There had been considerable enrichment on the part of various members of the nascent Perfecture, was what Hegelsy strongly suspected had happened. Treasures, money, favours, the secrets of the Duke's arcane vault and its locks. And their contributions towards the study of the Anchorwood, for what that was worth. The academics of the Gownhall had traded enough to be allowed to teach, even if their curriculum was curated by the Perfecture. A winking equilibrium had arisen that

Hegelsy had always loathed. *Not*, he assured himself, because he hadn't received any of that quid pro quo that he was sure had been going around. Hadn't even been able to *prove* any of it. As though his fellow officials had been laughing at him behind his back. *That Hegelsy – not even worth bribing!*

"There has been continuing unrest at the Gownhall since we arrested their scholar."

"Since *you* arrested him," Culvern pointed out, and that was true enough.

"It is not fit that we simply turn a blind eye to their heterodoxy. The man was implicated in a number of matters touching the heart of the Perfecture. And the student body has shown it does not accept the rational rule of just law. There are *slogans*. There are flags. There is inappropriate Maric nationalism. In the papers I sent for your approval, I itemised a long list of incorrectnesses."

"You are—" a shudder passed through Culvern's quivering, naked flesh "—*tedious*, Hegelsy."

"Let me do my job, and I will not trouble you," Hegelsy insisted. "Let me impose a military presence on the Gownhall, arrest their ringleaders, show them that they cannot thumb their noses at the law with impunity. It is not *proper*, Sage-Invigilator."

Whatever answer Culvern had ready was gagged back down. He gripped the sides of the bath and the water roiled. The spoiled-cheese stink intensified, and rancid shadows moved beneath his skin.

Hegelsy remembered the Old Duke when they'd brought the man out to hang him. A good crowd that day, the best he'd ever seen. Not just a respectable turnout from the occupation forces, but locals too. The Duke hadn't endeared himself to the people he'd squatted over. He'd been a great bloated hulk in sackcloth, standing on the scaffold. The swollen glands of his neck drooping like a fleshy cravat. Not a fat man by nature, not at all. Not a glutton's bulk. A curse, they said. From an Allorwen witch he'd despoiled. Or else another noble line he'd ended, whose last scion had spoken the fatal words. Or some traveller from the Anchorwood his people had waylaid, or even the Indwellers themselves. He wasn't short of enemies, the Old Duke. Plenty of candidates to land him with the curse that mortified his flesh even as he inhabited it. Had him rot and curdle and sour the air, and yet not die from it. Seeing him standing there, the rope lost in the suppurating baggage of his throat, Hegelsy had wondered that the man had been so keen to extend his life. *Were it me, I'd leap from the platform for the pure relief of it.*

And so they'd executed the Duke of Ilmar, but not the curse. It was tenacious, that thing. The moment the man's lopsided body had stopped quivering, Culvern had begun to show the signs. The Duke's last revenge, to pass his affliction to his conqueror.

"How! Many! Soldiers?" The words erupted out of Culvern like sneezes, spraying mucus and spittle across the room. "Someone sign him dispensation for thirty men, no more! Economic use of resources, Fellow-Inquirer. Basic principle of the Sway." Culvern forced an eye open to stare at him. "Thirty soldiers to be placed on *standby* for intervention at the Gownhall should circumstances merit. For the purposes of making targeted arrests against ringleaders inciting the student population. Further force *only* in response to action from the citizenry. Discretion, Hegelsy! Delicacy!" One of his servants was clumsily scribbling the requisition with gloved hands. "Now get out of my sight! You're bringing the migraines on early. Oh powers! Powers and regulations, bring me my medicine! My ointment!"

Hegelsy retreated with his hard-won papers before anybody could go for the ointment. Every effort of Palleseen medicine had proved unequal to the curse. It had already transcended death. There was nothing within Correct Thought that could put a dent in it, and Hegelsy suspected Culvern had ransacked the lore of Allorwen quacksalvers and Maric healers as well, behind closed doors. And rational medicine would triumph eventually, Helgesy had no doubt. The science was being perfected along with everything else in the world. But until then, Culvern would have to wait, just like the city of Ilmar and all the other fallible things. Wait, and know only that the curse tormented him, but it would keep him alive to appreciate it.

Ruslav's Master's Voice

The Vulture faction of the resistance was no better than the criminal Lodges, was what the Ravens told anyone who'd listen. Not entirely accurate, but only because it drew a hard distinction between the two that didn't exist. When Ruslav shatters someone's kneecap or breaks an arm, it would take a philosopher to say with certainty whether it was an act of crime or liberation.

When Benno stomped up the boarding house stairs to rattle a cudgel at his door, Ruslav was staring at the painting. Not on his wall. In the fire grate, in fact. He had matches in hand. He'd had them in hand, on and off, since he came back and found Lemya'd left the piece for him. He'd barely gone out. He'd absented himself from his usual haunts. He'd shirked his duties. Instead, he'd eaten Ellaime's tasteless gruel and drunk her bad tea, rubbed shoulders with the other boarders and not noted them. Except for Lemya, and she'd barely been about. The one time she had, she'd been too caught up in some worry of her own to see him staring at her. Trying to kindle in himself that sense of the Pursuit he wanted to feel. And it was there. But it was as though she'd grown away from him, or he'd grown up. As though the romance he'd wanted with her had flourished in some accelerated dream state while his back was turned, burgeoned and blossomed and died back. Retreated to some companionable *Ah, yes, I remember...* A fondness, a warmth of old memory, even though nothing had ever passed between them. And upstairs, the painting. The lone figure on its haunted mountainside. The ruinous castle. Nonsensical nightmare scene.

He felt the tug when he saw it, as though when going to woo Lemya he'd left his heart open, and all that hopeful flight of feelings had taken roost in the canvas instead. All well and good when it had been *hers*, but now it was *his*.

And there had been men before, but mostly just power plays, enforcing the hierarchy of the Lodges. Not these feelings. Not *this*.

He fingered the matches again. Struck one. Stared at – into – the canvas. The depths of perspective, the far mountains, the moon. Let the match go out. He'd had no fire in his rooms for two cold nights now, because this was what he'd given himself for tinder.

Then came Benno's feet and Benno's club, simultaneously welcome and aggravating. He and Ergice, come to rouse their good friend Ruslav.

He saw their expressions. Benno bold enough to enquire, faux-courtly, how Ruslav's lady was, trying to sneak a look past Ruslav into the room. Knowing only that the man in front of them wasn't the happy Ruslav of the consummated Pursuit. Something had gone wrong, and that was enough for them to enjoy. They'd forgotten who he was.

He couldn't let them see the picture. It wasn't even the oddness of its placement in the fireplace. He felt his inner mind was written there now. Imprinted on it. Impossible that Benno or Ergice wouldn't read him there, in large print. *A man made this, and Ruslav loves it.*

So he took offence instead. Always a reliable option. Picked Ergice up by the straining seams of her fancy coat and slammed the woman against the wall. Cuffed Benno hard alongside the head then half shoved him downstairs. And that was good. It reminded them of who he was, and it reminded Ruslav too. He was stronger and tougher than either of them. A Lodge bravo dressed sharply and loved like a poet but never shied away from bruising his fists against his enemies. Or his friends.

Benno stumbled down the stairs and put a foot into someone's full chamberpot, left optimistically outside their door. Then it was Ruslav and Ergice laughing at him, rather than him and Ergice laughing at Ruslav, and that was a restoration of the way of the world. Benno's look threatened murder, but then Benno was one of those people who made all sorts of promises they couldn't keep.

"Anyway." Benno, shaking his foot to get the worst of the piss off his shoe. "She wants you."

"Which?"

"Who can tell?"

It was Carelia. Today she was wearing a purple that was almost black, which meant Evene, wherever she was, had that pale silver-green on to subtly clash with her sister. Not the two of them enthroned, though. No great audience. Just her at the pit's edge, and the thing below. Her placement was a guarantee of their solitude. She'd never get so close to the brink if there was anyone within arm's reach to give her a push. The appetites of the Bitter Sisters' pet were politically omnivorous.

Evene was the sister Ruslav preferred to deal with. You knew where you were with her. Mostly it was wearing the boots that kicked in the doors of some shopkeeper who hadn't kept up his payments or the teeth of some operator who'd skimmed too much off the top. Evene hated everyone equally. Carelia hated the Pals more than her fellow Marics. Except – insofar as Ruslav could work out – for other resistance factions, whom she hated even more. And except for Evene, whom she hated most. It was a complex hierarchy of spite, and he had difficulty keeping up with it.

"You've been distant, Ruslav," she said. Benno and Ergice had put a space between them and him, just in case this was going to be one of *those* meetings. Already composing a decently lyrical eulogy in case they had to raise a final cup to him in some tavern tonight.

He shrugged. As if to make up for his silence, the thing in the pit rustled like a hundred years of cast-off snakeskins. Carelia beckoned.

"City's restless," she said. He advanced cautiously, skirting the pit's edge. Down below, the thing moved, its bird's nest of angular legs so dense he couldn't see its actual body. Its head, or the blunt grasping hand-with-eyes horror it had instead of one, meandered up one curved wall, smallest limbs scrabbling aimlessly, before it slid back down. Its long feelers weaved lazily back and forth.

"I heard, students," he said.

Carelia's expression showed just how little she rated the Gownhall and its cadre. "Pals pushing their noses everywhere. Difficult for anyone to do business. Still, they're stretched thin. All those officials lining their nests with soldiers. Big pissing contest up at the palace. Opportunities, perhaps." Just broken fragments of conversation, nothing for him to answer or latch on to.

"Herons are being difficult," she said, and that, at least, sounded like a sensible utterance he could be expected to reply to.

"You want us to go throw some in the river, Auntie?" The old term of respect, once just for any Maric matriarch, now fallen into the gutter with so much else.

"In hand. As you'd know, if you'd shown your face at court." She stepped back abruptly, leaving him closest to the pit's edge. For a moment, he thought it was going to be *that* time after all. Braced, ready for the shove, the shot. But someone else was coming in, a boy, just one of the junior recruits looking to become a soldier in time. Nervous – terrified, in fact – but refusing to show on his face the fear that vibrated every line of him. He had a leather sack, stained about the seams. When he stood at the pit's edge, the world held its breath as always. Even at the best of times the Bitter Sisters' mood could change like weather. Nobody was entirely safe, standing there. Not even the Sisters themselves. The thing down there had a reach on it. It had been known to be proactive about feeding times.

But the boy emptied the sack in – red chunks, and was that just a sheep or a pig, or had one of the Herons paid a hard price already? Emptied the sack and then got well back as the thing got to work.

"Pals everywhere. People think it's not business as usual," Carelia said, over the crunching and sucking sounds. The crack and splinter of bone. "Anchorage, tonight. Ruin-divers. Remind the old boy we get *ours* first. We *permit* them to scavenge." Standing close now, so that he was between her and the sounds of feeding. Advancing on him, and he had to keep his distance, and keeping face meant he couldn't just slide one side or the other. And the abrupt cessation of slobbering and grinding. Those whip-like feelers, groping their way up the pit side, suddenly interested in the conversation.

"I'll remind them," Ruslav confirmed, dry-throated.

"And a bonus. The thief. Fleance. If they can bring him out."

"Right. I'll tell them." The faintest contact at the heel of his boot. Carelia held his eyes.

"For Ilmar, Ruslav. Our heritage. Our city. Our revolution."

"Sure. Right. All those things." Nodding to show how thoroughly he agreed with her. A good patriotic Ilmari, him. "Revolution's got to be paid for."

He thought he'd got it wrong, then. That this would turn out to be one of the times she *didn't* want the reminder of all that went on, that made sure her fighters had weapons and bribes and safe houses as they waited for the great day. But then she smiled, keen as a knife. Smiled and turned and waved her dismissal.

And he kept his walk steady and unhurried for the benefit of Benno and Ergice, to show he wasn't in the least rattled. Steady and unhurried, and absolutely every step of it taking him away from the pit.

Jem's Reasons for Leaving

A slight woman, enough that Maric eyes find her childlike. Red-gold hair cut short and dyed dark every twelveday to make her more the local. Not that she'll ever be a local anywhere, or belong. She makes up her pale skin, too, to hide the glitter and the gleam of it, like butterfly-wing scales. She wears loose Maric clothes. And they stare, still. Stare and speculate as she serves them drinks, as though her touch might work some transfigurative alchemy for good or ill. All that work to have her appear merely odd and not unnatural.

The Divine City shared no land borders with Telmark, but its grey-blue sails had put in at every port since time immemorial. The Occupation hadn't changed that. The Divinati were a people the Pals held in something close to awe. Stories of the City had, it was said, been instrumental in inducing the scholars of Pallesand to perfect the world. If so, the Pals had learned exactly the wrong lessons from the place.

The Divinity was not an expansive state. Just the one city, on the coast to the south-east of Allor. A city of magicians, self-sufficient and insular. They had no fields. Not a one of them tilled or herded, toiled or spun, nor did they sully their hands with base conjuration of demons to work for them, or distil magical force to fuel their wonders. Instead, holding the world and its forces in an exacting balance, they lived lives free of want, devoted to philosophy and leisure. The Divine City where everything was already perfect. Why would anyone ever leave?

Jem had left. Travelled by ship and then river barge all the way to Ilmar, where a community of her kin did not in any way make her welcome. They sat in their handful of streets across from Mirror Allor and worked their phantasms and crafts for the locals, and tried to hang on to who they were, even though they weren't that any longer. Even though what they were trying to be couldn't exist outside of the Divine City. Jem slept in the slanted loft space above the Anchorage's rooms, because she hated the sour taste of the Divinate air. She hated the walk through the Ilmari streets with their staring eyes. Even though Langrice docked rent from her meagre wages.

The evening crowd was subdued. There were still Pal soldiers watching the Wood – even though the moon was down – and they came in sporadically for mulled cider or tea. The place went quiet when they did. She preferred it when everyone was talking. She could lose herself in the noise.

Langrice had said to keep the corner booth table clear. The big one with its ring of seats built into the wall, rounded out to give some privacy. She got Hellgram to evict people from it. Little Jem the serving girl wasn't force enough to budge the more stubborn of the local toughs and drunks, but Hellgram always managed. Jem had been in Ilmar for almost ten years now, and knew almost nobody outside the Divinates, but Hellgram she liked. Hellgram she could open up to, if only because he plainly just let most people's words sleet past him. He was safe, she'd decided. Not someone with loose hands or who'd put himself in her way while she was trying to clear a table. He only cared about his wife. She found the devotion touching – almost simple-minded in an otherwise resourceful man.

When she looked that way next, there was a man at the booth again. A gnomish little character with a bottle-brush beard and a Divinati hat – the folded-over kind with a tassel that she knew as a Third Degree Cap, but the locals called a sock. Her heart sank to see him, as it always did. She was no true magician, but she'd grown up in a city where the fundamental forces of the world were toys and playthings. She could see where they were twisted out of true. This man had a debt of luck on his shoulders. The world was bent out of shape all around him. As though, sitting at that table, he was at the bottom of a ravine with walls of loose scree looming above him and waiting to slide.

From the outside, the Divinate quarter looked orderly and perfect. Its inhabitants went about their business quietly. You never heard a raised voice. Families with neatly arrayed red-haired children. Elders sitting out in good weather to play chaq and barreau and mance. Teams of artisans painting houses this season's auspicious colours. *And it was a lie*, she knew. She could barely stand to be among them. A pack of desperate, clutching, feuding factions. United against the outside world, fractured and divided inside like a gut full of broken glass. They couldn't ever go home or recapture what they'd once known, or what their parents had told them about, or their grandparents. And every few years, another handful trailed their way upriver from the Divine City to remind them of what they weren't.

Jem went to the little man, face composed so he saw absolutely nothing of what *she* saw looking at him. Surely, this time would be the last, for him. Luck stretched too far, debt to the world paid. *But he's a canny little weasel*, she knew. Cheating dooms was his stock in trade, for all that *somebody* always paid. His name was Dostritsyn, and the booth had been held clear for him and his associates.

He had a pack up beside him. As big as he was, it seemed, rattling with tools and Allorwen charms. On a perch in a wire cage, a little tawny bird hopped and twittered.

"Aright," he greeted her, or at least the cup she brought him. Dostritsyn drank shark rum, and despite its legendary teeth, he never seemed to get bitten. "First, am I?" He always was. He wouldn't be the last. Because nobody went to the Reproach, and everybody knew nobody went there, and everybody knew someone who did. The most wretched crept to the edge to scavenge for firewood, because the furniture had been left in the houses. They edged into the fringes of the cursed district because there were intact roofs there to keep the rain off. And the bolder went further, because there had been rich families in the big houses, once upon a time, and they hadn't been able to take their treasures with them when they left. Some hadn't been able to leave at all. When the ruling classes of Ilmar-that-was had re-established themselves on the modern Armigine Hill, and the Duke-as-had-been had first raised the current Ducal Palace, their finery and wonder – and relatives – had been left behind.

And over the intervening generations, Ilmar being what it was, a whole suicidal trade had grown up around looting their rich leavings.

The Allorwen who turned up next were brother and sister, Grymme and Meraqui. They sat hunched in heavy coats despite the stuffiness of the taproom. Dostritsyn aside, the best ruin-divers were from Allor. The curse was slower to latch on to them. Their charms and wards were stronger. And Jem knew that she herself could have walked into the Reproach, if not with impunity, then at least with more safety than any of them. The invisible terrors of the place would have been apparent to her eyes. She could have danced through them and come out with an armful of valuables. Except the cold disapproval of her kin would have her returning to put every last item back. To rob the dead was unthinkable to the Divinati. In the Divine City, after all, nobody died before their time, and every single object was renewed and reused, over and over in an endless round. Perfectly in balance, nothing wasted. Which was exactly the problem.

And here came trouble. The three ruin-divers looked up and then looked grim. But there was always someone who wanted a piece of the spoils without taking the risks. Jem knew this one. He was one of Langrice's familiars of the gaming table. The thug, Ruslav. There was an extra twist to the man this time. Beneath the stain of violence that tainted the air around him like blood in water, there was a bruise-coloured flicker to his aura. Even as he sat down, shoving Grymme over not to make room but to make a point, something was eating at him.

She brought them drinks. Tried not to stare. Ruslav was making demands. Levying the old tax the Lodges charged on every piece of under-the-table business in Ilmar. He was clothing it in a flag. These were *Ilmari* treasures the thieves were looting. They should go to the *cause*. She'd heard it all before. Jem didn't do causes. But she did eavesdrop, seeing the air about the four of them twist and shudder as Ruslav bullied his way into taking over the conversation. Then Hellgram was at her elbow, his hand gently moving her aside.

Her breath caught at his touch. The world around Hellgram was absolutely still, uncluttered. Not as it had been back home, where life had been like living on a grid of chaq tiles, lines of precisely calibrated force everywhere, binding the Divine City together like a spider's elegant web. Hellgram wasn't from around here, far more of a foreigner even than she. He passed through the world without leaving ripples. She found the smile she kept for him, and just for him. His own was that distant, slightly puzzled thing that went no further than his lips.

Dostritsyn greeted him loudly, cutting across Ruslav, sensing reinforcements. And Hellgram wasn't dressed for work in loose long shirt and baggy breeches. He had a coat on, belts and baldrics. Knives and cannisters, and his glass-eyed leather mask hanging about his neck. The gear and garb he'd brought from *Where He'd Come From*. For a frozen moment, she thought this was it: he was going back into the Wood, going home alone. But it was bad in a different way: he was going into the Reproach with Dostritsyn.

Ruslav had obviously come to the same conclusion, and didn't like it much. He could put the screws on three ruin-divers easily enough. Hellgram was a different prospect. After all, he worked for Langrice, whose post at the Anchorage meant the Lodges were cautious of leaning on her. And Hellgram was a magician from beyond the Anchorwood. He wasn't frightened of Ruslav and his long-boned frame didn't flinch from the thug's fists or his reputation.

"What's this?" Ruslav asked. "Taking apprentices, old man?"

Dostritsyn cackled and drained his cup, waving it at Jem. When she came back with more rum, some détente seemed to have been reached, and she'd missed the details. Dostritsyn was shaking his head at Ruslav. "Eyes open, of course," he was saying. "Gone, though. Not a hope. Even the body lost, most likely." And she didn't care by then. Just wanted to pluck at the blue-grey of Hellgram's sleeve, to hiss demands at him that she was in no position to make, and he was under no obligation to answer. *Don't go into the Reproach*, she should say. *Not this time. Not with them.* Because she could see terrible fates spiralling over Dostritsyn's head like a storm system – surely the man's final strands of luck parting. Yet here he was chuckling with his two accomplices as though it wasn't his last night in the sane and sunlit world. And there was Hellgram, leaning back, watching. Not laughing – he didn't laugh. Just sitting at the edge of things, as he always did. So still. That was what she loved about him. Ilmar was a turbulent river, a babble of chaos and motion. And she remembered the Divine City, for all she'd tried to exorcise the thought of it. How elegant, so graceful. Perfection beyond the dreams of the Palleseen. Life in Ilmar eroded her with its constant churn, but if she stood in Hellgram's shadow, she could steal a little of his stillness.

One night, years ago, some drunk patrons had cornered her. She'd hunted inside herself for the will to make a struggle and fight of it, and understood she would just be meek and quiet, and hope they only wanted a little fun and not a lot of it. Hoped she could find a chance to squeeze past them with a minimum of human contact and it wouldn't escalate. But there had been seven of them, and they'd been drunk and angry and lusty and jolly and all those things together in a confusing welter of conflicting urges. Then Hellgram had been there.

He'd turned up not long before. Just stumbled out of the

woods, alien clothes, words, everything. Demented, desperate, calling a name that hurt the ears. Collapsing. Langrice had taken him in. She always did, with whatever came out of the Wood. Enough of them had paid her back, one way or another. And there he had been, out of his sickbed. Taller than anyone there, a looming long-limbed grappler of a man. Foreign in a way that put a dampener on their fun and games. And they'd worked themselves up to go for him, to start one of the brawls that happened even in the Anchorage. Doubtless, Langrice had been reaching for the cudgel beneath the bar even then. But he'd stopped them. Jem had seen his form, as a magician. He had one of his little trinkets in his hand, and there had been shadows everywhere the lamplight didn't fall, and the shadows had been full of eyes. Probably the befuddled Marics hadn't seen most of that, but they'd felt it and slunk off. And Langrice had offered Hellgram a job on the spot – just to keep body and soul together while he searched for his wife, obviously, though that had been years ago now and here he still was. Jem had watched the man fold down into a seat and stare at his hands, and felt the resounding quiet that surrounded him.

And loving a foreigner was absolutely forbidden. But feeling something for so foreign a foreigner as Hellgram was probably better than ending up with a Maric on the side, or a Pal – the secret liaisons so many of her kin maintained behind each other's backs. Even safer, when his own feelings were so dedicated elsewhere. She could pine for him with a purity that was never in danger of becoming something complex and earthy. Unless. Unless one day he gave up on his lost wife and rejoined the world, while somehow retaining that detachment she longed to stand in. To be quiet and still in his shadow.

And now, the Reproach.

At that point, even as she was trying to find a way to pull him away from the table and say, *No, not now, not with them*, Ruslav looked up and his eyes went wide, and he said, "You're in prison."

"Am I indeed?" asked Blackmane from behind her. He loomed like a wall, the sheer presence of him forcing Jem back out of the booth's entrance. He shunted everyone comically along until there was room for him. "I got better," he explained, the punchline to a different joke. "And why is that of interest to you, I wonder?"

She felt the air crackle and bend between the two of them: Maric enforcer, Allorwen magician. Neither of them in a mood to back down. Dostritsyn cackled again, tried to give the pair of them more room and physically couldn't. He was practically in Meraqui's armpit as it was.

Ruslav's gaze slid past Blackmane's shoulder, stuttered and cracked. He looked away hurriedly, ceding the field. A couple of Maric youths were standing there awkwardly. Nothing that should have knocked a hole in the bruiser's poise, except they plainly had. Students. Jem watched, fascinated, seeing the air tense and tangle between them. Ruslav and the girl, yes, but even more so Ruslav and the boy. Well-dressed, that one: every garment finely made and worn in calculated disarray. The long face of an Armiger. And Ruslav's eyes were on hooks, drawn back to him often enough that, at last, the boy noticed. Looked right back. Cocked an insolent eyebrow at the older man. *And?* His companion was hanging back, but he just sauntered in, his presence demanding a seat even though there was no possible room at the table, farcically full as it was. Blackmane was trying to talk business, but between Ruslav's distraction and the physical jockeying, he was having a hard time of it – the straight man in a comedy routine. Jem was suddenly about to laugh despite everything. An unforgivable public show that just *wasn't done*. Back in the Divine City, people smiled in careful, controlled ways. They put their hands together to show appreciation without ever being so gauche as to applaud. Like Hellgram, they did not *laugh*. Laughter was chaos and imbalance, just as weeping was. In the Divine City there was no need for either.

Then Hellgram stood up, unfolding all the height and bones

of him, enough to make the student boy step back. He slipped from the booth with a nod, leaving room for the young Armiger to sit, for his companion to hang at his shoulder. Blackmane shot the pair of them a hard look, a man who didn't want more hands stirring the pot he was trying to cook in. Ruslav sat back, the pressing bubble of his menace abruptly collapsed into watchfulness. The three ruin-divers expanded out a little to take up the slack, to listen to what Blackmane had to say. Most of the loot they hoped to take out of the Reproach – that part that didn't go to Ruslav's paymasters – would end up being fenced through Mirror Allor, where there were always appraisers for art and magical heirlooms and trinkets, and where the welter of forgeries and fakes and genuine antiques could disguise a lifetime of stolen goods. And if you wanted to sell in that market, you needed the nod of a man like Blackmane. One more oar in the turbulent river.

And there was Hellgram, standing in his foreign clothes, ready to go hunting madness. Jem sidled as close to him as she dared, right at his elbow, looking up at the hollows and planes of his gaunt face, his hair straggling down his high forehead. He flicked a glance at her, smiled slightly.

She felt desperately protective. She wanted to tell him off like a child. *Don't do this stupid thing.* Literally, in the speech of the Divine City *Do not be made a part of it.* It was all process and passive verbs, in that language. In the City, you did not *do*, you *were*. *Do not be this thing.* As though he was a timber in a ship bound for the seabed.

His eyes on her, still: the window into which she could speak slowly closing.

"Don't," she said. Already too daring, interfering in another's business. Tangling herself in the world, just as she'd always been taught not to.

"I've not searched there yet." That way he had, of having his words reach someone by speaking not over but under. Letting the argument between Blackmane and the students and

Dostritsyn close over his head like a hatch, so he could speak in the quiet space beneath.

"But—"

"She might be there. Trapped." That old, jagged edge that only opened up in him on this topic.

"But it's been years. The Reproach—"

"Will not touch her. We are of elsewhere, she and I. But what a terrible place to be caught in. I have to look."

And there was no wife, she knew. Not after all this time. And he could never let go, nor even lose hope. His devotion to his mission had never wavered, even as he'd made a kind of life for himself here at the Anchorage. As though any day, he'd find her in some unconsidered room, waiting for him, and be off back into the Wood. And she wanted him to find the love of his life, obviously. That would be balance and the restoration of the world's equilibrium. And at the same time, she knew he never would and was meanly glad of it.

The girl, the student, had just declared that she was going into the Reproach, and that was a surprise to everyone. Dostritsyn was sanguine. All one to him, and taking a lackwit stooge into the place was actually a tool in the kit of half the ruin-divers Jem knew. You wanted someone to attract the madness-lightning of the place first. Blackmane argued against it. Ruslav argued against it. Then her own friend was arguing against it, which had her turning on him, shaming him over some mentor figure they were doing all this for. "Who'll make sure of it?" she was demanding. "Him?" Jabbing a finger at the rum-sodden old man. More noise. Hellgram watched, impassive, letting it slide off him like rain from a riverman's coat.

Now the boy, the Armiger, had been guilted into saying he was going too, because the girl wouldn't back down. More farce, oath piled on oath, about who was braver and more patriotic than whom. Ruslav's face: haunted, horrified. A window onto a different man who'd been hiding out behind the thug's gaudy clothes and bluster all this time. Watching these two naïfs commit themselves to the asylum of their free will. And now *he* was going. He was going, to make sure that these thieves – cackling Dostritsyn and his Allor accomplices – didn't rob Ilmar of its treasures. He, Ruslav the patriot, would see to that. His eyes on the students, both of them, pleading *Don't make me do this.* Jem watched the knot of strings around the table bunch and pull taut, strain for escape, inextricably meshed. Each boast and brag covering a well of unspoken desperation. Roped together and staggering towards the abyss, carrying the great leaden weight of Dostritsyn's doom.

Blackmane stood, almost taking the whole table with him. A curt "You know what you need to do," to the divers. Staring at the students, who'd come there in his shadow and who hadn't been meant to sign on to the damned venture. Washing his hands of it, just a little strand of guilt and responsibility, that he'd somehow got them in this. More than she'd have thought, given his reputation. He pushed past, lumbering off on Langrice at the bar, his confederate of old. Someone he could unload on. When you carried the baggage of being Blackmane, there weren't many people you could talk to as equals.

"I'll take care."

She jumped. Hellgram, speaking quietly but heard still. Eyes on her, quizzical. And she wanted to explode. She wanted to tell him a thousand things about the way he carried himself and the way he dealt with people and most especially the way none of it touched him. Ilmar was a river, and he was a rock. The waters parted and closed, and he was not moved. And if he was absolutely committed elsewhere, that made him a safe person to love because he would never feel the same. Equilibrium. Sometimes being suspended on hooks was still equilibrium, and balance of any kind was better than constant shaking and motion. That was the teaching of the Divine City, after all. How terrible, how disruptive to the world, to love someone who might one day love you back!

In the City, of course, every love was requited. Every couple was quietly happy. There was no angst or uncertainty, infidelity or grief. But there were children. Happy children, brought up in perfect security. Always slightly too many children. The Divine City had an adult population of twenty-seven thousand five hundred and eighty-four. The perfect number. Exactly that many could be supported by the complex web of opposed forces that made the City such an ideal place to live. And when those children reached the age of sixteen years, they were examined, assessed for their intelligence and understanding and ability to become a part of the unchanging utopia they had been born into. And a very precise number who were found the most wanting were told that there would be no place in paradise for them, after all. That they were inferior, and so they had to go. Let the Pals seek to perfect the wider world by conquest and occupation. The people of the Divine City knew the limits of perfection. It was the ability to cast out your excess children into a bitter world, because there were always slightly too many of them, generation on generation. And Jem had not been good enough, and so here she was, tending bar in the Anchorage because *nobody* fit here. Not Langrice, not Hellgram, not anyone. Not here at the edge of the Wood, where the world broke open when the moon was up. And being imperfect, ergo unlovable, she touched the sleeve of the man who couldn't love her, and tried to bless him, and hoped he never, ever found what he was looking for.

Unleashing Hell

The Old Duke had been hated by almost everyone in Ilmar, and he'd hated most of them back. He'd hated the Armiger families who were waiting for him to die so they could fight over who got the palace and the big chair. He'd hated the Allorwen who couldn't cure his ills, and the merchants who tried to cheat him, and the Lodges who stole what was his. Most of all, he'd hated the Siblingries, because bad things were meant to roll downhill, and those worthies had the temerity to get together and try to push it back up towards him.

The sound of the maddened demon woke everyone within three streets of the factory. Not the volume of noise: if you lived in the Hammer Districts then the thunder of the factories permeated your very bones. Night shift and day shift slept with it. If the work ceased – the presses and foundry hammers stilled for repair or because the Siblingries were in dispute again – the quiet kept you awake.

The Tosthevar factory was stilled now, though not silent. The roar of complaints in the monstrous speech of demons was a foreign intrusion into the dreams of sleepers. Father Orvechin found himself awake, beside his wife, staring blankly into the darkness. Hearing all the mechanical sounds of the Hammer Districts at night plus that one unwelcome addition. The Tosthevar place was on his watch. He was dressed by the time they came to fetch him, shrugged into hardwearing overalls. Two straps crossed his broad chest: one for a satchel of his machine tools, the other stocked with what the everyday working man might carry to protect himself against demons.

His wife was awake, too. The whole street would be, listening to the bellows and the crashing absence of machinery. And they were both day-shift workers, one of the benefits of rank within the Siblingry. He had a foundry to oversee; she had a mill line to work on. Sleep was the due of the worker but right now it was a luxury. Someone had to sort it out.

He opened the door at the second knock. The foreman of the Tosthevar place and a handful of his underlings, breath spooling out in white clouds. He could pick out precisely who among them had the sense they were born with because the others hadn't grabbed their coats and were shivering half to death.

"Come in," he said. "Have tea. Tell me."

There was a fire going in the kitchen – wood he couldn't spare, but hospitality was important to the Siblingries.

"The new big mover," the foreman said. "Just broke. Turned over the whole press. Wouldn't stop for the wards. Nobody can get inside. Nobody can work out what's wrong with it."

"Broke," Father Orvechin echoed. "Banish it under terms. Demons break." Not this quickly, though, unless the Kings Below were sending up defective goods. The work destroyed everyone eventually: man, machine and demon. But they were supposed to be good for a certain number of hours. It was in the contracts. If they failed within their warranty, the Infernal Realms were bound to furnish a replacement, with penalties. And if there was one thing the Kings Below hated above all else it was paying additional charges.

"Not like that," the foreman said. "I mean, you hear the thing – it's on a rampage. Burned through the wards, though they left brands all over it. Listen."

The voice of the demon, echoing over the roofs. Unspeakable words, but words nonetheless, complex utterances rather than the raving of a beast gone mad.

Fortified with tea, they marched out again, towards the river.

A crowd had already gathered around the Tosthevar place – workers from inside, gawpers from without. Even a handful of Pal soldiers and Turncoats drawn by the noise, standing away from the rest. Orvechin glowered at them. No call for them getting involved.

And then, the one less welcome sight in all the world, here came Isvillich Tosthevar, son and heir presumptive of the owner. He looked as though he hadn't been to bed that night, but not for any wholesome reason. Fine clothes dishevelled and stained, and a little string of servants and hangers-on trailing after him like spatters of vomit.

"It's in hand," Orvechin told him, though it wasn't.

"This is unacceptable!" the Tosthevar youth shouted over the din. "We have orders! Boats waiting on the tide." And there wasn't a tide on the river because they were far from the sea, but the boy had doubtless heard the term from a sailor once and seized on it.

"It's in hand," Orvechin said, but the youth was shouting at the foreman, not him, browbeating and bullying, cutting wages and hiking hours. "Shoddy conjurations and poor craftsmanship!"

Father Orvechin stepped between them, forcing them apart. He was a big man and, although he wasn't young, time hadn't started to hollow him out or soften him. He worked at the machines with the rest. He was as tall as the Armiger youth, twice as broad, older. Isvillich, for his part, had the law. He could call the soldiers over. He could have anyone here whipped and beaten. But there were a lot more workers and idlers-who-might-be-workers than there were soldiers or Tosthevar lackeys.

The Armiger families had owned the labour forever. A few generations ago that had been farm workers, spread wide across countless little villages. But then the money had turned from land to manufacture. The mines had boomed. The foundries followed, then the mills and factories. The children of farm and field had funnelled into the cramped tenements of the Hammer Districts because that was where the work was. For the Armigers, it had been a boon, money hand over fist and a tame population of serfs to turn the cranks and get their fingers caught between the wheels. Each complex act of craftsmanship reduced to a score of unskilled stages that anybody could complete. No more fussy mastercrafters with their demands and standards. Every part of the machine replaceable, especially the human element.

But things had changed. Not in a night. Not anything approaching a revolution. But when Father Orvechin stood between Isvillich and the foreman, and said, "It's in hand," there was a moment when their eyes met. And the boy was drunk, and he could have had his people seize Orvechin and have him whipped. But something in the older man cautioned him, and he stepped back.

"See that it's dealt with. See that there's no shortfall. Or my father... My father will... You know what he will."

And Orvechin nodded, because Tosthevar the elder certainly *would*. Doubtless, there'd be docked wages and penalties, and he and the other senior Siblings would have to decide if *this* was where they downed tools or went slow or some other way of making the working population's displeasure known. Or did they let it go, like all the other times, husbanding their fuel for... when, precisely?

"Let's see this demon," he said. "And someone send for the duty hellieur."

They'd already been sent for, he was told, so at least someone had some initiative tonight. Orvechin pushed open the factory gates and stomped in.

He kicked through a slew of shifting, rattling objects. *Bones.* But not that. There weren't so many contracts about these days that meant you had to keep boxes of bones on hand. They were living in a modern age, after all. Most of the time you didn't have to feed them anything.

It was the Allorwen who'd changed everything. As the factories had begun to transition from the uncomplaining but limited drive of the river to demons who'd work harder and provide as much power as you could bind them to, the Ilmari factories had homegrown their own conjurers. They'd begged and borrowed and stolen the lore of it, and the Armigers had brought in Gownhall graduates who knew the sigils and how to compound the chalks. It had all been second-rate stuff, though. Orvechin was old enough to remember. But over the border, the Allorwen had demons serving their tea, pulling their grand carriages and building their manor houses. And so, long before the Pal invasion of Allor had brought in such an influx of refugees, the Armigers were hiring foreign conjurers in. Because they were better, but also because, by then, the Maric summoners had begun to sign up with the Siblingries. And suddenly, there were Allorwen everywhere, who got paid more and who knew the trade better, and everything changed. But not quite in the way anyone expected.

Buttons. He kicked his way through a great drift of spilled buttons, thinking, *Someone's going to have to pick those up*. And that wasn't demon work. Nobody was going to bind a demon to handle a broom. Kids and oldsters, and it wasn't as though the Tosthevars would be paying extra for the extra work.

There was a crash from the far end of the factory floor. The demon had upended something expensive. Father Orvechin turned to the foreman. "Check wards," he said.

The man peered up to the ash marks Orvechin had smeared on his forehead and cheeks, the oil-smeared signs on the front of his overalls and the back of his coat. Enough to give him a moment to get out of the way if the thing went for him. And people were killed by demons every day. Killed because they stepped into the demons' prescribed areas, or got caught in the machinery the demons were powering, or got careless in a dozen other ways. And this demon had broken its wards already.

He saw it down the ranks of the button presses. A vastly muscled thing, vaguely humanoid, horned head thrust forwards, absurdly small between its massive shoulders. The air around it caught fire in momentary gouts, shimmering and roiling with sulphurous smoke. They'd cropped its wings, which wouldn't have had room to unfurl in here anyway. They'd hobbled it with runed irons. There were a dozen smoking scars across its copper-coloured hide where the wards had bitten it. Excruciating pain to a demon, Orvechin knew. Usually enough to keep them inside. So had the wards been faulty, or the contract, or was this just a defective demon supplied in breach by the Kings Below?

Around that time, Aullaime arrived. Beneath the hem of her heavy coat, he saw the trailing edge of a nightgown. Her short hair stuck out in all directions like hedgehog quills. Her round-lensed glasses were askew. All very much the picture of a white-collar clerk hauled from blameless slumber. Save they told the same rumours about every Allorwen in the Siblingries. *Those Allors and their appetites.* Who knew what to believe? They'd always been disliked.

That had been what the Armigers had banked on, of course. Bring in the foreign experts, and you got three wins for the price of one. They were good at their job, they broke the power of the Siblingries, and all the ire of the workers could be turned against the incomers rather than upwards to their paymasters. A perfect arrangement. Orvechin still wasn't quite sure why it hadn't turned out that way. Knowing what he did about rich and poor, Maric and Allorwen, and just people in general, it seemed a perfectly good supposition. Even now, Aullaime was getting some filthy looks. And part of that was because, since Allor had fallen and they had all come over here en masse, relations really had soured. But people had spat at Allorwen feet even before, and still…

"Father," she greeted him, the formal title because there were others present. "I see we have a problem."

"Who did the contracts here?" Orvechin growled. The demon had seen the little deputation of humans. It dropped forwards, knuckles to the ground, peering at them through pupil-less white orbs. In the air of this world, demons were notoriously short-sighted.

"Varlechev," Aullaime reported promptly. Meaning one of the Maric conjurers. "He's solid," she added. "Wouldn't expect him to screw up. And Furenya oversaw the wards, so likewise. Quite the puzzle."

"Quite the puzzle," Orvechin echoed. The demon was sloping towards them, pointedly shouldering against the nearest press so that the machine's joints strained and complained. "So go deal with it."

Aullaime cracked her knuckles and took a few steps forwards. The stench of it, hot metal and sulphur, barely wrinkled Orvechin's nose. It was just the smell of the factories, of the Hammer Districts at large. With deft strokes Aullaime drew a sign on the ground – not even in chalk or oils, just making an empty shape where she'd pushed the spilled buttons out of the way. It wouldn't exactly hold if the thing charged, but it would hurt. Orvechin watched the demon to see if it was mad enough not to care, but it regarded the sigil warily. Aullaime's calligraphy was always top notch.

It spoke. Sounds like ragged metal tearing, nails on a chalkboard, grinding bones and guttural digestion. Human ears could not parse demon speech, or perhaps it was human minds. Aullaime had her chalks out, a wallet of worn sticks she poised her fingers over before choosing from. She drew eye-offending marks on the side of the nearest press, demon grammar and syntax coming to her with the ease of long practice. The demon slammed its knuckles into the ground, ruining an hour's wage of buttons, then lifted a slab of a hand, put a claw to the metal and melted a sigil into the steel. Its blind eyes bored into Aullaime.

"We have a dialogue," the hellieur said. Hellieur. It was an Allorwen word. Not a mere conjurer, but one who negotiated and assessed infernal contracts. A demon repairwoman.

"You're going to be all right?" Orvechin asked her.

"You just go clear the lollygaggers," she said. "Keep the owners off my back."

Orvechin strode out, leaving the woman exchanging hideous

hieroglyphs with the demon. She moved from machine to machine to do it, chalking in large, crisp lines that the thing peered at myopically. Its own replies were made in cramped, neat symbols, as though the thing was used to dog-ends and scraps to write on back home. And someone would have to put the time in to cover that up or buff it away, or it would upset the workers. The human people at the other end of the machines, who put the metal in and took the buttons out, and crawled into the teeth of the engines when there was a jam. Because the demons were strong, but they weren't *skilled*. They were just the raw motive power that kept the machines moving day and night, until even their unnatural sinews gave up and the conjurers went contracting for a new one.

"Get people heading home," he told the foreman, sitting down on one of the empty crates stacked outside the door. Isvillich Tosthevar was still loitering around, and Orvechin wondered how many ways he could say 'it's in hand' before the man got the message and went away.

"There will be penalties," the youth shouted over. "You find me the man responsible. I'll dock the pay of the whole shift. We have important clients. They'll make their displeasure known."

Father Orvechin mostly ignored him, turning a loose button over in his hands, running a thumb over the impressed quill design on its face. Important clients. Buttons for the uniforms of Pal soldiers. *We clothe them. We feed them.* He stood abruptly as Tosthevar came over. Orvechin waited. Looming. Staring. Utterly unamused, utterly uncowed by the man's family or money or aristocratic blood. His eyes like flint, less welcoming than the blank orbs of the demon. The Armiger's feet dragged him to a halt, and he seemed to recall business he had elsewhere in the city, and that was one problem dealt with.

After that, it was just the waiting, and wherever Father Orvechin planted himself in people's view, there were always those who wanted a piece of his time. The cost of being senior in the Siblingries. And he knew the main complaints, because

Correct Speech had been through half the factories down the river a week ago, looking for resistance sympathisers. Whether they'd actually found any, he didn't know, but they'd used the excuse to levy fines and penalties on the owners and that all got passed down to the working man. This family couldn't make rent, that one had the woman who earned their bread in the cells because she'd lamped the Pal Statlos who'd got frisky while searching her. Taking liberties, and when the Pals took your liberties, they didn't give them back.

And the rest. He heard the story of a factory foreman who'd been free with his juniors. He heard about a machine shop up on Liberation Way that was turning out shoddy work for Siblingry buyers, and a place where three kids had lost fingers because they didn't even slow the looms when there was a snarl. He heard about a canteen where the tea was always weak and tepid. He took it all in, made a list in his head. He'd get to it all, every last complaint. Because you worked a twelve-hour shift, hard graft, and even the kids did nine at a time. Then you went home and ate and had three words with your spouse, and you slept against the backdrop of thunder and sulphur. And then you did it again. And when that was your life, even poor-quality tea was a curse you could do without. And at least the Siblingries meant that he had a lever when he went to shift the world a little. Meant that a factory might be silent and empty come morning, a mysterious sickness might keep a whole neighbourhood home. Meant that any owner had to balance their greed for extra profit against the potential loss if they pushed too hard. It was a balance, and before the Occupation, both sides had found their equilibrium. Scales of justice where one arm was very long with a leisurely Armiger hand to push it, and the other was a stubby little stump with all the combined bodies of the workers hauling hard to drag it the other way. But better than it had been.

Now it was Mother Elvaer come to him, dressed in a man's working clothes, cap in hand. Come over out of Mirror Allor to mind the presses overnight. Not even a conjurer, but he guessed she was worried that any Allorwen on this shift would get the blame for what had happened. Except it wasn't that at all.

Had he heard about what was happening at the Gownhall, she asked, and he recalled abruptly that her daughter was one of the handful the Siblingries had wrangled scholarships for. That long-fought deal he'd hammered out with the maestros. Ilmari education for city children, not just Armiger third scions and the privileged kids of wealthy out-of-towners.

"Nobody's working there," Mother Elvaer said, and that didn't seem news to Orvechin, because who actually did real work at the Gownhall? Except that wasn't what she meant either. The place had come to a standstill.

"They say the Pals are watching it all the time now. Soldiers," she said. "After they arrested that what's-his-name."

Orvechin had heard something about it. He wasn't sure if he was supposed to care. The Gownhall wasn't his business. Perhaps the Siblingry students should just come home, he suggested.

"Someone said this is how it starts," Mother Elvaer told him.

"No," Orvechin said flatly. "This is *not* how it starts." Because that would be ludicrous, wouldn't it? Yes, there was a lot of paper in the Gownhall, but that didn't mean anyone would light the flame there. The great and roaring flame that they spoke of behind closed doors at Siblingry meetings. The moment of overthrow, when the Pals and their soldiers and officials would look out of their windows and see the streets crammed with working men and women, hammers and torches and upraised fists. And then the Armigers too, the owners and the exploiters with their long end of the scales, meaning Orvechin and his people had to pull with all their weight to get the balance shifted even an inch. It *couldn't* have its seeds in a pack of privileged students refusing to read another overlong word because their favourite pontificator was spending a few nights behind bars. And he said so, and he sounded convincing. But when she'd gone, he sat and brooded over it, telling himself over and over again it couldn't be.

Then someone said Aullaime was ready, and he stomped

back inside, trying to sandpaper the thoughts out from inside his head and not quite managing it.

Inside the factory, the conversation between the hellieur and the demon was scrawled in a wide circle across four presses, and the demon stood in the centre. Because circles were important. Demons crept out of the corners and edges of things, sometimes even without a contract where the boundaries were weak. But a circle bound them.

"Well?" Orvechin stared at the demon, and it stared right back. Quite calm now. Waiting for his responses to its demands.

Aullaime sat on the plates of one machine, hunched forwards to avoid the hanging workings above, looking drained. "Well, it's a mess, Vech." The informal contraction, because it was just the two of them and the demon didn't count. "But it's not our mess. The Kings Below have been busy."

He nodded gloomily, sitting beside her. "Meaning?"

"It says it's not supposed to be here. It wasn't in debt to the Kings, or theirs to dispose of. But they came and took it anyway. They had a purge. Rounding up the dissidents. Street to street and kicking in doors." And there were no streets or doors in the Infernal Realms, but some things always had an analogue.

"So?"

"So our contracts and work are fine, but the Kings stiffed us. We need to check every demon from this batch and double the wards, or there'll be more like this. Politicals. Organisers. Ringleaders. You know how it goes."

"I do," Orvechin agreed. He looked at the demon, wondered where it had stood, among its people. Whether it had listened to complaints about the poor quality of demon tea in the demon canteen. "So?"

"So I'm done. It's ready."

He nodded, feeling sick. "Bind it. But we need to go over the grievance clauses in the contracts. This is shoddy goods. I'll let the Tosthevars know they need to check the merchandise properly next time, or let us do it." With an emphasis on *let us do it*, shifting the lever on those scales ever so slightly, another finger's width on the workers' side. Leverage.

Aullaime pushed off from the press and went to face the demon. At a word, the sigils she'd worked into her end of the conversation flared bright. The demon screamed with rage and pain, shielding its blank eyes. For a moment, Orvechin thought it would break the circle anyway, just tear through her and him and the whole factory. But Aullaime knew what she was doing. The wards held; the demon was chained. From there, simple enough to bind it to the machines again, awaiting the word for when its brute strength would have the presses chattering. Although first, someone would need to come and set everything right and sweep up the mess. Always more work for the working men and women of the Hammer Districts.

The demon's face would haunt him. The look of betrayal, in a monster that had been negotiating in good faith. No amount of tusks and bestial features could disguise it.

When the Allorwen conjurers had come in, there had been what Orvechin thought of as the workers' miracle. Somehow, despite all the stirring and the rumourmongering from the Armigers' people – *They're here to take your jobs and corrupt your children and seduce your women* – a Maric labourer and an Allorwen tramp magician had looked at each other and seen what they had in common. More in common, nations bedamned, than either of them had with the toffs and factory owners and grand sorcerer-lords who bought and sold them. And that refusal to be divided had been the making of the Siblingries, and the leverage men like Orvechin had on the future of Ilmar. Hard-won and constantly eroded, but a handle on the world that he could turn and, sometimes, results came out of the other end.

But there were limits. Not that there wasn't a part of him that wouldn't have shaken that demon's taloned hand like a brother, but that would have been a step too far. And so, he watched the beast being enslaved to the mills again and knew that, even as he fought every day for a better life for his people, he was a collaborator in a larger war. And he hated it, and maybe there would come a day it would change, but for now, he needed the demon to work because that was his lever against the owners and the Pals.

Aullaime clapped a hand on his shoulder and left it there. Her look to him showed she knew and shared the sentiments. They were trapped in the same circle, for now. *We will be ashamed of what we did here, one day.* And at least, if that came true, it would mean things had got better. A better tomorrow bought with a succession of compromised todays.

"You get home," she told him. "Get the foreman to deal with the clean-up. I'll stay on until they're ready to start work again."

He nodded, still brooding.

"You've a meeting tomorrow night," she told him. "Siblingry business." And he hadn't, but he could have. He could tell his wife he had. There was always Siblingry business.

Her hand on his shoulder, the memory of her skin on his. One more compromise he'd fallen into. Not even the first time. He couldn't even say for sure his wife hadn't found out, just like she'd found out about the last one. Perhaps she knew and was just keeping it inside, like she did so much else.

"Siblingry business," he agreed, feeling that unique emotion that was guilt and shame and relief and anticipation. The demon that turned the wheels inside him.

Mosaic: The Hospitality
of the Varatsins

Don't let the resistance tell you Ilmar was ever unified or at peace
with itself. Only that the current strife is with invaders from
without, rather than between the locals. Before the Palleseen, it
was the Old Duke, whose last wickedness was to foist his living
curse onto the man who was hanging him. Before him, a sequence
of other Dukes, this or that Armiger family in ascendance, or else
a royal deputy when the succession became too muddied to be made
out clearly. And go back far enough, the family Varatsin. A name
the superstitious and the wise alike forebear to repeat.

Pull away from the band of ruin-divers and their hangers-on,
about to make their descent into madness-town. Head north
ahead of them, away from the Anchorage. Past Mother Ellaime's
boarding house where Yasnic bickers with God over who should
have the last biscuit. Through Gutter District streets where the
truly poor live, and then those poorer than they. Nobody who
has anything resembling work. Families that scrounge and
scavenge and steal and swing from the Donjon scaffold when
they're caught. And north, past ever more dilapidated buildings,
into sight of the firebreaks where Dukes past sought to stop the
spread of a peculiar malady with flame. Though that fire didn't
stop it, it's hoped time and ritual magic has. Nobody has ever

gone back to rebuild. Even the squatters peter out to nothing. And then you come to the Reproach.

And the houses in the half-empty, desperately impoverished streets closest to the Reproach are large. Grand townhouses now fallen to ruin – a few high-ceilinged rooms still fit for habitation, and the rest gone to rot and collapse. The houses beyond the scars of old burning are grander, or were. Great Armiger mansions, parks and little woods. A relic of an earlier age and a different line of Dukes who sent emissaries with seals and signets into the Anchorwood, and received delegates from distant and semi-imaginary shores. A time when the power of the ruling families had one foot in the arcane and the uncanny. At the heart of those grand houses, the palace-that-was, with its lawn and tourney ground, its follies and wonders. Of which the modern Ducal Palace, seat of the Palleseen Perfecture, is a mere shadow.

But just as nobody liked the Old Duke until the Pals strung him up and made him a symbol, nobody liked the ancient Varatsin Dukes either. Nobody liked the way they trafficked so freely with the things beyond the Wood. Nobody liked that this Duke or that Duchess had sourced a spouse from those distant places, or that some relative or other had married within a scribed circle, his bride a scion of the Kings Below. Or perhaps that's all just *post hoc* justification for what happened, when the other Armiger families cast down the Varatsins, exterminated their line, scattered their adherents and took over their palace and grounds, their parks and grand houses.

And then the Varatsins came back.

Shantrov Sirovar is, in the end, not going. He honestly hadn't wanted to go, but then Lemya had insisted that *she* was going because otherwise who would make sure they came back with what they needed? Who would stand for the city, the *cause*? And Dostritsyn had gummed at the stick of his pipe and said the more the merrier, and looked from Lemya to the little caged bird he had, but hadn't elaborated on his meaning. So Shantrov had felt somewhat trapped into saying that obviously he was going too. He'd shown them his sword, which he'd smuggled through the streets under his coat. Lemya had insisted he wasn't to go, and that had only made him insist all the harder that *of course* he would go. Then Ruslav had taken him aside and spoken to him. Everyone had waited for the big Lodge soldier to menace him or break the boy's sword or something similarly in character. Ruslav had just spoken quietly, though. He'd put his hand on Shantrov's shoulder. And Shantrov had come back and said that he would hold the fort here at the Anchorage and watch out for patrols and generally keep the home fires burning, and that would be his part of the venture.

Does that mean that Ruslav is going, then? Apparently, it does. And Ruslav is strong and has a number of unpleasant but potentially useful skills and has nerve, and none of that will necessarily help in the Reproach. In the Anchorage, he said he had to go, because someone had to, who knew what they were doing. Someone had to keep an eye on this naïf – meaning Lemya. Besides, he'd told Shantrov he'd see it through. Ruslav was a man of his word, everyone knew it. And the two thugs he'd brought along took issue with that, and so he went and boxed their ears and reminded them just who, of the three of them, was the mean one. And they said he was mad, and if he wanted to go piss in the asylum he shouldn't be surprised when someone locked the doors on him.

Does that mean Lemya is going, then? She'd sworn to it. She was glad Shantrov was out of it. She walked that curious moral tightrope which meant she had no qualms about putting herself in danger. For the city. For the *cause*. For abstract principles of truth, beauty and justice. At the same time, she would do her level best to deny the same perilous opportunities to her friends.

She was exactly the sort of theoretical revolutionary who'd stand between the batons of the Pals and the people of the city, just as she was the sort whose rhetoric would have put those people there for her to act as a momentary shield for, people who might otherwise have done something else with their zeal and their lives. So yes, she's committed, and now she has Ruslav as her right hand. She always figured him for a resistance man, and so she can leap to the conclusion that his current conduct is motivated entirely by that. In the others, she has less faith. The old man and his two Allorwen apprentices are thieves, out to pillage the treasures left behind when the Reproach was abandoned. And she isn't even sure *what* Hellgram is.

Hellgram, the man from the far side of the Wood, isn't looking for treasure. Not that he'd turn down his share of the take, but he has no expensive vices. He lives in a small room at the back of the Anchorage. He eats in the place's bare kitchen – whatever scraps are left after the depredations of the previous night's custom. And he's been to the Reproach before, several streets of it, but there are regions unplumbed. He must cross them off his list, and a ruin-diver's expedition is a good opportunity to do so. To find them empty of who he's searching for, and move on, grimly persistent. For Dostritsyn and his peers, he's a wild card. Hellgram has magic from beyond the Wood, tricks and toys nobody has ever seen. And the Reproach has no hold on him. He's not a part of its world. Dostritsyn is more than happy to have the hulking foreigner along.

Which brings us to our three professionals, out on what they don't know is their last run together. Most ruin-divers brave the Reproach two or three times. The first venture is tentative and fleeting, scarpering from under the shadow of the Varatsins with a handful of trash that will still – sold to Blackmane or some other dealer in Mirror Allor – pay the rent for a month, the tavern tab for a week or a gambling habit for a night. The second run, armoured in confidence, often ends in tragedy. Many don't return. Many return half-mad, maimed, shaken to their very soul's core. And rich. Just one piece of grand art, some Armiger's plaything crammed with magic that can be drained and repurposed, some lost tome of priceless poetry or lore. A prudent adventurer can live well for a year on that. Enough time to find some way of making money that never, ever requires them to go into the Reproach again. But some get a taste for it, or can't hold on to the money, or leave something of themselves in those streets that they go back for, but never quite find. Dostritsyn has returned from under the shadow seven times now. He's dined well on his stories of it and grown old with his own reputation. And still he goes back, his eighth venture. He must have made a dozen fortunes. Why risk his old bones and his sanity? Perhaps it's that the legend is the only thing left of him after all this time. If he isn't Dostritsyn the Daring, what even is he?

And then we have Meraqui, but that's simple enough. She needs the money. This is her third venture. She has parents and grandparents and sick aunts back in Mirror Allor. She has a little learning. She has a very desperate need to pay a variety of bills. Her creditors are not even the wages of high living, just of life. The constant grind that shaves the means from pocket and purse one slice at a time. She hands out paper charms to Ruslav and Lemya, just as she's bedecked herself with. Temporary warding written on them in Allorwen words, a product of the cheapest scribes, limited potency, one night only and don't get them wet.

And then we have Grymme. His third venture too, his second with Dostritsyn. Grymme has a secret. He saw something magical in those decrepit houses last time. He's told the other two: a real treasure. A glorious capstone to Dostritsyn's career, a payday to take care of all Meraqui's woes, if they can only find it again. But Grymme hasn't quite been frank with them. What he saw, back on that solo venture without Dostritsyn, was *too much*. He saw too far. He saw the revels of the Varatsins, and they spoke to him. He brought something out of the Reproach that wasn't treasure, but that sat in his mind and whispered to him. For Grymme, he's not just going into the Reproach. He's going *home*.

Now they go in.

The Reproach had been smaller, when it first manifested. Perhaps the firebreaks curtailed it – desperate lighting of a ring of streets around it, sometimes with the deranged inhabitants still within. More likely, it's the fifteen-inch sigils of bronze they buried at each intersection of that ring – a circle is a circle after all. Perhaps it's simply that the malign influence of the Varatsins has its limits.

They stand at the edge. The firebreak itself has long grown over. The circle has become a ring of weeds and energetic growth. In the brief summer, it's busy with insects, bright with flowers. Rats breed and thrive there, hunted by stray dogs and feral cats. If any of them are infected by delusions of grandeur, nobody knows it. On the far side of that green scar, the buildings rise again, some showing marks of burning, most with collapsed roofs. Moss grows in the cracks between bricks, forming an angular alphabet. Grass chokes the gutters. Adolescent trees push their branches where tiles and rafters were. The moon touches it all, a slender sliver of it. You don't want to see too clearly, when diving the ruins of the Reproach. Going in by daylight, for all it seems safer, was Statlos Shrievsby's first mistake.

It's all very quiet as they cross the no-man's land. Dostritsyn leads, head down. He has his caged bird hung on his back by his ear. Lemya wonders that the twittering doesn't drive him to distraction. He has his goat. He hadn't brought the goat into the taproom of the Anchorage, for obvious reasons, though he'd sent it a bowl of beer outside because he can be a considerate employer. Dostritsyn's slightly drunk goat, therefore. It trots along at his heels on the end of its string, yellow eyes goggling at everything. When they stop it chews away at whatever weeds and leaves are close, or else at the edge of Dostritsyn's coat. Why it doesn't just eat its own leash and then flee, Lemya isn't sure. She isn't sure why the goat. Nobody else finds it unexpected. She doesn't ask. She doesn't want to seem ignorant. Obviously, there must be a goat. It's probably an ancient tradition of the ruin-divers.

Into the shadow of the closest buildings. They're within the Reproach now. She expected to feel a chill closing over her, like stepping into water. Instead, being out in the overgrown firebreak felt exposed and, now she's under cover, she feels safer, outside scrutiny.

"That's how it gets you," Meraqui tells her, a low whisper in her ear. "You like it here, it tells you. You want to be here. You belong here. Don't let it. The place is poison." She's looking like she wishes she hadn't come. She wishes she hadn't come. But one jewelled chalice or spinning top, an ornamental sword or a portrait of some Varatsin scion, and she'll have the landlord off her back and pay her uncle's debts to the Lodges again.

Somewhere, not too close, there is a high peal of laughter. Mad laughter, barely human. Easy to imagine a face stretched beyond its limits, turned up to the night sky. A sudden flurry of motion out in the dark. Dislodged stones tumbling, shockingly loud against the backdrop of the silence. Then silence.

And music. Distant music on the still air. Just for a moment. Lemya shakes her head. Not sure if she heard it. Not sure if anyone heard it but her. Dostritsyn is listening to his bird. Forward, he signals.

Another street inwards. The sense of the place leans over invisibly above them to scrutinise its guests. The houses here have all been picked clean. The first ruin-divers had it easy. Each successive generation has had to risk more and go deeper into the Varatsin dream. They pause at a crossroads where an ancient fountain sits, full of thick, algae-scummed water and frogs. Dostritsyn, Meraqui and Grymme have a brief, whispered argument about where to go for the best leavings. Ruslav puts a hand like a ham on the old man's shoulder.

"This Pal woman," he growls. "Where's she going to have ended up?"

Dostritsyn gives him a pitying look. Where indeed? How is anyone to know? But Meraqui suggests one place; Grymme reckons she'll have gone only inwards. A lost Pal woman in the Reproach? It'll have lured her, he says. And, let's face it, he should know. The argument goes on, Ruslav shoving his ignorant oar in as well.

"The woman's lost," Dostritsyn says. "Yes, yes, we said we'd bring her out for Blackmane. We'll say anything. Why does anybody trust us with their business? We're thieves, Ruslav. You should recognise your own. Thieves, not rescuers. And there's nothing to rescue. The Reproach ate her a day ago or more. Madness."

Ruslav picks him up by the collar. "You will do. What you said you'd do. Old man." The knuckles tightening about Dostritsyn's coat are the victors of a hundred brawls. And the man doesn't care. Laughs in Ruslav's face. "She's lost," he repeats. "The longer we stay here, the more chance you'll be too. The weak and the unprepared go first, always. Why'd you think I was so happy to bring you along, son?"

Ruslav drops him, face writhing. Eyes casting back towards the firebreak and the outside world. He'd run then. If it was just him, he'd run, lie later about what had gone on. But it's not just him. It's Lemya. It's Shantrov. It's the feelings his head is full of. The Reproach will have to wait its turn if it wants him.

Lemya is watching Hellgram.

The foreigner has taken things from the satchel at his belt. A little square of waxed canvas spread out before him as he kneels. A tiny, hooded lamp with a steady green-yellow light like a firefly's. A brass compass. Four little cones of incense. A box of Ilmari 'Leaping Demon' matches. He lights the incense with brisk movements. Stares at the compass as its needle spins.

Stares at the lines of pale smoke that seem to make writing in the air. He has a book, dog-eared. She sees little tables there, set out in script impossibly regular, beyond any scribe's hand. He packs everything away again, pinching the incense out, turning a switch to kill the lamp, wrapping it all in the canvas. "There's a…" he says, and stops.

They're all looking at him.

"I don't have the proper words." His Maric has a faint, rough accent, clipped vowels, laboured consonants he can only clear by adding extra sounds as a ramp. *I don't khev the proper gworts.* "There's a disruption in the influences of this place. Something is holding out. That way." Pointing into the darkness.

"It must be her," Lemya decides.

"Holding out? A Pal? They don't know the first thing," Dostritsyn objects. "Still, there's good pickings that way. That's the palace grounds yonder." Grymme nods enthusiastically. A handful of ruin-divers have braved the palace itself, but not Dostritsyn, not yet. And what would his legend be if he left those stones unturned? Even if they don't venture within those walls, there are lodges and outbuildings, mausoleums and reliquaries. The Varatsin Dukes were profligate with their grandeur.

"Is it her?" Ruslav demands of Hellgram but the man only shrugs. It's something, is all. His divination has gone as far as it can.

"Rich pickings," Grymme echoes. "Fill our bags quickly." At his back there's a gurgle from the fountain. One of the frogs. Not the ancient mechanism finding voice and life again.

They go. One street deeper and the tumbled walls of the Ducal estate are in sight; they shrink back into the shelter of a crumbled house. The locals are coming.

A dozen of them, men and women and a child. Ragged, emaciated. They crest the rubble of a fallen home like animals, pause at the apex to let the wan moon touch them. Their hair is long and wild. The men have snarled beards like briars. Their flesh is bruised and grazed and pulled taut against their bones.

The moon finds their eyes, wide as plates; their teeth, bared in broad smiles. For a moment, one of them is looking straight at Lemya. One of the women, her dark hair a mass of knots and burrs, her clothes just five layers of torn rags. Eye contact, that Lemya flinches from. A smile. About to call her fellows to the hunt. But then they're off again, scattering down the rubble, now on two legs, now all fours. Hurtling off down the street at a tangent to the divers' course. Just mad people running madly. Except for one moment. Except, as they pass through the open space where the base of a fallen statue speaks of lost glories, there's an instant they are on their feet and dancing. Two, three steps of a pavane, circling each other with the grace of forest spirits, faces composed into a sublime and superior joy. Then scrabbling away like dogs. The night rings with their weird, hooting laughter. Lemya blinks. Nobody has reacted. She isn't sure what she saw.

At first it was just a little madness. Doctors were sent for. Then, as it spread, priests, magicians. Houses were burned. Bodies were exhumed for exorcism, from marble tombs and nameless pits both. Nothing stopped or even slowed the return of the Varatsins. And at last – under considerable duress from their peers – the three Armiger houses who had been central to the usurpation sent the heads of their households into the grounds of the Ducal Palace. They prostrated themselves, they confessed their fault – there were crossbows aimed at them, to ensure they did so. They promised all manner of reparations, for thus were ghosts laid to rest, in the histories and the tales.

Not one of them returned. Nor did most of the crossbowmen and other observers. Nor did the corruption of the noble district halt. That was when the new Duke, his court and all the Armiger families relocated across the river. That was when the western side of Ilmar began its descent into poverty, money leaching from it like water into sand. That was when they began to call it Varatsin's Reproach. Later just The Reproach, when the name seemed to conjure the thing.

Skip through several streets. Meraqui ranges ahead, into and out of buildings. Occasionally, the gleam of something in her hand, plucked from the rubble. Then, the wall of the Ducal estate, but it's fallen in more than one place. The trees within have had the time to bow and bully it over. The grounds, once landscaped and manicured, are overgrown, plenty of cover, plenty of chances for unwanted surprises. The denizens of the Reproach roam through it, skin pale in the moonlight. There are corpses. The divers come across three huddled by the breach they choose for entrance. Emaciated, stick-like, just skeletons with skin on. It's not that the curse doesn't want its recruits to dance and feast and enjoy all the good things, it's just there are no good things left to enjoy. Not to keep body and soul together.

Dostritsyn cackles, horribly loud. An echo of laughter comes from within the trees, but receding. They stare at the old man, waiting to see if this is *it*, if he's turned. He has found a necklace on one of the dead, though. A fortune in emeralds and silver. He holds it up to show the Lapwing crest cut into the largest stone. The bird of ill omen, never used by any family or faction since, in all the complex ornithology of the histories of Ilmar. He pockets it. A good profit even at the cutthroat prices of the fences and pawnbrokers. He listens. The bird sings to him. All, apparently, is well. It's his turn to screw his eyes up and stare at his fellows. Meraqui is telling over her garlands of paper charms. They're going brown, as though she's stood too close to a fire. Still good, she assures them. Still *efficacious*, as the Allorwen say. She's sweating. This isn't her first run; she should have developed thicker skin. Her hands shake when she thinks nobody's looking. Ruslav sees it. He doesn't say anything. His do too. He can hear music between the trees. Old music, drum and strings and weird wailing pipes. He sees stately gowned figures moving apart, together, across the neatly clipped grass. Blinks it back to the weed-snarled heath it's become, rubs at his ears until the night's quiet is restored. Lemya's hand closes on his arm, making him startle and draw his long knife on her. Her face is taut. She feels it too. Like a net, drawing close.

"We need to pick up the pace, old man," he says. "Can't keep waiting for you to catch up." Even though they haven't been.

"You're the one with the impossible requirements," Dostritsyn remarks. "I've got mine." Bringing the necklace out to shimmer through his fingers. The music ends with a flourish, round of applause for the minstrels, even though Ruslav thought he'd banished it. He realises Lemya's been tapping her foot.

"There's a tower," Grymme says. "Look." They can't see it. Ruslav climbs a tree: the man's correct. A broken tower, three storeys standing, and about the base of it a straggle of cadaver-people spasming in some manic scrum. A dozen, more. But harmless, surely. He could break them like sticks.

There's someone up in the tower. His eyes are drawn to it, as though the scene is a painting, the composition intended to lead him there. He sees that's why the wretches are there. Their faces turn up towards that high socket of a window. They're calling for her to come down. "My lady!" they cry. "Honoured lady! Your place is prepar'd!"

He drops down. Stares at Grymme. Stares at Dostritsyn, then Hellgram. "You knew."

The foreigner shifts the weight of his pack. He's been at some piece of magic himself. "She's there," he confirms flatly. "Or someone is. Someone not a part of this place yet." Putting his book of tables and calculations away.

"How?" Meraqui wants to know. "Some clueless Pal. How's she still *her*?"

"He means his *wife*," Ruslav spits. "The dead one."

Hellgram's face *is* dead, in that instant. Utterly still. Lemya stands between him and Ruslav, because to her it seems that his dead expression is going to send his dead hands at the other man's living throat. But Hellgram is calm. He's always calm. There's a hole inside him all the feelings go into. "Who knows?" he says. "But I must see."

"The score's there," Grymme says. "Such treasures as you never saw."

The bird sings in time to the music.

"If we're going," Lemya says. "We have to go."

They will go. For all the wrong reasons, mainly. That's when the voice rings out, "My noble peer, Lord Gauterin, what unlook'd-for pleasure is't to have you in our midst!" and it's too late.

They'll tell you the Reproach is peopled by the descendants of the Varatsins and their servants, who never left. Who lived on in rags and bore ragged children. Or the heirs and assigns of the others who went mad. By the heads of the Armiger families who never returned. By the soldiers sent to watch over them and make sure they didn't. And none of that is true.

Nobody goes into the Reproach. Everyone knows it. Madness to even consider it. Nothing worse in all the world. Except starvation. Except watching someone die for want of medicine. The riches of a bygone age sit there, picked at generation after generation but always another handful of jewels or an antique sword or enchanted tapestry to come out. People like Blackmane pore through old books and maintain a record of the great treasures of the Varatsin court yet to be found. A fortune tied up in each of them. And so, everybody goes into the Reproach. Everybody from the Gutter Districts who's desperate enough. The hungry, the tired, the indebted, the fugitives. And professionals like Dostritsyn and his crew, whether on freelance looting errands or sent skidding in on the coins of some Armiger family in the market for a new heirloom. The denizens of the Reproach always die, danced to death, starved to death, dead of exposure, or they murder one another. Or, as we're about to see, they surprise groups of intruders with ready knives. But the lure of free wealth is always enough to bring more, and so Ilmar leaks into the Reproach, and the place is never abandoned for long.

And more than that. You can hear it in your dreams they say, if you're needy enough to sleep in the streets close by the firebreak. If you're too imaginative and wild as a child. If you dream of yourself as an Armiger and buck your rightful place at the bottom of the world. If you *are* an Armiger, but some ancestor of yours brought Varatsin blood as an unexpected dowry. Just as well Shantrov *didn't* come, honestly. He'd have been lost already if he had. And so, they creep, in ones and twos and sometimes whole families. The Reproach sings like a siren on still Ilmari nights and is never short of an audience. And the Dukes used to place guards nearby to stop people, but then the guards went too. Some say that the streets within the firebreak – this is impossible, but they say it – are growing. Ruin-divers come out and say how the distances and the precise arrangements of paths change. How the Reproach is bigger now than it was. How their maps are useless. How streets that were on *this* side of the firebreak in their mother's day are on *that* side of it now.

The figure who speaks stands taller than the others. His Palleseen soldier's coat is only slightly torn by his cavort through the briars. The long face of Statlos Shrievsby splits into a delighted smile as he makes an ancient genuflection towards them. At his back, late arrivals to the scarecrow's ball. This one was a tailor's apprentice, that one a thief, the woman behind on the run from a brutal home.

The intruders are frozen, but Shrievsby strides forwards, one arm out in greeting. "I hadst thought mayhap we would not encounter thee!" comes out of his narrow Pal mouth, words the School of Correct Speech would have his tongue torn out for.

Ruslav kills him. He throws the knife he'd drawn and, though it's not meant for such abuse, it hacks a gash from Shrievsby's throat on its way past, and the man goes down. The scarecrows don't even react. His joyous expression flits from his spasming face and lands on the visage of the nearest. "Indeed, my lord, indeed," as though the murder had been a particularly good bon mot.

Lemya is hauling at his arm. The ruin-divers are already running. Dostritsyn has a look of almost amused disgust. It's always what these toughs do, when they brave the Reproach. They fight. They shed blood. They *engage* with it. "That's just opening the door on it," he used to tell them at first. Now he lets them do it, because the Reproach has a focus, and so long as there's an idiot around, it won't focus on him.

At first, they're fleeing along the line of the wall, just inside it, but then Grymme's ahead and calling, "This way, this way!" pulling them towards the tower, until they break from the trees into a night heavy with music.

The tower tapers five storeys into the dark. There is not enough breath on the air to stir the flags there. On the clear ground before it, the court of the Varatsins has gathered for a tourney. They sit on the grass, the lords and ladies in their finery. Antique gowns and fashions no longer seen in today's conservative streets. Drooping sleeves and coat tails; high-piled coiffures stabbed with bejewelled pins and combs; gowns that conceal the skin while revealing the shape. Fungal eruptions of lace at throat and wrist. Swathes of thick velvet like mould. They pass their elegant steps while the minstrels play, then stand back as the first jousters strut into the glade. A man, a woman, armoured in bronze-chased silver steel, sitting proud on the backs of their stamping steeds. In their hands, slender lances, blunted tips aimed at the heavens.

Lemya blinks, rubs her eyes. Finds she's taken three steps forwards, and nobody's seized her arm to drag her back. Everyone's fighting the same battle. She remembers herself and sees.

The starvelings, tottering about each other before collapsing to the ground like cut puppets. And here comes one upon another's shoulders, holding a withered branch aloft, even as a rake-thin herald cries out, "The Count of Osboryat gives challenge!"

And, beyond them – even as the armour gleams in the moonlight, and the count closes the visor on his helm – halfway up the tower, she sees a face. A plain, Pal face. Not Hellgram's wife, then. Not lost to the Reproach, either. Companion-Archivist Nasely, whom the Perfecture dearly wants back.

She has held out here, somehow, hiding and eating stale rations. Because of all things, Nasely is a creature of caution. When her superior, the late lamented Sage-Archivist, told her that they would be going into the Wood, she didn't want to. When she'd taken up a place on his staff, it had been with the expectation of no peril worse than a paper cut, occasional promotions and then a comfortable retirement. If she had to get posted out into the Sway, she would at least see it from the safe side of a desk.

When Ochelby informed her that he'd be bringing her beyond the Anchorwood, it was as though he'd personally taken her life and torn it into little pieces in front of her. And so, she'd done what she could. Instead of spending her time putting her paperwork in order like a conscientious clerk, she'd taken precautions. She'd shamelessly embezzled departmental funds to bribe Turncoats to direct her to where magicians might be found. She'd gone – hooded and cloaked and so suspicious-looking it was amazing she hadn't been mugged – into Mirror Allor and bought charms and amulets and relics. Under her robes was a whole extra garment woven from warded paper flowers and hearts, tin and brass medals, protective herbs and little dried bird feet. And half of it was doubtless flummery, but somewhere in there had been sufficient misdirection to keep her ahead of the beast. And now, she has the last of it in her hands, watching it blacken and fall apart, drift to dust through her fingers. Enough potency there, after she'd spent a small fortune on exactly the sort of people her department was supposed to be suppressing, to hold out. More protection than any ruin-diver could have afforded in a lifetime, and it has kept her safe just this long. And she's penned in this ruin of a tower – that the corners of her eyes are insisting is grand, and goes up above her where the moon should be. The beast is still out there, and now these horrible cadaverous people. Their cackling laughter, their elegant measures, the music. She can't blot out the music.

And then, below, something's happening. Even as the glittering knights salute each other, the lord of the revels makes himself known. The Varatsin Duke has arrived.

"Well," Ruslav says, "that's about the most mad-ass thing I ever saw."

"How do we get her out?" from Lemya, and Dostritsyn laughs at her, loud enough to rise above the skirling of the pipes.

"You won't even get yourself out," the old man tells her, "with that kind of thinking. We get the treasures. We get the preciousness. We get out. She stays in. She's lost."

"Look at her," Lemya insists. "She's not." And though the ragged court dances between stately grandeur and abject tatters, the woman at the window is constant. A dowdy Pal clutching her robe to her, the feel of a forlorn princess in need of rescue lent only by her surroundings, not by her self.

"Old man," Ruslav starts, but his knife was lost in the dark, and Dostritsyn's is out, weaving little eights between them.

"Son," the old man says, and then stops. Stares at the goat.

It's strutting. It stomps and tosses its head proudly. It rears, in a way goats don't. Nobody ever had a goat rampant on their shield, yet here one is. The ghosts of barding and caparison shimmer over its white coat. Its horns merge with the steel armour of a chamfron over its forehead.

"Oh piss," Dostritsyn says mildly, and lets go the string, as though the madness might travel up it. The goat canters off, head held high, a destrier seeking its knight. The bird attacks the inside of its cage, a hawk in miniature, keening. "We're out of time. Grab loot, get out."

"No," Lemya insists. Hellgram is standing, staring towards the tower as though it's crammed with dead wives waiting his inspection. Grymme steps forwards.

"My lords, my lords!" No trace of Allor in his accent. "See, see what guests I have aquir'd for your delight! New friends and faces for your revels!" Striding into the idiot's show of the tourney. Going home as the curse devours the last of who he was. The look on his face born of another age, some long-dust courtier copied from one unfortunate to another, until it burrowed into his mind and laid its eggs there. Whispering to his dreams. Devouring his self one morsel at a time. Hatching into its vacuous final instar.

They look up, all those grave, beautiful faces. All those emaciated skulls. The woods at their back are suddenly full of dance and motion, more of the graceful folk come to the spectacle. The lords and the ladies of a lost age. And, as there were never so many of the Varatsin court in life, now there are multiples. Two Lord Ystrovirs, a dozen Ladies of Tresov. Copies of copies of copies, each losing fidelity, until all they can do is parrot snippets of antiquated speech and dance until they die.

Ruslav has more knives, of course, and more than that. He draws from within his coat a short rod, socketing a gold tableth into it. A nasty little homegrown imitation of a Pal baton, cooked up by some Lodge hack-magician. Good for a couple of shots before it splinters itself to pieces. Dostritsyn's eyes are wide, but not for the reason Ruslav would have preferred.

"You can't use those things in here," the old man hisses. "It's like shouting."

Ruslav levels the weapon at Grymme's chest. The former ruin-diver shows no recognition. It's from after his time, now. He's just dancing backwards, gleeful as you please, and the revellers are coming to meet him.

When Ruslav looks back, Dostritsyn and Meraqui are gone. Cut their losses, professionals to the last. It's him. It's Lemya. It's Hellgram, his book in his hands, flicking swiftly through its pages.

Then the trumpets sound, and the oncoming courtiers are kneeling, twin ranks of them. The stamping, clattering knights salute. Grymme dances down the aisle and then casts himself into his own abasement. The lord of this place is come, cursed to never again know human shape. Somewhere, a maddened falcon screams in the body of a songbird.

Late that night – early that morning – a figure steps out through the riotous growth of the firebreak. The faintest line of dawn outlines the rooftop edges of the eastern sky, but the sun itself won't show for an age. More than enough time to get home and think up excuses to give to Blackmane. And the emerald necklace and the other valuables stuffing Dostritsyn's pockets will soften the edges of that conversation, he knows. Blackmane's a businessman first and foremost. They'll toast the lost together.

Meraqui didn't make it. She was at his back, and then she wasn't – her charms worn out, their strings breaking, the crisping paper exploding away from her like panicked moths. And gone. Dancing with the deranged. The way it always happens, on a ruin-diver's last run.

Enough money for a new bird, a new scapegoat. A new crew

of hopefuls. Always good to have someone less prepared than you. Gives the Reproach something to focus on while you're filling your boots. Eight runs now, and here's Dostritsyn, whistling, walking out of the Reproach with the hard little walnut of his mind still intact. Still himself; the man not even the Varatsins want paying homage to them. Off to retouch the gilt of his own legend, because otherwise people might see through it to the bodies he's left dancing in his wake and refuse to drink with him when he raises a glass to the dead.

Ruslav in the Teeth

Ruslav: a big man made small by the perspective that he's made a terrible mistake. He had looked at the wrong part of the painting. There'd been a knight on the road, lance and charger, bright as the moon. He let himself be seduced by that little pinprick of light, while Shantrov the artist had been focused on the great and inviolable darkness all around. The painting had been a warning that the dark is something to be broken against and lost in, not challenged.

Ruslav couldn't see the ragged people anymore. He tried, screwed his face up, peeled his lids back. Did everything but poke himself in the eye. Instead, there were only the courtiers, moving to the rhythm of music tuned to a minor key. Not even the regular antique garments now, but fantastical costume and masks. Beak-noses and fin-ears and manes. Inhuman eyes peering from the holes cut into inhuman faces. The kinsfolk and hangers-on and familiars of the court of the Varatsins. And Ruslav had heard all the stories. They scared him to sleep with them as a child, even though the name of the family was always omitted. The old nobility, who trafficked with things beyond the Wood and married into strange bloodlines. Who had been killed and burned and buried in unmarked graves, but who always came back. No matter how many times, how many borrowed bodies, you couldn't stop them dancing.

Around him, the Ducal estate was restored to its magnificence. The tower was faced with marble, its doorway edged with gilt.

Beyond it, the palace reached its spires avariciously towards the moon.

He had his rod levelled at Grymme. At the fish-masked capering thing he thought was probably Grymme, save that they blended one into another. There were so many of them, coming out of the trees. And now, their lord. Ruslav switched his aim, pointing the weapon at the heart of the shadow.

The Duke of the Varatsins took the shape of an elegant man in a great, trailing cloak, long hair lustrous past his shoulders, beard down to his chest, a great diadem set on his brow that was the most longed-for lost treasure in all of Blackmane's record books. Ruslav shot him, speaking the pirated word the tablethmaker gave him. A brief flare of gold momentarily banished the masquerade, showing ragged bodies all around, ribs straining the skin, cavernous starved eyes. It showed him what the Varatsin Duke was truly made of. He screamed.

That cloak, trailing off into the shadows: it was rats. His hair was rats, a tide of them roiling and fighting across shoulders made of rats. In the interstices of the rodents, Ruslav glimpsed bones, a skull. Not even a proper skeleton but just an assemblage of osseous struts and scaffolding worked like a puppet by the constant seething of all those tiny, enthralled bodies.

The hole punched in that composite mass healed itself by the simple application of more rats. The Varatsin Duke cared no more for the lost vermin than he did for the generations of the dead whose meagre flesh had fed his gardens. He bowed low before Ruslav, extended a writhing hand. The music swelled. The rod fell from Ruslav's fingers. He found he'd taken a step forwards, his own hand out. Some part of him was dancing to it all. Sir Ruslav of the Gutter come gallant to court. He reached out with the same hand that had held the weapon, wondering if he would feel cool skin or teeming bodies.

To dance would be a grand end to the evening, he knew. And to many other things. He wished Shantrov had come after all.

The thought was an off note in the orchestra. He pulled back, the knight in the painting again, surrounded by the dark but not lost to it. There was a weight on his arm that he shook at irritably, not recognising it as Lemya.

She had the rod, still partly charged. She was screaming in his ear, though the music was far louder. She wanted to know the word.

The Varatsin Duke stepped forwards, staring into Ruslav's eyes. His face was beautiful, the acme of Armiger elegance that later generations could only ape. The strings of his bloodline and marriage ties fell away like red threads into the night, connecting him to the city and half the families in it, high and low. He *was* Ilmar, Ruslav understood. He could no more be consigned to the past than a man could walk about without his heart.

He reached out hands that were gloved with fur. Ruslav heard Lemya whimper. She wasn't as far into the dream as he was. She saw more clearly. The Varatsin Duke cupped their chins, his smile all gentleness and welcome and utter raging idiocy. Fur twisted past fur behind his teeth. Mad little eyes glittered from the depths of his pupils.

"My lord, my lady, you grace us with your presence." A voice that scurried up from the depths of him, filthy with manners. Against Ruslav's cheek the Duke's hand seethed with motion, hard little points of nails, hungry teeth.

"Where," another voice demanded, "is my *wife*?"

The Duke broke away from them, rounding on this intrusion. Confronting something that could not just be *remembered* away into oblivion. Ruslav staggered back, hand to his face, feeling the scratches and nicks that the rats had left there. *He could have just eaten my face off, and I'd not have known.*

He took the rod from Lemya wordlessly, hoping there was enough in it for a second shot. She was yanking on his arm again, pointing.

Hellgram had undergone a transformation. Not into one of the capering court. If anything, he'd grown further than ever from it. He had a helm on now, of grey steel. There were lenses over his eyes and a point-nosed mask below them, nothing of his face to be seen. He had a blade in his hand that shifted uncomfortably against the eyes. His voice came muffled as he strode towards the tower, demanding his lost and perhaps imaginary wife. Ruslav didn't know if this was how the madness of the Reproach had finally touched Hellgram, or if this was the real Hellgram finally rising to the surface.

The nearest courtier swooped in, arms out to carry Hellgram off into a gavotte. The foreigner cut the figure down – naked scarecrow limbs showing in the instant the sword clove through flesh. "My wife!" he shouted at them all.

At last, something had ruffled the composure of the Varatsin Duke. Something that neither would nor could belong to the Reproach. Alien beyond the dreams of Ilmar.

"I banish you," the Duke's rats declared, and he seethed forwards. Hellgram cut him in half, more impatient at the interruption than anything else. Abruptly, all the component rodents above the Duke's waist exploded outwards, leaving a declining mound of scrabbling confusion, twined tails and bared teeth and sinuous bodies.

"*Damn* it." Hellgram's muffled voice, not even cursing the cursed Duke, just the whole quest – his doomed attempts to find this woman nobody had ever seen. And this was, Ruslav understood, one more place he'd cross off the list now. A place he'd staked his hopes on. The Reproach, that undiscovered country. Where better for a lost wife to be hiding?

The Duke came back, just rebuilt himself from bones and earth, branches and the tortuous connective tissue of the rats. He had a sword now, gem-hilted, the blade burning with ancient enchantments. Another treasure from Blackmane's books. Ruslav went to help by instinct, seeing the two uncanny blades cross, but Lemya was running for the tower.

He went after her, stumbling because the ground he saw wasn't the ground that was there. Ahead, Lemya tripped, staggered headlong through the tower door. Literally through:

it was closed, but she fell past it anyway. Ruslav understood he wouldn't be able to do that. He saw the door, so it was real for him. He was locked out.

She shouted his name. He closed his eyes, lowered his head like a bull, charged forwards.

He got it wrong, or half-wrong. His shoulder hit the old stone of the doorway with punishing force. Another few inches and he'd have brained himself. Instead, he spun through the doorway, the hammer-blow of pain briefly bringing all the moss and ruin into focus. There were stairs, carious and piecemeal as rotten teeth. He saw Lemya's heels disappearing up them.

He went after, practically climbing on all fours rather than running, because the going was so treacherous. He heard a tremulous voice raised above, a voice speaking Pel. He redoubled his speed, trying to catch up.

Lemya burst out into the third-floor room, reeling, out of breath. And there wasn't much she could have said, honestly. Nasely's scream of panic would have eclipsed any words, along with the flash of her own rod as she got the command word out. Nobody had told her she was being rescued.

Lemya took a glancing burn across the upper arm, her stumbling progress saving her. The trailing edge of the fire lashed Ruslav's cheek and crisped a hand's span of hair and beard to ash. And, because he was who he was, and lived in that world, he shot back without needing to think. That was what you did when someone shot at you.

Nasely screamed, and Lemya was screaming too – not in pain but at him. Because this was a *rescue*, and if there was a Rule One of rescuing, it was not to shoot the rescuee. And he'd winged her – hasty shooting and the constant confusion of where they even *were* had fouled his aim. Winged her, and she was running out of the room, up the stairs again, shrieking and weeping and leaving streamers of burning paper charms in her wake. They went after her at the same time, got in one another's way. Up above, cries for help in Pel mingled with weird mewling and broken ends of old Maric words. Ruslav, racing full tilt, had a revelation. Remembered something inconvenient.

He shoved Lemya back, sending her tumbling down the steps into Nasely's window room. Which had been the *top* of the *ruined* tower.

He'd shoved himself forwards, of course, because that was how it worked. He heard the Pal woman's scream. She had turned to shoot again, off-handed and awkward because he'd smashed her shoulder with his return shot. He struck the rod from her hand, but she'd got the word out and it discharged. The heat of it washed past him and set his coat alight. Then she took another step back and vanished.

He lunged. Almost straight-armed her in the chest because, just past where the wall wasn't, she was teetering on the brink with windmilling arms. But he had her, had a fistful of her uniform, even though buttons were pinging off it as the fabric twisted, shoddy work from the factories.

She bit him. Actually got her teeth into his knuckles. He roared, shook her. She laughed. A delighted smile cracked across her face like broken porcelain.

"Why, my lord! Such revels!" Nasely cried, old Maric words twisting their way out of her lips. Her eyes were terrified, disconnected from the rest of her.

His other hand shook, the rod in it was blackened, the tableth gone. Otherwise, he'd have spat the word and shot her, just from sheer revulsion. Instead, he hauled her back in, heedless of her ruined shoulder. Practically threw her down the truncated handful of steps to where Lemya was. The three of them stumbled down to the bottom of the tower, the walls sliding in and out – painted plaster and fine tapestry fighting territorial wars with mould and moss and denuded stone. They burst out into the open, Nasely sobbing, leaning into Lemya. Twitching in time to the music which now swept in on them from all sides. Ruslav was almost stunned by the reminder, *Oh yes, we have all this to deal with.* There was no sign of Hellgram, and the court was back in full sway again. At one end of the lists, there was a tall throne on which the Varatsin Duke reclined, and the throne was made of more rats, so that the edges of the whole rippled with constant busy motion. And yet he smiled. And there was a knight there. He was just a capering scarecrow on another's shoulders, but he was still a knight. Ruslav tried not to see the armour and the heraldry, but his eyes gave up. The cataphract stamped and steamed and lowered his lance. Ruslav drew his sword and readied his own shield. Lemya was shouting at him. He couldn't understand her words. They were all from after his time.

Nasely shrieked, high and annoying. It cut through even the Reproach, just for a moment. She broke from Lemya and ran, even as the knight began his thunderous charge. Nasely wasn't even running away from it, lurching on a course that would take her right under the hooves. Lemya, running after her, was bound for a similar fate. Ruslav just stood there, like the figure in Shantrov's painting. It was the painting's fault. It had let thoughts into his head. It had made him something that no sane world would have wanted him to be.

The thing Nasely was running from appeared then. They'd garlanded it with flowers and placed a halter of vines about its throat – or at least where that grotesque fish head met its body. It lurched from the trees with a dozen starveling figures hanging on and running alongside. What the Reproach had made of it in the interim, Ruslav couldn't think but, now its quarry was out in the open, it had remembered its purpose. The beast from the Anchorwood was charging for Nasely and Lemya, jaws agape.

It got the knight instead. A splintered moment as the lance rammed into it – Ruslav saw its scales torn open even though there was no lance, no knight. Then the stick figures were in its jaws, and it was turning madly, eyes goggling, seeking the source of its phantom pain. Lemya and Nasely were in the trees, still running. And here he was.

The Varatsin Duke stepped down from his throne, or at

least reshaped his struggling body until he was standing. His beautiful, verminous face was beatific as he looked upon Ruslav. There was an invitation there. He teetered on the brink.

Someone screamed from within the Wood, impossible to know which of the two women. He jolted into action, running after them, desperate to pick up their trail, feeling the claws of a century of decay and merriment snagging at his heels. He found Lemya crouching over the Pal woman, and for a moment he thought there was a murder going on. He'd not have blamed anyone concerned. Instead, Nasely was convulsing, foaming, clutching at the student. The exploded ruin of her shoulder was raw and red, splinters of bone jutting like hedgehog quills. What chilled him was that the wound wasn't Nasely's priority. What came from the Pal's mouth was a babble of Pel and old Maric, as though the words were fighting each other for possession of her tongue.

"Get her up," he snapped, speaking loud over the music. Lemya couldn't, so Ruslav had to, hauling the Companion-Archivist to her feet, heedless of how much it surely hurt her. She clawed at him. No, she had one hand in his, her arm about his waist, letting him turn her in the next steps of the dance. For a moment, he saw her clad in wine-dark satin, the glitter of jewels at her throat. Words rose in him: *You dance divinely, lady...* He champed down on them, ground them between his teeth, swallowed them back. Hauled Nasely through the trees, hearing the elegant calls of the court behind him. Ahead...

Ahead, the wall. The broken wall of the estate. And daylight. The whole night had gone, though it seemed impossible. The Varatsins had stolen time from him, buried it with all the unfound valuables of their reign. Morning had come, the sun clear of the horizon and muttering about the rooftops, the distant spire of the Gownhall standing like the gnomon of the city's sundial.

And they weren't out yet. Not past the firebreak. He had

dropped Nasely – she lay at his feet, laughing wildly, moving an arm that shouldn't be capable of it. Lemya was sitting down, exhausted, grey-faced. "What are we going to do?" she kept asking. He opened his mouth to say *Leave*, and *May I have this measure, sweet lady* flooded onto his tongue like vomit. They stared at each other. Her fingers amid the weeds moved with the drum. He plucked a ragged flower from out of the briars and placed it in her hair.

"Go!" shouted a figure, helmed, dark-coated, goggle-masked. A jagged discontinuity tearing through the glamour of the place. "She's not here! Go!" A man so lost, even the Varatsins couldn't find him. Hellgram ran past, then skidded to a halt and turned. He wrenched the leathery fabric of his mask down, exposing his gaunt, angular face. "What are you doing?"

Ruslav wanted to demand how he couldn't hear the music, the beautiful music. He wanted to label Hellgram with the moniker of some long-lost aristocrat and bring him into the dance. Hellgram was proof against it. Under the man's stern gaze it all felt like a child's dress-up game and he was ashamed of the mummery.

"Help me with her." His own words, briefly given uncontested sway over his mouth.

"Just go! Leave her or you're dead!" Then Hellgram was running, and Ruslav didn't understand. He picked up Nasely instead, hoisted her over his shoulders. Lumbered off in Hellgram's wake with Lemya at his heels. The world twisted around him. The paths all led back to the ruin of the palace. The music tugged at his ears and pleaded with him, *Stay! No, stay!* He felt the hook of it in him, barbed so it wouldn't easily be drawn. The eggs of the Varatsin dream were well and truly sunk into his brain and would hatch soon enough. Right now, he just followed Hellgram who saw none of it. Who trod that straight line through all the shimmer and the twist, until they were staggering out in plain morning light over the firebreak, trampling the bloom of the weeds and scaring the last of the feral cats. Ruslav collapsed on the far side, almost braining Nasely as he dumped her on the cobbles. She was making sounds – mewling, whimpering, laughing, wordless singing to the tune he could still hear inside his head, even though it was no longer coming in by the ears.

"What are you doing?" Hellgram shouted at him.

"I just need," Ruslav said. "Catch my breath."

Hellgram stared at him as though he was mad, and then the beast erupted out of the trees behind them, great blunt fish head splitting to show its underbite of jagged teeth. Ruslav hadn't understood what they'd been running from.

Lemya hauled on Nasely's good arm, cursing the woman. Something must have registered, some flicker of her skull's original tenant, because the Companion-Archivist was up and staggering, crying out. The beast had already built up a head of speed though, breaking into a full gallop as it crossed the open ground of the firebreak.

Hellgram had his sword out. It had come from nowhere – no scabbard for it nor room in the man's pack. Ruslav pushed himself up, a thousand pains competing for his attention. He hustled the two women ahead of him, shouting at them to take the narrower alleys. They were all injured, drained, snarled in the barbed music of the Reproach, but they ran. Behind them, Ruslav heard a sound like metal in terrible agony and knew it was Hellgram meeting the beast. He risked a look. The man was down – bowled over. The beast had a long gash across its head and flank. It reared improbably onto its hind legs, slammed down its foreclaws either side of Hellgram. He had a hand out towards it, some toy of his. A moment later, the monster had jerked away from him as though from a goad, abandoning him, hunting for its proper prey again.

Nasley dropped, twitching and spasming. Her voice rang out, loud enough to wake every late sleeper in the district. A scream, save that the words of an antique song were threaded through it. Ruslav got her onto his shoulder again, knees almost buckling.

Lemya was ahead, turning back for him. "Just go!" he shouted at her. "Just go!" Seeing her eyes wide at what was coming after.

Casting himself sideways into the narrowest of jitties, stumbling over the detritus of decades, barrel staves and rags and broken furniture. The beast came thrashing right after him, grinding its scales against the brickwork, even its flattened body hard-pressed to fit. He hoped it got stuck. He hoped it died there, and all the denizens of the Reproach's near shore came and carved off pieces for their breakfast.

Then he was out, still heading south. For the Wood, for the Anchorage, for Mother Ellaime's boarding house. Familiar places where the world worked in comprehensible ways, no ghosts or monsters. Lemya was ahead of him. The thought, *Damn me, we actually*—

The beast tore itself out from between the buildings in an eruption of jagged brick-ends and mortar that enveloped him. Shards and fragments danced from his back and Nasely's body. A fist-sized chunk of wall punched him in the back of the head and he went down, ending up with Nasely's weight across him as he writhed about to see the end. The beast loped towards him, shaking its scarred head. He had a moment then, staring at it. Wanting to demand of the thing *What do you want?* No hunter ever had such a single-minded focus on its prey, at such cost. It was ragged and torn from a dozen wounds. The blow Hellgram had dealt it should have warned off any predator. And here it was, bleeding, half its scales hanging off it, attention fixed on Nasely, and on him.

Lemya threw a stone at it, accomplishing nothing. She screamed at it, accomplishing nothing.

Nasely had stopped babbling and singing. Her head lolled. The bone showed white and jagged in her shoulder. Possibly she was already dead. He rolled her off him and tried to get to his feet. He had another knife somewhere, surely, or else a stick within reach. Or his fists. He was a fighter, to the last. He never backed down. He'd sink his damn teeth into the monster if that was what it took. He was the gleaming knight, and the monster was the whole dark landscape in every direction he looked.

It lunged, jaws agape, the whole front half of its body twisting sidelong, so its jagged sawblade teeth could close like a trap about his body.

Nihilostes Loses a Convert

*A short woman, hair the bronze-brown of dead leaves, sepia skin.
A pointed chin and eyes that always seem to be looking one way or
the other, never straight on. Baggy Maric clothes that can't quite
hide the foreignness of her. Not just the familiar unfamiliarity of
refugees from nearby lands, either. Her age could be twenty-five
or forty. Impossible for an Ilmari to guess at. And, hidden beneath
those layers, the tattoo that took two days of agony as she sweated
and writhed in the smoke of her ritual. The insect features of her
god.*

Nihilostes always brought tea. Superior tea. Better than they
had in any of the markets this side of the river. Certainly
better than Mother Ellaime kept in her high cupboards. And
if not better than the high-grade teas available in the markets
off Liberation Way, then at least different. Foreign tea, brought
to her by the secretive couriers of her sect. When she came to
Mother Ellaime's, she emptied out the samovar and refilled it
with fresh water and her own brass infuser, and made good tea
for everyone. That was one reason why Mother Ellaime put up
with her. The other was that Nihilostes was a foreign priest of
a dangerous cult who might do terrible things if someone cast
her out of doors. Either tolerate her presence, or else shop her
to the School of Correct Speech and be rid of her, but no half
measures. And finally, because Mother Ellaime had an Allorwen
pragmatism about her, there was always the possibility that a

foreign priest of a dangerous cult might be prevailed upon to throw a curse or some similar service, should the need arise.

"It is not," Nihilostes said, "a flying scorpion. I keep telling you."

Yasnic sipped the definitely superior tea. He'd poured out a libation for God, but God wasn't touching it. God had no truck with that foreign muck. Which made God sound very bigoted, but it *was* technically consecrated to a different religion, so probably God had a point. Probably Yasnic shouldn't drink it either, but it was very good tea.

"I still don't see the difference," he admitted mildly. They always had this conversation. When Nihilostes had first arrived, young and fervent for converts, it had been an argument. Now it was a running joke, because it was the one chain of hers he could yank and be assured of her rising to the bait. It was a clarification she was religiously obliged to make, apparently.

She'd brought fresh bread too. The scent of it filled Mother Ellaime's kitchen. The landlady was chewing around one end of the loaf, and God had the other. The middle was split between the two priests.

Apparently, the bread, being good Maric bread baked locally, was appropriate food for the divine. Yasnic had thrown that heel of it into the fire, anyway, which meant that God was now holding it in both hands like a child with an outsized melon, rasping away at the crust.

"Zenotheus is the divine scorpionfly, as you well know."

"Scorpion fly, flying scorpion." Yasnic shrugged.

Nihilostes gave up on the point of theology. "I mean, you don't get them here. The actual animal. Or even scorpions, much. If you did—"

"Well then, I suppose I'd know the difference. I saw you at that smithy on Morderitsin, by the way."

Nihilostes put on her secretive smile. "Perhaps I wanted to buy a horseshoe." There were, Yasnic recalled, no horses where she came from, across the sea. A land that had a bewildering

ADRIAN TCHAIKOVSKY

number of names – or perhaps just contained many different
nations or people. Some other place to which the Palleseen had
extended their Sway, which was why Nihilostes had arrived
in Ilmar with only a few words of Maric but a good grasp
of Pel. Her people's temples had been torn down, she'd said.
The gold and the relics had been carried out to decorate Pal
officials' studies or be rendered down for precious metals and
raw magic. The whole heart of her culture was being ground
out of her homeland like creases ironed out of a shirt. Except, it
turned out, that was like trying to eliminate a fungus by picking
mushrooms. Her people seemed to have a bewildering number
of gods and, before the Pals came, the big important gods had
spent their time trying to eliminate the little, subversive gods.
Her homeland had been a warren of little persecuted sects and
cults, all of whom seemed to do abominable things to each other
and everyone else they got their hands on. Nihilostes told him
the details with such a showman's glee that he suspected she
made more than half of it up out of whole cloth. Zenotheus
the divine scorpionfly was the god who laid eggs in the hearts
of kings, harbinger of upheaval and change, bringer of chaos.
Everything the Pals wanted to stamp out, and everything the
Mahanic Temple of Ilmar wouldn't want in the city, either. But
when the Pals had conquered her people and overthrown the
gods, Zenotheus and its fellow divine pariahs had fought back
by exporting their cults to every corner of the Palleseen Sway.
Nihilostes had converts, Yasnic knew. There were a lot of people
in Ilmar who wanted a bit of upheaval, change and chaos, and
a handful were desperate enough that even a foreign insect god
looked appealing. More so than Yasnic's God, certainly.

"I've backed a losing horse," he said. And she knew exactly
where his thoughts had taken him, putting a hand on his
carefully. She was good with other people's thoughts. He never
knew if it was magic or some gift of hers, or if his face was just
so eminently readable. He was a simple man, after all.

God stomped across the tabletop, his new blanket drawn

about him. He scowled at the hand. "That's improper," He pronounced.

"It's just a hand," Yasnic said. He felt terribly lonely. Nihilostes was watching him sidelong, as she always did. She didn't say anything. She didn't need to. He knew what she wanted, long-term. To Zenotheus, there was no sweeter prize than the priest of another deity to add to the fold. And she knew about God. She couldn't see Him, but she believed in Him. And that was a bitter irony, because nobody else did.

He thought she'd invite him to a service again, but by now she didn't need to say the words. The invitation just hung in the air between them. *Come along. See what it looks like from the other side.* She'd even offered to give him the pulpit, let him preach his own creed to her little scattering of angry, disaffected Ilmari. Give God the chance to take His own back. But Yasnic knew he wasn't much of a preacher. Not even as much as Kosha, his own teacher, who'd been weak enough at that game.

And it was so tempting, to give in. To just admit that he, Yasnic, was the worst priest in Ilmar, and he should just pack it in. Admit that what he really was, was a desperate beggar who somehow managed to hold down the cheapest room in the Gutter Districts, and that only because Mother Ellaime had special rates for priests. His divine vocation had become little more than a rent rebate. How blissful it would be to abandon all of the responsibility and give himself over to some alien insect god. And feel human contact, and perhaps even intimacy, as something that was his due as a human being. Needless to say, God forbad such pleasures to His priests for ancient and obscure reasons.

He must have looked wistful, because God kicked him for good measure.

Yasnic looked at God, and pointedly didn't move his hand. Nihilostes watched him with amusement.

"One of the big advantages about Zenotheus is that It permits Its followers to have a good time," she said, again with such a bead on his private thoughts that he might as well have a window in his forehead. "Its priests, too."

"Maybe one of these days," said Yasnic, because being kicked by God hurt surprisingly much, and then instantly regretted it. There would be penance, in his future. He looked up, catching a rare moment of direct scrutiny before she was eyeing him crookedly again.

Then there was a hammer at Mother Ellaime's door, hard enough to be the Pals come to arrest everyone. There was a fumbling at the handle, because Mother Ellaime always barred the door when Nihilostes was visiting, so the woman would have a running start out the back should Correct Speech come trawling for religious dissidents. The voice they heard was recognisably Lemya's, and it was Yasnic she was calling for.

There was a small crowd gathered ahead. Yasnic was already faintly out of breath by then. Running wasn't something he often had to do. Only the fact that Lemya herself was on the very edge of collapse had allowed him to keep up.

People parted. He saw the body. His gut plummeted, and he skidded to his knees beside it. "Ruslav... What even...?"

The man's torso was a welter of blood. His clothes had been carved open and so had he, and so much red sopping there it was impossible to know what was one and what the other. Yasnic couldn't think of any fate the streets of Ilmar had in store that might have caused such carnage. No knife, no baton-shot, not a runaway cart or a falling wall...

"You have to help him!" Lemya was insisting. And Ruslav clung to life with that tenacity Yasnic had remarked in the man. He was alive, conscious, fighting the pain like a drowning man trying to strangle the sea. Face wild, beard and hair matted with his own blood, one arm about his body though there were too many jagged gashes to ever be held closed.

"Oh, Ruslav." The man had always terrified Yasnic. A criminal, a thug, a thief, probably a murderer. And yet he'd liked the man, too. A man of strength and purpose, however malignly directed. To weak, directionless Yasnic, there was something admirable in the means, even if the ends went straight to perdition.

Nihilostes crouched down beside him, her eyes wide.

"There are beasts," she said. "In my home. Beasts that are gods that couldn't do a piece of work like that." But then her god was an insect, so what did that mean, exactly?

"Help him!" Lemya insisted, and Yasnic turned a watery gaze on her.

"I can't. I wish I could."

"You said you're a priest of a healing god. Well *heal*," she demanded. Ruslav was suddenly gripping his sleeve, pulling him close, eyes desperate.

"It doesn't work like that." A guilty glance at God, sitting at the very edge of Ruslav's spreading blood as though about to start finger painting with it. "I can only heal the faithful."

Ruslav tried to use him as purchase to jackknife up, mostly just dragging Yasnic's ear to his red lips.

"I'll... pay," he got out hoarsely. "Tithe. Donation. Pray. Name it."

"No, you'll..." He looked desperately over his shoulder at Nihilostes. "You can...?"

"Zenotheus is the Bringer of the World's Wounds." Awkward as a tradesman caught out in a matter of demarcation.

Ruslav's other hand had found his purse. "Here. Take it." Trying to give Yasnic money. But it wasn't about money.

"Ruslav, I'm sorry. I would... God heals the wounds of the faithful and demands" – gabbling his philosophy because somehow it was important he got the principles out before the man died – "demands they live by His strictures. No harm, no violence, a life devoted only to peace and the betterment of others. No exceptions. Ruslav, you are my friend." Not true, but he would have liked to have been brave enough to extend that hand. "But you are a violent man. I don't judge you." *But God does.* Best to leave that unsaid. "But you're not…" *Worthy.* And he glowered at God, and God, knowing his thoughts, glowered right back.

Ruslav sobbed something, and it might have been that he didn't want to die, and Yasnic felt that was a reasonable sentiment. He didn't want the man to die either. God wasn't about to start bending His rules, though. Rules and axioms were what wove gods from the cosmos. Cut through them and they sprang back into nothing. That was part of the useless burden of philosophy Yasnic had spent his childhood learning. Rules were important.

"I'm so sorry," he said again. "I…" He couldn't even lessen the man's pain. He was aware of the crowd gawking over his hunched shoulders, everyone from the neighbouring houses – men and women and children late for work in the factories – staring at this unexpected piece of street entertainment. Nihilostes, his enemy, the wicked cultist of the flying scorpion god, put a hand on his shoulder and squeezed gently. She rooted in a pouch and came up with a little clay phial with a wax stopper. "This," she said, "distances the mind from the body. Hunger, pain. Don't think it'll make much of a dent, but… Brings clarity of thought, too. Which may not be a blessing. But…"

He gave her a quick nod. Probably it was some filthy heathen sacrament, used in unspeakable rites. But if it would salve Ruslav's last agonies, and the man must have heard something of what she said because he grasped for it, gagged it down.

"I'll stay with you," Yasnic told him. Probably that didn't count as a balm. If their positions were reversed, he'd want someone to kick the insipid little priest down the street. "I'm sorry. It's…" Putting his hands gingerly to the man's wounds to demonstrate he had no miracles up his sleeves. "God's very clear. No men of violence. No blessings for those who love nothing more than themselves. He says what's the point in healing one wound so its bearer can create two more? Unless you're lessening the amount of hurt in the world, why heal anything? I mean there's about thirty thousand words of theology it's wrapped up in, but that's the kernel of it. I'm so sorry."

Ruslav shuddered, probably in disgust, said something, but it was just red bubbles at his lips. Yasnic sat back, finally met Lemya's accusing gaze.

"I told you," he said. "At the Anchorage. What even happened…?"

She collapsed abruptly – Nihilostes caught her before she jarred herself on the cobbles. She looked half-dead herself. There was a jagged line of char across her sleeve, exposing red, cracked skin beneath. Yasnic knew exactly where *that* sort of injury came from. His mouth thronged with questions, but who was he to ask them?

"I'm so sorry," he said again, to her and to Ruslav's body and to the world in general, and even to God who could frankly have used someone with more strength of character to be His final emissary to the world.

Ruslav rolled sideways and vomited out blood and blackish bile. That, Yasnic suspected, was the end. He sighed and bowed his head. God didn't have any prayers or rites to say over the bodies of unbelievers. Yasnic just closed his eyes and moved his lips in a way that made it look as though he had something sincere to say about the miserable situation. He did the same when he was begging, and it worked just enough to keep him fed and pay the rent. The crowd had gone absolutely silent. He suspected nobody was about to throw him a penny in recognition of his good intentions.

The strangled sound that came next was from Lemya. A choked-down sob. Nihilostes' grip tightened on his shoulder.

Someone laughed. It started off hoarse and raw but swelled out into a full-throated guffaw as ridiculously inappropriate as if a comedian had started up with *That Ruslav was so stupid…* The laugher had to stop to cough for a moment, but then went on. On and on, even as Yasnic frowned and screwed his eyes more closed and tried to hold on to the tragedy and the solemnity of the situation, because at least he could do *that*.

He couldn't do that. He was going to remonstrate. He, Yasnic the priest, was about to take someone seriously to task and have some *words* about propriety. He opened his eyes, drawing his pitiful ire about him.

Ruslav laughed in his face. "Got you!" the man shouted. "You and your god! Easy marks, the pair of you!" And Yasnic stared from him to the chalk-pale face of Lemya, to Nihilostes' wide eyes.

To God, who was shuffling His feet and looking bored.

"What?" God said. "He agreed. He did."

"*What?*" Yasnic demanded of God.

God – slightly bigger now, slightly less bedraggled – put His hands on His hips and scowled at him. "He heard what you said, and he agreed," He stated. "He's one of mine now."

Yasnic felt like shaking Ruslav, or possibly slapping him, not that he was allowed to do either. "You did what?" he demanded.

The thug's expression was a burlesque of piety. "I have come to the one true faith, rasophore. No more violence for me. All life is sacred." And a huge, exaggerated wink. "You had this hustle in your robes all this time, and you never said." Hands crossing his bloodied, torn clothes and the intact skin beneath. "I've got to introduce you to the Bitter Sisters. There's always one of ours getting torn up so bad nobody can put them together. You got yourself a job, rasophore. You got yourself all the converts you could ever ask for." Another big wink and a brutal grin. "Leastways, for as long as it takes to patch 'em back together, eh?"

"No," Yasnic said weakly. "That's not how it works. I'm so sorry, Ruslav."

And then the crowd, which had been a gathering murmur of excitement and wonder, was abruptly quiet again. Yasnic looked up and saw why. The whole spectacle had gathered more of an audience than he'd realised – than anyone had, given all attention had been directed inwards. There were Pal soldiers pushing forwards through the crowd. Because there had been a lot of blood and a lot of screaming and then a crowd, and so, of *course* some concerned citizen had let the Occupiers know. Or else they'd just been patrolling nearby and heard the ruckus. Either way, it was plain they'd seen all that had occurred. And there were whole departments of the Palleseen Sway devoted to exactly this sort of thing.

Ruslav was on his feet instantly. "Go," he said, and made to shove at the closest soldier, to focus their attention on him. *A remarkably valiant action*, Yasnic thought. Except Ruslav went pale, even as he started to move, and abruptly, there was a fresh trickle of blood on his chest, a tracery of the vanished wounds there like phantom scars. He went very still, and the soldiers laid hands on him, even as they pushed past to get to Yasnic.

"I'm sorry," the priest said, as he was seized. "You… can't just take it back. God doesn't work that way. You can't scam God, Ruslav, I mean…" *How did you even think that would work?* "You raise a hand against another, and it all comes back. That's how it works. Why do you think I don't have any converts? I'm sorry—" And then one of the soldiers twisted his arm behind his back, probably just to stop his appalling babble of useless talk.

God was looking meanly pleased with Himself. Ruslav had gone white as a sheet, ginger as an invalid as the soldiers pushed him about. They had Lemya too, mostly because she'd started shouting at them and at the crowd. Calling on them to rise up against their oppressors. Which was exactly the sort of thing the Pals were obliged to crack down on. Nihilostes had faded back into the crowd. He was glad of that. Except she caught his eyes and gave him a look, and he was dreadfully sure she was going to use this as the eggs of the chaos her god was so fond of. He tried to mum at her not to make a fuss or cause any trouble, but she was gone like a ghost, and then the soldiers were manhandling him away.

And the crowd wasn't happy, he saw. He'd always known this

day would come. That even he, least significant of all Ilmar's religious figures, would attract the ire of the Occupation. But he'd been secure in the knowledge that nobody would care, or even particularly notice, save Mother Ellaime who'd be put to the small trouble of finding another lodger. Except the crowd was ugly, and maybe Lemya's rhetoric had helped, but he had a bad feeling some of it was to do with him and what they'd seen. And they didn't understand. If they knew the absurd strictures God placed about His blessings, they'd likely be cheering the soldiers on. But they were ignorant, and so although the soldiers shoved through them and left, there were jeers and insults and angry words, and someone threw a stone. It hit Ruslav, but some of the soldiers still had a wary eye and a charged baton directed backwards as they retreated.

Going Home

A slight man, despite the rigours of deck life. The sort sent to monkey up the ropes or keep watch, rather than haul and carry. But fit for hiding, his riverman coat turned inside out for its dull brown lining. A clutch of hunger at his belly, of fear in his heart. The source of everybody's problems, most especially his own. Cut off from the river, cut off from his hunters, awaiting his moment. Whatever happened to Fleance the Heron?

In the early morning light, something was returning home. Slipping through the last few streets, squirming its fish-lizard body through the back ways. Remarkably quiet and discreet for a monster. Those who lived in those districts but had work were already abroad and gone, so saw nothing. Those who had no work to go to and chanced to look out and see that nightmare undersea visage, they closed their doors or shuttered their windows. They tried very hard not to have seen it. Life in the Gutter Districts was bad enough. And so, the beast passed almost peaceably on its way to the Anchorwood.

There were two Palleseen sentries stationed there, but they'd been up all night, waiting for their relief which was dawdling on its way to an unenviable duty nobody really wanted. The little stand of trees was no more than that. You could see clear through to the rocky countryside beyond. They felt like cats tasked to watch a painted mousehole. They were arguing about whether to go beat on the Anchorage door and see if they could menace a breakfast and hot tea out of Langrice. The beast trotted right past them. They only spotted it as it paused at the trees, baffled by the absence of any way *in*, truly in. They shouted; they levelled their batons. They squabbled over who should do what, before one of them ran off to fetch reinforcements. The broken body of Companion-Archivist Nasely dangled from the monster's jaws.

Fleance saw it too.

He had not gone into the Reproach. He had told the one riverman he'd been able to find that was where he was going, and to spread the word. Then he'd taken himself to the one place he hoped nobody would look for him. It hadn't been the Palleseen he'd been worried about, right then. The Bitter Sisters would be hunting him, and likely his own people as well. Probably there were Allorwen sharpening knives, too, since he'd pulled his big theft on their turf. He'd done a big thing badly, and then made it worse by losing the thing he'd stolen. In Fleance's mind, the whole city was after him for how he'd screwed up. He was the focus of everyone's ire, inside his head. And so, the thing he'd stolen, he needed it back.

He hadn't even quite known what it was. Just that it was valuable, and one of the Vultures had sent him after it. Then he'd ended up with the damned thing and understood what he was holding. Simultaneously the most valuable artifact he'd ever touched, and a death sentence. And then had come the Game, because Fleance never came to Ilmar without finding some way of being fleeced of everything valuable he had ever laid his hands on. The Game, and that damnable woman and the Allorwen chiseller and the rest of them, and *someone* had it now. Someone had his treasure, right when he needed it to get *out*.

And here he was, at the Wood's edge. And it was just a handful of trees, but Fleance was a small man, and he hid well. The Pals had been staring at these trees ever since their big man got killed, but Fleance had sneaked in while they were arresting the Wood's ambassador. He'd made himself a den in the dead leaves, under his spread coat, and waited for them to go away.

And they hadn't. And the Wood came and went, and he read the tides like a good waterman. He held to the very edges of it whenever the great chasm of space opened up between Ilmar and all those other shores. Because there were sharks in those waters; they'd have him in a gulp.

And now this. One of those very beasts, scarred and battered, coming to the borders of the trees. He heard the yells of the Pals out beyond it. Saw it prowl back and forth like a wolf in a cage. The vast round eye on the near side of its head tilted and swivelled until it fixed on him.

Fleance whimpered. Yes, its jaws weren't empty, but they were big enough for another corpse, and more besides. He shrank from it, as it picked its way forwards. That nightmare head cast back and forth as it nosed past the first trees. And if he retreated much further, he'd be out the other side and into open country.

No. No, he wouldn't. He felt the Wood flex and open up around him, the feel of the air changing as the trees unrolled into infinity at his back. The Anchorwood was welcoming home its lost child. He was caught between the monster and the depths.

Fleance crept backwards like a man with a cliff edge at his heels. The beast took two heavy steps into the trees. He could hear voices, flat Pel words fit only for orders and hard questions. The sentries' reinforcements had arrived, but it wasn't as though they were likely to help him.

Another lumbering step, and Fleance blinked. There was a haze coming up. Early morning in Ilmar, but this wasn't fog off the river. This came from the trees, chill and damp and smelling like autumn, gathering in the air to roll out towards the Anchorage and the city. He couldn't believe his luck. *I'm saved!* Except he wasn't saved from the beast which loomed, slab-sided, more than visible despite the gathering mist. He got to see every detail of how its jagged saw of teeth had carved up that body.

Then *they* were walking from the fog and the distance, standing at his shoulder, passing by his elbow. Half a dozen

Indwellers: their sightless wooden masks, their cloaks, their staves. The strings of snake oil and mummery they wore, that an Allorwen magician would have scoffed at, save that these were the masters of their own magic, from another place. He held himself very still, caught between terror and desperate hope.

They gathered before the beast, and he could see that something passed between them. One of them lifted a cloth-wrapped hand to trace along one of the thing's wounds, and it shivered. The Pel voices sounded very distant.

It dropped the body at their feet, shaking its jaws and scoring its teeth against the nearest trunk to rid itself of its burden. The Indwellers stared down at it, as though not sure what the precise etiquette was, when accepting such a gift. Fleance thought about his last and only view of the living woman: her back fleeing towards the Reproach with the beast in pursuit. It had been *days*. There was a whole history in between he couldn't guess at. It didn't help him. He didn't care. It wasn't a part of his story. Human lives lacked any satisfactory narrative. He had seen enough corpses to know that.

They were going. Some of them had already melted away into the mist, into the trees, back where they'd come from. The beast regarded him with a tilted eye, oddly philosophical. Its burden shed, it seemed subdued, as though it had expected more applause for its services. Then it was going, too. It brushed close enough that rough scales snagged at his clothes, and one lizard leg shunted him aside. He cowered back from the lash of its armoured tail, but it was dragging wearily, leaving a trail of blood across the leaf litter.

And the Indwellers were leaving, but they weren't all going home. A few were moving into the city, towards the Pals. He opened his mouth, for one absurd moment about to warn them. Except they were the Indwellers. What was he to them?

What were they to him, though? Cover, at least, just as the mist was cover. He was starving out here in the woods, and it was arrest on one side or monsters on the other. Out in the city, it was the Bitter Sisters and Blackmane and his creditors whom he'd gambled against and lost and made promises to. The whole wretched weight of it that had sat him down at Langrice's damned table in the first place. Although, if he dug deep enough to find true honesty, he could admit to himself that he'd have been there anyway. If all his bills were paid, it would only be like clearing a wall of old pictures so he could nail up new ones.

The Indwellers coasted on their fog that didn't even admit the existence of Palleseen soldiers. They walked not past but through them, by secret ways, and he followed. It seemed to him that the whole city was spread out like an unfurled sail, and the mist could reach any part of it, walls no more substantial than flattened-out creases. If he stepped away from them now, he would be anchored to the city again, where all hands were turned against him. He felt a wave of vicious frustration. He was a man wronged by fate, by the world, by half a dozen gamblers who'd conspired to rob him. Only the intercession of the Indwellers was keeping him from a dozen different fates. Easy for them, with their masks and their magic fog. And they'd betray him, too, he had no doubt. Abandon him for his enemies.

Unless, came the thought, and he slunk away in the Indwellers' shadow, thinking about what deeds the fog might hide.

Chains

Ivarn Ostravar: only a few days later, but a little more of the shadow, a little less of the man. It's not that prison food doesn't agree with him, though it doesn't. Information is what the academic is starved for. Since he sent his errand-runners to Blackmane, he's heard nothing from the outside world. In the interim, he's had his robes and good clothes taken from him, left in the chill and damp in shirtsleeves and breeches. Denied a razor, and if he wants to wash, he can choose how to apportion the shallow bowl of water they give him to drink. And in this time, Fellow-Inquirer Hegelsy has sent for him precisely once.

They had so far not prised his fingernails out or fitted tablethi to him and run currents of magical energy through his body. Nor had some burly member of the School of Correct Conduct taken a truncheon to him much. A few knocks and cuffs on the way to Hegelsy's study, to rattle him and put him off his game. A few more on the way back, to remind him whose house he was a guest in. The real festivities had yet to start.

The interview with the Fellow-Inquirer had been brisk enough. The man had been guarded, but Ivarn had sensed an odd mix of knowledge and ignorance leaking out between the questions. Obviously, the death of the Sage-Archivist was open knowledge, but Ivarn couldn't tell if Hegelsy knew his late colleague's warding bundle had been stolen. Which meant Nasely hadn't been recovered and interrogated by the Perfecture.

Which, in turn, meant the ruin-divers had a chance of taking custody of her, to be silenced or put up as surety as appropriate.

From there, Hegelsy had turned to the Gownhall, and that had been a little sliver of hope in an otherwise bleak room. Just a crack of it, in at a high window, but hope was hope. The student body had taken his arrest hard, apparently. The place was bristling right now. Ivarn had intimated that, were he released, he might calm things down nicely. He could even hear the speech he'd give, in his usual authoritative tones. Telling them to go back to their classes and books in such a way that they were left in no doubt he was still the Great Nationalist, ready to throw off the shackles of the Occupation when the time was right.

He'd need to shave first, of course. And change clothes. And bathe properly, the way the Armigers did. A herbal poultice and two properly treated tablethi heating the water to a fragrant steam. Or perhaps he should just go before them as he was, to emphasise the privations of his captivity. That might play better.

It had been a good offer, but Hegelsy hadn't been biting. The man had stared at him, and then started talking about the liberal arts curriculum. The literature the students were reading, which histories, what language. Always the Pal terror of any words not pinned dead on the page by their flat Pel script. And Ivarn had given all the standard answers, the ones he'd trotted out for more than one official in his own study, but each response had just vanished into the void of Hegelsy's expression. Each question had been spat out as though it was the first in a new line of inquiry. The man hadn't been interested in truths, nor even the convenient part-truths that Ivarn had offered him.

What he'd been after, Ivarn reckoned, was an *excuse*. What, after all, was a Fellow-Inquirer? Nobody's menial, to get to Fellow's rank, especially within the School of Correct Speech which even the other Palleseen departments were leery of. And yet, no Great Man, either. Not a Sage like Ochelby had been, or the current Perfector was. And that was Hegelsy's problem, Ivarn reckoned. A classic case of the middling man's thwarted ambition. He'd seen it in the Gownhall plenty of times – seen it from an elevated vantage, of course, given he'd vaulted up the ladder himself. Except, when a maestro of mathematics or antique linguistics found themselves without upwards prospects, they tended to either just complain about it at staff dinners or take their credentials to somewhere provincial where they could be lord of all they surveyed. When an official of Correct Speech felt the pinch of his too-tight shoes, there were cells and nooses and squads of bully-boy soldiers on the streets. And Ivarn was already behind bars.

He'd been moved, after that interview. Thrown half-stripped into a new and deeper cell. A windowless room with a single sullen lamp, charged by magic to give out a purplish-red glower every hour of day and night. The place had been a wine cellar once, he reckoned. It had a vaulted ceiling, and the walls were divided into alcoves. A wine cellar or some tiny retreat for miniature monks. Now it was Correct Speech's private cells, and he was sharing them with one other person. Or possibly a person.

They – the uncertain light gave him no clue as to gender – were a mystery at first, because the Pals had confiscated cloak and mask and staff, and all the trinkets and charms and pouches such folk were usually seen with. Their face was tattooed with patterns of triangles on cheeks and chin, though, and the patterns were familiar. There was no scholar of Ilmar who hadn't read at least the most accessible texts on the Anchorwood and its denizens. Even with that erudition leading him on, he still hadn't quite trusted the conclusion. He'd spoken to them, seen that face turn his way, so he could study the markings better.

"Are you of the Wood?" Best just to say it without prevarication. They had stared at him, expressionless. The faintest nod had crept into their body language, shown its head above the weeds then ducked back down. Other than that, they just sat and stared and didn't seem to see him.

"I'm of the… the houses," Ivarn pressed. The way the

Indwellers historically referred to Ilmar. Not *city*, not even *town*, just *houses*. The things people had come and built after the forest had been cut back to that one grove. And, as he was a scholar, he should have been bursting with questions about the Anchorwood and ancient times and all the scholarly quibbles he and his peers had debated. But his heart wasn't in it. There was an Indweller buried with him beneath the Donjon. Hegelsy and the Occupation had broken that ancient custom. *You do not lay hands upon them.* And yet, here one was: taken, beaten – he saw the bruises past the jagged patterns of the ink. And no crushing fate had descended on them. The Pals rolled on, and Hegelsy was ambitious, and it was going to end very badly. Instead of ancient lore, he asked the Indweller about recent history. What were the circumstances of their arrest? What had they seen in the city on their way from Wood to cellar? They stared at him and let his words run down their face and slope off their shoulders like rain.

And more than two days of this, no visitors, thin gruel and foul water. Enough time for Ivarn Ostravar, Maestro of the Gownhall, to wonder how he had so badly misjudged his estate, he who had thought himself so nimble in his dealings with all sides and comers. And then the rest were brought in.

Lemya, his protégée and catspaw, injured and filthy. Two others he didn't know. One was a monstrous brute of a man with the blood of two men on his carved-up shirt, yet none of it seemingly his own, his beard weirdly cropped on one side. Uninjured, but doubly filthy and so ragged their jailers would surely have to bring him more clothes rather than deprive him of the tatters he had. The other man was like the first's opposite, as though one rounded individual had been through some magic mirror or prism and come out as two. Small and mild and well-favoured. Halfway clean, and though his clothes were overlarge and had seen many owners, they were darned and patched with an artisanal neatness, not an inch of wasted thread or cloth. He met Ivarn's gaze and managed a wan smile.

"What happened to you?" he asked, because here at least was

news. Lemya started her tale and he had to stop her almost immediately. "You did what? You went where? *You?* You were my messenger to that villain Blackmane. He made you go into the—"

"No, maestro, but... I knew how important it was." Her voice trembled. "And I tried—I wanted to... We *had* her, maestro. The Pal woman. But she—"

"*You* went into the Reproach *yourself?*" Feeling the word echo about the close walls; feeling, almost, the place bend closer to them with that unwarranted repetition.

She just stared at him, sagged against the wall, pale from shock and loss and too many run-ragged hours. Ivarn Ostravar felt a worm of doubt move in him. He hadn't asked her. She'd gone for him. Was this his *responsibility?* One of his students had gone into the Reproach, because she'd thought it would help him.

"What was..." His throat dry. "What was it like?"

In return, he got her haunted gaze. "I can still hear them," she said. "All this distance underground. The music."

He recoiled from her. *It's not my doing,* he told himself. And it wasn't. He'd asked her to deliver a *letter,* for the gods' sake. Not plunge herself into that acid bath of the soul.

"And the woman, Nasely?" he asked, at last. There was doubtless a whole tale, between her going into that place and Nasely's fate, but he didn't want to hear it. "The Pals have her?"

Lemya just shook her head. It was the brute who answered.

"Dead. She's dead." He looked shaken. He kept touching his chest, his gut, the rents in his clothing. "Thing from the Wood came and got her. Just... She's very dead."

The slightest shiver went through the Indweller, and Ivarn waited for some pronouncement, but they just sat there, eyes on nothing.

Introductions were made, through Lemya. Ivarn; Ruslav; Yasnic. The Indweller had no name anybody knew, and volunteered none.

That done, Lemya sank back against one wall. She wouldn't look at him, and it was because she thought she'd failed him, Ivarn felt. He saw her face clenched to keep tears at bay. *The Reproach!* He remembered her in class, just some provincial merchant's daughter running to catch up, always at the front and a keen audience for his readings and lessons. The sort of flattering attention an academic rather expects from the young and impressionable. Listening with bated breath to the Ilmari heroic sagas, all that crisp alliteration and complex meter. And apparently, that had lit flame enough in her to drive her to idiocy. Though perhaps it was guttering here in the damp.

Her head had tilted back as she stared at the baleful light of the lamp. It shone off the shiny wrinkles of her burn scar. Someone had *shot* at her. In the *Reproach*. He couldn't quite get his head round the thought.

"Take it back," Ruslav growled, and Ivarn started. *Take what? My instructions to her? That damned warding bundle? All too late for either.* But it wasn't Ivarn the man was talking to.

"I don't want it," Ruslav spat. "Just... take it back."

"It doesn't work like that," Yasnic said in a small voice. He was pushed over to one side of his own confinement as though awaiting a cellmate. "I mean you could... *you* can *give* it back. Just... go back on your pledge. Raise your hand against the world in some way."

"No, just..." Ruslav gripped the bars fronting his cell. "Take the oath back. Leave me with a whole skin."

"It's not..." Yasnic cocked his head as though listening. "Severable, is the precise theological term. It's all one, blessing and stricture. I'm sorry. I... You can see why we were never all that grand, even in the old days. Why it's just me."

Ruslav's arms bunched as though about to shake the bars, but then a weird expression of fear came over him, and he retreated from them. "You've ruined me," he snarled.

"I'm sorry," whispered Yasnic.

Ivarn glanced at Lemya for clarification, but she was still

staring up at the lamp. Her chest moved, and that told him she still lived. Her foot moved, too, just a little. *Keeping time.* He shivered.

"This son of a bitch," Ruslav growled, and now he *was* talking to Ivarn, about Yasnic. "Don't listen to him. He's poison. He says he's a healer."

"I don't. I never did." Barely a protest, just a miserable undercurrent from the other man.

"Says he's a priest. A priest of… what was it?"

"God," Yasnic said shortly. But then, "Clarethism. Is what it's called. In the old books."

Ivarn laughed, a sound alien enough here that even the Indweller looked at him. "That old heresy's been dead for two generations or more," he said, with the authority of a senior Gownhall academic.

"Yes," Yasnic said. "That sounds about right."

Ruslav hunched forwards. "And do I… I have to pray, now? Sacrifice? Spread the word or it all… comes *back*? What did you sink me into, you little bastard?" But afraid rather than angry. "I just… I just got *out* from somewhere an invisible thing was trying to control my head. And now you've hooked me on just the same thing."

Yasnic looked at his hands, wringing together before him. "God has a lot…" A heavy pause. "A *lot* of strictures for His priests. But for His followers, no. Just… do no harm. Lift no hand against your fellows, nor incite others to. You'd not think it was such a burden, but… The world's a certain way, I suppose."

Ruslav's appalled expression suggested this was a fate worse than death. He sat back heavily, eyes wide like those of a frightened horse.

A day and a half later, a long stretch with only desultory attempts at conversation, the soldiers came back. Lemya started awake with a cry of panic, slammed her burnt arm into the wall and hissed with pain. Ivarn wondered if he could ask for medical help, but given even more basic things were in short supply down here, the gesture would likely just focus their attention on the girl. And here were more prisoners, so that now every nook had an occupant. One was a lean, angry-looking Maric woman, whose torn shirt showed a crude avian tattoo inked across her collarbones. Not exactly subtle. Ivarn saw the dagger beak of it. *Shrike*, he guessed, though the artistry was lacking. A resistance fighter. One of the murdering kind. Her name was Fyon, she said. She'd heard of him. Oh, not in a bad way. She knew he was a Gownhall man and that he'd been arrested, though. That one of the resistance's loose-blade killers had him on her list of reasons to slit throats suggested the crockery was sliding off the table up in the city, and faster than he'd thought possible.

The other two were Dorae and Tobriant, a pair of Allorwen. They'd been beaten harder than Fyon, because plenty of the Occupation force had done a turn in Allor and built up a solid head of prejudice. *Just ask Blackmane about that.* They knew Blackmane, of course. They were even peripherally in the same trade. Dorae ran a purported antiques shop, which was likely indistinguishable from Blackmane's pawnbrokerage save the original owners weren't coming back to reclaim the stock any time soon. Tobriant, older, stockier, was a cabinet-maker, which Ivarn interpreted as a forger whose work probably turned up with a fake pedigree in Dorae's shop. They didn't know precisely why they were here, and assumed it was just a bad roll of the dice as far as the regular Pal persecution went. Ivarn knew better. Hegelsy's people must be turning over every stall and barrow in Mirror Allor looking for the *thing* right about now. They'd finally worked out what had happened.

Then the soldiers were back, and Ivarn braced, because he'd been left to stew long enough, and surely Hegelsy had cleared his schedule for a proper bout of persuasion-with-menaces-and-thumbscrews. Except it wasn't him they were here for. Nor even Fyon, who likely had more than a few dead officials on her conscience. Instead, they hauled Yasnic to his feet and dragged the priest away.

Not Venom but Eggs

The harbinger of upheaval and change, bringer of chaos. Zenotheus, the scorpionfly god. Born of a land where its mortal namesake grows to the size of a hand. One of a litter of deities whose worship was driven out, wherever it was discovered, on the reasonable basis that they existed purely to undermine the status quo without bringing anything to replace it. Nihilostes has stood in the presence of her god. A little underwhelming. Bigger than a regular scorpionfly but still smaller than a human. Big gods attract the notice of bigger gods. There's a reason most insects are small. She has received her commandments direct from the mandibles of Zenotheus in the subterranean temple of her faith, surrounded by masked worshippers. She was one of many sent out to sow the eggs of disorder beneath the skin of the Palleseen Sway.

Zenotheus itself had not travelled with her. No invisible insect on her shoulder to keep her on the – not straight and narrow. The opposite. And of her fellows, the majority were caught, because the School of Correct Thought took up where the majority religions of her home ended. That she'd evaded notice this long was mostly due to inventive interpretation of divine instruction. Leave no place of power unburnt! Leave no document unaltered! *And she'd set fires and forged signatures in her time, but only when she could get away with it. Mostly what she did was get to know people.*

In a barrel-cluttered cellar beneath a Gutter District drinking den there was a long table where men and women went to talk resistance. Vultures, mostly, as the taxonomy went. The poor and disaffected whose politics mixed vengeance with pragmatism. Lodge people, many of them, and others were workers or ex-workers. Troublemakers at this factory or that mill. Couriers and delivery carters whose work meant it was always hard to work out exactly where they'd been or who they'd met. Dockworkers who knew how to get goods into the city via their Heron contacts. And sometimes, those goods were supplies the resistance needed, and sometimes, they were drugs or drink or other goods passing beneath the Pals' swingeing taxes. No hard line between the proceeds of crime and the funding of an insurgency, and it wasn't as if the cause could get by without money.

A handful of them worked direct for the Bitter Sisters who held sway over more of the Vultures than anyone else. Most of the rest paid their dues there. Nobody wanted to get on the wrong side of Carelia and Evene. One, barely more than a girl and exalting at being the focus of attention, had even been running word between the Sisters and the Gownhall. There were Pal soldiers stationed in three houses there, she said, but they weren't moving in. The students were singing the old songs. They had flags and banners with the names of Ilmari heroes stitched into them. Several of the faculty had been summoned to the palace to account for themselves, and yet the Pals hadn't made their move. It must be significant! Everyone nodded and fingered knife-hilts and drank.

And Nihilostes, sitting at the end of the table, observed that maybe the Pals weren't as strong as they had been. The Sway was always expanding. There were a dozen places she could name where the Pals had been seeding their agents and spies. After all, she was the foreigner among them, more well-travelled than even the Herons. *How thin the Pals must be stretched, by now!* And it was common knowledge their second biggest man had been trying to push the Sway beyond the Anchorwood, and been killed, and now the Pals were even at war with the Wood itself. An army of monsters might issue from between the trees the moment they turned their backs. If, say, something erupted within the city that demanded their attention. *Just think of that, eh?*

In a workers' canteen off Szechelm Way, Father Orvechin was receiving his own messengers. A delivery boy from a clothier's store on Ock Street who'd had his cargo searched by soldiers in the shadow of the Gownhall, and then the empty cart searched again after he'd made his delivery. The old man who kept the academics' furnace burning, through a demon contract fifty years old and counting, who said it wasn't just the students larking about. The maestros themselves were up in arms now, because nobody could get any word from Ostravar at all, and rumour was the man had died under the ministrations of the School of Correct Speech. Aullaime, the conjurer, stood up to say they were making arrests across Mirror Allor. She'd been held herself for an hour, just stood in the street with a score of others, questioned about all manner of disjointed things.

"They shut down the Brazylt Lightworks," said a big, shaggy-bearded man, a glassworker in good standing with his Siblingry. "All of us out. The owner's spitting feathers, but he's been compensated. Not us. Just blew the whistle, and we're on the street."

"You'll be back," Orvechin said. "The Brazylt place makes half the lamps they use for their fancy offices."

"Oh, certainly," said the glassblower. "But you know how it is. Once they come in, they never leave." And true enough. When the Pals showed an interest in a place, they'd have someone looking over the foreman's shoulder ever after. The Siblingry would be under scrutiny and under suspicion. Words would become guarded, meetings held elsewhere. And if the Pals' hand was clutching for the throat of the Hammer Districts again, that meant every new face was now under suspicion too. They always tried to get their people in, always a Maric tradesman or worker willing to turn on their own for Palleseen pennies. A winter of people eyeing their neighbours sidelong, Siblingry doors kicked in and people vanishing overnight. They'd seen it before.

"Someone's pointed them at us," said a mill-hand sourly. And maybe some Armiger had seen a chance to settle scores with the Siblingries now the Pals were all stirred up. Or maybe this was always going to happen.

And the Brazylt Lightworks dealt in tablethi, of course, and nobody there said whether some of those little thumbs of magic had ended up somewhere else. Whether the gold had been shaved and the goods adulterated so that a little trickle of arcane fuel might find its way elsewhere. Were the Pals just throwing their weight around or did they have the scent of subversion in their nostrils?

And Nihilostes, at the back, didn't have any right to speak. Barely an honorary member, save that, by her provenance, she was unlikely to be working for either factory owners or Occupation. But she leaned over to the solid woman beside her, a machinist at the mills and also an angry convert to the disruptive message of Zenotheus ever since her son had died in the teeth of one of the machines. *Malign chance: if you can't beat it, spread it.* Nihilostes made some observations about how the Pal hand was reaching, right now. Those iron fingers about to close, take away some fresh liberty, undermine the Siblingries. And all the while, the Armigers just stood there and wrung their hands and counted the factory profits, which hadn't particularly decreased since the Occupation. But right now, the Pals were being tugged very thin, weren't they? Thin and dry and taut, like paper on a frame. *And wouldn't it just take a match…?*

★★★

In a staff common room of the Gownhall, seven academics smoked thoughtfully.

Maestro Vorkovin, the music teacher, blew a phoenix-tail of smoke at the blackened ceiling.

"It would be," he said, "a very poor bluff, should they call it."

"Then it can't be a bluff," said Maestra Gowdi, who taught a Theory of Magic already half-undermined by the common practice of the Hammer Districts.

"It is," said a mathematician, "the precedent." He'd been saying very little else, in anyone's company, for several days. "A Gownhall maestro, just hauled out of his own study." Which meant it could be any one of them next. And perhaps the mathematician had some guilty secrets. Perhaps he had a relative with the resistance, or some side hustle that contravened one of the innumerable Pal ordnances. Or perhaps he just found that teaching maths in Pel made all the sums come out wrong.

"I went to the Donjon yesterday," Vorkovin said. "I waited. Nobody would see me. I couldn't see Ivarn. I know some of you have petitioned at the palace."

"They hate us," Gowdi said. "I remember. They wanted this place as their Perfecture offices. We tangled them in words and promises and logic. They love their logic and reason so much. Live by the sword, eh?" One of the servants came forwards with a brass plate, and she tapped her pipe out onto it. "We worked so hard to even continue to exist. To preserve ourselves and our freedoms. We found such a tightrope to walk, to maintain our way of life here." Nods around the table. "But what's it worth if they can just come in and *take*?"

"Precedent," the mathematician said again.

"We have to do—" someone said, and someone else trampled them with, "We can't! If we just… wait. They'll let Ivarn out. It'll all go back to where it was. We can't risk—"

"I don't know if we can hold the students back." It was stately old Maestro Porvilleau who taught geography and cartography.

Perhaps the least regarded of the entire faculty, but his words brought a chill silence to the room. The thought that they could chart all the wise courses they wanted, but it was for nothing if *they* weren't the hand on the tiller when the boat moved.

And Nihilostes leaned forwards. Not faculty herself, of course. Just a friendly face who visited the Gownhall from time to time. And she had access to the very best pipe-stuffing, some quite eyewatering blends from her distant home. Always welcome in this elevated company. There was so much *anger* among the students right now, she said. As a visitor, she'd been struck by the mood. The whole Gownhall was like a stack of tablethi waiting for the word to explode. She'd heard the names of plenty of maestros on their lips too, as she passed through the Gownhall to this august gathering. Teachers they respected for having the city and the nation's best interests at heart. And others, less committed, therefore less respected. She wouldn't want to be a Gownhall academic, right now, who went to the students and told them to just settle down and go back to their books. Better at least to wave a little Ilmari flag, just to show you were all of the same mind, eh? And at least some of the faculty *were* of that mind anyway. They had a tradition going back centuries, and it was under threat. And the Perfecture was *very* divided at the moment. The Perfector at odds with his own subordinates over what to do now they'd stirred the city up. *A show of strength and unity...*

And later, she sat in the little room she rented over a tea shop whose proprietor was all for chaos and division so long as one could also sit and have a properly civilised cup of tea. A concession Nihilostes was more than willing to make. She'd become very partial to a lot of Ilmari comforts and places and people over the years. And never to anything of the Pals'. Their hard, efficient and rational ideology had no give in it, and gave nobody the space to be themselves. Small wonder half their high-ups were undercutting it all for personal profit.

And one of the things she had become fond of, in Ilmar, was an enemy priest, a sad little adherent of a dying faith who'd performed a bona fide miracle in the street, almost by accident, and been carried off by the Pals. And that had recalled her mission to her. For Yasnic, who would hate the very idea of it, she was going to implant the seeds of chaos into every fertile mind she could find.

Conversations About God

God had once, according to Kosha, been very tall. There had been a proper temple – this was generations ago – and people had travelled from across Telmark. And after that, Kosha said, there had been a hospice where God had lived with His priests, and the sick had come to accept the tenets of the faith and be cured and healed and pieced back together. All that, still before Kosha's time. And after that, Kosha had just been able to remember when God, a suitably smaller God, had lived in a cellar under a house but still had something of a congregation. People came to give alms and thanks, and be healed, and take the pacifist vows that God demanded. Because God had once been freer with the healing, Yasnic suspected, but had regretted it when He saw what the beneficiaries of His healing had done with their health.

They took him from his alcove of a cell into what could best be described as a larger cell. There were no windows, although the lamps were a little brighter, covered with a different shade of glass so they appeared less red. It was not, he suspected, to put him more at ease. It was likely so the people who habitually worked in that room could see what they were doing better. It looked the sort of room where quite delicate things were done by people. To people.

They strapped him into a chair. 'They' were two soldiers, although one soldier, possibly half a soldier, would have sufficed, between Yasnic being weak, and theologically precluded from fighting back. He wasn't actually sure what God would do, should His last priest accidentally thump a guard while not wanting to be strapped into a chair. Yasnic had never needed divine healing before his ordination. He had no wounds to reopen, although possibly the nasty fever he'd had when he was five might come back. Given he'd been quite delirious with it, that might be an advantage.

Then they left him, alone as they thought. Although actually, they were leaving him with God.

God sat on the top of the bench that Yasnic's chair faced. Yasnic had a good view of that bench and the very neat array of implements and instruments on it. Probably the intent was to scare him, but in truth, he only recognised a handful. A select little cluster, organised by size, were plainly clamps and screws and hooks that had painfully obvious applications. The rest of the rods, lenses and jointed frames were too arcane for him to puzzle out.

God looked at him. That wrinkled, baggy face with its long beard and straggly uncombed hair. He should probably have procured a brush and burned it so that God could tidy Himself up. Although Yasnic suspected God didn't care about that sort of thing anymore. God's filthy grey robe was all holes and tatters, so probably Yasnic should burn a corner of bedsheet for Him too. None of which he had the money for, of course. And he had occasionally thought that he could just steal things for God. God didn't actually ban His priests from theft, although possibly because, back in the day, it hadn't ever been a necessary commandment. Kosha, however, had been adamant about how a priest of God should behave, whether or not God Himself had an opinion. Even with God sitting on the old bookshelf in the room they shared, shrugging.

"I'm sorry," Yasnic said to God. "I think this may be it."

God looked left and right at the apparatus. "What am I supposed to do?" He asked.

"I don't know. I'm sorry."

"When you go, what happens to me?" God whimpered.

"I'm sorry. I don't know. Don't you know?"

God didn't. He clutched His rags closer to Himself. "Orvost, the Divine Bull," he said.

Yasnic frowned. "Yes?"

"He was mighty. His brass hooves crushed the unbelievers. His priests had a temple with gold doors. *Gold*!" The thought mightily impressed God, evidently. "He blessed the warriors and brought sickness out of the river."

"Why would a bull god bring sickness?" Yasnic tried to shift to a more comfortable position on the bare wood of the chair, but the straps wouldn't let him.

"I don't know," said God. "Maybe he ate a river sickness god and assumed dominion. That used to happen a lot. What I mean is, though, where is he?"

"I've never heard of him."

"Nobody has. Not for hundreds of years." God's voice trembled. "Orvost! He was so mighty. We had battles. He would destroy the land, and I would heal it. I hated the bastard. But I never thought he wouldn't be there." God shook His head. "There used to be so many of us. But then you get Temples – because it works for the kings and dukes who want one place to go for divine favour, and that place is run by their cousin."

God had never talked so much. The divine presence sat at the bench's edge, withered legs dangling, staring past Yasnic into ancient history.

"We scared people," God said. "And then we bored people. And people wanted to get on with their lives and just have some convenient human-level institution to sanction their business deals and take their donations. People didn't want to have to *live* it all the time. And now these Islermen."

"The Palleseen," Yasnic corrected God.

"I remember when they were just Islermen with their sea and sky gods, catching fish and raiding. They were a lot happier."

And then God shut up, and two people came into the room at Yasnic's back.

"Right then," said one. "He's actually here this time." A man's voice, its owner pushing past the chair and giving Yasnic's arm a painful poke on his way to the bench. He had his back to Yasnic as he counted over the tools there: a short, broad man in shirtsleeves, breeches and stockings, the tight Palleseen style straining a little at the seams. "Which one's this, then?"

"They've left his head loose again." A woman's voice, younger and sharper. There were cool hands at Yasnic's temples, in the next moment, and straps he hadn't realised were there abruptly tightened across his brow.

"Please don't. I promise I won't fight," he said, abruptly very frightened in a way he hadn't been by the bonds at wrist and ankle. The unseen woman paused, then jerked the strap tight.

"He says he won't fight, Gadders," she noted.

"Makes our job easier, then," said the man: Gadders, apparently. "Is this the housebreaker? I thought they were supposed to be Allorwen."

There was the rustle of paper. "They did him last night," she said. "This is the healer."

Gadders had something multi-pieced in his hands, turning away from the bench but away from Yasnic as well, coming round past the priest's limited viewpoint, still just a broad suggestion of a person, a voice without a face.

"I thought healers were fat," he said.

"Why would he be fat, Gadders?" The woman sounded amused.

"If I could heal, I'd be fat. Not like I'd do it for free," Gadders pointed out.

"It doesn't work like that," Yasnic said. The pair of them went still at the sound of his voice, as though a piece of furniture had spoken up, or a cadaver. "It would be nice if it did."

"If you were a healer," the woman pointed out, ignoring Yasnic, "you'd be in that chair."

"No, no," Gadders said. "I'm interested. How does it work, then? Must be rules, I guess. Otherwise, you'd have people not being dead, all over, and then where would we be?"

"Well," Yasnic started, staring straight ahead at God and the bench.

But then someone else came in, and Gadders exclaimed, "Ah, tea at bloody last!" and that was apparently Yasnic's window for a theology lecture gone. He did indeed smell tea, and to his nose, it was cheap tea, the sort that Mother Ellaime bought, not the very superior tea his friend and enemy Nihilostes brought round.

"I don't suppose," he asked, in a quavering voice, "I might have some tea? Just a little tea?"

Someone was at his ear. The woman. The uncomfortably hot rim of a cup was pressed to his lower lip, and he sipped awkwardly at it, managing a couple of mouthfuls. It was slightly better tea than Mother Ellaime provided.

"Thank you," he managed. The woman made a noncommittal noise.

"Riechy," Gadders said, "they have given me the cup with the chip in it again."

The woman, Riechy then, made an equally noncommittal noise.

"I bloody asked them not to. I—"

"Cut your lip on it last time," Riechy said, along with him. "Except your 'last time' was three months ago now."

"And they're still giving me this cup."

"Because you complain."

Gadders drew in a breath, and Yasnic felt himself warm to the bickering, ready to weigh each of them up and take sides as appropriate, but then, the man let out a sigh at all that was wrong with the world, slurped his tea – carefully, Yasnic presumed; from the intact side of the cup – and said, "We'd better get to it, then. Waste of time, if you ask me. Get the plate, will you?"

Gadders screwed something to the back of the chair that

extended past the sides of Yasnic's head. He felt the hard metal press of it, like the feet of some raptorial insect. Gadders sucked at his teeth right at Yasnic's ear, tutting. Fumbling for some tool to help him tighten the apparatus. Meanwhile Riechy was at the bench again, just her back. The same clothes as Gadders: shirtsleeves, breeches. Uncomfortably tight to a Maric eye. Her hair was longer than he was used to in a Pal, pinned into a bun. He saw her struggle with it as she pulled goggles over her head. When she turned around, she had a square piece of smoked glass before her, edged in what looked like lead. Her head, through it, was a hazy suggestion of form, the round lenses of the goggles like owlish pools of darkness.

"Prepped," Riechy said.

"Clear," from Gadders, behind him.

"Discharge," she told him, and for a moment, the room was plunged into a wrenching deep gloom that simultaneously allowed Yasnic to see every tiny detail of it, save through the glass that Riechy was holding in front of his face, which was the utter void. In the next instant, all was as it had been before. Riechy passed to his left, out of his view, and the two of them retreated a little.

"I thought…" Yasnic said, still keeping his voice very polite. "I thought that…" And it wasn't as though he had much to contribute, but he felt a desperate need to make himself a part of their conversation, to be a *person* and not just an object. Because anything could happen to an object. "I thought you were going to be torturers." And a little laugh, even. *Ho-ho, what an idea! All friends here, aren't we? Although only one of us is strapped to a chair.* God was standing up now, staring past Yasnic at Gadders and Riechy.

"He thought we were torturers," the woman echoed.

"Fancy," Gadders muttered, obviously engrossed in something else. "I mean, occasionally. Or they let us hold the nipple clamps and tighten the nut screws. Different department, though. Wouldn't give me the chipped cup if I was one of those Correct

Speech lads, I bet. Do we need to do this again? Doesn't look right to me."

"It's fine. Don't overcomplicate things." Riechy was right at Yasnic's back, briskly removing the whatever-it-was from his head and the back of the chair. He kept getting glimpses of her hands: pale, narrow fingers with bitten nails painted black. A weird, personal affectation for a Pal official.

"I mean, it's there," Gadders went on. "I thought matey here did something serious, though. Half a dozen reports of 'man brought back from the brink of death', wasn't it? From *this* milquetoast?"

Yasnic would have nodded in agreement if he could. "I'm sorry," he said, before he could stop himself. And he was sorry. He wished he could have been a more impressive priest for them. For God, too. For everyone.

"The beneficiary got brought in too, didn't he?" Riechy said. She was at the bench again, setting down the collapsed frame of the thing with a rattle – not where it had come from, so presumably Gadders was the neat one. "Haul him up and run some divinations, if you want."

Ruslav. Who had surely suffered enough, what with the injuries and then the unwelcome cure. "No, no, there's no need," Yasnic said. "I did heal him. From almost death. I'm sorry."

Riechy turned. He saw that below her owlish goggles was a slotted leather mask, nothing of her face visible save a grease-smudged forehead.

"He's sorry," she told Gadders.

"Glad someone is," the man replied. He came round with the glass plate, still staring at it unhappily through his own lenses and mask. "This is poor, frankly. I reckon… twenty?"

"Thirty. I bet you. Thirty-five," Riechy said. She seemed the more upbeat of the two. Yasnic decided he liked her more.

"Can I see?" he asked. They froze again, and he realised that neither of them had really looked at him. Not at his face. Not in the eyes. "Please," he added.

There was an awkward moment, as though he'd made some dreadful faux pas at an Armiger's fancy luncheon. The two sets of goggles exchanged a look. Gadders thrust the plate in his face again.

There was a silhouette there, of a head. Probably his head, from context. No sign of the chair-back at all. Cheeks, ears, wispy hair, and around it a kind of smoky aura painted onto the glass, and beside it…

God. God was at his shoulder in the glass. Not a silhouette, but as though an artist had got his dark and light pigments mixed, a monochrome image in reverse, but recognisably God.

"That's… Do you see that?" he asked.

Gadders snorted. "Do we see that, Riechy?"

"Wouldn't be much point doing this otherwise."

"That's God." Because, after Kosha was gone, nobody had been there for God except Yasnic. Nobody else was allowed to see God. Which was probably intended to make God important and exclusive, but when it was just Yasnic and God, Yasnic felt it just made Him very lonely.

"This is amazing," he said. "You could… can you… see Him now? Right there." He twisted a finger to point.

Another look between the goggles, and then Riechy, at least, followed his indication and stared in the general direction of God who glowered back at her, fists clenched.

She shrugged. "A little. For the next minute or so, while the energy's still bouncing about in here. Like a little smudge there. That's him, is it?"

"Him," Yasnic corrected, giving the word its correct weight. "God, yes."

Gadders snickered. "'God'," he said. "Always with the 'God'. These Marics! But don't worry, you'll be rid of it soon."

"What?" Yasnic asked.

The man had another folding device up from the bench now, walking round out of sight again, attaching parts of it to the chair and swearing occasionally when he had to fight with it.

Riechy had brought out another frame that she was fitting to the arms of the chair. A set of wooden pigeonholes fixed so that they were all Yasnic could look at. With brisk, bored movements, she was fitting dull little objects into them. Rounded lozenges of pewter-looking metal. Familiar from across the city since the Occupation. Uncharged tablethi, grey and lustreless.

"Twenty at best," Gadders said from behind him. "It's not as if it's a grand totem."

"Healed from death," Riechy reminded him. "I'm putting the full fifty in, and we'll see what we can squeeze out."

"We end up with two score half-charged tablethi, it's your fault."

Riechy made a rude noise and kept on clicking the lozenges into place until the rack was full.

"What are you doing?" Yasnic asked them in a hoarse voice, though he knew.

"Decanting," Gadders told him. "Obviously."

"Do him the talk," Riechy prompted.

"I will not. You do it."

"Been too long. Can't remember most of it." Her goggles showed Yasnic his own aghast face twice over. "Whole thing we had to learn. Cleansing you of your superstition. Relieving you of the burden of your mistaken beliefs. Repurposing your relics and whatnot for the greater good. Progress. Reason something, something. But it's all bunkum. It's about these, isn't it? So we stopped doing it, and nobody came and told us we had to start again. It's just decanting, is all. It's not worth all the ceremony."

"You can't," said Yasnic, and *now* he struggled against the straps, though he couldn't loosen them even slightly. "You can't decant God. I need Him. Please, I'm all He has. He's all I've got. I've lived all my life…" And the horrible, guilty thought of all the things he could have been doing, if he hadn't had God to look after. The religious strictures he wouldn't have had to keep. He could have gone mad all over town, starting fights and falling in love with people. Instead, he'd been stuck looking after

God and obeying God's rules. "Please," he said, staring at that little, haggard figure now standing on the bench. "You can't."

"We're bringing you into the age of reason, age of ignorance, liberated from antiquated belief systems, blah-blah," said Gadders. "You're supposed to be grateful. Ah, there we go." And whatever part of the mechanism he'd been having trouble with clicked into place. He came round the front again, spooling out what looked like braided silk thread that he wound about a line of keys projecting from the side of the wooden rack.

"Right, this, then lunch," he said, and Riechy nodded.

"Please," Yasnic begged them. "I'm sorry, but please don't. There's got to be another, something else, some different. Please, no." Staring at God, right into God's tired old eyes. "Please. I'm sorry. I'm so sorry. Please."

"Look." Riechy put a hand on his trapped arm. "It'll be for the best. You'll see." Sounding genuinely sympathetic. The doctor telling him the arm needed to come off to stop the rot.

"You don't understand!" Yasnic shouted at her. "He's my God!"

She retreated from him as though he was rabid. Her body language said very clearly, *there's no helping some people*. Then she and Gadders both backed out of his view.

"Prepped," she said.

"No!" Yasnic shouted. "No. God, no!" Trying to throw his body left and right and barely straining the straps. Trying to rock the chair, but it was fixed to the floor. Shouting and howling and wailing fit to wake all the many dead the Donjon surely boasted. And at the back of all of that, wincing, bracing, waiting for the moment when the blade came down and cut his faith from him.

"Bloody hell," said Gadders, long-suffering. "I said *clear!*" he added, over the row that Yasnic was making.

Riechy jumped up and put the bench between her and Yasnic. Around that point, Yasnic's breath gave out, and he wheezed to silence, leaving Gadders yelling, "Clear!" at the top of his voice. And then a pause, in which something ghastly and rank crept invisibly through the room. Riechy was standing very straight, like a soldier, and Yasnic heard Gadders yelp and skitter weirdly off to one side.

"Sage-Invigilator. Magister," the man said, sounding strangled. Yasnic sympathised. Abruptly the close, windowless air in the cell was unbearably thick, curdling into an appalling reek of spoiled meat and unwashed flesh. Someone stepped heavily in, shoes scuffing and dragging a little.

"Go," a voice said, and the two torturers or engineers, or whatever they were, didn't look back, just bolted out of the room.

Yasnic, still securely bound, tried to bite back a whimper. The immediate panic he'd felt a moment before was now an icy, existential dread. *Something* was behind him. Something that smelled like it had died a long time ago, advancing with a limping gait until it stood right behind the chair. The stink of it made Yasnic gag, gorge tunnelling up through his throat like prisoners fleeing thrown-open cells. He tried to jackknife forwards, couldn't; was left with the thought that, if his stomach revolted, he might choke to death.

"Nobody seems to know your name." The rough, greasy voice sidled to his ears on breath that brought a doubled resurgence of the reek. "Not my people. Not the Ilmari out there shouting for you." A hand, gripping the back of the chair, making the wood creak as the man leaned his weight on it.

"Yasnic," the priest squeaked.

"And I thought you wouldn't cooperate," the voice said heavily.

Breathing through his mouth still brought the stink to Yasnic's nose, and coated his tongue with a sour, metallic taste. "You're the Perfector," he got out. He couldn't remember the man's name. He'd heard of the man's fate, though. A familiar one, to the Ilmari. Everyone had felt it a great blow against the Occupiers, when it had happened. The last and only decent thing the Old Duke had done for his people.

Abruptly, the hands behind him were working, unlatching the straps: head, wrists. Leaving him to deal with his own ankles, which he did, so he could jump away and stand where Riechy had done, the bench his inadequate shield. God jumped down and lurked at his heels, peering out.

The Perfector, Sage-Invigilator Culvern – the name came to him unbidden and unwanted – was a big man, wearing one of those Pal robes that didn't hang much past the knees. His legs beneath it were bare, mottled with broken veins and discoloured with greenish swellings. His hands were the same, the knuckles a diseased topography of warts. His face was lopsided and lumpy, like something carved inexpertly from a gourd and then left out too long.

"Come," he barked, and then just turned and left, trusting to Yasnic to follow. And there were soldiers outside, faces tightly clenched as their lord and master walked past. And there were no other exits. He was hardly going to stay in a torture chamber, was he? And yet, it took most of his courage to step out and walk in the man's eyewatering wake. The odour was never still. The moment Yasnic's nose had the measure of it, some new offering entered the mix, ranker than the last.

They went to a study, very well-appointed. He'd heard the Perfector spent more time over at the Ducal Palace, but this was plainly his lair when business brought him to the Donjon. Yasnic could tell instantly which parts of the room the man favoured. The wood and upholstery of the desk's rich chair were stained and eaten away. There was a yellowish semicircle spread out along that side of the desk, warping and peeling the varnish. At the window, a rainbow smear across the glass showed where Culvern stood most often to stare out at the Donjon's enclosed yard with its ever-present scaffold. There was even a discoloured trail across the rugs showing the exact paths the man used to move about the room. An assassin with no sense of smell would find half his work done for him.

Culvern let himself down into the chair with a sigh of relief. There was another chair across the desk from him, and though sitting there would bring Yasnic's nose closer to the reek, it had the advantage, over its counterpart in the cell, that it lacked any kind of restraints. Cautiously, he sat. God clambered up and crouched on the near side of the desk to him like a little gargoyle.

"You're the healer," Culvern wheezed, and Yasnic felt his heart sink. *This* conversation, then. And honestly, he'd been expecting it sooner or later. If not with this man, then some sick old Armiger, some Lodge chief who'd taken a knife somewhere slow but sure. Someone powerful and desperate.

"My name is Yasnic," he said. "Sage-Invigilator, sorry. I am a priest."

Culvern nodded. "A priest who heals."

No. And yet, there were doubtless reports from the patrol who'd seen it all, plus any of the other onlookers who'd been dragged in for a statement. The yellowed paperwork on Culvern's desk, blotted with fungous prints where his fingers had rested too long – probably it was all about Yasnic.

He shrugged.

"There was a little crowd outside earlier," said the Sage-Invigilator thickly. "Calling for the healer. Do you want me to send you back to them?"

That opened the door to the line of rhetoric where the man rubbed his hands like a mummer's show villain and asided *In pieces* to the booing mob, but Yasnic didn't feel this was one of *those* conversations. Not that he could trust the Sage-Invigilator one bit, of course. But even so.

"They want me back, sir? Sage-Invigilator? Magister, I mean, sorry. Is that right?"

"You have become a momentary hero to them. Although none of them seems to know who you are. You and the man you healed. There are people in Ilmar even now demanding you be returned. I have received" – he coughed, brought something foul into his mouth and swallowed it back down – "*letters*," he got out, as though the very idea was disgusting. "My subordinates will ask me what we should do. Should we descend on them with sword and baton? That would quiet them. Or there is the option of magnanimity. Unconventional and somewhat against

Correct Thought, but it remains in my quiver. Do you want me to be" – another throaty cough – "magnanimous, Yasnic the priest?"

Yasnic saw how it would all go, then. Not a man for prophecy, nor serving a god who habitually granted it, but he saw. "I know what you want."

The mad little pig's eyes that squinted out of Culvern's head glared at him balefully. "It isn't exactly a conclusion that would command high marks in an exam," he spat out. "Look at me."

Yasnic made himself look.

"You Marics gloat and leer. You sing songs about the stinking Perfector. You tell each other it's a judgment from your filthy city. But I choose to look on *you* and see more, Yasnic the priest. I choose to see an educated man of refined sensibilities. A man whose religion sees to the healing of both rifts and wounds, rather than the inflicting of them."

"In that, magister, you are correct," Yasnic said. He felt very calm one moment, utterly panicked the next, the waves of fear alternating with the nausea he was still fighting. He desperately wanted to go over and open the window.

Culvern slapped his hands palm-down on the desktop. Yasnic half expected the putrid flesh to quiver like thick liquid. "I suffer!" the man declared. "Every day, every hour, I suffer. I disgust my fellows. I disgust myself. My flesh eats itself and is never consumed nor sated. My skin erupts and weeps, priest. I am cursed with a perpetual affliction. As you well know, you and every other Ilmari. You rail at me, yet none suffers like I do."

Yasnic nodded. "I understand, magister."

Culvern lurched forwards at a perilous angle over the desk, making the priest rock back in his own chair. "I'm not asking you" – spraying strings of spit – "to understand. Unless that understanding leads you to a *cure*." And he sat back down abruptly, coughing, retching, the ripest egg-sized lumps on his face peeling back and running with translucent yellow that dried in seconds. "Your city did this to me," he got out. "I'm owed a cure." And he didn't need to say how he'd exhausted every other option, from rational Pal medicine and wards all the way down to the shiftiest snake-bleeders in Mirror Allor. And now a healer, a miraculous near-resurrection on the streets, with witnesses.

"I have healed seven people in my life," Yasnic said. "They're all dead bar one. That one is in your cells, and I fear he'll be dead too, soon enough. There is a cost to it. A cost you will not pay."

"I will pay," Culvern groaned. "I have the Perfecture's treasury at my fingertips. I will sign a draft for whatever sum you need. I will give you to your public, the healer who even the dreaded Occupation could not hold! A legend, priest. You'll have them flocking to be your followers. I'll let your friend go. Or all of them! Damn Hegelsy and his corkscrew schemes. Even that lanky, treason-talking academic. Even the Indweller!"

Yasnic nodded miserably, sinking lower in the chair. "Yes, that would be nice," he said. "But that is not the price I mean."

"Then ask!"

"My master, Kosha, he was taken by the Old Duke. Word reached the palace about the last two priests of a god. Perhaps it was one of our disenchanted followers who let him know where we were. This was years before your people came. My master was invited to the palace. I saw the paper. Folded-over and written in gold. Except it was delivered by the Duke's guard, and so, it wasn't the sort of invitation one says 'no' to."

"Your Duke," Culvern growled, "deserved what he got. I do not! Look at this!" Peeling away a strip of shrivelled skin from the back of his hand.

"I won't defend the Duke," said Yasnic. "Suffice to say he made the same demands of Kosha that you have made of me, and received the same answer. Will you become a part of God's following and abide by his rules?" Asking the man who headed a crusade against all gods and beliefs whether he would bend the knee at God's lonely altar. But Culvern just nodded. Which left the only real rule God had any interest in enforcing.

"Will you do no harm, with the wellness and life that God grants you?" Yasnic asked.

"I will do only good," Culvern said. "You people must understand: the Sway *is* good. The greater good. The greatest! We are purging the world of a sickness, just as you can purge *me*. A sickness of ignorance and superstition, inefficiency and vice. What is a higher goal than perfection?"

"God is less concerned with goals than means," Yasnic told him. "You could live a life devoted entirely to base pleasures and selfishness, if you could do so without bringing harm to others. God will heal nobody whose health only increases the harm in the world. That is His rule. I've argued with Him over it. Shouting all night, because it's *absurd* to expect such conduct of anyone."

"I will harm nothing and nobody," Culvern promised, impossible to separate out how much of his own words he believed.

"A hundred writs and orders cross your desk every day, or are enacted in your name, Perfector," Yasnic said. "Men are beaten and imprisoned, hanged, deprived of their property, tortured even."

"Wicked men," Culvern insisted. "Criminals and those who would bring disorder to the streets of Ilmar."

"God doesn't care. God judges those He heals, and nobody else. You can't control the ripples once you've thrown the stone. You can only choose not to throw the stone." A line from Kosha's teaching, dredged up now. And probably Kosha had said the same to the Duke.

"Then I will," Culvern hesitated, wrestling with the sheer size of the obvious lie he was about to tell, "do no harm." A hunted look in his narrowed eyes. "I will leave the choice of such things to my subordinates."

"They are still your subordinates. Just as a Lodge Aunt whose hands have not a spot of blood on them still owns all the wrongs her people dole out when the protection money is slow." And probably comparing the Perfector to a crime boss was a hanging offence in itself. "And – I need to make this clear because last time I didn't and I'm responsible for what will happen." *To Ruslav. Who I scammed, in essence, because I didn't tell him the rules.* "The moment harm is done, by you or originating from you, it all comes back. I've seen it happen. The sickness, the injuries, the curse. All of it, as though it was never gone, worse sometimes. The very instant you fall from your vow." Ruslav might be dead right now. Might have lunged for the guard bringing their food, say, or tried to thump the Allorwen in the next cell through the bars. And that would be it. He'd be torn in a hundred places as though the teeth of the beast had only just left him.

"No!" Culvern was on his feet again. "There is always a way. Call your god up. Explain to him that he must come to the aid of his priest now. He will make an exception, this once. And in return – what do gods want? A temple for your new adherents, free of scrutiny from the School of Correct Speech? He can have it. Speak no sedition, and you can heal all the city, priest. Heal and spread your creed. Peace and healing. Who would be opposed to that? Our aims are not so different, you see? When we have brought full perfection to Ilmar, all shall be peace, and no harm shall be done to anyone. We want the same thing. But your god must start with me. Priest, I have lived with this for three years! I can't bear it anymore." And his agonised voice must have been audible for three rooms and a corridor on either side, but the Perfector plainly didn't care. "You can't imagine what it's like to live like this! Cure me!"

Yasnic glanced at God who had His thin arms folded and His lip curled. God had weighed Sage-Invigilator Culvern in the balance and found him wanting.

"I am sorry for you, magister," he said.

"I don't want your sorrow!" Culvern roared at him. "What good is your sorrow to me? Will you weep little tears onto these boils and heal them up? Will your sobs clear away this *smell?*"

"Vow to me that you will harm nobody, by any means, nor countenance harm done in your name, and you will be healed," Yasnic said. He was going beyond his brief now, and God was shaking his head, beard whipping back and forth. God didn't want to heal Culvern. But God had rules, and if the man actually became a convert and gave up violence, then Yasnic felt he would have God over a theological barrel.

"How?" Culvern railed at him. "We can't bring perfection to the world without the threat of force. We can't rely on the threat of force unless they know we will follow up on it. If I lived by your rules, the Perfecture would collapse in days. There would be rioting in the streets. Buildings burning, murders! Anarchy! Isn't it better that we hurt *some*, and keep an order that protects so many more? Your god must be reasonable, priest!"

"Yes, well, we've had that discussion." Yasnic looked miserably at God. "He isn't reasonable. He says he can't be doing with all the ifs and buts. He only judges his own, meaning me and anyone He heals. But he judges them hard."

"I am a Sage-Invigilator of the School of Correct Appreciation," Culvern told him. "I know what it is to judge. And when we have brought perfection, then we will be able to be rigid. But now... your god must see that I am not some gutter brigand." He lunged, and though Yasnic tried to writhe away, Culvern had the priest's coarse robe between his oozing fingers, dragging Yasnic in until they were face to face. And it would have been a strong face, Yasnic was sure. A good chin, an intellectual brow. They always said the Old Duke had been the most handsome lad in Ilmar, in his youth. Before he'd brought the curse down on himself. The Old Duke had lived a life busy with wickedness. Few people had shed a tear when the Occupiers had broken in the door of the Palace and hauled him here to the Donjon. Certainly, Yasnic hadn't. Kosha had been hanged, after all. If Yasnic went to that stained window, he'd look down on exactly where it had happened. Hanged after a conversation that had doubtless gone exactly like the one Yasnic was having with the man who'd hanged the Duke.

And, in the moment of that drop and stretch, the Duke's body had been left unblemished. A middle-aged man, a little paunchy but not unhandsome, a well-turned leg, features of traditional Armiger elegance. Although pop-eyed and red-faced and dead, of course, what with the noose around his neck. And the curse had manifested in Culvern.

Culvern, who now slobbered into his face, "Tell your god—"

And Yasnic closed his eyes against it and said, "No."

"We'll decant him." No shouting now. A steel hiss. "We'll render your divinity down into tablethi and use them to shoot every Ilmari who demands we release you. We'll hang you from the scaffold and draw the puissance from your corpse after everyone's had a chance to see what your high principles bought you. I'll hunt down every one of your congregation and string them up shoulder to shoulder, even if I have to leave whole streets, whole *districts* empty, you hear me?"

And Yasnic laughed. Despite himself. Despite everything. Laughed in the face of the most powerful man in Ilmar at the thought that the scene Culvern described would look any different to the solitary execution of Yasnic.

Culvern threw him across the room. Rotting and foul, the man was still strong. Yasnic collected the chair on his way, and then broke it against the wall. Dazed, he sat up, waiting for the next assault.

The Sage-Invigilator had already closed half the distance. His distorted face was purple with rage, seeping from a dozen ruptured boils. He'd stopped, though. There was another Pal in the doorway. A lean and narrow-shouldered man with a face twisted into a parody of disapproval at all this unseemly commotion.

"Sage-Invigilator," the man breathed, "we have duly appointed officials whose job it is to brutalise the prisoners. You need not lower yourself to the task."

"Hegelsy," Culvern spat. He was no less angry. For a moment, Yasnic thought he'd go over and strangle the life out of the smaller man.

"My prisoner, Sage-Invigilator," the newcomer, Hegelsy, said patiently.

"Hang him," Culvern spat.

Hegelsy blinked. "Excuse me?"

"A public hanging. Have Correct Conduct round up an audience. Let them see their healer swing. Let them see the fruits of superstition. Him, and all of his. All the scum you've been hoarding. The Indweller even. Let them see what happens to those who strive to hold back perfection." But he was staring straight into Yasnic's eyes, even as God ran over and ineffectually tried to help the priest up. Staring into him and telling him silently *You have killed them, you and your god.* Doubtless, waiting for the begging and pleading, the recanting. The healing, that wouldn't ever come.

"Please," Yasnic whispered to God.

God shook his head, bared his teeth. "Never." As tyrannical for peace as the Pals ever were for control. "No exceptions."

"Not for me. For yourself. For the others."

And as for Hegelsy, Yasnic saw a dozen arguments rise up on his face and be put back in their boxes, replaced by a speculative look. "Hang them all in public, Sage-Invigilator?"

"Show this city what it means to be under the Sway." Culvern stumbled over and kicked furiously at Yasnic. "What it means to *laugh* at us." His voice breaking on the word, an open wound in the sentence through which Yasnic could see so much suffering, given and taken. A soul like a cancer.

"I'm sorry," he said, for the he'd-lost-count time today, and then soldiers were bustling in to drag him off. To drag him past Hegelsy who was already looking at him as a scavenger might a corpse.

Breaking Things

Ilmar is seeping into him, replacing him piece by piece with locally sourced materials, erasing what he was. Hellgram and his wife had been soldiers. They had become lost. Their skills and gear had got them through the Wood. His foreign clothes are darned with native thread now. His language, that nobody knows, is rough on his tongue. He dreams in Maric, or even Pel. He hopes that all the little pieces of him he's losing are still out there. Perhaps they've gone ahead of him to find his wife.

Hellgram had dragged his feet back to the Anchorage after the expedition to the Reproach. Bruised and battered, grim. No need for Langrice or Jem to ask if he'd found what he was looking for. Langrice knew he wouldn't. No point telling him that though. And Hellgram was a perfect employee otherwise. He'd do any job, and if he was no master at anything, he learned and had quick and steady hands. He could sew, hammer, paint, chuck out the kind of drunk who could be chucked out and face down the kind who couldn't. She wasn't entirely sure what Hellgram's wife had brought to the package, honestly. The woman must have been waited on hand and foot. Plus, though he wasn't exactly *popular* and didn't really have friends, he'd accumulated a fair amount of respect among the various groups and cliques who used her taproom to plot their villainies and acts of resistance. She was constantly brokering his services, and that brought her a trickle of coin and got Hellgram into places he hadn't searched yet. Which would have been a perfectly equitable arrangement if his wife had been out there somewhere for him to find. As it was, Langrice had to admit to herself that she was exploiting the man's monomania, but he didn't seem to mind.

She's dead. Or never even made it through the Wood. After all, she only had Hellgram's word for that. Easier for him to tell himself she was out there, as though someone could just get their foot stuck in a hole for five years and wait patiently for darling husband to come free her delicate ankle. Easier that, than accept he'd abandoned her to the mercies of the Anchorwood. *Or else she's running from him.* She'd entertained that notion more than once. That the relationship had been a lot more one-sided than Hellgram let on. That he hadn't found her because she'd put as much distance as possible between them the moment his hands were off her, and had never stopped running since. And Langrice wouldn't say that Hellgram was a mean customer. There was no sign of that kind of anger in the way he dealt with her or Jem or anyone. Except, Langrice had been with someone once, and she knew exactly how, when you took off your public face and turned it inside out for private use, it could end up a very different shape. There was something cold in Hellgram. Usefully cold, if she was honest. He'd not shirk at dirty hands or wielding the cudgel. But if he was motivated by love, then it was the sort of sharp, narrow love that he'd do anything for, and not in a good way.

Right now, he was buying eggs, which hopefully shouldn't need knife or cudgel. Although, the day before, the farm whose stall she usually bought from had turned out to have a printing press and a stack of pamphlets stamped all over with ravens and hawks, so no more eggs from that direction. If she wanted her accustomed breakfast and her customers' favourite hangover cure, Hellgram was going to have to hunt for something less romantic than a lost wife. And he'd come back with eggs, she knew. Eggs and change from the money she'd given him. He didn't care about money. Perhaps to him it wasn't real money, not being stamped with whatever strange kings and provenances his lost homeland espoused.

Late afternoon in the Anchorage. A thin crowd. Jem was at the bar, talking a sullen Ilmari girl through where everything was and what to do with the money. The kid wouldn't work out, Langrice decided. There was always a disaffected local who was pariah enough to come asking for a job. Or else, one who understood just what a meeting place and melting pot the Anchorage was, and reckoned they could profit from it. The former never stuck it out. They discovered the cold shoulders they'd been getting up to that point were nothing once you took the Anchorage's coin. The latter stuck it out precisely until they'd got whatever deal they'd been angling for, and then quit once better prospects had been secured. Or they got knifed for sticking their nose into dangerous people's business. Fifty-fifty, either way.

Quiet enough that she could take the weight off her feet. She poured herself a mug from the good barrel, then a second, and stomped both over to the table where Blackmane was haggling with a couple of rivermen. They were Herons, Langrice knew – honestly, most of the river trade had some hand in the smuggling that kept the other resistance groups fed and equipped, and fenced away downriver any loot too hot for Ilmar's own markets. They stopped when she arrived, staring suspiciously, but Blackmane rapped on the table to get their attention.

"Gentlemen," the big Allorwen rumbled, and they scowled but went on with their talk with Langrice sitting there. Nothing incriminating said, but she could sniff it out, locked up in their talk of *the goods* and *sealed deliveries* and *material*, neat terms for contraband and black market tablethi and crates of swords in hidden holds.

When they'd gone, Blackmane shook his head, as though dealing in such matters was beneath him. She wondered what he was getting from it. Likely, some trinket or antique or Allorwen heirloom would stick to his fingers as he allowed his kin and their places to channel the goods to where they needed to go. She hoped he hadn't started actually funding the resistance. The day Blackmane went hard for a cause other than his own skin was the day he went soft.

"You have a shop," she pointed out, as he sipped the beer and wiped foam from his moustache.

"You try doing business in Mirror Allor right now," he complained. "Soldiers all over. My stock in trade got turned over three times in three days. Looking for, well, *we* know what. And just because they found nothing didn't mean items of my inventory didn't walk out of my door for free each time. No, my dear, I cannot be seen talking to suspicious river types on my home ground right now. So here I am."

They shared a moment of quiet then, their uneasy relationship squatting invisibly on the table between them. He'd sell her, she knew, if only there was a market. She'd sell him – and there *were* markets – if it made more sense than just keeping him around. But while he *was* around, he was good company. They went way back, and it wasn't as though the Allorwen cared much about an establishment's uncanny revelation.

"Bad out there, people tell me," she said quietly.

"It will pass," Blackmane decided, peering into his beer as though it was divination, then draining it. "Endurance is all."

"Bet you're glad you did your stint in the Donjon already. Crowded in there right now, I hear."

He chuckled bleakly at that. "Three days ago, you'd not find anyone in Mirror Allor who hadn't been stopped and shaken down, and one in five seen the inside of some kind of cell. Obviously, I heard the howls of protest from outside the district, all you Marics decrying the way the Pals treat us. And now it's your turn. They've shaken us villains until there's nothing left to fall out, not coin nor guilt, so they're off doing it to you fine upstanding citizens, and suddenly, it's a tyrannical liberty."

"So cynical," she noted. "Some of the crowd I get in here are saying this is the one. The pin that cracks the bridge. What with the Gownhall, and now, I hear the Siblingries are talking. Lots of knives being sharpened for the Pals. You should enjoy that."

He gave her an old, old look. "It's so strange, the way that when the Pals are on the advance, then there are people breaking windows and bones in the streets of Mirror Allor, and when the Pals get pushed back, the exact same. It's just what clothes the people wear is different. Besides, this isn't *it*. These students and idealists and bird-wearers you get in here, everything's *it* for them. It's always the uprising tomorrow. Only when tomorrow becomes today, the uprising stays tomorrow. Convenient that way. It's like always having the dinner but never needing to wash the dishes."

She nodded, and they shared the smile of two people on the far side of middle age who no longer had to believe in things. That was when Hellgram came in.

He had eggs, cheese, ham and news, depositing the first three in the kitchen and serving the last to their table.

"A hanging," he said.

"Pshh," Blackmane scoffed. "That's not news."

"The healer, they said."

The Allorwen shrugged. "One less charlatan in the world. Right now, Ilmar doesn't need another reason for people to go around throwing stones." He caught Langrice's look. "What? You don't agree? Some mad miracle man turns up, makes a big public show of some fake restorative. His bad luck the Pals took him up before he could start selling his patented cure-all."

Hellgram had a poster, though – the thin, grey paper the Perfecture used for its official proclamations, torn at the corners where he'd pulled it down. There were faces there, reproduced in that neat, slightly stylised Pal way that still left them quite recognisable. Langrice looked over them, recognised most of them, sniffed and sat back, not sure what she thought. It was more than just business as usual, that was for sure. Both in the identities of the condemned and the fanfare of the announcement. The victims weren't even being smeared with regular crimes, the way the Pals often did with resistance fighters they caught – easy enough in most cases because it wasn't as though they had to invent the crimes. But this mob weren't being called murderers or thieves. *For Working Against the Perfecture*, said the poster.

"These two went with me into the Reproach," Hellgram pointed out.

"Then count yourself lucky they left you in the street before the Pals found them," Langrice told him. "Ruslav. There always was a hanging in his future." The student girl was presumably just collateral damage. Stringing up one of the Gownhall's protégés was a predictable play by the Occupiers, to remind the student body and the faculty just who held the big stick. They hardly needed to waste the rope on her, given who else's likeness was sitting there. The sight of Ivarn Ostravar dangling from the scaffold was going to either set light to the whole of the Gownhall or throw a very cold bucket of water on it, and she couldn't decide which was more likely.

Blackmane stood. She blinked at him warily.

"What?"

"Business to attend to, my dear," he told her. "A sudden rearrangement of matters I thought could wait till later. A night to be spent in unsavoury negotiations. Because tomorrow, they hang my long-time acquaintance Ivarn, to whom I owe *so* much, and I wish to be there to see that they do it properly."

The Second Murder

A chill. A cold space. Who'd ever thought of it, that such a place was even there? Between the walls, or within them. The fog was all, its obscuring shroud. What you couldn't see needn't impede you.

Johanger Tulmueric lived in Ilmar six months of the year. The wrong six months, from his perspective. The cold winters up here, and then his cartel had him back home for the hot, still days that the Ilmari chill always left him unacclimated for.

When in Ilmar, he had a good suite of rooms over the cartel's tradehouse, sitting between Liberation Way and the Mahanic Temple. All very pleasant but, at the same time, very expensive. It wasn't as though he would be compensated for all the high living the district practically required. Which was why his preferred haunts were decidedly west of the river. Where he could wear shoddier clothes that weren't so ruinously expensive to clean or replace; where he could fetch up in cosmopolitan dens like the Anchorage and play a sharp game of chaq behind closed doors for high stakes. And if the next cartel envoy noticed that certain objects of art were missing from the tradehouse displays, well, Johanger would have made his fortune and gone home by then. It wasn't his fault the buy-in at Langrice's games was high, and he didn't have the budget to go acquire an armful of relics and antiques out of his own pocket.

Right now, he was keeping to his rooms, though. These wealthy streets were safe enough, but Ilmar was going through one of its periodic convulsions. Between the locals and the Palleseen, it wasn't safe to be a foreigner on the streets right now. Even a Loruthi, whom the Ilmari tended to like, and the Pals were generally leery of, as nationals of a large and powerful state outside the Sway.

And it was a shame, but he knew it would all settle down. Some rioting, a little arson, some optimistic speeches about freedom, a brutal crackdown. And he didn't have to *like* it, but it was someone else's problem.

The servants having retired to their rooms below, he shuffled in slippers and dressing gown into his lushly carpeted bedroom and found someone already there.

A young man, skinny frame almost lost in a great cloak – not the usual baggy Ilmari fashion but clothes plainly made for someone else. A robe that hung in folds like a dying man's skin. Tangled strings of oddments and animal bits. And a mask hanging about the man's throat. *Is he in costume as an Indweller?* The oddness of the thought actually got in the way of Johanger's shock, and he didn't shout for the servants. Then the man was across the room in an insect-quick skitter, a knife at the merchant's throat. Behind him, the air was grey and hazy. *Has he set a fire?* But there was no smoke in Johanger's nose, just the stale reek of body and clothes equally unwashed.

"Where is it?" the man demanded. Johanger was still not quite able to take him seriously, dressed up in ill-fitting mummer's wear. A face, pop-eyed and rictus-mouthed, taut and pale and... familiar.

"You were at the table," Johanger got out. "The riverman."

"Where is it?" the skinny creature demanded. The knife cut, a bead of pain at the merchant's throat.

"You had the..." That unexpected treasure. Who had ended up with it, though? Nobody. The Game had been abandoned. The first match to the whole string of fireworks currently going off around the city. "Why should I have it?" And at last, something of the man's manner communicated itself through all the strangenesses. A terrible desperation. A madness. "I don't have it. Why would I have it? Just – put away the knife. You need money? I have money."

"I need *out*." There were tears in the man's eyes. "I need it. My treasure. Where is it?" And, past his shoulder, Johanger could see pulled-out drawers, his fine clothes in tangled piles on the floor, his medicine cabinet rifled. Nothing taken, everything in disarray, a most single-minded search.

"It's not here," he told the knife that his whole world was focused down to. "I never—" And the words stopped coming, just wheezing to nothing in his throat. For a moment, he couldn't understand why. The knife was gone. Surely, that was a good thing. Except the knife was very red now. Red and wet. The riverman in borrowed clothes was pulling away from him as though the sudden openness of Johanger's throat was something Johanger himself had done, some Loruthi defence mechanism designed to horrify and drive away potential threats. And then, his body caught up, and there was pain but not for long.

It was the Indwellers' fault, after all. They'd murdered the Sage-Archivist. And Fleance didn't care about some Pal high official. He wore the Heron, after all. He was a proud fighter for Ilmar's future freedoms. Let the Occupiers all be strung from their own scaffolds for all he cared. But when the man had died and his idiot servant had come howling out of the woods, it had broken something. Some chain of events he'd been in control of. He'd been about to win the Game, earn enough to blunt the teeth of all the creditors who'd been hounding him. The Ilmari who'd taken to hanging around the docks – his own river kin who'd loaned him all he was ever going to get and would send him over the side with weighted pockets if he couldn't pay them back. Everything was going to be set right. Then the Indwellers had done what they'd done. And yes, there were other details.

Contributions to the course of events that he himself had been involved in. The thoughts squirmed in his head like eels, impossible to hold on to.

The Indwellers. He'd followed them out of the Wood, into the city. In the fog, at the heels of the very last of them. And they'd gone... places. Cold places. Not the Gutter District streets he knew, between the Anchorage and the river. Under and over and around. As though when the fog rose, it didn't just creep where the buildings weren't. The fog went *everywhere*; it was just people couldn't see the other places it went because the buildings got in the way. But the Indwellers knew about the fog. They walked in it. They went where it went. The other places. The buried halls, the tombs, the fragments of forgotten chambers. The ghosts of forest groves long fallen to the axe. Places that didn't exist anymore, save that the fog remembered. And who knew that the Indwellers didn't just dwell *in*? That they didn't only wander the paths of that here-then-gone forest, but elsewhere too. Perhaps everywhere. Ilmar was just the immediate step beyond the Wood, on the way to older, worse places.

They'd taken Fleance to the edge of those places. To the precipice. A bridge over a howling chasm, and landscapes on the far side that would make the Kings Below weep. One by one, they'd crossed, and he knew he'd followed them too far. He had to stop, while he could still see the shadowy outlines of walls and windows, not those cliffs of teeth, those tormented eyes!

And he'd reached for the shoulder of that last Indweller, the one whose heels he'd been dogging. *Take me home*, he'd begged, but they'd ignored him. And it was follow or be abandoned in this netherworld with the fog leaching away. He'd grabbed the shoulder, pulled, felt the cloak slip. He'd fought with it, the furs, the robe, the bony body beneath. Feeling it squirm from him, boneless, double-jointed.

And the knife. His knife. Knowing even as he drew it that it wasn't for the abandonment. It was revenge, justice for them bringing this misfortune down on him. It was envy, for they could walk anywhere, and thanks to them, there was nowhere in the world would welcome him home. Stabbing, once and again, and more. The point sinking into that mass of furs, as though there was nothing of substance within, and yet the Indweller collapsed. Collapsed and, with it, the last of the fog left Fleance in a dead-end alley with the rattle and thunder of the Hammer Districts just streets away. In an alley, with a corpse.

He'd taken the furs and robe, the trinkets and fetishes and mask. Hidden in them, feeling a terrible doom over him, so that he dared not look into the sky. Knowing that only one talisman had the potency to salvage a new life from the mess he'd made of the old one. As though the perfectly reasonable desires he'd had before the knife came out had become branded onto his brain, all other thoughts pared away. And with the cloak and the mask and the rest of it, the fog. Seeping in from nowhere, opening the city to him. Knowing that each step he took through the cold, lost places would devour him just a little more. But if he could get the ward. If he could only get the *ward*, then surely, he could find a way back to the man he had once been.

The Loruthi merchant didn't have it. Fleance tried to remember who else had been at the table. Faces swam in his mind, twisted into caricature. His hands shook. The knife went red and wet back into its sheath. He couldn't find the door to the room but that didn't matter. The fog seethed out from the bloody furs of his cloak, showing him the way.

Dancing on Air

In the Pallesand Archipelago, there were no executions. That would imply criminal acts, and everyone knew that the Palleseen were sailing into their Thousand Years of Perfection. Even the persistence of the Temporary Commission of Ends and Means was entirely focused outwards. Of course, plenty of people disappeared across the Archipelago. They just weren't there, and all reference to them was removed. Their name would only ever be found in one place, a carefully curated list of all the people who didn't exist and should not be mentioned. The list was necessary when prosecuting anyone gauche enough to mention them, because you had to have something to refer to, to know what it was to which nobody was permitted to refer. But these weren't executions. This was just the operation of perfection. Outside the Archipelago, however, the officials of the Sway tended to retain the crude local forms of punishment. Among the imperfect, a public show had been found to be efficacious by the Commission.

The next morning, they were marched out to the scaffold. Dorae hadn't even been interrogated yet. He'd spent his time in the cell carefully constructing the arguments, inducements and bribes he would offer his questioners. What he could afford to let go, what he might be able to borrow from cousins and business associates. He was, after all, just a dealer in old tat. One of half a street of them in the heart of Mirror Allor. He was the friendly bobbing face who twinkled and beamed and joked

– appropriately subserviently – with middle-class Marics who thought they were daringly avant-garde for visiting the quarter to browse. The Pals had some kind of wasp in their ear right now, and as usual, they were taking it out on the Allorwen. It would pass. It always did. It wasn't the first cell he'd seen inside of, and he knew some of the guards at the Donjon by name.

Except here they were, him in his shirtsleeves and loose trousers, shivering in the chill of a lead-grey morning. And there was the platform, there the overarching beam. And there the ropes.

Tobriant, the woodworker, started fighting when the wan sunlight of the yard hit them. Protesting, "I didn't do anything! I'm not the right man! I'm just a carpenter! I just make cabinets and chairs!" The guards cuffed him. One of them called him an insurgent. They tripped him onto the hard cobbles and then kicked him and hauled him up by twisting his shoulders back. Dorae was fairly sure Tobriant was exactly that, a tradesman caught up in something that was nothing to do with him. He wouldn't even age a fake to up its sale value. Dorae knew because he'd asked the man, when his usual counterfeiter-of-goods had ended wrong way up in the river. Tobriant had been horrified. Everything he made was *his*, carved with his knotted serpent mark. It was high-quality, and how *dare* Dorae even *suggest*? He was blamelessly honest, while Dorae himself had hidden resistance fighters and fugitives in the back room of his shop more than once, and their pamphlets and loot as well. And if he'd been taken up for *that* then, well, some kind of judicial logic would have presumably been served. He hadn't, though. They didn't know about any of it, but they were going to string him up anyway alongside Tobriant who'd never broken a rule in his life.

There was a crowd gathered, he saw. They must have been coming in since dawn. Plenty of soldiers on the walls and the scaffold platform, all with batons slanted in their arms. Another row of the grey Pal uniforms between scaffold and crowd, these with swords and cudgels. If it kicked off, there was going to be a bloodbath, but why would it? He knew the Ilmari; they loved their executions. It was the pressure valve of the city's kettle, always had been. The Old Duke had turned the hangings into his circus. In his time, there had been peddlers with fried meat and children's toys and beer around the edges of the yard – though the Pals hadn't approved of that. The crowd right now didn't look like they were there for a good time.

He stumbled as he went up the steps. The executioner, Hoyst, was at his elbow immediately, grotesquely solicitous. "Wouldn't want you to sustain an injury, eh? A fellow could break his neck." And Dorae thanked him, by knee-jerk habit, because you got used to saying thank you to the Marics and the Pals who despised you.

He squinted down the line, feeling the prickly temper of the crowd swell and roil past the soldiers. Wondering who it was that had changed the mood. Who was so important that they'd broken the Ilmari love of lethal street theatre?

The academic, surely. The severe, dignified old man, who even now was putting a good show on, standing tall and straight with his arms tied behind his back. Head up, long nose jutting at the sun. If they gave him a chance to make a speech, he'd make a good one, Dorae decided. Except that was another of the Old Duke's traditions the Pals didn't approve of. It wasn't just him, though. He had his adherents – students aplenty there, and some Gownhall faculty in their distinctive robes and flared, square-topped hats – but some other hook was twisting in the gut of the crowd.

It wasn't the Shrike woman, Fyon. Probably she had some resistance brothers and sisters who'd regret her passing, but anyone who went Shrike was digging a grave and not inviting mourners to the funeral. And if it wasn't Ostravar the Gownhall maestro, then it wasn't the student girl either. Dorae could see her on Fyon's left, shifting and shuffling, feet moving rhythmically, even as she stared out across the crowd. *Desperate bravery*, he thought. Scared out of her wits, but she knew exactly what the moment demanded. He'd seen similar resolve in a painting he'd sold once, one of the old Maric masters. His heart went out to the girl a little. She was so obviously out of her depth. And the crowd was ignoring her, just as they were ignoring the thuggish lout who'd been railing and sulking in the cells. And as for the Indweller – if they really *were* an Indweller as Ostravar claimed – nobody knew who they were, and they didn't even seem to understand what was happening to them.

It was the skinny little man, Dorae saw. Yasnic, the man who'd been taken away and then brought back, along with the announcement that they all had a morning appointment. The man who had got them killed, then. Except he was so meek and miserable Dorae could hardly hold it against him. Even now, he just stood there before the ugly crowd with his head down. They were, it seemed, here for him, almost as much as for Ivarn, and he didn't even acknowledge them.

Hoyst was going down the line now, his usual caper, slipping the rope about Tobriant's head and checking its fit, attentive as a tailor. Then to Dorae, "Is that comfy, sir? The silk, as requested." Because Dorae had paid the extra. He'd denied himself a lot of luxuries in life. Why not treat himself now? "Splendid, splendid." The hangman's quick fingers adjusting the rope, twitching the hem of Dorae's shirt out of the way. "We endeavour to provide a neat and final service here," Hoyst said briskly. "A minimum of fuss and unpleasantness."

"Thank you," Dorae said, and Hoyst danced on to Ivarn, having to reach higher because the academic stood so tall. The executioner's showmanship had taken over from the silenced speeches of the condemned under the Perfecture, but there was a twitchiness to his movements right now. The crowd weren't laughing. He wasn't used to that. His checks became more and more perfunctory as he went down the line.

About Yasnic's neck they'd hung a sign, he saw. He had to lean forwards and sideways to get a look at it, but it seemed inexplicably important to know. He didn't want to get hanged with the mystery unsolved. And it was written in Pel, Dorae's third language and not one he was comfortable with. "Healer," he spelled out eventually, with some diacritics that indicated possession by the reader. "Your healer," then. And Dorae had missed some key news, that had been slow to filter into Mirror Allor, so he didn't understand that at all. The crowd did, though. Or some of them. They obviously did feel some proprietary interest in this healer and didn't like that he was about to get the drop and the dangle. But a whole extra crowd was filtering in at the back, now, and they were the more usual Donjon yard speculators, here for the show and not the unrest. And there were all those soldiers, four times as many as usual. Dorae felt the fulcrum of circumstance tilt the crowd's mood back and forth, until it was sliding towards the near end of sullen unrest, rather than over into action.

So much for that, he thought.

Some familiar faces in the crowd, he saw. Some other Allorwen, come to see their countrymen die. He tried to catch eyes, mouth some last message. There was too much going on. Then there was Blackmane, a little mountain in the crowd's sea, burly and brooding, barbarous in his fur coat, his fierce beard. Nodding to Dorae, to Tobriant. But then his gaze, too, passing on. Not the healer. Ostravar. Fixing the Gownhall man with a particularly keen needle of a stare.

Hoyst had them all fitted for collars now, executing a flourish of a bow to a crowd that wasn't in the mood. Retreating to the levers. Dorae shifted his feet, feeling the trapdoor move slightly in its frame. Aware of Blackmane's relentless gaze, even though he wasn't its focus. The student girl gave a choked little breath, shoulders shaking. Fyon spat suddenly, painting the back of a soldier's jacket. He turned, furiously, about to vault onto the scaffold and cudgel her. And perhaps that might have been it. That might have somehow put a match to the oil. But the man just smiled, almost sweetly. Looked from his club to the rope above. *What can I do that won't get overwritten by that?*

There was plainly a lot going on, Dorae had to admit. A lot that didn't concern him. He felt that he should draw this to someone's attention. He really shouldn't be here in this august company. As though he was some bit-part actor who'd taken the wrong entrance and ended up standing where the king was supposed to come in. The focus of attention, just for one brief moment, when he'd only ever been supposed to carry a spear or swell a crowd.

The healer lifted his head, staring. Not, apparently, grateful they'd turned out for him. Appalled, rather. Shaking his head. *Go home, go home.* Ostravar, having exhausted his sang-froid, now starting to shake, clenching his lean jaw, blinking rapidly.

"It'll be all right," Dorae said to him. The man stared at him, for a moment just outraged at being addressed by someone so outside his social sphere. As though there should be separate lynchings for respectable academics and Allorwen tradesmen. Then a collapse of his dignity into a wry humour.

"Will it? Ah well, I'm reassured then."

Beside Dorae, a Pal soldier lifted his baton – not in the sense of aiming it with lethal intent, though the meaning was fatal enough. Lifted it, and the crowd quieted, conditioned to the act. Slammed the butt against the planks of the platform. One. Two.

Dorae, who had been very calm through all of this, felt a great upswelling of panic and misery, as though all the years that he should have had, the time with friends and family, the joys and wonder, they were all crowding on the far side of that uncrossable division the rope was about to make. Thronging there and wailing that they would never be, snuffed out from the future by Dorae's weight and the twin inexorabilities of physics and biology. Three. He heard himself whimper. Tobriant was openly weeping. Dorae wished his hands were free, so he could grip the man's fingers in his own. A last moment of solidarity. Not going alone into that grand dark.

The baton came down a fourth time. The crowd was utterly hushed, staring – some keen, some aghast, all of them caught in this moment as though each one of them was on their own taut rope.

"Please," whispered Dorae, and then the baton made its fifth descent. Hoyst's trusties hauled the levers in perfect unison, practised as clock-tower figures. The trapdoor beneath him was suddenly no longer beneath him, and he dropped, strangling, into the void.

Through the Bottom of a Bottle

Langrice. Tired, mostly. Tired in peacetime because everyone brought their squabbles to the Anchorage. Tired right now because the squabbles had got loose all over the city, and neutral ground was one of those ideas that's grand on paper. Watching Jem sweep the floor. Counting last night's take, separating out the coins: this for the Anchorage and its many needs, this for bribes and protection, this for wages, this for her. To vanish away to that secret place where she keeps the money. More than one inebriate or chancer has tried to find the legendary hoard Langrice surely has hidden around the Anchorage somewhere. They say she leaves thieves tied up in the Wood, her own special offering to the monsters. But what, after all, is she saving it up for?

She'd expected a band of thugs. She hadn't expected Aunt Evene herself. The woman marched in with a spatter of rain and, although likely the foul weather made it safer for a major figure in the Vultures to be abroad in Ilmar, Langrice felt she'd brought the deluge with her. Part of her escort.

And the escort was that band of thugs, right enough. A dozen Lodge soldiers, their mismatched finery bedraggled and drenched. Big men, lean men, vicious-looking women. And overcloaks and baggy layers of clothes meant a Pal patrol might not have seen the swords – even the batons that a couple of them carried. More likely any stalwarts of the Occupation who spotted this mob had looked the other way. Oh, Hegelsy's boys from the Donjon garrison might be all fired up with ideology, but the regular patrols in the Gutter Districts were realists. They preferred prey who couldn't fight back.

"Where is she?" Evene demanded. "Show me." She threw her wet cloak onto the nearest table, upsetting a lamp that Jem scurried to rescue. Beneath, she had a cuirass of velvet, bulked out by metal plates sewn into it. Dark blue, studded with rivets whose heads were old bronze coins.

Langrice had been in two minds about sending the messenger, when she'd made her messy discovery. Under better circumstances, she might have been more circumspect. With all that was going on right now, though, she didn't feel up to trying to get rid of a body and then concocting a story to explain the absence of a living person who'd absolutely been hiding out in her upper cellar just the day before.

Hellgram had made the discovery, which was good because he was the least squeamish person alive. It'd take more than a stabbed-up corpse to rattle the man. Down there in the first cellar, behind the false wall: that bespoke space Langrice made available to Carelia and Evene, and any other bold patriots who had something they didn't want the Pals to get their hands on. In this case, the hot goods had been Cheryn, also known as Fish for obscure reasons. Not even a stranger to Langrice: a regular at the Anchorage. No great hardship to stow the woman – still alive right then – in the hidden space and give her a little beer and some vittles. Cheryn had been an ambassador for the Vultures, meaning she went off with a roving brief and cut deals with Herons and Shrikes and various Lodge families. And because she'd been Evene's picked woman, she went and collected money from shops and drinking dens who were desperately keen to contribute to the effort against the Pals. Because not being patriotic was one of the chief causes of catching on fire.

What with the increased Pal activity right now, Langrice reckoned a number of slightly singed businessmen had been pointing fingers, and so Cheryn had gone to ground. Specifically,

Evene had arranged for her to hole up in the Anchorage out of harm's way until things blew over.

They trooped down to that first cellar, the boots of all the Lodge boys heavy on the steps. Langrice operated the catch, feeling like a tired old magician demonstrating how the trick was done. The counterbalanced wall, the barrels moving aside with a grind and a shudder that said the mechanism was old and in need of maintenance, much like her. The reveal. She and Evene stared at each other, two women of an age, of long acquaintance. Not friends. Langrice didn't know precisely where she sat on the Bitter Sisters' list of grudges. It had never been high enough to get a summons to the Fort. Perhaps this had boosted her up the page a few names.

Cheryn was dead. No medical examination necessary. There had been a fight. Her own knife was clear of its sheath, spun across the floor of the little den. Someone had stabbed her with maniac zeal, a dozen wounds if there was one. Blood across the floorboards, seeping between the cracks. Her last meal overturned, part eaten. What little floor was clear of the pool of red was marked with sanguine footprints. Not as though the killer had been much into concealing any clues. Except the footprints didn't go anywhere. The rest of the cellar was clean of them. No suggestion anything was amiss until Hellgram had come down to take out the chamber pot.

Langrice explained this to the flint of Evene's expression, hearing her own voice, calm and measured. Very aware of all the blades – even just the *fists* – of everyone around her.

"It's like someone just appeared in there and left the same way, Auntie," she finished.

"Who knows about the wall?" Evene asked.

"Me and my staff. A fair few who know this place is here – you and yours, a couple of Herons. But not the workings of it."

"Go fetch her man, the one who says he found it. The foreigner," Evene ordered, and a couple of her people clumped back up.

"You and Cheryn," Evene noted, a trailing half-sentence hunting for something to get its teeth into.

Langrice made a noncommittal sound.

"She turned up at your table, didn't she? Langrice's famous high-stakes invitational. Liked her chaq and hazard," Evene considered. "Let me guess, she had something up as stake you really wanted to walk away with? Or were you fool enough to give her credit?"

Langrice made herself a study in calm, weight canted to one foot, thumbs hooked into her apron strings. "You think this was me?"

"Or your man, on your orders. He's cut some throats in his time, hasn't he?" And then her people were trying to bundle Hellgram down the stairs, although he was a lot stronger than he looked and made the descent rather more on his own terms than they'd intended. At the top of the stairs that idiot girl, Jem, was peering down worriedly. Langrice wanted to snap at her to go away, except that would just bring her to Evene's attention.

"Foreigner," said Evene, the arch-patriot, champion of Ilmar. It took four of them to force Hellgram to his knees. He wasn't even fighting them properly, just mutely pushing back against whatever pressure you put on him, by instinct. At last, they had him down, staring at Evene with a kind of brute, animal defiance, not even understanding what was going on. And Jem was halfway down the stairs rather than just going away like a sensible girl should.

"I didn't give any orders," Langrice said, still the very picture of composure.

"Then maybe it was some personal grief he had with her." Evene bent low and stared into Hellgram's angular face. He stared right back, just the way you shouldn't with the Bitter Sisters.

"He's not like that," Langrice said softly. "He's not all there, it's true. Wife died and he won't stop looking for her. But he wouldn't just knife someone." *Unless she did something to his wife, or he thought she had. Then he'd paint the damn walls with her. But no point going there in this company.*

"This place stinks," Evene said. And it did. Death and bowels and blood and stale beer.

"Now you've seen what there is, we'll clean up."

"Stinks," Evene repeated, and her people were pressing in, more than ready to push Langrice herself down beside her servant. "Too much turning up and vanishing here, or in that Wood of yours."

"That's just this place. You know how it is, Auntie. How it's always been. You know we've always been here for you. Hiding your people, your goods. I'm Ilmar-born. I want the Pals out of here same as the next woman." And, true, she'd tell the Palleseen patrols how she was a law-abiding citizen, peace and order and waving a little flag for the onset of perfection. She'd tell anyone anything, frankly, if it got them out of her face. But it wouldn't inconvenience her if she never had to speak the ugly, artificial words of Pel in her own taproom again.

Maybe Evene saw that in her – or Langrice's vain belief in it, whether or not there was any real substance to it. Or maybe Evene just weighed her up and reckoned a live Langrice was still useful enough not to feed to her pet. But Hellgram…

"He's useful." Seeing Evene about to say something, to order some violence to balance out the random violence that had happened without her say-so. "You know how hard it is to get staff here."

Evene snorted derisively, then she was striding up the stairs. At the top, she must have made some signal, because one of her people thumped Hellgram across the back of the head and then kicked him in the gut when he was down. Another two slopped into the bloody room and took Cheryn's body between them. Perhaps the dead woman would be interred somewhere with all resistance honours. Perhaps she'd get fed to the pet.

After that, Langrice heard them troop out. Jem, who'd finally found wisdom and retreated, hurried back down as soon as the path was clear. She fussed over Hellgram, offering him an arm like one of those little pick-birds trying to lift a crocodile. Hellgram didn't seem to register her, or the fact that he'd just taken a boot to the solar plexus. He got up like an automaton, all focused inwards.

"You'd better clean up," Langrice told the pair of them. "And get some herbs down here for the smell. Nobody likes a taproom that smells of shit and dead people." And she left them to it, only thankful that Evene didn't know about the *other* cellar.

Orvechin's Boots

They were good boots, solid, but you could never get them clean. The muck of the streets, and then the grime of the factories – the smoke, the oil and grease, and that peculiar tacky residue you got where demons were held for any period of time. Scrub all you like, you'd never get it out. And he had. He'd tried. All his life he'd been cleaning boots that would never take a shine again. Something of a metaphor there. So they became a badge of office, those big, steel-reinforced, hardwearing boots. Dark with honest muck.

But there was one advantage to boots like that. You got to trek that working man's grime onto the fancy carpets of the Sirovar family, or any of their Armiger fellows. You got to stamp into their hall, after the liveried flunky who'd grudgingly let you in. Knock toe and heel together. Leave them with a reminder that you'd called. Orvechin, doing just that, grinned within his beard, despite the gravity of the occasion. And he knew he was making work for working people – none of the Sirovar blood would be on their knees callousing their hands with caustic soap. He knew that being a maid in the Armiger district was work, and for the same masters who owned the mills Orvechin worked in. But there was a part of him that would always feel being 'in service' was a betrayal of where they'd come from, and he'd just have to live with that. And so would they.

When word had found him, he'd not been home. Meeting with the Vultures, he'd told the wife, only he'd ended up in

Aullaime's little room round the back of the Ropa Street mill-bank. They'd come there looking to see if she knew where he was. Thirteen well-placed Siblings had been taken up earlier that night, the Pals kicking in doors like they hadn't done for over a year, just yanking people out of bed. For working with the resistance, they'd said. And sometimes that was true, and sometimes it wasn't. The only common ground had been that each of the victims had been organising, spreading the word – getting work in mills and factories where the Siblingries didn't have purchase and giving people the talk over lunch or tea-break. And now, they were all 'resistance fighters' and locked up in the Donjon.

Aullaime had taken all this in and then said she could probably find Father Orvechin, she knew a few places to look. All said with her still in the doorway because the only place she'd need to look was in her own bed right then. Orvechin had let the big old work boots of them clump away before leaping up and dressing, quick as he could. He and Aullaime and Petric Lesselkin of the Scrapherd Siblingry met with a delegation of men and women, all rushed out of their beds and into one of the clothiers' warehouses.

All because of the hangings, was the general feel. That big public execution had been the Pals' way of sticking a toe in the river to feel the current. People had grumbled and scowled, but not a stone had been thrown. It wasn't about the nooses around those necks, it was the rope they had about the throat of the city. They'd tightened it another turn, and nobody had stopped them. So they were going to go on twisting that rope until someone stood up and showed them it was more trouble than it was worth. The Allorwen had felt the pinch, and the Gownhall, and now it was the Hammer Districts' turn. The old game of choke the millhands into accepting less, so the factories would pay out a little more. And, Orvechin was grimly aware, it wasn't as though they'd loosen that noose without a great deal of pressure being brought to bear. It would only get tighter or, at best, stop getting tighter for now. The two modes of the Occupation.

The Hammer Districts had been on a knife edge for days now. The delegates told him that most of their shifts were ready to act. To Wield the Hammer the most effective way. Orvechin could see a confrontation with the Pals rolling towards them like an avalanche. The best way to survive it would be to have it break on something before it reached them. *We need allies. We are the city's spine, but the city's more than us.* And so, he'd be talking to Vultures, doubtless, and the rest, but first, he'd sent the best turned-out messenger hotfoot over the river with an invitation. He'd already been ready to travel when the word came back that *he* was very welcome to attend at the Sirovar townhouse, but the matriarch of that clan was not going to get her own fancy footwear dirty in the streets he called home. Oh, put more diplomatically than that, but Orvechin knew exactly what she had meant.

Petric Lesselkin had one of his apprentices bring a cart up. It was used to hauling a load of scrap, ruined furniture and masonry spoil, so it tripped across briskly enough with just the driver and three passengers. And then Orvechin got to teach the salutary lesson that, when you met with the Siblingries, you chose between cleaning your pretty shoes, or your expensive carpets.

They were ushered into a living room or a sitting room or parlour or some other word for a fancy space to meet people in. He saw the precise moment when Vidsya Sirovar registered the trail he'd tracked in, but he'd give her credit for mastery of her expression. The wince lasted only a fraction of a second. There was a table laid, and little ornate chairs that looked like his bulk would smash them to matchwood but bore him with nary a creak. All of it done as though he'd called around after luncheon, and not in the small hours of the morning.

A neatly ironed servant brought in a samovar on a trolley and poured out tea that probably cost a month's wages a cup.

Orvechin sipped. It was good tea. It wasn't as good as it was expensive, and he reckoned that, never having had bad tea, Sirovar would never appreciate it like he did.

"I mean obviously, I've heard." Vidsya Sirovar was younger than most of the Armiger matriarchs. Her aunt had been the real power, and had held on long enough that several elder siblings had moved out of the city or just passed away. And then she died, and abruptly, the big family mantle was about these slender shoulders. Vidsya was well known across the city as a hedonist, a drunk, an ineffectual rake. All of which was only about one part truth to seven of carefully manufactured image, by Orvechin's estimation. But she wasn't the iron lever her aunt had been, which might have moved the world.

"You've heard. Good." Orvechin sipped the tea, making himself the weight of the world plonked down here in her fancy chair, not going anywhere. Aullaime was leaning back in hers, making the legs groan. Petric was looking at the bottom of his cup for a maker's mark. You got to know your domestic goods, in the scrapherd trade. Orvechin had seen the works tea-set the man kept, twenty rescued pieces, chipped and glued back together, each exquisite, all mismatched.

Their twin silences wrestled each other over the table. Vidsya had put on a vacantly polite look, covering whatever wheels were turning in her mind. Orvechin judged it was on him to advance matters. He couldn't make her sweat until he'd turned up the heat.

"Something should be done," he prompted, and she clicked back into social motion like an automaton with the key turned.

"Obviously, something must be done," as though it was a novel notion unrelated to his own words. "Once the sun's up, I will send people to the other... houses."

"Ravens," Orvechin filled in. "We know what parts are within the casing, Lady Sirovar." Making it a compliment with just a hint of a barb. *We know you're more than just an addled aristocrat. But also, we* know. "And you and your fellows will..."

"There is pressure that we can bring to bear, don't you worry," she told him. "The old families have been usurped by the Occupiers, it's true, but we retain capital. Influence. There are enough within the Perfecture who will listen." And seeing the judgment in his look, "I know, I know. But until the day comes that we can rise up effectively and drive them out, these little victories—"

"My people want to Wield the Hammer," he said flatly.

"Absolutely not," said quickly enough that she'd plainly known he was headed there. Aullaime shifted, making her chair complain, and Petric put the cup down.

"My brother's in the cells," the scrapherd said. "They broke three doors before they got the right one, terrified a dozen families. Beat him in the face with a fist and then took a baton to his back when he was on the floor. Didn't even say what it was he'd done. Took him off bleeding. Slapped his wife when she asked a question. His children saw, your ladyship. And he was just one of many. And saving your ladyship's blushes, but you've done a mite more to earn that cell than he ever did, if I hear right." Stopping just the right side of a threat.

Aullaime nodded. And they'd been hauling her kinfolk out of Mirror Allor for days before this. And Orvechin gave that an uncomfortable moment's thought, that he'd not considered taking action over *that*. Because they hadn't been Siblingry. Not *ours*. And now, Vidsya would be looking at him and making the exact same calculation.

"It's what we have. Wield the Hammer. Boots on the street. Show them they can't just take."

"You're only going to alienate my fellows. The Armigers – the *Ravens* – can't support you just walking away from the factories. A free holiday and dead mills isn't revolution, Orvechin."

"Your family owns the title to seven mills and Petric's scrapping yard," Orvechin said. "And that doesn't mean what it did before the Pals came, but it still means that if someone should drop this fancy cup and crack it in two, it'd be our sweat and toil paying for a replacement. So you could say to the Pals: these workers are *our* people. We support their right not to be hauled away, beaten, tortured, *hanged*. You've heard the Pals have got a new thirst, where hanging's concerned."

"You can assume I'm generally informed of matters that are wider public knowledge," she said acidly, and he preferred that to all the dancing around.

"So." Orvechin put his hands on the table. "We both know, your ladyship, that, west of the river, a lot of folks lost their *respect* for Armigine Hill back when you didn't ever tell the Old Duke no when he was off on his whims and predilections. And then, after the Occupation, you lost your pre-eminence, but that respect's been slow coming back. And I hear you. You've been making sure your generosity is felt in the right places. I've heard men and women with a raven badge under their collar or inked on their wrist give a good talk, about how you and yours will lead the charge, when the day comes. So, it's time to stand up. Even if it's just accepting a twelveday without the mills turning out coin for you."

"Revolutions cost," Vidsya told him.

"How many teacups do they cost? How many carpets?" Petric asked angrily. Orvechin shot him a look, and he subsided.

"Look, I'm sympathetic," Vidsya said. "If it was just *us*... Many of the Armiger families are a lot less committed to the cause than the Sirovars, Orvechin. I keep them in line because I don't try to pick their pockets. This is... not the time. Soon. When the city is all pointed in the same direction. But right now—"

"I understand," Orvechin said, "your cousin is at the Gownhall."

She went very quiet, very still.

"Shantrov," Aullaime filled in.

"That's the fellow. I've seen him down at the Anchorage often enough. Singing the old songs that you can't fit Pel words to. In the thick of it. And at the Gownhall now, for sure. And *that*'s a boil that's about to burst, one way or another."

"It won't come to that. It's… tense, I know. But the faculty will keep the students in line. It'll cool."

"They hanged a Gownhall maestro and one of the student body," Aullaime noted.

"That they did," Orvechin agreed. "That's a lot of heat for a pot that might or might not have been about to cool." Seeing her ashen, despite her poise. "I don't much rate the scholars for more than hundred-penny words most of the time, but now…"

"What are you *asking*, Orvechin," Vidsya hissed.

"We Wield the Hammer," he told her. "We march past the Gownhall. Show the children there they're not on their own. Show the Pals. Like you say, it doesn't need to come to more blood. But if they see us go past, they'll see just how much blood they'd have to wade through if the shooting started. We Wield the Hammer, and maybe you up here on the Hill could see your way to getting your hands dirty. If not taking to the streets, then sneaking retainers into the Gownhall who can fight. If not men, then weapons, ammunition. There's no grand house within spit of here that doesn't have a stack of batons and tablethi hidden in a cellar or an attic. And if not that… you and I, Lady Sirovar, we both know how it goes when the Hammer's taken up, when the mills go still. How your noble peers, Raven or not, respond when their work doesn't get done. We know your people take to the streets *then*. Spies, provocateurs, threats to workers, threats to families. But this time, it's not about you and us. It's all of us against the Pals. I'm asking you for solidarity. I'm asking you to stop your peers trying all the old tricks to break us up and slow us down. You know how to win a fist-fight, Lady Sirovar?"

"Enlighten me."

"Your man grabs your right hand, you give him your left. He takes that, you get your knee into his progenitors, saving your blushes. You use your elbows. You bite, ladyship, if you have to. Now your Gownhall, what's that? An elbow. We're the right fist, sure enough. But you need to commit your whole body. So the Ravens are the head, you say? Maybe this time at least bare your teeth."

"You've made your point," Vidsya said sourly. "Who'd have thought a millwright would be such a hand with metaphor."

"It's all about assembling pieces into something that does what work you need from it," he said. "You've a lot of strings on your fellows, your ladyship, and we've sent to you because you're best respected of your peers. The only one my people have any faith in. We can't sit in our homes and wait for the next round of boots and batons. We're Wielding the Hammer for Ilmar, and we'd like to believe you in the fine houses remember where your address is located. Because it'd be a sorry page in tomorrow's histories if not."

He drained the last of the tea, pushed the chair back, tried to ignore that Petric had just slipped a silver spoon into his sleeve. "You call on all the contacts you can, inside the Perfecture, your ladyship. You tell them a dozen different ways to back down. But you back us. You let the machines go still and the demons sit idle, maybe even give a statement that you *understand*. Do it, and we'll remember. Take the Pals' side, and you can bet this fine house we'll remember that too."

The Price of Rope

The Old Duke would exhibit the bodies for a twelveday sometimes, but otherwise, relatives or friends would get them back to say farewell in a more private setting than the circus of a public hanging. The Palleseen had retained his method of execution, but didn't hold with sentiment. The furnaces of the Donjon doubled as incinerators. The dead were never seen again. Save in those cases where the deceased was a magician or had been in prolonged contact with the arcane. With those cadavers, the Palleseen reclaimers decanted what puissance they could into tablethi before the fires claimed the rest, a process identical to the way the Hammer District scrapherds dealt with broken goods. Nothing was wasted.

It was the music that woke her. Muffled, distant. The tabor and the pipes and the intricate whisper of the strings. She felt the rhythm of the pavane twitching through each muscle of her in turn, like a faithful dog tugging at her hem. She let it pull her back and forth in the drowning depths of semi-consciousness. It would, she knew, be good to dance. And she knew there were reasons she mustn't. A price that all the dancers paid. But that knowledge was eroding in the ever-changing meter of the music, and she couldn't hold out forever.

And at last, the sway of it pulled her past a critical threshold and the pain made itself known. Her neck, outside. Her throat, inside. Bruised and raw. She jack-knifed up, coughing, each racking shudder an agony as air sawed like sandpaper in and out.

Lemya remembered being hanged. And now she was in a gloomy place. A buried place. A single candle, across a cluttered space. The ground strewn with corpses.

She let out what would have been a scream but came out only as a rasp. Staggered upright – she'd have fallen but the dance caught her, moved her feet *just so*, and she made a graceful half-turn, arms out for balance or for a partner. And stopped, the music receding, the memories encroaching, of where that music came from.

Suddenly very afraid.

The gloom offered the shrouded suggestion of a single door up a flight of stone steps. The candlelight, an island in a sea of darkness, showed her a table, two hunched figures. The light half lit their faces, making them seem piecemeal, half-people.

She chose the door. She chose wrong. She stepped on one body, kicked another, jarred her knees on the steps as she tripped. It was locked anyway, wouldn't even shift in its frame. She didn't have the throat to yell but no matter because she didn't know what might answer. *Am I dead? Is this where we go when we die?* The Mahanic Temple preached that the obedient and meek went to a bright place to be with god. Lemya would be the first to admit she hadn't been much of either. But the unruly and the proud just… went. Fell into oblivion as though death was a trapdoor. But what if there was a dark place below, undreamed of by theologians, where the unworthy dead ended up?

It seemed unreasonable for such a place to hold corpses. What was the point of dying and coming back as a corpse? Also, a lot of unworthy people must have died over the years, and even in the dim light, she was fairly sure there were only five of them.

The closest one, the one she'd trampled, was Ivarn Ostravar. As she watched, he shifted, long face clenching as he moved towards wakefulness. No more a corpse than she'd been. Her mind was still pulling itself together, letting her crawl out of the morass of speculative theology and back into the material world. *Not dead.*

She wasn't dead. They'd hanged her, and she wasn't dead. Nor was Ivarn Ostravar. *The resistance! They saved us!* And she had no idea how they'd done it, but done it they very obviously had. She must be in some safe house, and any moment, someone with a bird badge, a Raven, say, would come through that door and tell her she'd passed. She'd been judged worthy, a patriot, someone who'd give their all for Ilmar. They'd give her a sword and a plan and send her back to the Gownhall to light the first fires of the inferno that would sweep the Occupiers out of the city.

But until then…

She looked towards that solitary candle. One of the figures waved tentatively, and she picked her way over, looking down at the faces. There was Ruslav, and there Yasnic. There was that fierce Shrike woman, twitching irritably. There, one of the Allorwen men they'd brought in shortly before the hanging. And, at the table, the other one. Tobriant the woodworker, she recalled. And, with him, the strange person with the painted face that Ivarn had said was an Indweller.

They had an upended barrel as a table and crates as chairs, and Lemya joined them and croaked her name when it turned out the man had forgotten it.

"Has anyone come?" she asked. Nobody had.

Tobriant had beer. There was a cask of it set out, with clay cups, and he passed one over.

"Helps the throat." He sounded rough, but nowhere near as bad as her. She drank gratefully.

"Do you have a name?" Back in the cells, the Indweller had said nothing, but there had been plenty of others to fill the silence. Now they just stared back, a slight smile on their face as though they'd not heard what was being asked but were too polite to say so.

"You speak Maric?" And Lemya tried Pel, then some halting Allorwen and a few words of Loruthi. The Indweller's smile didn't change. A sense that they weren't *there*, hollow behind the eyes.

Fyon stalked over, eyeing them all suspiciously. Tobriant's offer of beer took the edge off her hostility.

"Your people saved us," Lemya told her. "You're resistance, aren't you?"

It turned out Fyon didn't have people. She had a cause, but like a lot of Shrikes, the bird's wings were just a banner of convenience. She'd got into the Donjon to kill the Fellow-Inquirer, she said. She'd disguised herself as a servant. Plenty of Ilmari worked there. Except they'd picked her up, probably because she made a terrifying-looking housemaid. She had only got near Fellow-Inquirer Hegelsy after she was in chains. And then had been the cells and the scaffold, and now this.

"I'll go back," she said. "I'll find another knife and go back for him."

"There's got to be a better way," Lemya said. "Just random killing, how will that bring about a wider revolution?" Settling in for the sort of argument she'd always enjoyed with other students.

But Fyon just looked at her. "It sees him dead. What else is there?" and that wasn't exactly the cut and thrust of academic debate Lemya was used to.

The awkward moment was lost in the horrified wail from right behind them. Fyon leaped up, smashing her cup against the barrel's rim. Lemya thought it was an accident, but then the woman had a razor shard of it in her hand, ready to cut up the trouble. Except the trouble was Yasnic. He was up, his hands yanking at his wiry hair, actually yelling at the low, shadowed ceiling. She thought he was having a fit, tried to pull Fyon back when the woman stomped angrily over to him. She drew back to slap him, but Yasnic collapsed into her, sobbing into her shoulder like a child. Fyon convulsed and thrust him away, abruptly not wanting to even assault him in case madness was contagious.

Lemya went to him instead, wanting to console him, wanting him to stop making noise in case something bad came. "What is it?" she demanded. "Yasnic, it's me." Now there was sound to give it cover, the music was coming back. It got in through your feet and your ears. It had got into her. A song they'd been playing for generations back within the circle of the firebreak. And so long as the song went on, the party in the Reproach never ended. It was in her like a worm...

"Yasnic!" She shook him. "Talk to me!" Making him her concern and her focus because that way there was less vacant space in her head for the song.

"He's gone!" Yasnic told her.

"Who?" Looking across the remaining, stirring figures. Everyone accounted for, surely.

"God," Yasnic said simply. "They took God from me."

She blinked at him. "What?" But his answer was the same, and all her attempts to characterise it as metaphor withered in the face of his grief. So he *was* mad, then. A quiet kind of mad, until now. And wasn't being hanged a reasonable excuse to escalate your instabilities?

Ivarn lurched over then, and Lemya gave him her crate and got him some beer. He blinked at her, recognised her, nodded. Asked the obvious questions about the where and why of their situation. She confirmed the resistance had rescued them, and he seemed less convinced than she'd have thought.

"Rescued you, I imagine," she added. "The rest of us were lucky we were with you. But it must have been you. Or... Ruslav?" He was with the resistance, wasn't he? But it fitted her worldview far better for Ivarn to have been the catalyst for their salvation. The great man of letters, the authority on Ilmar's glorious traditions. Of course he'd be why they were all still breathing.

Dorae was sitting quietly by Tobriant by then. That left only Ruslav, who sat up suddenly, cursing. Staring at them all with baleful rage.

"What the piss?" he demanded. "Who are—" Memory fell on him like an anvil. "Oh." He accepted her help to get up, took his own measure of beer, the dregs of the cask. Made a rattling sound in his throat. The raw weal about his neck spread into a mottled bruise from chin to collarbones. They all had it, members of a select society. She could feel her own as a quick hot pain whenever the collar of her shirt brushed it, a dull ache the rest of the time. Duller than it should be. Between that and the long sleep, she reckoned they'd been dosed with something. Something that made them appear dead enough, perhaps. And then, between scaffold and fire, they'd been rescued.

She felt a different fire within her. A joy. *This* was how it was supposed to go. The resistance, like an invisible hand moving its pieces around the city. The elegant and daring schemes of its great minds, inexorably undermining the Occupation, until… the *day*! The *uprising*! Victory!

"Damn me!" Ruslav suddenly rasped. "What's that? What am I seeing?"

She didn't know what he was seeing. There was nothing there, for all his eyes were fixed on it. Not his feet, but something beside them. A scuffed space of stone. Ruslav recoiled from it, went to kick out at nothing. Stopped, face suddenly going pallid even in the wan candlelight. He sagged, swayed. She helped him over to a barrel, and he sat down, holding his stomach.

"Oh god," he said. "You fucker, priest. What have you done?"

"I told you," Yasnic said, from close to the candle. "I'm sorry. No violence. I'm sorry."

"Not that, you bastard," Ruslav spat at him. "I mean *him*."

"What?" Yasnic stood.

"Little hairy sod in rags. I'm seeing him, right there. About yea high. Like someone's midget grandad."

"You…" The intense joy on Yasnic's face seemed to brighten the dingy chamber. "That's… God, Ruslav."

"What?" The thug stared at him. "Your god?"

"Well, I mean, technically *our* God. Your and my God. I…" At Ruslav's elbow now, peering around. "I can't see Him. They were going to decant Him. That's what they do, with anything of power. You know how it is. Old wands, magic mirrors, rings of power. Gods. For their lamps and their engines, their instruments and their weapons. They'd have made God into ammunition for their batons, Ruslav. But because of you, He had somewhere to go. You kept Him safe." He seized on Ruslav's arms, practically jumping up and down like an excited child. "Tell Him He can come back, now."

"Tell him yourself," Ruslav said.

"I can't... I can't see Him." Yasnic looked around as though suddenly aware of his audience – and everyone else was watching, with a variety of bewildered expressions. "I always... He was always there. Ever since Kosha died. It's... strange. Not seeing Him."

"Right," Ruslav said, plainly out of patience with the rigmarole. "Sling your hook, you. Back into your priest's pocket, pint-size."

"Please don't talk to God like that," Yasnic said mildly. "But yes, please."

An awkward silence. Even grim Fyon was hanging on every moment of it. Ruslav's face took on a hunted look.

"Piss," he muttered. "He says he doesn't want to."

"What?" Yasnic asked.

"You bloody well get," Ruslav told the ground near his feet. "I'm done with you. Sod off with you." And then he stopped and looked aghast and said, "You son of a bitch."

"Ruslav, *please*," Yasnic said, and then, "But... what did He say to you?"

"Bastard said if I want rid of him, I know what I can do, and he hopes I enjoy being opened up all over again. Grinning while he said it, the little turd. Yasnic, I don't *want* this. Do something." And then he recoiled from his own feet, his features crawling with frustrated rage and revulsion as, presumably, God made some additional demands.

"Says... he's tired of... I am *not* saying this. I won't, I... All right, stop *whining*. Says he's been a burden to you. It's about time you had some of your life back. Is what he says."

"But I... I'm still your priest!" Yasnic, on his knees, trying to find the piece of floor his invisible God was standing on. "It doesn't change anything. And Ruslav isn't... You can't make him live like a priest. He's..." A weirdly prudish moment. "Lusty."

"What's that mean?" Ruslav demanded. "Wait, you can't—"

"Bringing pain into the world in any way," Yasnic agreed. "Which includes *that*. Apparently." The slightest edge of bitterness.

Ruslav looked from Yasnic to God. "What? You never—"

"It's not an uncommon sacrifice for a priest to make," Yasnic said, trying for pious righteousness. "Please come back, now. I'll... get you another blanket. A good one. I'm sure someone has one to give me. I'll find more money. There'll be better food. Please."

Ruslav stared. "So I can still...?"

"You're not a priest," Yasnic confirmed. And then, to the patch of floor, "He's not a priest. He'll do things You won't approve of."

"But when I do, *he*'ll be there watching," Ruslav said, and then once again recalled their audience. "What?" he bellowed. "You never saw a man have a crisis of faith before?"

Fyon smirked, and Ruslav took a step towards her. She stood, more than ready to throw down with him right then. Except he stopped. Tears came into his eyes. "This isn't fair," he muttered, then rounded furiously on the ground at his heels. "He's laughing at me! Yasnic, your god is... nasty. Your god is a nasty son of a bitch. I thought he was all about healing."

"That doesn't mean He's *nice*," Yasnic said, still kneeling, now almost fumbling over the floor to where God had apparently strayed to. "You try healing humanity for centuries only to see the same hurts over and over. He's sick of us, I think."

"I'm sick of him," Ruslav retorted, and then the door opened.

The lamplight from without was blinding, their visitor just a broad silhouette. Then a woman's voice said, "Looks like they're all on their feet, anyway," continuing some conversation nobody had been privy to. "All's clear. You'd better come up."

"Langrice?" Ivarn said.

"The same. But before you start getting all teary-eyed, maestro, I'm just providing lodgings. Come up and meet your benefactor."

And then she was out of the doorway, leaving it open for them to stumble into the glare of one lantern turned low, and then haul themselves in stages up the scale of illumination until they came out into the midnight taproom of the Anchorage. Blinking in the unthinkable radiance of half a dozen guttering lamps. Langrice had retreated to the bar, leaning there with Hellgram at her back. Lemya felt a sudden stab of guilt because, after the man had been knocked aside by their monstrous pursuer, she'd not had room in her head to wonder how he'd done. Better than her and Ruslav was the plain truth.

The taproom itself was clear of patrons, save for one. A solitary hulking figure sitting at a table, watching balefully as they emerged. Blackmane.

They all knew him, save the Indweller who'd followed vacantly along but showed no signs of recognising anything. There was a moment in which he just stared, and people either stared back or avoided his gaze, but nobody *said* anything. Ivarn broke the détente, stepping forwards after a glance to Langrice.

"Blackmane, my dear fellow, you—"

"Later, with you," the big man told him. Perfectly cordial but admitting no negotiation. And then a sentence in fluid Allorwen, that was like Maric with the hard edges filed off, and which Lemya interpreted as: *You two reprobates, come over here.*

Dorae and Tobriant did so, the latter giving one backward glance to their comrades in adversity. They sat awkwardly, chairs somewhat back, a distance between them and their countryman. A little respect, a little fear – a man who'd placed himself half outside his own district and people, and who dealt in questionable things. They spoke in Allorwen, and Lemya's grasp of the language was rusty. Seeing her frown, Ivarn leaned in to translate.

"He's telling them they're dead. Dead as far as the city goes. And I suppose we all are, for that matter. He's—"

"Their families," Lemya filled in. She'd followed that much.

"Yes. They're coming here. And some money. And he'll take the rest for his shop. I'll bet he will. Something about it going to help the others. Hrm." He didn't sound as though he had much faith in Blackmane's community spirit. "He says they need to get out of the city. He... Oh."

Blackmane had brought out a roll of cloth, unscrolling it across the tabletop. Two objects there: string wrapped around sticks and herbs, decorated with trinkets and charms. A prickly incense smell crept into the taproom. For a moment, Lemya didn't understand what they were, but the Indweller twitched, just once, as though the scent had evoked a deep-buried memory.

"Are they...?"

"Ritual wards for the forest," Ivarn confirmed. "Not exactly the finest. Not like the last one I saw." A thoughtful pause. "Enough, perhaps. If the Indwellers will even act as guides after what's happened."

"But they'll be all right now, won't they?" Lemya glanced at their fellow's tattooed face and blank expression. "Now we've brought their kin back."

"I don't know what we've brought back," Ivarn admitted frankly. But then it was plain Blackmane had finished his business with the two Allorwen. They were retreating to another table with the ritual wards. Lemya wondered what it had cost him to get them. Or what Mirror Allor as a whole had stumped up. Because such things were in circulation, but they were vanishingly rare, even the cheap ones. And there were fakes aplenty, although she guessed being fooled by a forgery wasn't likely to happen to a man in Blackmane's trade. And since the things had been aired there had been a tension in the room. From Ruslav. From Fyon. People used to taking what they wanted, seeing a treasure handed over so casually.

"Now," Blackmane said. "Maestro Ostravar, my old gaming

fellow. Let me have a look at you." He stood, shoving the table back to give himself room. Ivarn stepped forwards to meet him, leaving a distance between them.

"I knew you had your tricks, you old sorcerer. I can't imagine how you managed this one."

"Oh, you'd work it out," Blackmane said. He was smiling, but Lemya couldn't work out if it was friendly or not. "I was saving something for that one time it wasn't your fun and games saw me on that scaffold."

Lemya blinked at that, unsure what he meant.

Ivarn just faced up to it, gestured at Dorae and Tobriant. "You and I are alike. We both hold our communities sacred, do we not? I will go a long way to preserve the history of my people, their artifacts and treasures. I'm sure you'd do the same for yours." He was taller than Blackmane. The other man was far more massive, but he still had to look up.

"Well then, I hope you don't mind one of those priceless treasures being spent to buy you breath for those fine words, maestro," Blackmane said.

"You rescued us through the relic trade?" Ivarn asked, amused.

Blackmane's smile widened, though its precise character remained obscure. "Oh, a very precise and specific application of it, my friend. A very particular collector. The one man with the skill and the opportunity to make certain *modifications* to the mode of execution, so that you could be hanged, and yet not to death."

Ivarn touched his raw throat. "He cut it close then. Hoyst, the executioner?"

"My old friend Hoyst," Blackmane agreed. "Always happy to see me. He and I are very close these days, thanks to you. And what I had, he couldn't resist. He is a scholar of his profession, after all. And I laid hands on the very rope the Pals used to hang the Old Duke."

"I would... not want to handle that," Ivarn mused. "The curse..."

"Oh, it's absolutely crawling with the curse," Blackmane agreed. "A death, a curse, an unrequited vengeance. I handled it with leather gloves and still it brought me over in chills. A most puissant artifact, albeit of interest only to very specialised buyers. I dread to think what Hoyst will do with the thing. Make a shrine and worship it probably. Perhaps Ilmar will see a new god of neck-stretching in a few years, eh?"

"That is something not to be thought on. Still," Ivarn went on. "It was good of you, to make this gesture. Our old acquaintance."

"Hmm," said Blackmane, cocking his head to size up the academic. "As to that, yes. Where is it, Ivarn?"

"Where is what?" And Lemya could hear the instant evasion in her mentor's voice.

Blackmane's smile was abruptly not cloaked at all, but a predator's bared teeth. He lunged forwards, very fast for so big a man. He had Ivarn in his grip before the academic could dance away, hoisting him clean off his feet and then bringing him down into a tabletop so hard the wood flexed like a wave.

"Where is it, Ivarn?" Blackmane shouted. "The thing you took! The thing you *promised* me. You *know* what!"

"You didn't—the Pal woman died!" Ivarn got out, fighting Blackmane's hands at his throat. He kicked at his attacker, got a knee up under the pawnbroker's gut that did absolutely nothing. Lemya rushed forwards, but Dorae and Tobriant stood as she did so, mutely backing their countryman. And of the rest, Langrice was still leaning on the bar as though a senior scholar wasn't being throttled right there in front of her, and nobody else was intervening. It was between the two men, old scores nobody else had the right to interfere in.

"You'll lawyer me, will you?" Blackmane roared. "I have you here for one reason only, Ivarn. That you pay your debts. You live because you have a thing I want, that you have no right to. It's not one of your 'artifacts and treasures'. It's a Pal thing. But I will have it from you. You'll tell me where you stowed it. Because the Pals went through your rooms at the Gownhall and broke every case and tore up every book, and I *know* they didn't find it."

"They..." Ivarn sagged. "They did that, did they? Shrievsby, the swine. Damn it."

"Every last valuable stolen, every vase smashed, every picture ripped from your walls," Blackmane confirmed. "So where did you hide it, you old fraud?"

"Stop it!" Lemya shouted at his broad back. "You can't talk to him like that! He's a great man!"

Blackmane looked over his shoulder, not releasing an inch of his grip. He stared at her as though one of the chairs he'd overturned had piped up with a complaint. He didn't even recognise her. Not as the student who'd come to him on Ivarn's errand, not as a human being at all. She'd won a moment's respite for Ivarn, though. And a silence for the room, waiting.

"They didn't find it," Ivarn said, grimacing, "because it wasn't there. It wasn't there" – a deep breath – "because I never had it. I thought... well, when I sent this girl as my messenger to you, I half expected you to laugh in her face and tell her it was already in your possession."

Blackmane stared into his eyes as though hunting down the least flicker of falsehood.

"You don't," he said at last, "*have* it."

"I never did," Ivarn confirmed. He'd completely relaxed now, accepting that, if the man was going to beat or strangle him, there was precious little he could do about it. "I was desperate. It was Correct Speech, Blackmane. The *Inquirers*. Lemya, I certainly never meant to put you in danger. You know I didn't mean for *you* to go... there. Just people who were already going and might bring back something that could help me. And now you've *got* me out of there, Blackmane, and you see me for what you've always called me. An old fraud. In this, at least. I don't have it, though I could sorely use it now. I give you all my title in it, as I said. For what that's worth."

Blackmane hunched around him, as though every muscle

was tensed to just tear Ivarn in half. Then it all went out of him, and he straightened up, actually dusting his hands off. "You never had it," he echoed. Disgusted, but Lemya felt it was more at himself than anyone else.

Ivarn sat up tentatively. "Don't think you've wasted your efforts. A debt. I acknowledge a debt. And these kin of yours, you saved. And…" A vague gesture at the others: Fyon, Ruslav, the rest, as though even Ivarn wasn't really sure what they were good for.

"A debt? You? You think I'd take your marker? You've got nothing left, Maestro Ostravar. You're a dead man with nothing but the clothes they hanged you in." Blackmane turned away. "Who has it, or who's sold it, or who's come into possession of it, then?" A complaint aimed entirely at himself. "How many people has it passed between by now, and I've not heard a *whisper* of it. Something you could buy half the Gutter Districts for, and *nobody's* talking."

"Well, there were—" Ivarn started, and Blackmane rounded on him.

"Oh, I know. Don't think I haven't listed just who was there. And I'm following the news of them with *great* interest. As should you." His meaning was clearly opaque to Ivarn, though Langrice nodded.

"Well then," Blackmane said at last. "I have a shop to tend. Some of us work for a living." All that rage creeping back into him like a crab into a shell, until you could see only the very tips of it. He faced the lot of them square on. "You're on your own now. You're all dead. The moment the Pals understand that isn't true they'll not rest. You know how they are with unfinished paperwork." And then more Allorwen to Dorae and Tobriant: telling them to stay out of sight and wait for their people. Telling them, she thought, that he hoped what they had would be enough to get them through the Wood, when it next opened.

And then he was turning, shouldering through the door and

out of the Anchorage, leaving a Blackmane-sized silence in his wake.

Ivarn, aware that there were still plenty of eyes on him, brushed down his clothes. "It's becoming dangerous to be a guest at your table, Langrice."

She gave him an odd look. "More than you know."

"We have to go," said Lemya. Nobody understood her. "To the Gownhall. The students. We have to get you there, maestro."

Ivarn looked at her, smiled uncertainly. "I don't see that there's much to be gained there. You heard the man. All smashed or stolen. A lifetime's worth of curation. My personal collection. And what the Pals didn't seize, I've no doubt my fellow faculty took for 'safekeeping'." He sat on the edge of the table he'd so recently been splayed over. "I need to consider my options. The capital, perhaps. If I can get out of the city the regular way. Or else…" He looked over at Dorae and Tobriant. "Perhaps there's enough of an umbrella for one more."

"No, maestro," Lemya said impatiently. "They need you at the Gownhall. They were up in arms when you were arrested. After they vandalised your rooms, even more. They – we – need you. A leader. Someone to rally around. To show the Pals that they can't just trample over all the glory of Telmark and Ilmar."

She was aware of a definite character to the echo, after that proud declaration. Not the awestruck audience of a master orator but sheer blank bafflement. Ruslav, Yasnic, Langrice, none of them with her.

"We have to resist," she added, in case they hadn't worked that out. "The Occupation. We can't let them run roughshod over our past. You taught me that, maestro."

"Lemya," he said gently. "You understand that we use the word 'Occupation' because that is exactly what they have done. Run roughshod over our past, as they continue to do over our present. You… are old enough to remember this. It isn't ancient history that needs to be taught and interpreted."

"Yes," Lemya agreed. "And we have to drive them out. Out

of the city, and then out of our lands. All the way into the sea and back to their islands. Retake what's ours, maestro! Because I remember when they came and overthrew the Duke, and everyone thought it was out with one and in with just the same. Who cared, back then, that there was a Pal sitting in the Ducal Palace, and not some Armiger? But it's not like that, is it? We buy our goods with Pal coins and in their weights and measures. We pay their taxes and get accused of their crimes. And one day, the Mahanic Temple will outlast their patience, and then we'll only have Pal gods, which means no gods. And one day, it won't just be official business and judicial proceedings and formal proclamations that have to be in Pel, but it'll be all the books in the schools and all the trade in the marketplaces and then even the thoughts in our heads. They'll take away all we have and melt it down for its gold and its magic, and then we won't ever get it back. The last person who remembers who we were will die, and then we'll be gone. We'll be Palleseen, and perfected. We'll just be more of *them*. And so, we *have* to resist. We're ready to resist. We, the students, the Gownhall. We're waiting for you to come back and hoist the banner, maestro!" Hearing her voice ring back from the walls, feeling her heart soar. Hearing that music loud at her back, the horns and trumpets of another age. Because the denizens of *that* place were many things, but they were Ilmari too.

Ivarn's eyes were wide. For a moment, she thought she'd lit the flame in him. But then he said, "You're mad, girl. Yes, Ilmari culture. Maric literature. We husband it. We keep it close. We do our best to preserve it. Because if the Pals ever came with a will, what do you think we could do? Their soldiers, their weapons."

"Our hearts!" Lemya cast back at him. "Our courage. They're nothing but hollow men. They believe in nothing; they fight for nothing. Their whole perfection is a nothing! If we show them that we will not be erased, I *know* that they will break. The Turncoats will cast off their uniforms. The people, the Armigers, all the birds, maestro! All of them. But it has to start somewhere.

Somebody has got to tell them *No*, while there still *is* someone. Or else we're less and less until we're gone! Now's the time, maestro, and you're the man!"

"Is that what you believe?" he asked her.

"Isn't it what *you* believe?" she demanded. "I heard it in every lecture you gave, about our history, our poems and songs, our legends."

"Then you heard an echo inside your own head," he told her flatly. "You're mad. Go home. Go back to your farm or village or wherever it is your people are from. Because if you push down this path, you'll earn nothing but a grave, and not a solitary one." And then he shrank back because Ruslav was abruptly looming before him, not quite the great bear Blackmane had been, but not far off. He flinched back from the raised hand, but then the man shuddered and snarled – not at Ivarn but at his feet again, that invisible ball and chain. "Just once!" he demanded – begged, almost. And then, turning his back, "Yasnic, your god's a bastard!"

The priest just hugged himself, looking utterly bereft. Ivarn abstracted himself from Ruslav's shadow and said, more gently, "Go home, before you just make things worse."

Lemya looked at him, and swallowed. Her mouth opened a couple of times as the words got drowned on their way up. But she wouldn't give him the satisfaction. *I went into the Reproach for you.* And he'd just say he hadn't asked her to and tell her she was a fool.

"I'm going," she told him icily. "I know my duty to my country and my people. I will go to the Gownhall and stand alongside my brothers and sisters. For Ilmar. Against the Occupation. Because someone has to."

Ivarn's look seemed to suggest that *No, nobody had to*, but she shrugged it off and turned to bid a bitter farewell to the rest of them.

"I'll go with you." Ruslav looked daggers at Ivarn. "I'll… I'll help. I'll find something. I'll build a barricade. You'll let me do that, you hairy streak of piss? I'll help you, and that artist boy, right?"

"Thank you," she said, and then Yasnic was shuffling forwards. She wanted to tell him he didn't have to, but of course it wasn't out of any obligation to her. Ruslav was taking his god away from him, and he couldn't bear to be parted from a divinity he couldn't even see any more.

And one more. Fyon, the Shrike. The murderer. Lemya looked into her eyes and saw that, of all her varied audience, *this* was where her words had landed.

"You're going to fight the Pals?" Fyon asked her.

Lemya nodded.

"Good. You, barkeep. Got a knife?"

"And cloaks or something." Ruslav picked at the shreds of his shirt.

"Anything else?" Langrice asked sourly, but she waved at Hellgram. "Go get the lost property."

This turned out to be a big trunk that the foreigner lugged into the taproom. It was full of clothes, mostly poor quality and cut, but all manner of styles, even a Turncoat's jacket. More than a few had rust-brown stains and suspicious holes.

"Sometimes the customers leave things," Langrice said, deadpan. "We collect them up, in case anyone comes back for them." And this was the Anchorage, after all, on the very shores of the uncanny. Who knew what was possible?

They found enough clothes that halfway fitted, enough hats or hoods to go around. Ivarn watched sourly, sitting at the table where Blackmane had almost murdered him. At the bottom of the trunk was a miscellany of pipes, tools and short blades. Fyon took a knife for each hand, and Lemya took a single wicked-looking stiletto. God's two chosen abstained, one willingly and the other with a lot of scowling looks. With that, they were ready, and with a half-measure of night left before the sky lightened, they took their leave.

Evidence

Companion–Monitor Estern. Companion: reflecting his middling to low standing in the Palleseen hierarchy. Monitor: reflecting his being listed within the School of Correct Conduct, one of the five fingers of the Palleseen hand that was slowly clenching around every part of the world it could get purchase on. A greying man, his hair and everything else about him. More than happy to have his little fiefdom within the Donjon carry him over to retirement. Which is why today came as such a shock. Today started very badly for Companion–Monitor Estern, and became considerably worse when Fellow–Inquirer Hegelsy took a personal interest. Fellow: meaning he outranks Estern. Inquirer: meaning he brings down the menace of Correct Speech, the thumb that has the authority to rap all the other knuckles.

Estern was shifting from foot to foot like a man with an urgent appointment with the privy. Hegelsy didn't care. The Companion-Monitor was one of Culvern's long-time appointments here in the Impounded Evidence Office of the School of Correct Conduct. It was a job with almost no responsibilities, other than not losing the keys, and plenty of pay and status. Time the man was taken down a peg or two.

The Impounded Evidence Office had been raided overnight. Raided with extreme prejudice and by uncertain means. Estern had not lost the keys, though Hegelsy was considering summoning the man for enhanced enquiry procedures, just to restore some much-needed diligence and discipline. The door hadn't even been locked, for the very good reason that some of Estern's people had still been working there. None of them was in a position to explain what had happened.

There were two new Monitors there now, carefully going through all the accumulated miscellany of goods and gear confiscated from everyone who got brought to the Donjon. There was a lot of it. Some of it dated back to the earliest days of the Occupation. Hegelsy had an itch that told him he could narrow down their search, though.

"There was a fog," Estern explained. "I saw it myself. I came down that corridor there, from the... from the refectory." Meaning the man had been fixing himself a midnight snack and doubtless not recording it against his resources docket. "And there was this, well, I thought it was smoke. But I couldn't smell any smoke. And so I had to go and look, of course." Plumping himself up, trying to be the *conscientious* Companion-Monitor. "And the door was shut, and I called, and nobody answered. And there was this mist. Just, fading away. And when I opened the door, the room was full of it, but by the time I got back with reinforcements, it was mostly gone."

Hegelsy wanted to make some jibe about needing reinforcements against the weather, but there were bodies on the floor, and so perhaps that had been a fair call on Estern's part. Two bodies. Not dead. The Companion-Archivist who'd examined them said they were breathing, physically healthy, not asleep, not even unconscious, exactly. A whole tableth's worth of medical instrumentation said their minds had just been emptied. Nobody had devised a rod that let you *read* someone's thoughts – how useful that would be to Hegelsy's people! – but just knowing if the mind was there was a longstanding side effect of various other tests. Here, it was absent. The mist had wiped both of them clean.

"This third," he prompted.

"Cohort-Monitor Riggel, magister."

Hegelsy considered how close 'Riggel' was to the Maric verb for squirming, and decided it was just as well the woman had been tucked away here off the streets. Except, now she'd vanished. Oh, there was a search underway, in case she'd demonstrated hitherto unevidenced skills at stealth and evasion, but he'd already run through the routes from this room and the time since anyone had last seen her. It didn't seem likely.

"Check the effects of the most recent prisoners under my authority," he told Estern's people. They paused, looked from their direct superior to everyone's worst administrative nightmare. Estern wasn't exactly going to kick up a fuss about demarcation, though, and nodded. They paged through the lists of their holdings, until they came to entries where the ink wasn't quite so dry. He had already spotted Ivarn Ostravar's Gownhall robes over in the racks, and watched Estern's people migrate over there and check. Because the oddest part of this whole incursion, after the mist and the mindless bodies, was all the things that hadn't been taken. Impounded Evidence had a lot of valuables, although Reclamation eventually got anything which held power that could be squeezed out. A resistance adherent here could have got away with a lot, or just set the place on fire. And they hadn't.

Estern's people found one thing that had been taken. And although they'd still have to go through absolutely everything else to tick the proper boxes – a tedious process Hegelsy had no intention of denying them – he reckoned that was it. A very targeted theft. The Indweller's mask that they'd taken from the creature they'd arrested at the Anchorage. The one that had presumed to lay down the law to the Palleseen Sway. And he'd had the creature hanged with the others, as per Culvern's orders. And now something had come and mind-murdered two people and vanished a third, and all they'd taken was the mask.

We should burn the grove, he knew, but that wasn't policy. There were far too many armchair perfectors back on the Archipelago salivating about new lands to bring the Sway to, just like the late Sage-Archivist had. And now the Indwellers had effectively declared war on them. Who knew what would come out of the woods next? An army of monsters? A mind-destroying fog that would cloak all the city and put the Reproach in its shadow? Some horror nobody had ever encountered before?

The next morning, first thing, he summoned two of his peers. Both the senior heads of their Schools within the Perfecture of Ilmar; both mere Fellows, like him. Neither of them particularly Culvern's creatures – hence the lack of promotion. Fellow-Monitor Brockelsby, Estern's superior, was pouchy and sour, condemned to disfavour in a provincial backwater when Hegelsy knew he had familial ambitions back home. Fellow-Broker Nisbet of Correct Exchange was a woman so thin she seemed almost two-dimensional, pale and sickly looking. She had risen to her rank without any connections at all by being meticulous and pedantic and very hard-working, and her career had then stalled because those traits were all very well in a subordinate, but nobody wanted her in a high enough position to look over their shoulders.

"I can't help noticing we're two Schools short," she said. They were in Hegelsy's own office, a place nobody much wanted to receive an invitation to, given Correct Speech's correctional mandate. That they'd come so early and so readily, without any interdepartmental games, suggested they had more than half an idea what he was about.

"As for Erudition," Hegelsy said, "they're still in a mess after Ochelby." He had to stop because Brockelsby apparently considered that funny, though from Hegelsy's perspective it was lamentable. "And Appreciation, well… I wanted to talk this over with my peers before considering whether we should trouble the Sage-Invigilator."

He had their attention. Possibly because they were weighing up how much they could sell him for, should he start talking open insubordination. Which he was about to.

"You're aware I have people currently committed around

the Gownhall, with Culvern's blessing." Bringing their mutual superior down to earth by invoking the man's name instead of his rank.

"Aware but not sure what the *point* is," Brockelsby complained. "Just let them tear their robes a bit. It'll go away. It always does. Students." The derision of a man not fond of books.

"That is a common opinion across the Perfecture," Hegelsy agreed. "Now, Nisbet, if you would recount for our colleague's benefit what you told me yesterday. When you asked me to redeploy those troops elsewhere."

"Ahem. Yes." Nisbet looked as though she wanted to consult her notes of the meeting so as not to misquote anybody. "My informants within the banned labour associations known as Siblingries tell me they are about to 'Wield the Hammer'."

"Smash the mills?" Brockelsby asked, frowning. "Well then, you *should* redeploy. We can't have that kind of vandalism. You know how much this city needs to export to keep them happy back home."

"The Maric workers' saying translates as 'the most effective way to wield the hammer is to stop using it'," Hegelsy explained patiently. "It means they'll down tools."

"Well, that's almost as bad. Put in a request for my people to go down there and break heads. Culvern'll approve it."

"I have no doubt he would. *Eventually*." At that point a junior aide came in with steaming kava and vineroot biscuits, the one a vice from home that Nisbet prized, the other an imported luxury from elsewhere in the Sway that was a favourite of Brockelsby's. An interdepartmental peace offering. "They will march, according to Nisbet's informants. That's how these things go, apparently. When they don't work, they don't just sit idle. They take to the streets and make sure everyone knows they're not happy. According to our information, they'll likely march all the way up to the gates of the Gownhall."

"Where your soldiers are," Brockelsby noted, spraying crumbs. "Convenient."

"Where the students are," Nisbet said. "So that they can show solidarity."

"Hrmm." And even Brockelsby was getting it by now. "Your own informants… Who else is in on this?"

Hegelsy shrugged. "I'm sure those treacherous rats up on the Armigine Hill are waiting for their moment to swoop in and taken credit, raise bird flags over the spires of the Gownhall. And as for the rest, they're a murderous rabble always after an excuse for civil disobedience, aren't they? And my people will be tied up making sure none of those excitable students spill their ink. I wouldn't give much for your regular patrols anywhere west of the river. And there's more. The Wood."

Brockelsby sighed. "We should—"

"I know, I know, and I'm very much of the same mind. Have you read the reports from Impounded Evidence?"

Likely those reports hadn't even reached Brockelsby's desk yet, and the man wasn't exactly a quick reader. Hegelsy sketched out what had happened on Estern's watch. He didn't even need to exaggerate.

"The first move along a new front in our war with this city. With a dangerous new enemy. We have a watch on the Wood now, but it's just a single squad. Since the Sage-Archivist stirred them all up, we could be facing *anything*. So, from where do we pluck this additional force, to guard against that? From the troops we'll be using to bottle up the students? From those who will be putting out fires in the Gutter Districts? Or those confronting these workers and their odious demands? And, when we're stretched so thin on all these fronts, *that* is when the rest will decide their time has come. It's been three years since we liberated this city from its own foolish ways. They've forgotten the order of things. They are going to undo all the careful steps we've taken towards perfection. Unless we act swiftly and decisively."

"Sage-Invigilator Culvern—" Nisbet started.

"Is distracted," Hegelsy said. "His… affliction consumes him.

Not just his body, but his mind. We all know this. I'm not saying… well, perhaps I *am* saying he is not fit to make the appropriate decisions in this moment of crisis. Culvern prevaricates. He is not well. The thought of making hard decisions pains him. It is on our shoulders that this responsibility lands. Leave it to Culvern, and the city will be overrun before he gives the order."

"I see why this is such a select meeting," Nisbet said primly.

"You want our complements to reinforce your own," Brockelsby said heavily. "Our people on the streets, without proper authorisation."

"To save the city from itself," Hegelsy confirmed. "As for authorisation, the Perfector's most recent orders to me permit 'Further force in response to action from the citizenry'. I think we can agree that's what we're seeing. And I will take full responsibility. You'll have that in writing."

Nisbet's lip curled. "Meaning you'll take the pat on the head if this goes well."

"And the fall if it does not," he said, like iron. "And if – *when* – we re-establish proper discipline and control over this city, your names will be appropriately flagged within the minutes of the action: instrumental in preserving the Perfecture and the Sway."

"Do I take it you have some Sage-Inquirer's robes already picked out?" Brockelsby asked acidly. "And perhaps a half-written speech for when you accept the Perfector's seat here."

Hegelsy's smile was knife-blade thin. "Should the Temporary Commission see fit to so honour me, I will of course have a mind to the promotion of my fellows who have shown themselves capable, dedicated and efficient in times of crisis."

And, simple as that, he had them. Just so long as the city didn't boil over before he put everything in place.

The Day Gets Only Worse

Ivarn Ostravar. A shadow of his former self. Still in the shirt and breeches they hanged him in, gingerly fingering the weal about his throat and wondering what kinds of high collars he's condemned to, to hide it. Will he be able to secure a position at some seat of higher learning in the capital or perhaps southern Mahamar? Or will it be a schoolteacher's stipend for one of Ilmar's great scholars, or private tutor to some Armiger's brat? And eventually, someone would recognise him and recall he was supposed to be dead, and then, perhaps the boot at the door. Another high collar for him, and this time one he couldn't take off at the end of the day.

The Divinati girl, Jem, had brought him tea. Not even good tea. And he didn't much like the way the big man, Hellgram, stared at him. The foreigner with his narrow eyes and bony face. The two Allorwen stared too, when they thought he wasn't looking. The only one not deeply interested in him was the unmasked Indweller he'd shared Hegelsy's cells with, their slight smile no more than wallpaper over a void.

Langrice had them all down in her second cellar again. Above them, the early evening of the taproom was subdued, plenty of drinkers but nobody boisterous. Hard drinkers drinking hard against a backdrop of the city holding its breath. No students, he guessed. No academic hedonists out on the razzle and still burning the oil left over from the night before. He wondered if Ilmar's tavern trade would survive.

He wondered what would survive.

Langrice came to check on them. Sat herself down with a mug of something hot that smelled proof enough to catch fire at room temperature. Ivarn shied away from her.

"You too?" he demanded.

"What?" With that nasty half-hidden smile the woman was prone to.

"I taught them better than that," he told her.

"What are you blathering about?"

"The distinction," he insisted. "Between stories and reality. The things that happen in books. The way life is."

Langrice gave him a measured look. "That right?"

"I am a maestro of the Gownhall."

Her look suggested it wasn't worth as much as he thought.

"I am a custodian of Maric culture," he said. "Without people like me we'd live like travellers in a fog. Our footprints lost to us the moment we moved forwards. Where we came from, erased."

Langrice made a sound. Neither positive nor negative, just a grunt to show she was in some way part of the conversation.

"But you don't save the past by burning down the present. You save it by preserving it. Keeping it safe. Burying it, hiding its light, if you need to. Until it's safe to bring it out again. You *compromise*."

Another noncommittal sound.

"Will you *say* something?"

"Old man, I don't know who you think you're having this argument with, but it isn't me." Langrice got up. "Let me know when you've worked out when you're going, and I'll mark up your bill."

The sight of her heedless retreating back incensed him.

"That's it for you, is it? Coin? Nothing of the city, nothing of what you were born to? You're a fit custodian for this place!"

She stopped, turned lazily. Her gaze told him she knew exactly who she was, and more: she knew who he was. She exited without a word, leaving him in the centre of the cellar, shaking with undirected rage. The gazes of Tobriant and Dorae bore into his back.

He rounded on them. They were, after all, Allorwen – didn't even belong here in his city. He could safely give them the edge of his tongue, they who were more wretched than he.

There was a curious haze between them. For a moment, he thought one of their fitful candles had set something alight. Or was it some Allorwen sorcery…? As though the very fog he had conjured in metaphor was rising up for real between the flags of the floor.

The two Allorwen had noticed it as well. He saw their wide eyes through the murk. Not their doing.

The Indweller had stood. Their eyes were unseeing. Their mouth opened, and one hand reached halfway out as though expecting someone to take it. Then all animation went from them again. Whatever was here, it wasn't here for them.

"Where is it?" a voice hissed.

Ivarn turned. A man was there, who hadn't come through the door or down the steps. A skinny little man half lost in a fur cloak. About his neck, a wooden mask. Upon his face, a dreadful, tortured look; each muscle of his expression pulling against the rest. And despite that, a face Ivarn had seen before.

He had a knife, and there was dried blood spattered across the robes he wore, sticking the tangled strings of amulets and beads to his chest. His eyes were wider than should have been possible, and never still.

"You were there," he said, his voice jagged as a sawblade. "You took it. What did you do with it!"

Ivarn held out his hands. "I don't know what you—"

"My *treasure!*" the man howled and leaped. He had Ivarn by the shirt with his free hand, whirling the scholar around as though they were dancing. His thin frame was grotesquely strong. And Ivarn knew him then. The Heron from the Game.

"I haven't got it!" he managed. "Please, I never had it! It was just to trick Blackmane!"

"You're lying!" the man shrieked at him, raised the dagger, then convulsed away from Ivarn, clutching at the mask about his neck. "No!" he hissed. "No, I won't; you can't make me! I won't do it!" Speaking to nobody.

"Listen to me." Speaking with all the scholarly authority he could muster, clutching for the man's name but unable to remember it.

"Shut up!" And it wasn't clear whether the Heron was talking to Ivarn or the unseen interlocutor. "I can't hear myself with all the whispering!" For a second, he stared into the scholar's eyes with a desperate, naked pleading. "It's getting stronger," he said. "It won't let me go. I need *it*. I need protection. I made a terrible mistake. I'm being hunted by, by... and it's right here! It's with me, and I have to... *Where did you take my treasure!*" And without transition, he was at Ivarn's throat, the blade raised, lips so far back that Ivarn could see not only teeth but all his gums.

Then the Heron was across the room – not of his own volition but because Hellgram had thrown him there. He bounced off the far wall and came straight back, knife first and face knotted into a paroxysm of fury. "I need it back!" howled from deep within him without the apparent intercession of lips or tongue. "Shut up! I won't! I need it!"

Ivarn squawked and fell over backwards. Hellgram had left the door above open when he came down to see why their hidden guests were making so much noise. The scholar bolted for the stairs, feeling the cold wind of a knife strike at his back. Then Hellgram and the Heron, wrestling over the blade, cannoned into him, spinning him round and slamming him down against the edges of the steps. Ivarn cried out and covered his head. A wild flourish of the blade nicked his forearm. Then Hellgram bunched his limbs like a spider and threw the Heron off, grinding Ivarn further against the hard stone.

The madman howled, appallingly loud in the close quarters. One hand raised the knife to hack down, but the other was wrestling with the mask, as though trying to hold it as far away as possible without actually taking it from around his neck. Hellgram had something out from a pocket that gleamed between his fingers like a glow-worm. With a series of swift motions, he drew something in the air that glimmered, silver-green and side-on to everything else in the room in a way that hurt the eyes. The Heron screamed at it, stumbling away.

The fog, which had receded, was abruptly back in force, seething in from beyond the walls. And then clearing, as if Ivarn's eyes had misted and he was blinking them clean. The ugly, wire-sharp sigil Hellgram had drawn pulsed and faded and was gone, and the world was better for it.

Foreign magic, Ivarn thought. *Something from beyond the Wood.*

Hellgram turned. A feeling human being would, Ivarn felt, have helped an injured man up. The foreigner just stared at him as though not sure why he was even there. No human warmth or contact.

Langrice appeared in the doorway. "What in the Realms Below is going on here?"

"The Heron." Ivarn sat up, feeling a corrugated pattern of bruises all the way up his body. "He was here, by magic. He tried to kill me."

"He came in mist," Hellgram said, and that seemed to mean something to Langrice.

"He wants his trinket," Ivarn moaned. "How many people do I have to tell that I don't *have* it." He quailed before her stare. "I *don't.*"

"I hit him with a Forbiddance," Hellgram said matter-of-factly. "But it won't hold long. He's not of the Wood, nor of here, nor anywhere."

"He's going to come *back*?" Ivarn demanded.

Hellgram just looked at him.

"I can't stay here," he told them. "He knows where I am now. I have to go."

"I'm not stopping you," Langrice said. "Only, I thought you didn't have anywhere."

There was only one place that would shield him, Ivarn knew. Oh, he could flee the city, for sure. Or try to. There would be Palleseen eyes at every gate, and he had been very publicly executed just a day or two ago. He had always prided himself on the distinctively aristocratic lines of his face, how he dominated a room or a debate. His august presence. If they took him again and threw him in a cell he couldn't run from, he might not even live long enough to get killed the legal way.

His own rooms and prized possessions were gone, but the Gownhall was a great store of history, much of it still steeped in old power. He could think of half a dozen relics of Maric pedigree with protective enchantments. Wards and armours and banners. There were people there who'd help him. His students, his peers in the faculty. And he could talk them out of whatever foolishness they were about and turn them to the far more important task of hiding and protecting *him*.

"I have a duty," he told Langrice, drawing all his old dignity around him, "to my fellows. To my city. My voice is needed. I have languished here long enough."

Her look suggested she saw through him as though he was no more than the evaporating fog, but she called for the lost property trunk when he asked. He walked out of the Anchorage in a borrowed cloak and scarf and shoes and set off across town for the Gownhall, trusting to the gloom of evening to hide him.

He skulked through the Gutter Districts, seeing far too few people on the streets. A boon for a fugitive in hiding, but still it spooked him. There was a silence in the air that he – a man used to more salubrious locales – did not identify as an absence of distant thunder. The mills had stopped.

There were Pal soldiers standing idle on the far side of the Portbridge. He stopped for a moment in the shadow of an alleyway, wondering if he could cross elsewhere. He tried south along the river, because there were always boats shuttling between the factories of the Hammer Districts at all hours. Except now, apparently. And at last, the echo of the stilled factories made itself known to him. No crowds, not yet, but clusters of working men and women in the streets, talking. Staring at him, the interloper from another stratum of life entirely, as if he were foreign as Hellgram. Angry looks, suspicious glares, as if he was a spy. In some factories, he could hear a great susurrus, as of packed meetings of robust and discontented people. Ivarn was a man who'd lived within the shelter of the Gownhall much of his life. He had a terror of the mob, and what he heard in the echo of the stilled factories brought torches and clubs to his mind. He retreated along the banks until he was at the Portbridge again.

And would he go north to the old Rathbridge? A long detour through increasingly impoverished and dangerous districts until he walked in the very shadow of the Reproach. No. He would cross here, his walk brisk and casual, a man who had every business being there.

And the soldiers watched him pass, a dozen of them, but their concern wasn't with any one man, right then. They didn't even stop him. *And better here than at the Gownhall, surely. Let them keep their vigil.*

But there were soldiers at the Gownhall, too. He didn't even see them. He was in sight of the familiar gates, his home, his sanctuary, with the last gleam of sunset. Though his feet were rubbed raw in his borrowed shoes, he actually broke into an arthritic run. There were faces at the windows there, peering out. They'd see him. They'd open up for him. He was practically waving. *It is I, Maestro Ostravar! I have returned in your hour of need! I bring wise counsel!*

And then the arresting call in Pel. "Halt! Present yourself for inspection!"

He made two mistakes, firstly to run faster, and then to stop. Because he was a fugitive and simultaneously an orderly man who had confidence in law and reason. Making himself instantly suspicious in the eyes of the soldiers, and then allowing them to catch up with him.

He abruptly had a semicircle of them around him, the

charcoal uniforms of the Pals and the light grey of their Turncoats. A Statlos was staring at him, demanding his papers. Which, of course, Ivarn didn't have. They didn't tend to furnish you with identification at your own hanging. It was assumed that everyone involved was sufficiently sure of who you were.

"You need to let me into the Gownhall, Statlos," he assured the man. "I'm just in time to prevent a great foolishness. Believe me, I can get everything calmed down in there. If you'll just let me in."

"You what?" And Ivarn had made sure to use the most exacting Pel, but from the look on the man's face he might as well have been speaking High Arcane Divinate.

"I appreciate this is unorthodox, but you'll be aware the student body is whipping itself into a ridiculous frenzy in there. Just in there." *Just twenty paces from the goddamned gates and they stop me!* "Right there. Which is why you're here, of course, Statlos. But I can put it all back in its box, I assure you. They'll listen to me."

And the fatal question, "Who are you, then?" to which he had no good answer. And then one of them, one of the Turncoats, was peering at him, hooking Ivarn's scarf down. The beam of a lantern flashed blindingly into his eyes.

"I know him," the Turncoat said. "He's that Gownhall master. Ostravar. Probably he can talk to them." And the worst of it was, the man obviously thought he was helping Ivarn, and somehow hadn't caught up with recent news.

And for a hopeful second, he thought the Statlos might be similarly ignorant. The officer actually got as far as, "Well in that case," before recollection clicked into place. "Wait, wasn't Ostravar the one they hanged?"

"I'm... his brother." Even as he said it, Ivarn couldn't quite believe himself. *I've become a character from one of those terrible plays.* And he saw that they didn't believe it either, for which he couldn't blame them. They hadn't quite got to the conclusion: *This man is supposed to be dead by judicial decree.* But they were plainly at: *This is suspicious enough to kick up the chain of command*, because the Statlos said, "You'll come with us, then."

That way was cells. That way was noose or knife, and Ivarn knew you didn't get to cheat death twice over. Even once was more than most managed. In that moment, the decision he made, against a life of sedentary scheming and study, was *Flee!*

He ran for the gates, and then he was on his face on the cobbles, a whole new set of bruises across his front to match those Langrice's stairs had imprinted on his back. One of the soldiers had just stuck out a baton and caught his heels with it. It had been that easy to bring all his plans to ruin.

"Right, you." The Statlos stood over him, and he had his own baton half levelled, just enough to be a threat, while making the point that Ivarn was no threat at all. And then they were looking up, recoiling as the Gownhall gates opened and a mob of students surged out.

The soldiers levelled their batons, but to their credit, they didn't just start shooting. Ivarn, on the ground, heard the Statlos demanding that the students back off. Stating that they were taking this man in for questioning. Inventing seamlessly that the fallen academic was wanted in connection with a string of crimes.

Lies, Ivarn thought. *I thought they were supposed to be the law.* A wretched book-bound man's complaint, because the law had always been something that had protected him, or that he'd used to his own advantage. *They're supposed to play fair, aren't they?* And the lies just bounced away, because none of the young bravos who'd sallied forth from the gates were interested in listening to Pel right now.

One of them stood right over Ivarn and cried out to all the world, "It's Maestro Ostravar! He's alive!"

"Back away!" The Statlos, with his baton practically up a student's nose. And the lead student calling out, "Ostravar! Ostravar!" It was one of the Armigers, Ivarn recognised. Shantrov Sirovar. Ivarn always made a point to learn the names of his better-heeled students. You never knew when you might need to solicit a bequest.

He tried to tell them *no*, but he wasn't entirely sure which side he was on right now. There were hands trying to help him up, but *up*, right now, seemed more dangerous than just getting stepped on. He saw the soldiers shoving, the butt of a baton raised to strike. Then the Statlos discharged his weapon into the air, doubtless relying on the crack and sizzle of it to cow the lot of them, mere children that they were.

Shantrov had a sword. It was an heirloom piece, decorated with family arms and Ilmari heraldry. The goldwork gleamed beautifully in the lanternlight. Illegal, of course – not as a weapon but as a piece of the city's memory. The boy had put a point on it, though. It ran the Statlos under the ribs and barely slowed for it. The baton practically hit Ivarn in the face as it dropped from the man's fingers. He had a clear view of Shantrov's expression, ashen with the realisation of what he'd done.

And then it was the scrum, boots and shoes coming down on and around him, so that he just curled up and shielded his face and his belly. He heard a woman scream and another baton discharge. There were three times as many students as soldiers, though. A whistle sounded. Reinforcements would be hurrying over, but not in time to intervene.

Two or three of them helped him up, and he swayed, his aches overlapping from head to toe. The soldiers were running. The soldiers were *running*, save for the Statlos and one other, who were lying in blood on the cobbles. The students were cheering, and some were claiming the dropped batons. A greater roar of triumph sounded from the walls and windows of the Gownhall. Some of them were shouting his name.

Mosaic: Wings

Pull away. Soar on the wings of whatever bird you choose. Carry the word across the city, fleet as thought. The Gownhall flies the banner of the Dukes of Ilmar, the Phoenix of the Kings of Telmark! Your flaming wings carry embers and sparks to the tinder-dry districts of the city! The blood of the Occupiers is shed before its gates! Revolt and uprising! Ilmar forever!

A spark.

Orvechin has been arguing and bullying and shoving among his fellow Siblingry leaders all day. Tomorrow, they march, except everyone had a different route and mood and intent in their heads when the word was used. Only now, when it's almost too late to do anything, does he find that out. Some – those who've had relatives and friends taken up, or lost their positions for agitating, or for whom the straitened wages have bit into who gets fed at mealtimes – want broken windows all the way to the Ducal Palace. Some want peace and banners, saying that the mere showing of their faces will be more than the Pals can resist. Warning how the Pals will answer violence for violence more than the Old Duke did. And a hundred shades between. Everyone must have their say and Orvechin has a headache from people shouting at each other all morning.

And then some apprentice or other runs up shouting, getting caught up onto someone's shoulders, getting passed from worker to worker, until she's set in front of Father Orvechin and

CITY OF LAST CHANCES

the other senior Siblingry folk. Saying that there are dead Pals outside the gates to the Gownhall. Gabbling it so the words come out forwards and backwards. They practically have to shake the apprentice before they understand what's happened.

There was a fight. The students carried the day. Flags like flocks of wheeling birds decorate the sky above the Gownhall. The Pals just look on and wipe their bloody noses.

It's Father Orvechin everyone looks to. There are plenty more voices saying they should parade past the Gownhall gates tomorrow. Show the students what real resistance looks like. Plenty of others saying the march should avoid the square like the plague, and for exactly the reasons you'd avoid the plague. Both voices shout louder now, both causes strengthened by the news.

History teeters on Father Orvechin's nod.

He nods. They'll muster up and show the students the solidarity of Ilmar.

No sooner do they have Ivarn past the gates than the reinforcements turn up, summoned by the whistle. Lemya watches from a ground-floor study window, propped open, as though she's just an inattentive tutee on a summer day. Beside her, Hervenya has adopted a peculiar position, lying at an angle up a bank of cushions laid on a chair and footstool so that barely more than her eyes and the top of her head protrude past the sill. The impression is as if she'd been washing when some intruder blundered into the bathhouse, and she'd sunk beneath the suds to preserve her modesty. The reason for it all is the baton she has levelled out of the window, a gleaming tableth pressed into its slot. Lemya had been startled, on her return, to find more than a score of the weapons in student hands. Not, as it turned out, the spoils of a skirmish with the Occupiers, but a stash some faculty member had been hiding.

Supposedly, Hervenya's family out in the country go shooting birds once a year, and so she knows what she is doing.

Lemya herself has a crossbow, and a long pike taken from the grand ceremonial dining hall they only use twice a year. Emlar showed her how to sharpen it to a proper point. His people are cutlers among other things.

Lemya's people are sheep farmers, which doesn't seem to be overly applicable. Unless you count trying to get large aimless groups from one place to another, which she has been doing.

She hadn't even been part of the group that rescued Ivarn. That had been Shantrov's expedition, and he was a hero now. He'd struck the first blow against the oppressors with his family sword. She'd been in the kitchens grabbing a bite to eat, and by the time she'd run out into the quad, it had all been over. Then the call had gone out that more soldiers were coming. They'd barred the gates, and everyone had taken to the windows or the precarious walkway atop of the wall.

A score of soldiers conspire down there: the patrol that Shantrov had sent packing, plus another. They confer, well within sight of the students. Then another two men turn up lugging a ram between them. For regular domestic doors the nail-shod Palleseen boot would suffice, but for a portal as grand as the Gownhall gate, they have a special tool. That's a Pal trait: they always devise something nasty for any given job. The ram is a metal-shod wooden cylinder with four brass handles and a socket in its fist of a head for a tableth. When they bring it against the gate with the right shout, the magic will discharge and the gate will take the brunt.

Five or six soldiers stay back with levelled batons and the rest just go in mob-handed, ram first. There is very little hesitation or pre-planning about it. They're angry, they're going to teach these students a lesson, and the gate isn't going to be in their way for very long.

Hervenya swears, levels her baton and says the word inscribed on the tableth. It's a Pel word, though, and her Pel is rough, and it doesn't go off, just sparks a little. A handful of cracks sound from nearby windows, and then a return shot strikes dust and stone chips from the wall above them. Lemya hastily copies Hervenya's sprawled position.

The other student is still trying to pronounce the activation word. Lemya tells her to aim, then says it herself, bent close to the little gold lozenge so it can hear her. The explosive percussion of the baton has her leaping back, ears ringing, and Hervenya lets out a surprised cry. For a moment, Lemya thinks she's been shot herself.

"We got one!" Hervenya's yelling, though. Then a glittering bolt passes through the window, over their heads, and obliterates the face of a past Gownhall bursar. In portrait form only, thankfully.

"We got one," Hervenya repeats. And then, "I killed him."

Lemya feels herself teeter on the same abyss. At what point, when her parents had scraped together the fees to get her an education, did she imagine this was what she'd be learning? *For Ilmar!* she thinks, though. "That dead Pal down there," she tells Hervenya, "could have lived and grown old and died in Pallesand, on the Archipelago. He came to our city to make us his slaves. He's his own judge and executioner."

Hervenya looks at her for a moment, then nods. The tableth is a little blackened but still good, high-quality decanting. She levels the baton again.

Below, the soldiers try to get the ram to the gates, because once they're inside, things will be far more in their favour. Someone douses them with a big tureen of what looks like hot soup, presumably whatever had been on the boil at the time, and that scatters them so that they drop the ram. As they come back for it, another two are picked off by baton-fire and crossbow bolt, in among a host of misses. Then a very expensive bottle of the maestros' aquavit goes arcing end over end with a lit rag stuffed in the neck, to explode in flames and sharp glass shards right in their midst. A roar of triumph goes up, that sounds as though the Gownhall itself is exalting. The soldiers hesitate, caught in the open, flinching back from the fire.

The gates open. Nobody will ever admit to it being their idea later. It could have been a fatal mistake on the part of the defenders. The soldiers are thoroughly off their stride, though, jolted out of being the attackers and not at all ready to become defenders. Before they can form into any semblance of order the students are on them, with at least a couple of maestros in their midst. In the vanguard of the charge runs Fyon, the Shrike, with a long knife in each hand, howling for blood.

Lemya knows her moment. She manhandles herself and her pike out of the window. She'd taken a tapestry from one of the upstairs common rooms – not really a flag but it has about a hundred different birds tessellated across it in faded dyes and tarnished gilt thread. She shouts "Ilmar!" and "Freedom!" and waves the flag, and when she finds a panicked soldier in front of her, she tries to get him with the sharp end. The tapestry weighs the pike down too much, and she misses. He's already showing her his heels then, baton dropped so he can run faster. They're all running, weapons left behind. The students swarm out into the square that faces the Gownhall, whooping and cheering and lashing a few barbed insults at the slowest of the Pals to keep them moving. For a moment, after the soldiers have gone, it all seems about to fall apart. As though everyone might just go home now, and in the morning, the whole city would agree never to speak of this again. They look at one another, the thought *What have we done?* bold on every face. And she wants to wave her flag, to give a speech, to lead them in a rousing chorus of *The Peak and the Port*. Not even the obscene student version but the real words, that the Pals banned with so much else. But who is she and who would listen to her?

But she knows who they will listen to. He stands in the gates now, staring out at the raucous students with a haunted look. As though he's about to evaporate like a night-phantom. But Lemya goes to get him, catches at Ivarn's sleeve and pulls him out into their midst. Calls for silence, because Ivarn Ostravar, the resurrected, is going to speak. Is going – she says pointedly – to remind them of who they are. The glory that is Ilmar: its storied history, its pride and its place in the world. Ivarn Ostravar, the patriot, the hero, come back from the dead to lead their city to freedom!

She sees Ivarn's eyes like an animal's in a cage. He's a man tied to a stake with the flames desperate to feed on him, the naked enthusiasm and adoration on all sides. He will either rise to the occasion, she knows, or the moment will destroy him. He'd never have respect again, not of others, not his own.

He draws himself up to his full height, hands held out for quiet. His voice tolls out, that voice she'd loved when it told the epic sagas of their people, the literature, the elegant phrases. And Ivarn is, she knows now, a survivor first and foremost, and so she's put him in a position where he can only survive by clasping to the cause at last. She will make the man a hero of the revolution whether he wants it or not. She'll make him the thing he always held himself out to be, and never really was. She listens as he speaks of glory, eyes glittering with tears of sincerity. Does he truly believe it? She can't know, and it isn't important anymore. His listeners do, as though, from his mouth to their ears, the words enact that greatest of all magic feats and engender something from nothing. Ivarn Ostravar calls out for the freedom of Ilmar and the future listens.

Another spark.

Vidsya Sirovar has been closeted with some select handful of her peers. The messengers, who rode fleet carriages from Gownhall Square far faster than any apprentice's short legs, chased each other about Armigine Hill until she could be located. So prepared and intent on her planning is she, the news of events actually happening comes to her late and finds her

ADRIAN TCHAIKOVSKY

unready. From that moment, though, there is a steady shuttle
of intelligence between the Gownhall and wherever she might
be found. She flits from townhouse to townhouse, speaking
urgent words with those members of the Armiger families who
paint themselves most as Ravens. Who channel family coin into
the pamphlets and ideologues and bribes that make up their
resistance. Junior members, like Vidsya; cadet branches. Those
who love something beyond owning land and buildings and
businesses.

They talk in rapid, worried tones of what it might mean
and where it might go. The latest news from their informants
among the Siblingries, or in the Donjon or the Ducal Palace.
What they should *do*, now this sword has actually been drawn?
They've talked so long about the proper channels of opposition
and overthrow (orderly, cautious), the form a newly established
revolutionary government should take (their guiding hand
upon the tiller), the laws and the protections for old and
valuable things (such as families and estates and bloodlines)
that must not under any circumstances be burned down in the
mad rush to freedom. And now they're confronted with the
match already lit.

Decisions, hasty, not unanimous, are made. Some flee and
barricade the doors of their houses, trusting to nothing but their
own staff. Vidsya continues to receive her spies and messengers
as the first day dwindles into night, and sends messages out of
the city by routes she prays the Pals won't intercept, and tells her
people to ready her carriage.

Ruslav shifts desks and chairs out into the square. It's something
he can do. He can even do it angrily, slam them down so hard on
the cobbles that the wood splinters. He can lift a hammer, too:
nail planks and furniture together with a vengeance. God has no
brief for the wellbeing of woodwork.

Sometimes, God is on the things he moves, standing there like a wrinkled gnome, swaying to keep balance as Ruslav hauls His pulpits about. He tries to dislodge God, but the little creature has the agility of a monkey.

They are making barricades around the square. Ruslav isn't sure whose idea it was, but it seems a good one. If they let themselves get bottled up in the Gownhall itself, it will be rats in a trap when more Pals come. And they're singing and drinking – God didn't mind him commandeering a bottle either – and dancing around. A lot of students have their arms about each other. It's amazing anything is getting done at all. He sees the staff there, too. Old men and women, some of them just standing around aghast, others putting their backs into the work. Some with swords or batons that must have been their own personal property. Others just with reservations.

It's full night by the time a jumble of desks, chairs and cabinets front each approach to the square. Nothing that will hold against a determined assault, by Ruslav's estimation, but it'll give cover and slow a charge. Although, a lot of the students say it won't come to that. The city will rise with them. The word must be racing down every street in Ilmar like wildfire.

Ruslav listens to them talk, exhausted, still drinking. His Ilmar is cellars and backstreets, gambling dens, shaking shopkeepers down when they don't come up with their dues. It's bareknuckle fights and swaggering, boasts and knives and dying young. He's already older than most of the kids he grew up with ever had the chance to get. His Ilmar is the Bitter Sisters and the thing they keep in their pit. These students seem to know a different city, one he'd never had the chance to visit before now.

Then he sees Shantrov.

The youth is being paraded around on the shoulders of his peers. He has on an antique military jacket from before the Occupation, threadbare maroon cloth with the gold frogging and epaulettes coming loose. His sword is in his hand, waving and weaving as though he's trying to fight the sky. Shantrov, the artist. Ruslav feels a strange kick inside him. He'd thought he might try to go find Lemya, talk to her about what they'd been through. The Reproach, the cells, the hanging. God. Because he needs to talk about it and who else is there? Not Yasnic, that long streak of misery, that's for sure.

But here is Shantrov Sirovar, the Armiger. The child of privilege and hero of the hour. They dump him down at last, and Ruslav expects him to rush off and find some other group of students to sing and cheer with. Instead, the youth just stands there, sword a weight at the end of his arm. Head down, looking lost. It's a look Ruslav knows. You saw it in Lodge recruits who'd been through their first harsh initiation. Break a man's fingers for stealing from the cause. Break a woman's windows and counters and spill her goods on the ground before her children if she's been too friendly to the Pals. Beat a debtor, shave a head, dump an informant in the river with heavy pockets and boots. And then, afterwards, you saw them understand the life properly. And some of them passed through that moment in an eyeblink and were fit for that life up until it killed them. Others needed a moment, to understand what they'd done and who they'd become. Shantrov has killed a man. Ruslav, who has enough deaths and beatings on his conscience that he can't even remember the first one, understands.

He goes over. He hadn't known how to approach the man before. Now Shantrov is adrift, and it brings him down to Ruslav's level.

"I know you," Shantrov says, though he had to be prompted for a name. "You went with Lemya into the… that place." A shudder. And he'd wanted to go with them, but at the same time he'd been glad not to. "They hanged you. They hanged all of you."

"They did a crap job of it," Ruslav says. Not exactly the poetry the youth is expecting, but it prompts half a smile. "So you stuck someone, I hear."

Something retreats in Shantrov's face. He nods.

If this had been some Lodge tyro with blood on his hands for the first time, Ruslav would have shamed him for feeling bad, got him drunk, mocked his qualms, told him the victim had it coming. Or given the lad a kicking, failing all else. He sorts through his toolbox.

"Listen," he says. "I'm useless, in this. I can't fight anymore. It's…" God is standing right there, looking smug, and Ruslav won't give Him the satisfaction. "It's a curse." Let Shantrov think it's something he'd brought from the Reproach. Anything better than a bad bargain with God. "But *you* can fight."

Shantrov looks away. "I don't know that I want to. It's not like… you know, stories. Poems. Heroes."

"I saw your art." Ruslav feels that kick inside him again, just thinking of it. "I bloody *loved* your art. That one you did. With the man on the horse with the castle and the moon and thing."

"That doesn't narrow it down much," says Shantrov, with a weak smile. "That's kind of all I do. The maestros despair."

"I don't care." Ruslav is aware he's very close now. God is at his heels, shuffling like a bored child, wanting to go elsewhere.

"Do you want to see my studio?" Shantrov asks.

"Yes."

He watches the student's back, seeing the inturned shoulders, the slight shake and falter. The weight of a dead man slung there still, loose-jointed limbs swinging back and forth. Someone who's never killed before, leading someone who'll never kill again.

And then the studio. A tall room – there are post-holes halfway where another floor had been before it rotted. Canvases hang in patternless profusion all the way to the ceiling, some mostly blank, some pencilled or part-painted, a few complete. Variations on the same scene. That radiant figure, sometimes afoot, sometimes mounted on a horse or some more fantastical beast. The looming castle or ruin or temple. Once or twice, the rolling crests of waves coursing in from a midnight sea. Sometimes the moon, sometimes grey clouds from which its silver light emanates dully. Once – Ruslav feels the colours like a blow under the ribs – the unexpected sanguine of a sunset. Always, the knight dwarfed by the scale of the landscape. Always, he remains undaunted. Every line of him, armour, lance, steed, defiant against the great darkness that crests above.

Shantrov sits on a high stool, watching him, hunched in that ill-fitting military coat.

"The thing is," Ruslav tells him, eyes constantly sliding from him to the paintings, the exposed anatomy of how they come together. "It isn't like that." Meaning the knight, shining in the darkness.

"I know that now."

"It's never like that. Those stories are balls, frankly. Made up so people can pretend their grandfathers weren't bastards. But that doesn't mean you don't have to do it."

Shantrov's shoulders hunch more.

"Listen," Ruslav says. "I killed a man because he insulted me to my face, before my people, and you can't let that lie. I broke Benno's nose because he thought he could push me and not get pushed back. I hit a woman with a chair in front of her husband, because she'd been holding out on us. I opened up an old man after he told the Pals we'd been after him for protection. Which we had. And I had to do all these things. The rules of who I was. They were good reasons to me, right then. You come and tell me I was overdoing it, and I'd have laughed. And then I saw that goddamn picture of yours, and I wanted to be *that*. That son of a bitch on the horse. All gleamy bright. Ready to put that pig-sticker into someone and *know* it was the right thing to do. And I knew I'd never be that, and I'd never been that, and your bloody picture was just showing me how all the times I'd done all those things, I'd never had a reason. Not a good one. Not one to make up for the actual things I'd done. You hear me?"

Shantrov nods, eyes wide.

"You stuck some bastard Pal. Just ran that fancy sword of

yours into his guts and let his life out. And you thought it would be all like these glittery sods, and it wasn't. It was the darkness instead, right?"

Another nod.

"And of course it was," Ruslav says. "Because the sword's only shiny until you shove it into someone. After that, it's messed up like everything else." He pauses. "I had a lesson. I had a point, to all of this."

Shantrov shifts down off the stool, staring at him. "I wanted to be him too." A flip of the hand towards a knight that was half bold argent paint and half pencil-line wirework.

"You killed someone to save your man, Ostravar," Ruslav tells him. "You killed him because he's a Pal and an Occupier, and his people came burning and trampling over it all three years back and never went away. And you're right: it doesn't turn you into your man there on the horse. But it brings you a main sight closer than I ever got. And you know what, I really loved hurting people." He finds the words hard to say. "I used to talk the noble and the honourable, how we had to make people respect us, how it was our right. Like we were the shadow-Armigers, the reflections to all you nobs on the Hill. But it was because it felt good. And now I can't have that. And…" Aware Shantrov is right there, in arm's reach, staring at him with a slight smile. "So long as you don't love it," he finishes awkwardly. "You're him. On the horse. He doesn't love it either. But he knows he's got to do it."

"You're not getting a lecturer's post here any time soon," Shantrov says softly, and kisses him. Ruslav twitches away, more from the sudden jolt of emotion than anything else. From elsewhere in the building, he can hear singing. Celebration, an almost desperate cheer.

Tomorrow's going to be bad. He should go. He's no part of this. He's a neutered thug, of no use to anyone. A dog without teeth.

He lets his hands rest on Shantrov's waist, burrowed under the student's shirt to find skin, the leanness of him. Brings him down among the paint pots and the sacking. Above, the half-made knights keep blind watch.

The word floats over the roofs of Ilmar, touching down, setting things aflame. Like hearts. Or hissing in a brief complaint of steam where it meets those that have no burning in them. Fellow-Inquirer Hegelsy's heart is ice, but he suffers a little heartburn anyway. Midway through his post-supper paperwork – all those warrants and writs and orders of seizure won't just stamp themselves! – one of his staff raps neatly at the door. The people he set to watch the students have been routed.

"Have been what?" he asks blankly. And it is a word in Pel, but not one he ever thought to hear applied to servants of the Palleseen Sway. Perhaps he wants his officer to go away and come back with some other verb more befitting the dignity of the Perfecture. But a second 'routed' joins the first, and then, hot on the heels of that, a new knock. A new staff member, jostling elbows with the first. The reinforcing patrols, gone scurrying to the alarm whistles of the original combatants, have been… Something in Hegelsy's stare forbids the use of the word, for all the second messenger can't even know what's been said. Have been forced into a less than orderly retreat, the officer concludes awkwardly, Pel not being a language well-suited for circumlocution.

Hegelsy feels two wolves inside him. One knows only ambition, the other knows only fear of failure. He has brought this about, but he thought he had more time. Has Brockelsby mustered his troops already, or are they all still scattered across the breadth of the city, because the man won't hurry just because Hegelsy asks it? Has Nisbet called her people from the customs yards and the counting houses and the Ducal treasury, or is she still meticulously completing the orders in her pedantically over-exacting manner? Somewhere, he hears Culvern laughing at him. The reek in his nose is that of disgrace, worse by far than the odour of the Sage-Invigilator.

Word is that the students are barricading Gownhall Square even now. His heart, that icy organ, races fit to fracture. He writes and seals his orders one after another. His hand shakes, and he can't tell which wolf has got its teeth into it.

Yasnic decides he'll leave very quietly, without bothering anyone. Then he has to ask for help to clamber over a barricade, which rather spoils that. But he doesn't feel he can stay.

There is going to be a great deal of violence on the morrow. The Palleseen can hardly let this student insurrection be. It isn't even that he didn't think the students had no chance. There's a whole city out there, and everybody chafes under the Occupation. Perhaps this *will* light a fire to burn the Pals all the way back to the coast. Perhaps the end of the entire Palleseen Sway starts right here at the Gownhall in Ilmar.

But he can't. He's lived his whole life avoiding the brutality that seems so commonplace to everybody else. He's seen people die and be hurt and hurt other people. And sometimes, he's even tried to help, asked them to take God's strictures into their lives. Seen the miraculous healing the divine power could wreak. And then seen it all undone. Within minutes, within hours, within days perhaps. But violence is like a drug. They can't resist it. Eventually the wounds come back. And in the end, he became sick of seeing it. He understood God, earned his place as a priest of the world's least regarded religion. Why heal, if those you heal only turn to their neighbour with a raised fist or a knife? Why help, if all you help is the spread of misery in the world?

Yasnic would have liked to see the faith back when it was stronger, hundreds of adherents, dozens of priests. Most of all he would like to have seen God when God still had hope. When God healed in the belief that healing others would enact a change for the better in the world. Before God became jaded with the constant backsliding of His flock. So that, in the end, He chose this crotchety and senile retirement, clinging on to His last priest and, now, his one unwilling convert. Complaining that He was cold. Sharing the scraps that Yasnic could beg and whine for. Healing nobody for fear those He healed would just do more harm.

Beyond the barricade, he turns to the students. "I hope it all goes well," he tells them. Utterly vacuous sentiments but they seem to take it in good faith. They cheer him and raise bottles. "Healer!" some say. He tries to wave the word away but they won't stop saying it. Perhaps they think he's going to heal the city or something. He has become a sign and portent of some worse or better age waiting in the wings.

He puts the Gownhall at his back and walks off down the street, heading in the direction of the Gutter Districts, the Portbridge, Mother Ellaime's boarding house, all his usual haunts. Feeling the city tremble around him, waiting for what the morning will bring.

After a while, God catches up with him, running until He reaches Yasnic's heels, then matching his pace. God's last priest looks down at Him, seeing the creased and wizened face.

"I thought you preferred Ruslav," Yasnic needles, because he can be mean too.

"He's going to get killed," God says in a small voice. "I don't want to see that. And also..."

"Yes?"

"He was happy. And I was going to spoil it for him. Just sit there and stare, and put him off. And I..."

"Yes?"

"I decided he should be happy. My follower. My convert. Before they come to kill him. So I have come to my priest."

"Yes, I'm very lucky," says Yasnic. He thought he'd be happier, having God back. Things returning to the way they were, and soon enough, the city will get over its current convulsion, and he can creep out and just begin… *living* again. If you can call it living.

It feels to him that there is something more he should do. If not a religious duty – and how could it be, given God is right there and not demanding it of him? – then a wider moral one. Because he likes Ruslav, and he likes Lemya, and he even likes Ivarn a little, and he liked what he'd seen of the boisterous students, and it was all going to go horribly wrong. And he is clear of it. It won't touch him. He and God will be just fine.

"I want a drink," he says, and God agrees that, minor forbiddances notwithstanding, it's a good idea.

Sparks, falling in the Gutter Districts, the Hammer Districts, all that close-leaning housing west of the river where the Pals only go in force. A swarm of messengers converge on the underground Fort where Carelia and Evene make their lair. One by one, gangs and cells and factions, the Lodges and the Vultures, report what's going on in the city above. A patchwork army of the greedy and the dispossessed, the lazy and the desperate and the patriotic. The Vulture has a hundred heads, and many do whatever they want, but the rest look to the Bitter Sisters.

As the Last Calm Night draws in towards midnight, and the city holds its breath, Nihilostes, priestess of chaos, watches all these strands come together. Sees the two near-identical women argue among themselves, and unite against all comers. Feels that something is being forged here, even as the factories go quiet above. Zenotheus, Scorpionfly God of Chaos, seems to crouch at her back, rubbing its legs together in a frenzy of anticipation. She has no idea how much of this she's wrought, and how much would have happened anyway, but she'll happily take the credit.

★★★

"I've lost God," Ruslav says.

"That," Shantrov tells him, "is an odd thing for a man to hear."

There's a moment when Ruslav is going to come clean about God, but given that the divine presence has become an absence, there doesn't seem much point. He lies back on the mound of sacks and books and stolen upholstery that Shantrov threw together. Sure he'd seen this in his future, but with him and Lemya, after his Pursuit had finally reached its desired conclusion. After which, he'd just go whistling off until a new prospect caught his eye, and he began the process again. He doesn't feel the same, right now. It must be the art, all those partway creations of Shantrov's imagination surrounding them. Lending meaning to trivial things, the way art always does.

"What's the hour?" No windows in the studio, just one bluish lamp burning out its stored magic on a wall.

"Small hours," Shantrov says. The student is watching him without expression. He's so young, barely twenty. Ruslav, an old man of twenty-eight, feels ancient.

"I can't fight with you," he whispers. "Tomorrow." And he hasn't explained why, and somehow Shantrov hasn't asked. Just like nobody pressed him on how he wasn't dead despite the fact that some of them – there for Ostravar or Lemya – had seen him dance on air as well. Oh, he waved it away, or made some passing comment about mysterious rescues, but not sufficiently to satisfy even a passing curiosity. And yet they accepted it, because it's a time of signs and portents and miracles. There is a healer in the city who could bring back the dead. The iron rule of the Palleseen can't even be relied upon to get an execution right. No questions, because to pry into the reasons and the logic of it would be to pull the miraculous apart and find, no doubt, the mundane and the reasonable behind it. And there is no give in the mundane. There is no 'perhaps' or 'what if' in it. It hits you, and you take the blow.

What if we win? Perhaps tomorrow will be better. These are the thoughts for which you kept the miraculous in your back pocket. What hope, otherwise?

Then someone's calling Shantrov's name, down the hall outside. The boy twitches, then scrabbles to his feet, pulling on breeches. One of his fellows is at the door a moment later, peering in without knocking and not at all surprised to see Ruslav there.

"Someone here for you," runs the message. "At the gates. Says she's your cousin or something."

Ruslav dresses too, the borrowed clothes he got from Langrice, that weren't slashed to ribbons and covered in his own blood. And he regrets, now, that he left the rags behind. They were relics of the marvellous, after all, for all *that* miracle is going to be short-lived. Because tomorrow the Pals will come, no doubt, and how long can he sit idle for? What will be the provocation, the one that'll make him throw a punch or take up a knife and lunge. And rupture. And restore the rational and the real, even as he dies to the mystically repatriated wounds inflicted by the jaws of a monster.

Because it is night still, and not yet the harsh light of tomorrow, he can laugh.

He knows the woman at the gates. Vidsya Sirovar, last seen across Langrice's gaming table. He hadn't even connected the shared surname.

"What is it?" Shantrov asks her. "Have you brought help?"

"Help," the woman echoes. "I've a carriage past your fellows' barricades, Shantrov. We're going, now."

Shantrov stares at her. "Well, no," he says reasonably. "I'm staying. With my comrades. Tomorrow, we fight."

"Shantrov, what do you think is going to happen, if the Perfecture comes in force?"

"A fight," he tells her. "We fought them already yesterday. We'll fight them again tomorrow. And it won't be just us. The city will rise." He lunges forwards, catching her by the hem of her coat. Ruslav sees the fine satin lining gleam in the lanternlight.

"You know it's true," Shantrov says. "Cousin, I know who you meet with. I know you're not blind to the screw the Occupiers turn on this city. You've been working towards this for years."

She pulls back, looking at the other students and Ruslav as if they, at this extreme, might turn informant. "Yes, I know," she says, exasperated. "Years, as you say. And that's why I need you to come with me, Shantrov. You think we haven't made plans, your kin, the others. I've sent to the estates. Family and retainers are on their way even now. Mercenaries, laid in for this moment. I won't deny we looked for it later, but the preparations were made. And I want you to lead them, Shantrov. I want you to come through the gates with the cavalry at your back. Because the city will need you, after, and so it will need to see you."

Ruslav sees Shantrov's slouch evaporate. "You're serious?" he demands. "They're coming?" And the word is being passed from student to maestro to student. Not just the city, the nation is rising!

"But you have to come now. You've seen all that's happened. I want to you tell it to them," Vidsya insists.

"Ruslav..." Shantrov turns to him. "You should come too." And it's plain Vidsya isn't keen on that, and who could blame her. Who'd want a failed criminal soiling her nice Armiger coach? And he might have said yes, and to hell with Vidsya's sensibilities, except that her words have got to him, too. Miracle words that hold open the gates of hope. Turning the wheel of the world, so that when the sun rises, it will light a transformed landscape where things can be better.

"I've got somewhere I need to go," he tells Shantrov. "I can't fight, but I can help. I have people I can speak to; aid I can bring."

He watches Shantrov leave. Walks with him and the elder Sirovar to the barricade and sees them over it, to where a fine coach is indeed standing, two horses stamping and steaming in the night's chill. They are demon-breeds, he sees, their coats metallic in the wan light, their heads jutting with horns. Nothing will pull as tirelessly.

Before Vidsya's judging gaze, the comrades don't kiss, but clasp hands. Then the two Armigers are climbing in, and the coachman cracks a whip that bears the words of the demon steeds' contracts burned into its leather. The beasts flinch from its touch and then are off.

Ruslav watches until they're out of sight and then makes his own exit. He knows where the Bitter Sisters will be holding court, and he has news for them.

Drinking Alone

There were Allorwen who worked in the factories, who were even then filtering out to the Hammer Districts. There were a few Allorwen students at the Gownhall, mostly not locals. The night after the Gownhall uprising, though, Mirror Allor was strangely calm. The quiet of something that knows it might be prey whichever way things go, perhaps, but also the quiet of a neutral country, or another time.

Yasnic had found a drinking cellar still open, dangling at the very skirts of Mirror Allor on the far side of the Portbridge. He'd scurried in there at first because there had been soldiers. Blocks of them forming up in side streets, individual patrols coming together. A quartet of them had even stopped him, demanding to know why he was on the streets. But he was plainly going *away* from the areas they were interested in, and he'd just told them he was going home. After they'd moved on – just a few shoves and a cuff across the head to remind themselves of who they were – he'd felt terrified of venturing much further. The night seemed to be filling up like a sunken room. There was enough danger to drown in.

And so he found the Pledge, which was a subterranean taproom run by an Allorwen family whose many members rotated shifts behind the bar so it never closed. He slid a single coin over the counter, received a single measure of harsh spirits in return. There were others there. A few quiet locals and more

Marics than he'd have thought, given the hour. The finer clothes of one table identified them as Armigers' servants, probably on their way back from darker pleasures. They were responsible for most of the noise, already quite drunk. Elsewhere, Yasnic saw sombre, serious-looking men and women in hardwearing clothing and overalls. They talked in low voices, scowled, drank and waved for more. Nobody had hailed him out as the miraculous healer. He'd thank God for it, except God was right there.

God hopped up on the tabletop, stuck a dirty finger in Yasnic's cup and licked it. "As a sacrifice," He said, "it's got something going for it."

"It's forbidden." Yasnic wasn't sure why he was reminding God.

"Only to priests," God pointed out. "Do penance later."

Yasnic just stared at the cup. Once he'd drained it, they'd want him to leave. He couldn't afford another. He should have asked for beer, though he couldn't remember actually having a choice about what he'd got. Perhaps he'd looked like a man who needed something stronger.

"I'm scared," he confided to God.

The divine presence looked at him uncertainly. "There, there," He tried. And then, "What do you want Me to do about it? You're out of it. That's good."

"Not scared for me," said Yasnic, though he was. He always was, honestly, at some baseline level. "Ruslav, Lemya, the others. You know Ruslav. Your follower. Singular."

"There's still you," God sat on the edge of the table, thin legs dangling. "And he didn't want me anyway. And he's going to die."

Yasnic nodded.

"There are better ways to learn a language," one of the Armigers' men brayed out, "than one word at a time!" For some reason this was hilarious to his companions who practically fell off their chairs.

"The same word over and over," said another, the moment the mirth was flagging.

"Vinchec, don't step on my *joke*, you wretch. Get your own."

"I was just saying, to be strictly accurate, actually, that—" And then the interrupter looked up, because Yasnic had come over to their table. "Piss off, beggar. We've got no coin. We're flat broke, aren't we, lads?"

"Not a stone token!" the others agreed. "Spent it all on whores and demons and demon whores!"

"I was just hoping to hear you explain the joke," Yasnic said mildly. "Seeing as you were going to."

"Oh, you have an admirer, Vinchec," said the joke-maker. "Don't feed him. He'll follow you home!"

"Home," said another. "We should be going now." A little uneasily, as though only just understanding how far past midnight it was.

"Nonsense," said Vinchec. "My dear fellow, my dear fellow. We were discussing the parlous state of *education* in this city, what with the, you know. And my friend Pravil here, had the wit to say, well, you understand on the curriculum of most institutions there's a certain emphasis on language. In this case, for the purpose of this witticism, Pel. And if you were a student, let us say, wishing to learn the language of our fellows in the Perfecture, as it were."

"Oh Vinchec, just get to the point!" Pravil rolled his eyes theatrically.

"Well, he was saying there were easier ways to learn, than with just one word. Because of the tablethi, don't you know? You've handled a baton, hunting, eh? Say the word, unleash the magic, pop, bang, eh? Only, my point was that, strictly speaking, because it's always the same word for these Pal weapons, you'd learn, you see – you'd learn even *less*!" And trying to raise the table in more laughter for a quip now thoroughly desiccated.

"In what possible world," Yasnic asked, "would that be considered funny?"

"He knows you!" cackled Pravil. "Vinchec, he knows you!" And then choked on his own words when Yasnic passed his accusing gaze across the table. God was plucking at the hem of his coat, but he ignored it.

"There are men and women taking up arms against the Palleseen Sway right now," he told the table. "They are... brave, and young, and of your people. And you're making *jokes*. Why aren't you out there with them? Why aren't you all rushing to the Gownhall with your family and your friends, with your... swords and your hunting batons and all of it. To show them that you're with them."

"My dear fellow, you say that as though everything's so simple," Vinchec started, but Pravil just stood up and said, "Well why aren't you?"

Yasnic opened his mouth, closed it. *Because I'm a priest. Because I'm forbidden violence. Because it would rend my heart, to see it. Because I'm useless.* And Pravil sneered and gave him a push, just a very genteel shove, barely any force to it. A dismissal, though.

Something heavy hit the table, hard enough to rattle the ranks of their empty cups. It was a short-handled hammer, a solid workman's tool. The big woman who'd dropped it down there stared without love at all of them.

"Drink up," she said. "Move on."

Yasnic babbled an apology out of instinct, but the look she turned on him made it clear, somehow, he wasn't included in the injunction. The Armigers' men squawked and clucked, but then downed their cups. When they tried to leave, a solid man was in the doorway.

"Didn't see you settle your tab," he said. And when Vinchec rooted in his purse, "Good of you to offer to pay this fellow's as well."

A protest formed on the man's lips, but the thought that he might end up paying for *everyone* at the Pledge if he objected must have occurred to him. He emptied change over the counter with an ostentatious flourish, and dumped a handful of coins in front of Yasnic too. Then the whole table of them were scurrying out.

Yasnic tried to thank the man and the woman, but they weren't interested in him any longer. Probably it had just been the incessant noise that had stirred them, not his words. But he could get another drink now. In fact, there were coins to spare, even after all manner of tabs had been settled. He had a second cup and a third, and his pockets were still heavier than they'd been in months. Nobody seemed to mind, or even pay him any heed at all. He felt as though he was moving through the world like a ghost, incapable of affecting the events taking place all around him.

"You're not going back," God told him. "It's too dangerous. I could lose you too. Where would I be then?"

"I don't know," Yasnic said dully. "Actually, I don't. Where would you be, if there was nobody left?"

"I don't know either," God said in a small voice. "I don't want to find out. So you get that down you and then go home to bed. It'll be fine tomorrow. It'll all look better."

"It won't."

"It will if you don't go to see." God folded His arms. "You are my priest. I am protecting you, like I am supposed to. I forbid you to go back."

"I wasn't going to go," Yasnic confessed to God. "I'm not brave enough." Screwing his face up to force the tears back – a cup and a half of liquor, and he was about to bawl his eyes out! "I like Ruslav."

"Man's a thug."

"And Lemya."

"Woman's an idiot. And corrupted."

"What?"

"There's a curse in her like a fishhook. How long do you think she can go, before it reels her in? It was in your thug, too, save I healed him of it. And now you need to stop thinking about them."

Yasnic downed the cup, aware that he was now outstaying his welcome. "Go back," he said.

"No, you're *not* going back," God said patiently.

"I want *you* to go back to Ruslav," Yasnic clarified. "Help him."

"What do you imagine I can do? The moment there's a fight he'll swing a punch and then he's dead to Me. And everyone else. Yasnic, I don't want to see it."

"Go and help him. You're his god."

"Not through any informed choice of his or Mine," God insisted. "It was just you sticking your nose where it wasn't wanted. I didn't ask for him as a follower! He's everything I despise. Violent men spreading violence, infecting others with their ways. Like a disease."

"He is yours," Yasnic insisted, but God just looked away and stuck His lower lip out like a rebellious child.

"I am giving you one last chance." Yasnic stood up, staring down at God, feeling his head spin a little. He couldn't remember when he last ate.

"Or what?" God sneered. "Going to get tough with me now? Quote scripture? Oh no, you never even *learned* it. Kosha tried to teach you, but you could never remember."

"I'll show you." Yasnic wagged a finger in the face of God, to the amusement of everyone in the Pledge. "I'll force you to go to him." Probably people talking to invisible dwarves on tables wasn't new in the drinking cellar.

God made a noise unbecoming of divinity. "You are a terrible priest," He pronounced. "And mostly what you are is weak." A shrug. "But then I'm a terrible, weak god. We fit well together. Let's go home. I'm cold."

"No," Yasnic said, and then he was marching out of the Pledge, God at his heels. Not west towards the boarding house, but deeper into Mirror Allor, turning from the suspicious glances of the locals, trying to remember the way through the narrow, tangled streets.

Until at last he found the door with its painted ring of

flowers. No other sign, but those looking for solace here needed nothing more.

Yasnic took a deep breath and stepped into Mother Guame's circle house.

The place was quiet, but full. The front room, where patrons waited their turn and set out their requirements, had a lot of people in it who didn't look the type. A handful of men, a few more women, children. They all had satchels and sacks. Yasnic blinked, wondering if he'd somehow stepped into the wrong house despite everything. And there were soldiers, he saw. Or at least a couple of Pals, a woman officer and a young man, uniform jackets open, drinking.

He stuttered. Suddenly, it all seemed a terrible idea.

And then Mother Guame herself was bustling over, weaving around the bags and some fitfully sleeping children. "Why, sir!" she greeted him. "How good it is to see a new face!" She looked strained, pale. "Forgive the, ah, clutter, sir. Just some temporary arrangements. But you, sir, look to be a discerning man. A man who seeks a very particular release. My other guests have just finished up." A half-nod in the direction of the two soldiers. "I will have my girls mark out the chalk for you and draw up the contract. Just give me in my ear what your particular wants are…?"

She leaned close, sweat and stale perfume and weariness. He swallowed. God was pulling at his coat again, and Yasnic yanked the hem from His hands.

He said, "I've heard that… you can… Only I can't. I'm not allowed. Forbidden. Except, I heard that you can…"

Understanding came to Mother Guame's face. Perhaps even a mote of sympathy. "Sir," she said, "you've come to the right place. And we have such contracts prepared." A hand on his arm, more human sympathy than he felt he deserved, so that he almost broke down then and there. "You wouldn't be the first," she said, "to find it difficult."

He gave her the coins that Vinchec had dumped on his

table. All of them, not counting. And possibly it wasn't enough, but Mother Guame seemed willing to take what was on offer. And God was shaking his leg now, complaining, threatening, warning, but Yasnic just shivered at the thought of what was to come, the great sacrilege of it all.

The Bitter Sisters

The Hammer Districts. Hours before dawn, and the streets are beginning to fill. An air of festival. Banners, some new, some dusted off from the Old Duke's day. Embroidered symbols of their craft; dancing figures linked elbow to elbow. Or a flag of iron grey on one side, rust red on the other, a vertical bar of blue between. Stone and steel and the river. Occasionally, an older device, a rosette of trees touching crown to crown. The forest, before it became just a grove at the edge of a city. Men, women and children hold the flags. Most have turned out in work clothes. Some have thrown on a little carnival show. There are fake Indwellers with paper masks. There are comedy Armigers in caricatures of last generation's fashions. They sing the old work songs that came into the city with the fieldhands when the factories first opened. They have hammers and work knives and staves, boathooks and billhooks and weighted ropes. Sometimes, the difference between a street party and a riot is in the provocation. But there's one corner of the Hammer Districts where the mood is quite different.

Ruslav pushed through the crowds, skirted them, not sure what it was about. The factories had gone quiet. The city seemed to be slowly turning upside down. Was it a street party? Was it an army? The answer to any question seemed to be 'yes' right then, as though they were in some festival season where all the forbiddances and restrictions were lifted. They weren't his people, though. He could only press on until he reached the yard outside a certain mill whose underground spaces weren't used for storing goods or raw materials. The Fort of the Bitter Sisters.

There was a fair crowd outside the Fort, too, and these *were* his kin. They were the street-soldiers, the sworn men and women who collected dues and broke bones and enforced the harsh honour of the Lodges and their ruling Aunts. They were the Vultures, the groundswell of resistance drawn from every disaffected villain on the streets of Ilmar. People who wanted to strike against the Occupiers, and maybe against the Armigers, or even just against anyone who'd held them back or told them no.

Benno saw him, and hollered out, "Ruslav?" And then his name was being passed back and forth across the crowd. "Ruslav! It's Ruslav!" And he remembered he was supposed to be dead. Twice over he was supposed to be dead.

He hadn't known what kind of reception he'd get, coming here. He'd been absent without leave, and that was a bad look for a soldier in any army. It turned out that, behind his back, he'd become a figure of myth. A shining knight. What had they heard, after all, told mouth to ear in increasingly garbled versions? That Ruslav the swaggerer had been found cut to ribbons outside the Reproach. That he'd been miraculously healed. That he'd been arrested by the Pals. That they'd hanged him – some had seen it with their own eyes. And here he was, obstinately not dead. The best of both worlds: resistance hero and martyr, and still walking around to enjoy it.

"You son of a bitch!" Benno whacked him on the arm, danced back to evade the counter-blow that didn't come. "You faked it!"

"He died! I saw him dancing!" someone insisted, and someone else said, "He sold himself to the Allorwen, and they brought him back!" or "He's got a demon in him, making his body go," or "Is he just going to keep coming *back* now? Can we never be rid of the bastard?" Laughter, cheers, slaps on the back, his name on their lips.

"Listen," Ruslav told them. "What's going on? What happened to the factories? What are you all waiting around for?"

"Where've you been?" Benno demanded, but someone pointed out he'd been dead, so fair enough, he might not be best informed.

"They're Wielding the Hammer," someone told him.

"They're marching on the palace," from someone else.

"They're going to the Gownhall," from a thin woman. "Going to fight the Pals." And some found that hilarious and some cheered it. Ruslav felt a treacherous sliver of hope in him.

"Why are you all standing around here, though?" he pressed, wondering just how many miracles he could expect. "Don't tell me you're marching too?"

"Balls to that," Benno agreed. "Aunties called everyone in. Something big."

"Oh big, all right." *A great big knife in the back of the Perfecture?* The thought gave him an ugly jolt of anticipation, but it was followed by the phantom pain of the monster's teeth. The reminder of where he'd be if he enacted even the least shadow of that retribution. *But I don't have to act. I just have to talk. Am I allowed that?* He'd try, and find out. "I need to speak to the Sisters."

"Oh, they'll want to speak to you," Benno agreed. "Make way! Get out of the way, you turds!" Pushing and kicking just like Ruslav couldn't, anymore. Clearing a path, so he could get inside and descend to where the Bitter Sisters were.

When he shuffled into that circular room it was just Evene there, half the Sisters but all of the bitter. A couple of her people were reporting to her, kids who looked too young to have swords thrust into their belts, decked out in ragged finery like they'd raided their parents' old clothes. He caught a few words from their half-broken voices, talking about Pal soldiers on Misnost Street and the Ockernov. Then she'd dismissed them with a flick of her fingers, turning to face him across the pit. Evene wasn't dressed for court, he saw. She had a long brocade coat on, but beneath it was a breastplate, as much of an antique piece as anything hauled down from the Gownhall walls. One side was etched with some Armiger family's device, but the whole was so rusty and discoloured he couldn't have said what family. She had tassets, too: little waterfalls of articulated plates from hip halfway to knee, and her tall boots were fronted in metal. She had a basket-hilted sword and a couple of short rods holstered at her belt.

For a moment, her face was without expression. She could have shot him there and then, and he'd have had no warning. Then she broke into a smile.

"That accounts for all the cheers. You're dead, Ruslav, haven't you heard?"

"Someone said as much," he told her. "Nobody gave me the message."

"You found your way back to us."

"I did, yes."

Evene nodded, strode partway around the pit. He heard the thing below pace her with a whispering scuttle, steeled himself not to look. "Good timing. We need everyone we've got. Busy day tomorrow, Ruslav. Work for everyone. Where've you been?"

"Gownhall."

She stopped. "That so?" Appraising him. She had eyes that saw through most things, he knew that from long experience. She must see something of what he'd gone through, that he wasn't the man who'd once run her errands and beaten her enemies.

"Those kids, they gave the Pals a bloody nose. I was there. You'll have heard, but I saw it all."

Another few steps round, still with that echo from the pit. Her gaze weighed him thoughtfully. "Well, I've heard a dozen stories, and they none of them match up. So maybe you'll tell me, before Carelia comes back and we need to start the circus."

And he told her, aware that it was just one more story. It wasn't truth, because that would have required a broader perspective than his two eyes and his two ears. And besides, he exaggerated. He made the students like the knight in the painting and the Pals like the mountain, except the knight had won. They'd sent all that darkness scurrying away. Once, when they'd grabbed Ivarn. Once, when the soldiers had come with the ram. Then he told about the barricades and the stolen batons and the sheer furious enthusiasm of it all.

"They were scared," he said, meaning the Pals, except perhaps also the students. "And I came—"

"Because this is your place," she finished for him. Her head cocked. He heard a murmur – voices echoing down stairwells and tunnels as people came in from outside. "And we'll have work for you."

"Give me twenty with swords," he blurted out. "Give me fifty." Feeling the first keen parting of his wounds, as though the violence he was envisaging was pushing against the inside of his gut, forcing apart the invisible sutures of God's grace. "Swords," he whispered. "Batons. Knives. A hundred." His shirt was wet. "Two hundred, and we'll drive the Pals out of the city, Auntie."

"Will we?" she asked, and then people were funnelling in, pushing and shoving for a good view but not too close to the pit edge. Carelia stalked over, her coat white leather with copper trim, her armour banded lorica edged in brass, and a hatchet at her belt. Ruslav retreated, feeling the strained lines about his body relax, sag back together. There were a few spots of red seeping in through his clothes. God was not amused, wherever He was. His new convert had reached the very edge of apostasy.

He reckoned it was just about all of the Bitter Sisters' people there. The crooks and thieves and enforcers with their extravagant hand-me-downs and mismatched street foppery. The lean, hard men and women who wore the Vulture mark under plain cloth and talked of resistance, and basically did the same work as the others, just sometimes to slightly different people. Here were his two hundred and more so. Add this band of brigands to the Gownhall's defenders, and the Pals would never shift them.

There were a handful there not of their own free will, he noted. Men and women, civilians by their look, plus old Brachalven who'd led the Sisters' efforts over Yennitch Park ways, and some foreign woman who looked halfway familiar. He sidled and ducked his way over to Benno, but before he could ask, the Sisters were talking.

"So a mob of you turned up this evening gone, with news," Carelia said, her voice ringing across the chamber and silencing a dozen separate conversations. She left a beat for the echoes to die into, then continued. "And you've all been up there jawing at each other like a lot of old men, and not one of you knowing the full truth. Half of what anyone's said to anyone else just misheard or speculation or outright made up." Staring hard enough to make the hardest gangster shuffle.

"There's a pack of robes and books at the Gownhall who've thrown down with the Pals. And you all saw the Siblingries have lifted the Hammer and are about to go parade about like it's the Duke's birthday revels," she went on. "And there's Pals mustering right now at the Donjon, according to Gorvachec here. And there's Pals getting together in that park with all the shops, off Dustravaier. And a whole bunch of them headed for the Anchorwood too, because the Pals somehow managed to declare war on the Indwellers or something. Not even the Old Duke managed that one."

A little laughter at that.

Evene took up the slack. "So it's time we got our talons and beaks dirty, don't you think?" Some cheers. "And we've had plenty come saying we should go raise the Old Duke's flag on Armigine Hill and sing *Beauty on the Revein*. Muster up and follow into battle like the old days." More shouts. A head of steam gathering in the room around them. Swords rattled in scabbards. "Or head to the palace and string the Perfector up, see how he likes it." Whoops and yells, a few blades drawn to flash about overhead. Evene looked sour, or perhaps it was just what her face relaxed into. "You're welcome to try, but don't forget what happened when *he* did the same to the Duke. I hope you like perfumed baths." And laughter, perfectly anticipated. The more enthusiastic whoopers and wavers suddenly chagrined.

Ruslav felt as though someone was winching his guts tight within his body. *Come on*, he thought. *Get to it. Give the word.* They were shoulder to shoulder down there, pushing in from the back, shoving back from the centre. An army.

Carelia had taken a rod from her belt as Evene spoke, and now she pointed it at one of the prisoners and spat a Maric word. The weapon flashed and old Brachalven was pitched backwards out of the grip of the men who held him, a charred gash in his temples and across the top of his head.

"We've been lax," she said, in the resulting silence. When one of her people moved to kick the body into the pit, she shook her head. "No. It stays hungry. Old Man Brach wasn't keeping our secrets as he should. Bags of Pal coin and someone covering his game-table debts. Not just him." Looking over the other ashen prisoners until she met the defiant tilt of the foreign woman's chin. "Someone's always ready to sell you out or use you. I've no doubt there are others here, not fingered yet. You might want to decide where your loyalties lie. What's best for the city and your own continued health." For a moment, she was looking straight at Ruslav, who knew his own loyalties were split, but her eyes passed on like crabs picking over a littered shore.

"It's time we remembered who we are," Carelia said. "We're Ilmar! We're the Gutter Districts. We are the people who were given nothing and took everything. Who are we?"

And, because nobody had rehearsed it, she relied on Evene to crow back, "Ilmar!" rather than some spontaneous unity within the crowd.

"And what's our banner, sister?" Carelia demanded. "Is it the Shrike that goes mad with murder until they tear its wings off?"

"No!" Evene barked.

"Is it the Heron that flushes itself down the river like a turd at the first sign of danger?"

"No!"

"Is it the Raven that croaks about who its father was and tells us how wise it is?"

"No!" And by now, everyone had learned the drill.

"Who are we?" Carelia demanded.

"The Vulture!" managed at least half of those present.

"Who inherits the streets?"

"The Vulture!" Everyone, now.

"*Who inherits?*"

"*The Vulture!*" So loud they could surely hear it over at the Ducal Palace.

Carelia held up her hands, and the crowd subsided again. Ruslav had his mouth open to say, *Then we march on the Gownhall!* The only thing that stopped him was knowing he couldn't go with them. Not lead them, nor carry a sword to anyone's order. He had come like a ghost, full of warnings and pleas, but insubstantial as a cobweb. A man who couldn't fight was less than a man.

One of the others spoke, though. They'd got their sword out to flail it over their head, eyes wild with fervour and red with drink. "Which do we take first, Auntie?" he asked. "The ones at the Wood or the ones at the hall?"

There was an argumentative but eager echo as everyone told their neighbour just what they thought the answer should be, but Evene clashed her blade against Carelia's and that silenced them.

"Not either," she said. "The Gownhall, what's that to us? Spend our blood for some children whose daddies bought books while we couldn't buy bread? The Wood? It can look after itself, or it's not worth looking after. Let the Pals burn it and deal with what comes out. The Siblingries? How often have they snubbed us and looked down on us, as if what they do to buy bread is any better. Let them and the Pals claw each other's throats out. The Vulture's no raptor to be flown off anyone's wrist. Nobody's foot soldiers, nobody's flag. When there's blood spilled, the

Vulture *feasts*. Watch-houses, customs lockers, treasury offices, jails. Informants and collaborators, them who sell to the Pals and them who serve them. We'll claw the Pals' guts out while they're off getting blood on their uniforms. We'll take their pay and burn their papers and teach their friends what it means to be loyal."

Ruslav felt that inner winch turn, until it hurt. "What?" he said. "No, wait." Too quiet to be heard, but he was about to say it louder, draw the fatal attention of the Sisters, save that someone else did it first.

It was the foreign woman. Some immigrant shipped in from elsewhere in the Sway. She writhed in her captors' grip and was abruptly free. They fell back, clutching at stung fingers. "Listen to me!" she shouted. "This is your chance! The city is yours, yes! But you have to take it together! Or after tomorrow, it's just corpses in the streets and the boot on your throat again. Your chance is *now*!"

"Ah, yes." Evene stepped around the pit's edge almost daintily. She had a rod in her hand, too. She pointed it at the foreigner, but then jumped it to the left and put a hole in the chest of the next prisoner along, singeing one of the people who'd held him into the bargain.

"Informant," she said, and then her aim passed on to the next, and the rod flared again. "Collaborator," she said, of the woman she'd just killed. And so on, down the line, swapping rods as the first one's tableth drained. "Informant. Profiteer. Traitor. Traitor. And you, I forget what you did, but this is for you." A line of corpses, the last two arrested in mid-flight as they tried to batter through the crowd, because their wardens had got well clear of Evene's ire.

"And you." Back to the foreigner. "We know you. We've followed you to fancy parlours and shop floors and beer cellars. A priest of some bug god, here to stir trouble you'll never have to pay for. Tell us how to live and when to die, and call that chaos?"

"Freedom!" the woman shouted back. "Come together, and you can break the Pals! Not just pick at their leavings!"

"Nobody's foot soldiers!" Evene shouted her down. "Nobody's flag! We have our own bug god here. Put her in."

The foreigner's voice was lifted abruptly, louder than it should have been, and something flashed into being over the pit. A glittering winged thing with vast eyes and a scorpion's tail lifted in threat. The crowd eddied back, screams and yells blending into a monstrous roar of fear. But someone had their head screwed on, because the phantom was gone in the next moment, and the foreigner was in the pit.

She tried something, some bug charm of her bug god, but the thing in the pit didn't care. It had smelled the death above it, but received none of the expected bounty. It tore into the woman with its claws and fangs, folded its carpet of limbs about her, and that was that.

"Listen to me," Carelia said. This time, she was definitely fixing Ruslav with her stare. "We are the Vulture. There's barely a uniform west or east of the river save where they're fixing to throw down. Where we went only in darkness and under a cloak, we go now in daylight with drawn swords. The belly of the Occupation's bared for us. Why play dare with its teeth? You all sort into your crews and listen up. Each one of you gets to go put the mark somewhere. Some office where there's just three knock-kneed clerks and a Turncoat propping up the desk. Some fine fellow who wins the love of the Pals by selling goods to them on the cheap that we could never afford. Some moneylender who bankrolls their vices. Some brothel where a Fellow of the Schools keeps his fancy mistress. They all thought they were clear of us, but we've been making a list. Each crew gets its target. Go do your work. Take what you take. Break what you break. Teach them it doesn't matter if the Pals were guarding their shopfronts and fine front doors yesterday, not if they can't be sure they'll be there tomorrow. You teach them the Vulture knows how to wait."

Ruslav just stood there, the crowd swaying him, feeling hollow. Hearing the names roll out – a crew, a target, a set of orders. As organised as any military campaign. He never knew they had it in them, this love of detail. This memory of every petty slight and refusal.

"Ruslav, your crew," Evene said. "We asked you to bring that Allorwen in some days ago, and you failed. So the man got himself arrested. He's free enough now. Up and down the city making deals. Gathering a chestful of money and toys like a man with the rent due and the landlord at the door. Blackmane owes us a mirror, and more than that. Get your gear together, and I'll be out to join you when I've given these villains their work. It's time that Allorwen chiseller gave a proper and final accounting. Time to hold his feet to the fire."

Ruslav had no particular love for Blackmane. Yes, the man had saved him from the noose, but that had been a side effect of his fencing with Ostravar. And Blackmane didn't *have* the ritual ward that Fleance had lost, or else he wouldn't have gone to such trouble on the expectation that Ostravar could give it to him. He didn't think the Sisters would listen to him, or that it would change anything if they did. Blackmane was a foreigner with money and an attitude. He would be right there towards the top of their list, regardless.

His crew trooped outside, even as the remaining layabouts crowded closer for their own briefs. Ruslav could feel those invisible sutures tensing and flexing across his torso, as though he was caught in a net of wires and yet couldn't stop pulling against it. "This is mad," he said.

Benno looked at him and grinned. "Right it is," he agreed. "Upside-down town. Ilmar's pockets getting shaken out for us to pick over.

"No, listen." Ruslav rounded on them, braced for the return of the pain. "We've been up against the Pals three years. Getting in weapons, getting in money. Making anyone who gets cosy with them regret it. And right now, we *can* fight them. We can *win.*" Feeling the first slick warmth of blood as his skin began to part, fighting back a whimper. "How can we be Ilmar and Ilmar be ours when we're not lifting a finger?"

"That's what we've been doing?" Benno laughed uncertainly. "We're making bank, Ruslav. We're making people remember why they pay rather than pushing back. That's what we do." Spelling it out as though to a slow child. "Since when did you give a piss and a fart about it?"

Ruslav goggled at him, wanting to declare *But I always...* Except... *But I did. In the abstract. We all knew it would come, though...? Some time, in the future, the day... And until then... We're the resistance. We're not just...*

Benno snorted and cuffed him, dancing back with his guard up because Ruslav always clouted back twice as hard.

Ruslav stared at him, frozen, feeling his skin pulled taut. He had the sense that Yasnic's god was sick of him. Wanted him to die and be out of the way.

Benno gave him another shove, as thoughtful as a student experimenting. Ruslav staggered, caught himself. Opened his mouth. There was a wondering look on Benno's face. In it Ruslav could see every time he'd knocked the man down, kicked him, tripped him, slapped him. Humiliated him in front of the others, just to make himself bigger.

He remembered Yasnic's instinctive *I'm sorry* to anything and everything.

Then he was on the ground. Benno had hit him in the face, but awkwardly. He'd gashed his fist on Ruslav's teeth, and now there was blood slicking his shirt. He wanted to scream at God for the injustice of it. Benno's boot came in and took up his attention, and then they were all at it. He hadn't realised they all hated him so much. Then he understood it wasn't even *him* they hated. If he'd come up swinging, they'd have been drinking together happily enough by that evening. It was weakness they hated, and he'd hated it just the same, before God had made him weak.

He managed to get to his feet after Benno kicked someone else's leg when they both went for him at once. They eddied back, ready for him to regain his fighting spirit, but Ruslav just ran. Ran from the great mob of his former fellows. Dodged through the streets where the Siblingry march was just preparing to set off. Slowing to a stagger as the jeers fell behind and the bruises caught up with him. And there, on the Portbridge, he found God.

God. Stunted, straggling, clutching a blanket to Himself, staring at Ruslav mournfully.

"I'm going to the Gownhall," Ruslav told God. "I'm going to be with them. Even if I can't fight."

God looked as though He might argue, but Ruslav had no energy left for theology. He just staggered on, past God, over the bridge. After a while he heard the patter of feet as God ran to catch up.

Past the Threshold

In the mists of time, the power of the Armiger families had been simply that they bore arms. The fighting elite, who defended the lesser folk, and therefore ruled them. After that, it was land, the agricultural engine of a simpler time. It was power and influence at the courts of dukes and kings. It was factories and mines, driving a new age of prosperity and poverty. The Armigers transformed from feudal overlords to industrialists, coming to new and uneasy equilibria with the people who had tilled their fields and now turned the cranks of their mills. Every Armiger house had a fancy motto and fine words, but in truth, there were only two maxims they clung to. That they must survive. That they must control.

"How many are they sending us?" Shantrov asked. He'd tried to hang his head out of the window of the coach, but Vidsya had hauled him back in. As though he'd be recognised, when the coach itself bore the livery of the Sirovar family. The quartered shield with harp, crossed scimitars and doubled shells. And there should have been an owl, of course, but after the Occupation, the Armigers had repainted their coaches and re-liveried their servants, because to publicly display a bird in your heraldry would bring Correct Speech to your door.

"How many?" he pressed. Vidsya was half out of her seat, though, leaning close to the grill that let her communicate with the coachman above.

"Go around, then," she ordered. "Just bring us to the Portbridge the quickest way. Get us across the river."

"Where are we meeting them?" And the Sirovar estates were west of the city, true enough. Shantrov would rather have marched in through the main gates as befitted a grand liberator, but if the stalwarts his family had dispatched had to creep in through the Gutter Districts, then so be it. He could recruit more fighters along the way. Whole neighbourhoods would flock to his flag, weary of the Palleseen boot.

Vidsya settled back. She looked as though she was at least two nights behind on sleep, drawn and gaunt. Her clothes – the elegant but practical outfit she might have ridden to the hunt in – were creased, the lace at her throat unravelling slightly where she'd caught it on something. She stared at him with an exasperation familiar from most of their family get-togethers.

"I could use some armour, perhaps," Shantrov said, because he wanted her to understand that he could be practical too. "And will our people have a spare baton they can lend me, do you think? I know I'm not the shot you are, but still—"

"Take off that ridiculous coat," she told him.

He looked hurt. "This was worn by—"

"Take it off."

Frowning, he shrugged out of it. The old Ilmari general who'd first honoured it had been broader across the shoulder than Shantrov anyway. "What do you have for me?" he asked. "Something in our colours, then?" *With the owl restored to its rightful place, surely.* A boyish grin that she didn't return.

"Oh, come on, cousin," he insisted. "A ghost of a smile, perhaps, for the freedom of our city!" No room inside the coach to flourish his sword, so he settled for rattling it in its sheath. "Who did you get to bring the troops here? Is it Uncle Osten? It's not Jerivic, is it?"

Vidsya stared at him.

"It's not, is it? Jerivic?" The coach lurched in a turn, and

Shantrov felt his sense of solid ground go with it. "Vidsya, what's wrong?" One hand on the brass of his scabbard, the other clutching the long-dead general's coat.

"Oh, for god's sake, Shantrov," she snapped. "Nobody's coming. Surely you understand nobody's coming. That was just for *them*. So they'd let you go."

He actually smiled, waiting for the punchline. "No, but really." Her unwavering stare bore into him. "Vidsya, really."

"Shantrov, you are my cousin, and I love you deeply," she said. The unspoken words *but you are so stupid* hanging there between them. The coach took another turn, juddering on cobbles. "And that is why you are going back to our estates until all this is over."

"But I need to be a part of it!" he said instantly. "The liberation! You can't just keep me away until it's all won!"

"Until it's all won," she echoed. "Shantrov, it will be dawn in perhaps two hours. When it is, the majority of the Perfecture garrison will move in and crack the Gownhall like an egg. Trained soldiers, who defeated the king's army and every Ducal levy on their way to Ilmar, and then took the city gates in two days. The same men, Shantrov. And though the main army has moved on, the garrison they left will be more than equal to the task of putting down a few students."

"Turn the coach around," Shantrov said.

"Don't be an idiot."

"They need me, then. They need me to—"

"Lead them? Do you think that'll help? Do you think the inspiring presence of Shantrov Sirovar will turn the tide of battle against all the odds? The only thing you'd accomplish is to get yourself killed, and you're my *cousin*, Shantrov. My aggravating idiot cousin who doesn't have the sense he was born with, but you're family."

He made a game try of getting out of the coach then, for all it was rattling along at a fair pace. The door was locked, though, and as he fumbled for the latch, she just grabbed him and yanked him back into his seat. They sat there, swaying, knee to knee and gazes locked, his accusing, hers blithely pragmatic.

Then she frowned, because there was music on the air, swelling even as she registered it. Horns and pipes and drums, and voices raised in somewhat discordant song. And the coach was slowing.

She took up her cane and rapped at the roof of the coach. "What is it?"

The muffled voice of the coachman reached them. "It's the bridge, ma'am. It's choked."

Shantrov took that opportunity to try for the window. He actually had it open, head and one shoulder wedged into the gap, before Vidsya hauled him back with a hiss of exasperation. Ahead of the coach, the Portbridge was completely full of people. A grand procession of them was marching, banners and flags and solid-looking men and women. Children, too. Though their clothes were muted canvas and leather and denim, their faces were bright in the light of the bridge's lamps. As though, as they crossed the river, west to east, a glorious future was rising ahead of the sun.

"It's the people!" he crowed. "They've risen!"

"Sit down," Vidsya snapped, and then, to the coachman, "the Rathbridge, double time. We'll cross the river there." Sounding rattled, and he'd have thought he'd take pleasure from that, but her anxiety was catching.

"But they're going to help the Gownhall," he tried.

"They don't give a damn about your idiot friends," she told him.

The coach lurched off again. Shantrov cast an aggrieved look back, then an accusing one at Vidsya. "You always talked resistance," he told her. "Throwing off the yoke. Restoration of Maric rule. You talked freedom, Vidsya. And Aunt Sachemel before you. I used to creep down and eavesdrop when the other families came to our house. It was all plans for when the city would be ours again. What happened?" A snarl, because he wanted to hurt her, wanted her to turn and fight him rather than just staring through him. "When did the Pals buy you?"

She laughed at that. "Is that what you think? Shantrov, you were sent to the Gownhall to get an education. How did it make you so dull? Ilmar will be free of the Pals, cousin. The city, and our nation, will be returned to their rightful governors. And it will be done by our efforts, I can assure you."

"Vidsya, they are fighting *now*!" And if that was an exaggeration, the margin of error was only an hour or so. "And those people on the Portbridge, they'll fight too. The city is rising, and where are we? Where are all your conspirators now?"

"You mistake what you have seen," she told him, "for the city."

He sat back, blinking at her.

"Shantrov, if the Pals left today – if they were driven en masse from the city – who would that leave in control? Who is placed to fill any vacuum? Yes, we have been working towards a restoration of Maric rule ever since the conquest. Careful plans, Shantrov. Raven plans. Plans that involve other cities, the nation as a whole, revolts in other conquered territories. When the day comes, cousin, the right people must be in place to take command and preserve order. *Order*, Shantrov. What's out there isn't order. It isn't the restoration of anything. If the Pals left today, the Vultures would ransack the city. Criminals and thugs. The idlers and malcontents we saw on that bridge would tear down the factories that are their very livelihoods. They'd eat their fill from the city stores and never ask who would refill them. No Duke, Shantrov. No leadership. Just a pack of warlords squabbling over the spoils and looting the warehouses until the Palleseen army came to recover the city."

"You don't know that. There are people at the Gownhall. The maestros—"

"You think the city would magically unite behind a philosophy teacher or a professor of antique literature?" she demanded. "Shantrov, you don't know the Bitter Sisters. You don't know the Vultures. We have plans that will see this city free. A new, strong Ilmar, our glory restored. Can you imagine how it would be if the Pals lost tomorrow, and we had to go cap in hand to the table and concede every demand a Siblingry agitator made, or some Vulture Aunt? They'd take everything we've built since the nation was founded, Shantrov. They'd rob us of our factories and houses, our land, our heritage. They'd tear it all down in the name of their freedom. They'd chant the city's name while setting fire to everything that makes us what we are."

The coach jolted, and there was a creak and a thud as the coachman fought for balance.

"You are telling me," Shantrov said, "that you think we could win, together, against the Pals."

"I am telling you that whoever might win, it wouldn't be *us*," Vidsya corrected him. "The Gownhall, that you were willing to die for a moment ago – yes, one of Ilmar's greatest institutions! Do you think *they* would preserve it and its traditions? The townhouse you lived in: do you think they would let your young cousins grow up in it? There is nothing that you love in Ilmar that they would not cast down, because it's something they were denied. The Pals are a curse, and their occupation will end, but until then, they at least maintain civic order. They can be reasoned with and bribed. We've got more in common with them than with anyone on the streets today, believe me."

Because he didn't feel he could look at her anymore, Shantrov's gaze went to the back window, the receding streets of the mercantile districts. He saw something dark topple from the top of the coach, just a shapeless flail of cloth that tumbled past and then was no more than a dark patch on the dark road, lost to the last dregs of the night.

"Vidsya—"

"I promise you," she cut him off, "you'll get your chance. You'll ride into the city at the head of an army, or else you'll be the phoenix that rises from the ashes of the Gownhall. It will all be worth it. But not today, Shantrov. Today, I keep you safe, so you can be the hero when it's time. When we're ready."

Above, they heard the whip crack, and the coach was abruptly accelerating, rattling dangerously through the streets. Shantrov heard alarmed cries, early morning pedestrians leaping aside.

"Slow down, you fool!" Vidsya called, but then they were skidding into a mad turn, teetering on one wheel as they spun onto the Rathbridge. The side of the coach swiped against the bridge's rail in a splintering of wood, and Shantrov was amazed they didn't lose a wheel. And the Rathbridge was dilapidated and old. It had been the grand thoroughfare from east to west once, but that had been before the Duke and nobility had evacuated to the palace and Armigine Hill. That had been before the streets to the north had become the Hammer Districts, and the city's bustle and money had been drawn up to where the mills were being built.

"Vidsya. Something's wrong," Shantrov said, gripping his seat for purchase. They were careering through narrow, run-down streets now, the houses on either side half ruined, less and less suggestion of occupation. All broken windows and rotted doors forever ajar.

Another corner, and this one too perilous for the coach's abused balance. They tipped, skittering on a single wheel rim, impossibly stable for a drawn-out second. Tilting, the traces dragging askew at the demon steeds. Shantrov heard the beasts complain, shrieking more like hawks than horses. Their hooves skidded and sparked against the flags, slithering in the mud and moss. The coach crashed onto its side, Vidsya's knee ramming into his stomach and the hilt of his own sword punching him under the chin. The shrill complaints of the horses were abruptly silenced.

Vidsya was cursing the coachman, struggling to disentangle herself from Shantrov. She reached up for what was now their new ceiling, threw the bolts back and braced a foot on her cousin's leg so she could fling the door open.

"You idiot, what were you thinking?" she demanded, and then

someone reached in and hauled her bodily out. *The coachman,* Shantrov thought, and then she screamed.

He fought his way up through the doorway, snagging on shards of splintered wood, getting his sword hilt tangled with the frame. Outside, there was a flat, grey light over the city, the first breath of dawn. His cousin was fighting.

A wild figure had hold of her. They'd rolled off the coach past where the horses should have been but weren't, at the very edge of an overgrown dyke where the ruinous buildings left off. Even as Shantrov fell out of the coach, Vidsya was on her feet. Her attacker clung to her, shorter than she and agile as an ape.

"Give it to me!" A thin lost voice on the wind. "You took it. I need it!" A man in costume, it seemed. As though he'd latched onto the coach from that festival crowd down the Portbridge and been carried all this way. A beggar got up as an Indweller.

Vidsya threw him off. He landed on all fours, screaming now, not even words. Shantrov saw his cousin's cane flash, raised in threat. The mummer shrank back, clutching at the wooden mask about his throat. Shantrov saw his fingers go white, as though he was striving to break the thing in half. The beggar shook his head, snarling to himself. *No, no, I won't.*

"Wait," Vidsya said. "I know you—"

He leaped. There was no prologue to it. He sprang at her, as though there was red-hot metal at his back. The cane spun aside, and Shantrov at last saw the dagger in the man's hand.

He ran forwards round the wreck of the coach, fumbling with his sword that was jammed in its scabbard. Vidsya wrestled with the man for a moment, and then he was hacking at her, screaming, demanding she give *it* up to him. Weirdly rational, even as his blade bit across her upraised hands, cut away at her fingers and then drove past them. "I need it! They're hunting me! I need it to keep me safe!"

Shantrov had been ready to charge in, blade drawn and heedless of danger, right until the dagger plunged into Vidsya's breast. The arc of her blood killed the valour in him. The maniac way the man continued to carve at her body, shouting demands at ears no longer listening. The *real* of it, far more than when he'd put his sword into the Palleseen officer. Seeing someone he knew turned into meat. Then the man looked up.

His face was contorted as though multiple invisible hands had hold of it and were trying to shape it like clay. He clutched the mask still, fingers like claws. "She didn't have it," he said, quite cogently, even calmly. "You've got it."

"No," Shantrov whispered hollowly.

"She gave it to you. You must have it. Please." As though he wasn't elbow-deep in Vidsya's blood. "I don't have much time. It's going to make me. I don't want it to make me. I need it." Two opposed *Its*, the one at the man's heels, the other that he was so desperate to acquire. Neither of them anything Shantrov understood.

He had his sword out, and every fencing manual agreed that a man with a sword should always out-master one with just a knife. Then the madman straightened up and grinned and advanced, and Shantrov found himself backing up. Not even wit enough to put the coach between them, just retreating from the whole bloody horror of it. The man's terrible, piteous expression; the wreck of the coach and his cousin. The ground abruptly sloped behind him, and he lost his footing, tumbling back into the overgrown scar separating the almost abandoned streets before him from the completely forsaken district at his back.

The madman gave out a high, catlike wail. Shantrov scrambled back, snagged on briars and thistles, the hard edges of fallen stones raking him. He regained his feet, still putting distance between them, so the whole house-wide span of the overgrown firebreak was between them.

The madman stared at him, pacing along the edge of the break. He whined and swatted at the mask about his neck. "Give it back to me!" he called. "I need it. Quickly! I need it." But he would not cross. And Shantrov understood, then, where he was, and what had happened to the horses.

The madman's eyes flicked past Shantrov's shoulder, into the shadows of the fallen buildings, the opportunistic trees. "You can't have it!" he shouted. "It's not fair!"

They'd done more than just burn buildings, Shantrov knew, to contain what lurked here. There were wards made of inscribed bronze, buried in a ring about the whole district. An unbroken chain to cage the curse of the place. And still potent, clearly. The demon horses had evaporated like morning mist when they'd run into them. And the madman: whatever possessed him, he would not cross it. He just begged and wheedled, and whatever he was trying to negotiate with, it wasn't Shantrov.

"I haven't got it!" he shouted at the man. "Whatever you're after, it's not here!"

Utter agony, in those demented eyes. "It's *him* then," he hissed. In that moment of distraction, his off-hand almost had the mask up over his face, and he fought it down, spitting and snarling.

Shantrov heard the music, then. Or became aware of it, understanding that he'd been hearing it for a while. There was, he knew, something at his back. Someone. And, though the dawn was limning the rooftops of the city, the darkness around him was only growing greater. The madman was receding, as though a fog was rising up to swallow him. He'd only been a sad creature with a knife, after all. There were worse things.

Something rustled, right behind him. The sense of those furs you put on when regal ermine had long since rotted away. The music was louder now, and at the edge of Shantrov's vision, emaciated figures danced, hand in hand, long lines of them winding their way in and out of the ruins and the trees.

"I only ever wanted to save the city," he told the last dregs of the night. It seemed inconceivable how many things had gone wrong for him so swiftly. He wanted to wake up and be within the Gownhall again, his new lover beside him and Vidsya safe at home. And if death came, it would be a clean death against the Pal batons or blades, or even at the end of a rope. Not this.

And a voice, the ghost of one, borne by the breeze that came at his back. *But I am of the city too.*

The first light of dawn lit him, leaping over the rooftops to dazzle his eyes. Behind him, he sensed the great shadowy edifice of the Reproach looming. A scene in which he knew his place.

But the voice said, *No.*

He hung there, its shadow lapping all the way to his heels. "I will turn and face you," he said. "That is what the knight does. I am—"

My noble Lord Sirovar, it finished for him. *Long generations have passed since you last graced us with your company.* He could hear the crowd now, venturing out of the choked streets. The scuff of their bare feet, the whisper of their rags. The slow, soft music. But the voice said, *Do not. Do not turn. Do not listen to us.* A strain like wire strung between the words as though it fought against itself. *Do not be a part of the picture, lord, not yet.*

As though he stood with his back to a great dark cliff, and only the tumultuous sea below, the crash and murmur of it. How easy to tilt backwards, just an inch, until the hungry grasp of the world took over.

Still, that voice in his head, that he *knew* should be wheedling for him to do just that, and yet was not. *We know you of old, my lord, for all you have been absent from our court. You wish to take up arms against the foes of Ilmar. You dream of drawing a blade to defend the city.*

"Yes." And he had drawn his sword, but never was there a more useless weight of ironmongery than the thing at the end of his arm.

Do you think you are alone? You are not alone.

"I know." His feet desperate to shift with the drum's beat, his back prickling with the need to turn and see the horror of them.

Do not, it told him. *Remain yourself for just one task more. Please. Then we shall make you our general, our champion. You shall carry our standard and lead our armies. We shall defend Ilmar together. We shall reclaim all our lost honours and titles, my lord. But do not become one of us, until you do what is needed. Never before has one come so readily to the very brink of us.*

He asked: "What must I do?" In his ears, the drum had gone from pavane to martial rattle.

It told him. So simple. The undoing of all things was so wretchedly simple.

Blackmane's Reckoning

To the Marics he was what they thought of as an Allorwen. Dangerous. Secretive. Powerful in ways that had nothing to do with the regular structures of civic Ilmar. A man to complain about or despise right up until the point where you needed to sell or buy something exotic. Then he was your man, and you cursed him for the hard bargain, but you took it. After which, you were free to despise him again. Just some crooked Allorwen, and you couldn't trust them. None of the Marics considered that the other Allorwen saw him the same way. The dodgy, chancy man who dealt with Marics and Pals, sold their secrets and traditions. Who they needed, even though they told their children to avert their eyes when he walked by.

There were children in the front parlour at Mother Guame's. As unnatural a fit as anything Blackmane had ever known. Children in their coats, bags and satchels tied to them with string, luck charms about their necks and wrists. Other relatives sat at tables normally only patronised by men and women craving the delights of hell. Or at least of those denizens of the Infernal Realms who specialised in that sort of thing. And he'd conjured them himself, in his day, in his youth. In Allor, it had been an initiation into the adult world. A behind-closed-doors yet respected tradition. For the first wave of refugees into Ilmar, it had become just one more thing they could trade for coin.

Mother Guame trudged over. A long night of her trying

to square this particular circle. The expectations of her clients against what she owed her people. He knew what that felt like.

"How many?"

"Seventeen."

Blackmane winced. "That's no good."

"You want me to turn one away? One of the children, perhaps? They're all in enough trouble, Blackmane." Except, of course, she was speaking Allorwen and said his name properly, his old title. *Lord of the White Manor.* From when he had been worthy of it, and not this shadow-self. "If it's not the Pals after them, it's someone else."

Seventeen was ill-omened. You never started a venture on the seventeenth day, or laid a table with seventeen items, or travelled as one of seventeen companions, even for part of the way. Except that was back when the world was sane. It wouldn't be the first bad-luck stricture he'd breached since coming here."

"One of your girls, perhaps," he tried. "Or you, even."

"I'm too old. I've built something here. I won't call it a life, but it's something." Mother Guame shrugged. "Reverse our positions, you'd say the same."

And she wasn't wrong. But still. "It's too many," he decided. "Our protections will be spread too thin as it is. Find one family to stay behind."

"As to that, you just wait here." Not letting him off the hook even slightly. Then she was gone, and one of her hostesses turned up, offering tea. He took it, took a seat at a table away from all the hopeful travellers, aware of their eyes on his broad back.

The other man at the table looked up, started, got halfway up, sat back down. Blackmane was about to tell him that, if he wouldn't drink with an Allorwen, he'd come to the wrong establishment. Then recognised him.

"You," he growled, suspecting a trap, for a moment; trying to work out the angle. "You're the priest." The skinny little one, who'd been saved from the noose as part of Ostravar's job lot.

The man – Yasnic? – gave an uncertain smile. "Not anymore."

Blackmane eyed him, then looked sidelong at their surroundings. And true, Maric clergy had odd ideas about abstinence. The chuckle he gave vent to was mean – he, a man of broken vows and ruined faith, always took joy in seeing others fail to meet their own high standards. Not a part of himself he much admired, but it was there. "So much," he said, "for your oaths. They were brittle, in the end?"

"Aha, no," Yasnic said, taking no offence, sounding a little dazed. He'd got his money's worth from whatever the girls had conjured up, Blackmane decided. "No, the oaths were… iron. I couldn't break them."

"Then…?" Slurping at the tea, taking this free entertainment for what it was.

"The… workers here."

"Call them demons," Blackmane needled nastily. "Or whores," and then he let himself be silenced by the priest's look. A moment of seeing himself through the other man's eyes and not liking what he was looking at.

"I always heard a succubus could bewitch you," Yasnic said quietly. "Lure even the most resistant to, what was it, succumb to their wiles? Make a willing slave of the strongest and most virtuous will. That sounds like the way the balladeers would put it, don't you think?" He was smiling. It made him look younger, though not exactly young.

"Someone had a good night," Blackmane said, feeling sour. Mother Guame was coming back. Blackmane finished his tea. He wanted to say something that would spoil the ex-priest's mood, because surely, a Maric wasn't *allowed* to sit here, having enjoyed the house speciality, and still pretend to virtue. Then he considered that, back in the old country, the business of this house *was* a kind of virtue. It was the renewing of old bargains and the celebration of life and the exercise of an ancient craft. It was spirituality more than physicality. Was that what Yasnic had found here, somehow? Abruptly, he had a need to sit and talk more with the man, but dawn was on the horizon, and his time was up.

Mother Guame's lips moved, but she didn't say whatever words were bunged up in her. Instead, she pressed something into Blackmane's hands. A neatly wrapped bundle: carved sticks and silver wire and faded old cloth surely torn off the hem of a once-fine gown. And magic. He could smell it. Another warding bundle, the real thing. Worth a small fortune at today's prices, from anyone trying to get out of the city the old and eldritch way.

He raised an eyebrow at her. How many turned tricks, how much ritual chalk, how many bribes, to acquire such a thing, and then just to give it into his hands. Hands that were anything but safe – surely, she knew that. Was this something she'd been husbanding against her own need of it, or bought at seller's prices when she'd heard what was going on? He'd likely never know.

"All right, then." Because what could he say, exactly. Given his diminished state, he had no words large enough to cover the gift. "Get them together. It's not far to the Anchorage."

There were troops mustering near the Anchorage, but the inn itself wasn't their focus. They were forming up at a camp nearby, where a street petered out into a mud track, and the houses turned their backs, and it was just the cleared common and the little stand of trees that was the Anchorwood. They'd hauled some heavy goods all the way out here from the Donjon, he saw. There were two cross-sectioned barricades of spiked wood protecting them from any sudden move by the trees. In the gap between the two barriers, they'd set up a Palleseen Hand, an ugly thing with its stick fingers stabbing forwards. Its knuckles and wrist were set with strings of tablethi, a fortune in stored magic. Blackmane had seen similar contrivances the day his home city had fallen to the Pals, all those years ago. The gates and the walls had both bowed before them quickly enough. He imagined the rapid fire of the Hand turned against the beasts of the Wood. Would even the Anchorwood's magic survive such Palleseen ingenuity?

Not my business, he decided.

A couple of sentries called out – something between an enquiry and an order. Too much to hope that he'd get such a pack of strays under cover before they were noticed. The Pals strode over, just a couple of soldiers in dark jackets. Their faces said they'd not appreciated being handed the graveyard watch and wouldn't mind enlivening it with a few arrests and a little casual brutality. Blackmane put the others at his back and waved at the uniforms, as cheerily as he could fake. *Good morning, chill isn't it, how are you both, my friends?* And they would know him or know him by reputation or not know him at all.

Their eyes ranged past him to the others, the bags and boxes. "What's this?" one asked.

Just after a drink, officer. We all came down with a thirst at the same time. The children also, yes. You know how we Allorwen are…

He met their suspicious eyes. "There is a disturbance in the city," he said flatly. "Violent people. When there are violent acts on the street, they find their way to Mirror Allor eventually. But not to the Anchorage."

He was telling the absolute truth, to avoid having to tell them the truth. After whatever chaos was unleashed, there would be plenty in his quarter who'd suffer. No doubt about that.

And if they'd taken names, perhaps they'd have recognised some. Those whom the Pals had on their lists – and mostly for helping or supplying or hiding the Maric resistance, not that it would stop the Vultures breaking windows and cashboxes. But Blackmane knew the Pals. Ilmar was no grand posting, and nobody wanted to be near the Anchorwood if they didn't have to be.

"Expensive," one said, "to drink there." A laboured aside, ostensibly to her comrade.

"I've heard so," Blackmane agreed. "Probably you will be off shift soon after dawn. You should not deny yourselves." A brief sleight of hand in which Blackmane was the magician and the lead soldier his charming assistant; a handful of pennies passed so that any watching Statlos would see nothing. And then they were on their way, the jaws of the trap propped open by greed. *And the Marics curse me for being tight-fisted.*

Langrice met him inside. She looked sour, but that was just how her face was. Shave his beard, he'd likely have a kindred expression most of the time.

"This is more than you said," she observed.

"Dorae and Tobriant's kin. And some others. And then some others," he told her. And he had the seventeen here now, and with the two fugitives already in the cellar that made nineteen, still not the most auspicious of numbers, but it was *better*. It wasn't openly asking the world to kick his shins and trample his toes. "How are the charts?"

She hadn't liked it when he'd known about the charts. It was a look behind the curtain, puncturing the mystique of the Anchorage and its chain of keepers. But there were calculations you could do, regarding the moon's course and an antique Maric calendar and the seasonal ebb and flow of background magic. There was a book, many-times repaired and rebound, passed down the line of those unfortunates who'd taken up the mantle of harbourmaster at the Port to Nowhere. It let you know when the Wood would open.

"Tonight," she told him. Her man, Hellgram, was taking Blackmane's charges downstairs, to that hidden cellar beneath her hidden cellar. It would be crowded, but it would only be for one day.

She hadn't named a price, yet. That worried him. He didn't like owing people, though in this life, who could avoid it? He especially didn't like owing Langrice. It wasn't that he didn't like her. Well, he didn't *like* her, but then he didn't like anybody. He respected her a great deal: intelligent, resourceful and ruthless when she needed to be. Exactly the sort of person you didn't want to owe.

"How many d'you have?" she asked him.

"Four, now." The wards, scavenged, scrounged, gifted, stolen.

"Back in the day," she said languorously, "tuppenny wards like that, you'd want one for each of you. Not four between, what is it, twenty?"

"Nineteen."

"Ah well, that makes all the difference."

Better the beasts than the Pals. Better tooth and claw than the cells below the Donjon, the Inquirer's toolkit and, at last, the noose. Better this chance. And steeled himself against it. And perhaps there would come word, from a far city on the other side of the Wood, about new starts and new lives. Or perhaps no word would come, and he'd tell himself, *It's the distance. They're busy. It doesn't mean they didn't make it.* Or, knowing him, he'd have forgotten, moved on to some venture more reassuringly selfish. Thoughts of the refugees gone like smoke.

Like smoke.

"Is something on fire here?" he asked, blinking to clear his sight but finding the air still hazy. His senses twanged with the exercise of power: the impression of a space extending beyond the walls and all the way past the western horizon. *The Wood, it's opened already?* Almost that, not quite. Langrice hissed. When he turned, there was a figure standing between them and the door. Gaunt and angular and raggedly robed, but he didn't know it, not until it spoke.

"It's you. Both of you. One of you has it."

Fleance, Blackmane recalled the name. The Heron. The bad gambler.

"I need it. It's mine." The man stepped towards them like invisible hands were moving his legs. But quick, too. A stomping stagger that closed half the distance across the taproom in a heartbeat.

"Everybody thinks I have this thing," he said, his throat dry.

Fleance had been no magician. Blackmane would never have set out to rook the man else. And yet, here he was, walking through walls, emerging from *elsewhere*.

"What," he asked thickly, "have you done?"

"The Loruthi didn't have it," Fleance said flatly. "The Vulture didn't have it. I searched them. I searched inside them."

Blackmane backed up a step, making a subtle crooked gesture that watered his eyes. Seeing Fleance, a man draped in the flayed skin of a spirit that crawled about his shoulders.

"The Armiger didn't have it," Fleance went on. "The Gownsman didn't. And I'll go back for him. I will. I don't want to forget about him. But he didn't have it. He said he didn't. A maestro of the Gownhall. He wouldn't lie to me." His knife was in his hand, glinting and shifting, as though some part of the place he'd walked through clung to the steel like a fungus. From behind the bar, Jem let out a squeak of alarm but did nothing more useful.

"You know all this, you'll know I don't have it," Blackmane said reasonably.

"Listen, no listen, but *please*!" Fleance said, another skitter of steps closing the distance then swaying back, fighting like a fish on a line. "Allor sorcerer. You have to. I need it. It's strangling me." Pawing at his throat, eyes bulging. "I can't be safe until I'm safe."

"What did you do?" Blackmane demanded again.

"The robe. The mask," Langrice offered. "It's obvious."

"You killed an Indweller."

Fleance snarled, trying to round on both of them at once and somehow managing it, as though two of him were hazily overlain on the same space. "I *had* to! I had to do it. They were leaving without me. I had to escape. And now I have to escape *them*, before they – get – me – too." He wrestled each word out as though hands were at his throat, then he was at Langrice. "You!" Shrilling, castrato-high, weirdly inhuman. "Give me!" The knife flashed back, and she grappled with the wrist, biting at his other hand that was groping for her throat. Blackmane lumbered in and just swatted the Heron away, or that was the intent. He ended up with the skinny murderer clinging to *him* instead, tenacious as a stain.

"*Where is my treasure?*" shrieked Fleance.

Hellgram exploded up out of the cellar stairs, already fumbling about at his belt. He got something out, some trinket or toy of his, but Fleance bunched like a frog and sprang clear across the room at him. His blade cut a wide arc and slashed open the palm of Hellgram's hand, scattering his implement in a spray of bright blood. The foreigner fell back with a yell, more of surprise than pain, and at last, Jem was out from behind the bar. She almost got herself gutted, but she was only concerned with getting to Hellgram who'd curled about his damaged hand like a spider. With an animal sound, Fleance remembered who his enemy was.

He came at Blackmane faster than the space between them should have allowed. His body fought itself. The knife and its arm remained entirely his, but the rest of him was wracked by tides and countertides of muscular spasms, a battlefield where Fleance the defender was making a fighting retreat. He cannoned into Blackmane, the blade cutting away hanks of fur from his victim's cape while his off-hand choked himself with his own collar. Blackmane got a hand on the knife-arm's bicep and tried to hurl him away, but Fleance's bandy legs pincered his waist, heels digging into Blackmane's kidneys like bony thumbs. Then the man had his left hand under control again, clawing a fistful of Blackmane's shirt. He was trying to writhe his other arm from the Allorwen's grasp, and Blackmane saw elbow and shoulder just dislocate and distort, contorting through impossible degrees of freedom.

"Help me," Fleance said, quiet and calm and human. "Quickly, please. I need it."

"I don't *have* it!" Blackmane shook him furiously. "I never had the cursed thing!"

Fleance whined through closed lips, high enough to hurt the ears. Tears ran down his face. "They're coming for me," he got out. Then his arm was free, and Blackmane couldn't recapture it, the knife waving in triumph before drawing back like a theatrical murderer preparing his audience.

Langrice, whom Blackmane had thought fled, was abruptly at that elbow. Reaching, but not for the quicksilver razor of the knife. Fumbling for the mask instead. Fleance saw what she was at just too late. His face collapsed into a burlesque of horror, mouth open to howl the negative. Then she had one hand on the painted wood and one on the back of his head, and she practically mashed the two together to get the mask over Fleance's face.

He collapsed like a puppet with its strings cut, clattering down at Blackmane's feet in a tangle of limbs.

Blackmane took a long, ragged breath, feeling over himself carefully, just in case the knife had gone in somewhere despite it all.

"You and I," he said to Langrice, "are going to have a conversation."

She'd stepped back. There was a very pointed distance between them. She nodded.

Hellgram sat up. Jem had his hand bound in what looked like green and gold paper, crossed over with purple tape. A Divinati thing, Blackmane guessed. Some cast-off tatter of that enviable magic of theirs, that they'd neither share nor teach. And she was the least amputated finger of her exclusive little homeland, but apparently, she could still tie a bandage.

"Where's the ghost?" the foreigner asked. He looked waxy pale with pain. "Where did it go. It was riding him. I saw it."

"Good eyes you have, to see the invisible," Blackmane murmured, but Hellgram just said, "Yes." Perhaps in that lost war he claimed to have fled from, ghosts were just one more weapon.

"The ghost," Langrice said, "is still here."

Fleance's body made a *huff* sound, and Blackmane was weirdly certain it hadn't drawn a breath since the mask had gone on. It shivered. Hellgram stared at it, edging backwards, his slashed hand drawn close to his body and the other one outstretched as though to grasp for a knife. *Found something you've not seen before, have we? Some homegrown nastiness not a commonplace of your wars?* Blackmane considered.

Fleance got up. There was very little in it of the leverage one might expect of human limbs pushing against the pull of the ground. Rather, just as he'd collapsed with a marionette's abruptness, here was the puppet with its strings pulled again, rising to its feet and quivering.

Blackmane had never seen this, despite it being absolutely a local delicacy, magically speaking. Heard of it, certainly: read accounts, but there were matters you didn't pry into. The girl, Jem, was looking horrified and sketching some half-remembered warding in the dirt of the floor. Langrice, however, was composed. Grim, but unsurprised by any of it.

"Do you know," she said clearly, "where you are? What you are?"

Fleance's masked face tilted back and forth. It wasn't clear where he might be seeing from, but by Blackmane's reckoning, it wasn't him doing the seeing.

"Can you hear them?" Langrice pressed. She'd done this before. All part of her mystery, that came with being keeper of the Anchorage.

Another sound came from beneath the mask. Sighing, less like breath than wind through branches. And then a recognisable word. "Restoration." Not Fleance's voice.

It seemed to satisfy Langrice. She sagged back down onto one of her own chairs.

The masked figure – not Fleance, Blackmane decided – just stood there, swaying slightly.

He got as far as "Well," before the others came in. He heard the feet, the bustle of movement, expecting more Indwellers come to claim their errant kin. It was an intrusion of a more prosaic nature. Evene came in first, in all her pirate finery, sword drawn and a dozen of her bullies at her back. Langrice got to her feet hurriedly, then backed off when the tip of that sword and a couple of batons ended up pointed in her direction.

"What business?" she asked. "Or are we not square after your woman died? I thought we were square. You know it was none of my doing."

"Oh, there are a lot of things about this place I don't *know*," Evene said, though her eyes were more on Blackmane than Langrice.

"That's how it is. You know how it is," Langrice said levelly. "Always has been. You know this is nobody's turf, here. Not the Pals', not the Duke's, not the city's. You always found that useful, when you had someone to meet or something to hide."

"Right," Evene said. Her people were fanning out around the taproom. "You think I'd interfere with the Wood?" A blithe smile that turned nasty. "Much, anyway. Benno, Shevorn, go scout out below. Let's see if anyone else is hiding or storing, shall we."

"That's—" Langrice started, and the rod jutted back in her direction, and she bit off the sentence and swallowed it.

"Meeting, though," Evene went on. "I do want to meet someone. I want to meet a fat Allorwen dancing bear who owes me a magic mirror and a magic ward the Herons stole, that never made their way to me."

Blackmane closed his eyes. Opened them. He'd never had the ward, but he'd had the mirror, until Ostravar had abstracted it while Blackmane enjoyed the hangman's hospitality. Just one more piece of Maric history for Ivarn; a broken contract with the Bitter Sisters for Blackmane. *I should have strangled the old man when I had him.*

There was one tile he had left to play. He met Langrice's gaze and was gratified to see her face go dead and hard. *Yes, you understand me, don't you?* And he didn't think just coming out with his ever-so-belated realisation would save him, as opposed to just spreading the trouble. Selling Langrice to them wasn't the answer. *Or else I'd do it*, he assured himself. *But that's not the long game, here.*

"Well, you've met him," Langrice said. Evene's people had Hellgram and Jem backed into one corner. They'd been leery of the lanky foreigner at first, but his injury emboldened them. A couple of others stared warily at the masked figure, but if Blackmane was counting on rescue by Indweller magic, he was disappointed. It just stood there.

There was a commotion from below, which rolled up the cellar stairs and into the taproom. Blackmane had been silently hoping Hellgram had fitted everyone into the lower cellar, the more secret one, but apparently not. Here were Dorae and Tobriant and Tobriant's wife and another man, a glassworker whose name he couldn't even remember. Dorae had a hand to one eye, and that plainly represented the measure of resistance they'd been able to put up.

"New staff, is it?" Evene asked.

"You see how busy we are." Langrice shrugged around the taproom, crowded with Lodge soldiers.

"Auntie, look." The one called Benno was proffering something, and Blackmane's stomach dived to his boots. The wards. All four of the wards. The things he burned so many favours to get hold of. Evene raised her eyebrows, then looked over at Blackmane.

"My, we *do* have something to talk about, don't we?" she said sweetly.

"Langrice," Blackmane growled.

"Why don't you and he have a seat, Auntie?" Langrice said, with the proper and formal honorific. She indicated a booth table. "I'll have Jem get some tea on. Or stronger. You know Blackmane. He always has an angle. I'm sure he has something for you."

"I don't think so," Evene said softly. "Your offer's much appreciated, but it's my turn to host. Blackmane's cordially invited to the Fort. Our tea's not so fine, I'm sure, and we lack the view, but the company makes up for it."

Two of her people went to lay hands on him. He bristled, growled at them: they were big, but he was bigger, and a sorcerer too. Let them fear all the curses he was in no position to spit at them.

"You don't want a ruckus," Langrice said. "Not with the Pals out there."

Evene looked at Dorae and the other fugitives. "Is it *me* who doesn't, you think? Besides, we weren't exactly shy coming in. We made well sure they saw us and our pieces. They're not here for us, if we don't make trouble for them. Though they'd have fun with your clown here." She actually prodded the Indweller's chest, and they swayed. "Burn anyone wearing a mask, right now, I reckon."

"You know how it works here," Langrice continued. Her eyes were more on Blackmane than Evene, waiting for him to open his mouth and drop her in it, but her voice was admirably level. "That I am who I am, that I wear the mantle I do. I talk to everyone. I'm the go-between. The third party. Sit down with him and make a deal. You know, if I hear it, then the Wood will make sure it's honoured."

It was part of the mystique of the place and its keeper. Blackmane, for all his lore, wasn't sure if it was true or not. And yes, the Anchorage had seen its share of oath-breakers, and a lot of them had met a miserable end. But then, so did everyone else. That was life. Yet Evene had grown up with the same stories, as had all her people. The woman narrowed her eyes.

"Fine," she said, and Blackmane dared to start relaxing, already plotting the web he'd have to weave to get the wards back and walk free from the Anchorage and come out on top, outwit the lot of them. Then Evene said, "We'll take you, too. We are good hosts. Another guest won't strain us."

"And these, Auntie?" Benno asked, shoving Dorae into his fellows, but Evene wasn't interested in them. She didn't care about Hellgram's wounded-wolf snarl or Jem's wide, frightened eyes. They just goaded and kicked until Blackmane had shambled out under the dawn sky. Langrice, they let walk in his wake, though doubtless they'd have been rougher if she'd hesitated. The two of them exchanged a look, out in the open. She'd got herself this deep into the mire on his account. He'd not given her away to Evene. They were notionally even.

The Palleseen soldiers watched them depart, more than one baton directed their way. Evene had been right, though. Their focus was definitely on the Wood right now, as though sunrise would conjure an army of monsters for them to repel. But it didn't. However convenient that might personally have been, no horde came through. The trees would not be a port to distant lands until nightfall. And Blackmane and Langrice were going to the Fort to be the playthings of the Bitter Sisters.

Mosaic: The Spark

The Gownhall. It has survived a series of bad, indifferent and even illiterate Dukes, a paper tax and periods when the Ilmari populace viewed all learning as suspect sorcery. It has survived Ilmar being inducted into the Palleseen Sway, with its narrow rules on acceptable scholarship. The faculty would say you cannot extinguish the flame of learning. A close reading of the available primary sources suggests that those governing the Gownhall have always found a compromise. When the Pals invaded, there were dinners and fine wines, half-kept assurances about regularising the curriculum. Most of all, there was the siren lure of the Anchorwood. "We have studied the Wood and its ways for generations," they said, seeing the greed in the conquerors' eyes. "Would you throw all of that away?"

But now, the day is here. Pull out, then. It's too much for any one pair of eyes to see.

Full dawn finds Lemya at the barricades. She still doesn't have a baton. Her country family didn't shoot, not for sport nor sustenance. She has her flag and a sabre from the fencing team that Emlar's put an edge on. She's never fenced, either. There are a lot of Pals out there.

Mostly, they're the regular soldiers. Someone with a spyglass says they're the Donjon garrison. There are some detachments of Turncoats, paler uniforms and the implication of treachery making them targets the moment any shooting starts. Lemya wonders if that's why they were brought in.

They have a presence on every street leading to Gownhall Square, but they've concentrated their forces on two opposing approaches. Hard for divided defenders to support one another but, Lemya considers, much harder for split attackers to do the same.

A shout! It's started. She almost falls off the classroom chair she's sitting in, fumbles automatically to make sure her flag is flying properly, as if that's anyone's sane priority. A skirmish and a scuffle in one of the buildings overlooking the square. Everyone has a weapon to hand, looking up anxiously. Then a handful of Pal soldiers are bursting out onto the street, in full view of Lemya and her comrades. They're running, though. Legging it almost comically back towards their fellows. A moment later, a handful of students appear at an upper window. One of them is waving a Palleseen cap in the air triumphantly. It's Fyon, the Shrike woman who was strung up alongside Lemya. Her idea, to get people into every building with a view of the square. Just a handful in each, but the Pals plainly had the same thought and hadn't expected to meet the enemy there. Someone throws down a handful of batons the fleeing soldiers dropped, and now there are more students armed, though ammunition is going to be a problem. A cheer goes up across the square, and the Pals hear it.

They do. Fellow-Inquirer (soon to be Sage-Inquirer, surely) Hegelsy does, and scowls. Every soldier that came back without their weapon is sent for discipline. If he'd got his people placed to shoot down into the square, perhaps he would just have ordered an immediate advance and trusted to superior Palleseen discipline to have the business rolled up by midday. The enemy, after all, are only children and a few old men and women.

He doesn't have to be here in person, of course. He isn't a

military field officer. He has people for that. He is, however, exactly that sort of superior who won't leave his subordinates to do their jobs. And, perhaps, wary and wise enough about the treacherous ways of the City of Bad Decisions. He's studied the history of his current posting. It seems to him that, before his people came to impose order and common sense, the Ilmari were fully occupied fighting each other and falling victim to curses. *They should be thanking us with tears in their eyes.*

No immediate charge at the barricades with ram and portable artillery, then, not until the overlooking windows can be counted as friendly territory. He has time, though. He has planned today very thoroughly, and his allies are in place across the city. When the various other disturbances are either dealt with, or have failed to materialise, Nisbet and Brockelsby can come and reinforce him, and finish matters here, if anything is still outstanding. He can be patient.

He lets the morning lag as his people get themselves into place, cautious, hidden from the aim of the students. Moving door to door, until he has a noose around them, ready to bite into that final ring of buildings and then the barricades themselves.

He sends to Nisbet for an update on where the factory mob are, whether they've even crossed the river. Then he feels it's time to engage the students again, and if not with arms, then with words. When could these academics ever resist the chance to exercise their jaws, after all?

"Send in our terms," he decides. Small chance of an actual surrender so soon, but for his report, he can at least include that he made the attempt.

The Palleseen flag of parlay is halved black and white, simple enough that even their enemies can understand it. The two halves mean *Either, you accept our terms, or you fall.* Beneath it, a squad of soldiers and their officer advance, ramrod straight, under the aim of the students' batons. Just as nobody shot the runners earlier, nobody shoots now. The students are young and scared and hungover, or else still somewhat drunk. Very few of them have slept – some are sleeping now, to be woken with a kick and a curse if fighting starts. Overnight, they have drained the Gownhall cellars and sung increasingly incoherent songs, made pledges to each other, made love, all that. They have written their own terms and demands and constitutions, debated fiercely what the future should look like. They've invented a hundred different Ilmars – restorations of the old and impositions of the new. And then dawn came, and the Pals with it. In the cold light of day, after all that intellectual exercise, nobody wants to speak the first killing word.

The officer steps forwards, unfolding his orders, eyes flicking to the high windows. It would, after all, only take one joker with a baton to cut the man's military career short.

"By the authority of the Perfector of the city and environs of Ilmar," he declares, "those dissident citizens currently arrayed under arms are found to be in breach of the following sections of the Charter of Correct Thought, namely..." He looks from the paper to his audience and judges that a long dry list of numbered paragraphs is not going to play well to this house. "Namely... several such ordnances," he glosses. "By said authority of the Perfector and the Schools of Correct Thought, you are hereby commanded to disperse to your dwelling places and abodes with no further violence. You are required to dismantle such obstructions to the streets and thoroughfares as you have erected. You are required to surrender such arms and implements of violence as are in your possession and in all other ways comply with the very reasonable dictates of the Principles of Correct Thought as laid down in... the usual places." Another throat-cracking chunk of liturgy avoided because nobody's in the mood this morning. And nobody's much impressed, either. *Is that all you've got?* hangs in the air. But that's just the preamble. His orders give him a carrot and they give him a stick. Or perhaps, just a selection of sticks of various sizes.

"If these very reasonable requirements are complied with," he continues, hearing his own voice echo from the walls and from the far side of the square, "then the Perfecture shall require only the following in reparation. That leaders of the insurrection to the number of seven" – it says 'seven (7)' on the paper, but he doesn't know how he's expected to read it like that – "surrender themselves or are surrendered by their fellows into the custody of the School of Correct Speech who confirm that they shall hear all their grievances and supporting evidence before passing the malefactors to the School of Correct Appreciation for release or sentencing as is deemed appropriate." He pauses, hearing the gathering anger of his listeners. They don't feel that the Perfector or Correct Speech are in a position to make demands. He presses on. "Those others under arms who effect a prompt surrender and concession to these terms shall receive a general amnesty under the special dispensation given to the School of Correct Appreciation. However, if no such general surrender of arms and submission to these terms is made," he informs them, his voice edging a semitone higher as he braces himself, "then may it be known that upon any subsequent surrender after the commencement of a pacification action as defined in... as... after a fight" – grinding his teeth at the loquacity of his superior's pen – "then such leaders under arms as may be apprehended, to the number of no less than twenty – twenty – shall themselves face immediate execution, and any and all others who are found to have participated in unlawful insurrection against the Perfecture shall be liable for arrest either immediately or at any time thereafter, to be tried and sentenced at the discretion of the Schools of Correct Thought."

And he's done, and braces himself, but nobody shoots. In fact, somebody is coming over the barricade. A man whose bald head is intricately inked, wearing scholarly robes but looking ferociously piratical for all that. A sword at his hip and walking as though he's more than used to it being there. Maestro Vorkovin of the music faculty, not that the officer would believe it.

He has a scroll in one hand, and he waves it at the officer in an admonitory fashion, as though the man is a student late for class. His own voice – he has a fine baritone – echoes all the way back to the Gownhall buildings and ahead of him – far enough that even Hegelsy can make out the occasional word.

"The faculty and student body of the Gownhall of Ilmar are pleased that the Perfecture is open to a non-violent resolution and reasoned discussion of grievances," he announces in Maric, and then says it again in mostly decent Pel. Thus informed, the officer feels the man is somewhat misrepresenting the tenor of the Palleseen ultimatum, but Vorkovin isn't done.

"I have here a number of requirements that the faculty and student body have agreed must be met before a peaceful resumption of regular academic life can be contemplated. If you would be so kind, perhaps you would convey me, as an ambassador under your flag of parlay and according to paragraph one thousand seven hundred and ninety-two, brackets nine end brackets, brackets three end brackets of the Charter of Correct Conduct and section eleven of the ninth appendix thereto," and each sentence given in two languages – the Maric longer and more shaded in meaning, the Pel hard and flat and economic. "I would welcome the opportunity to present them to your commanding official."

The officer's orders don't cover this situation, but the point of Correct Thought is that there's always a default response, and in this case, it's to kick it so far up the chain of command that hopefully he'll never have to see it again.

A lifetime of performance, teaching and faculty budget squabbles has given Maestro Vorkovin a good game face. Inside, he feels like an hourglass nobody's going to be giving a second turn. He's not slept, strung wide awake on a diet of strong tea, nerves and medicinal pipe-stuffing that he's currently on three times the recommended dosage of. Last night (when he'd added brandy to the mix) things seemed very different. He sat up all hours with Gowdi and Porvilleau and a rotating cast of students hammering out just what it was that they actually wanted, now they were up in arms. As is so often the case, the *casus belli* had arrived before anyone was ready, and now they had to justify it *post hoc*. But it wasn't as if people didn't have sufficient grievances against the Perfecture or things they wanted changed. The main struggle had been trying to produce something that balanced the increasingly idealistic demands of the students with anything he reckoned the Pals might even give the time of day to. In the cold light of this day, he feels he could have pushed back further. There are a lot of Pals out there, and every one of them has a baton, and they have some Palleseen Hands too, which will chew up the barricades quickly enough. In his mind, the Occupiers must be raring to throw their soldiers into the teeth of the fight, while he and his fellows need time. If he and Hegelsy could have been candid with one another they'd find their positions have a lot in common. From Vorkovin's perspective, there is help coming. The Armiger families are bringing in their retainers from outside the city (they aren't). The general body of resistance fighters across Ilmar will be gathering towards the Gownhall (they won't). Of the factory march and the Wielding of the Hammer he has only the vaguest notion, but they *are* coming, which is about to have a profound impact on his embassy.

The demands themselves, argued over at such length and in variously rational states of mind, mostly relate to the students' own grievances. Revolutions always go from the specific to the general if they're given the chance. The students want an expansion of the curriculum, the restoration of a bibliography of banned texts, formal exceptions that permit teaching of all subjects in Maric. They want specific freedoms for particular Ilmari institutions to preserve their Maric identity rather than just being moulded into the Palleseen likeness. Later on, after they'd gone back to the cellar a few times, they'd added demands that Mirror Allor be guaranteed certain rights and protections, and a paragraph regarding freedom of religious worship that Correct Speech would never permit and that the Mahanic Temple would probably have some issues with too. Demands that Correct Conduct follow its own rules when arresting people and that Correct Speech not be permitted to mandate exceptions to the proper treatment of prisoners. It had all seemed perfectly praiseworthy at the time. And if it's all antipathy to the very essence of the Palleseen Sway, well, Vorkovin has spent all night talking people down from demanding the dismantling of the Schools of Correct Thought entirely. He's also had to explain to a succession of excitable students that they couldn't really demand reparations for the unlawful execution of Ivarn Ostravar given the man in question was sitting to his left, very obviously un-executed. Certainly, Ivarn had been very keen *not* to remind anyone in authority that he was supposed to have a longer neck and a shorter life than had turned out to be the case.

As they march him past the ranks of silent soldiers, all of them staring ahead at the barricades while eyeing him sidelong, he silently rehearses all the subsections and paragraph numbers of Correct Thought that deal with their intricate parlay rules.

He sees a table set out ahead under a hastily erected awning, because the weather is no respecter of occasion, and the first spots of rain are just lancing down. He recognises Fellow-Inquirer Hegelsy, which confirms the rumour that Correct Speech is running the show. Everyone's least favourite School. The man is smiling, though. Perhaps that's a good sign.

A stir runs through the soldiers. Just a slight one, like wind brushing across a field. Vorkovin catches up with the cause a moment later. His own thoughts have been drowning out the world, but a new sound creeps up on him. A murmur, a susurration, a rumble. The sound of many voices – some of them raised in song. Not close, but not far. Not all the way across the city, for sure. This side of the river and getting closer. Some of the soldiers start glancing away when their officers aren't watching. Looking west towards the source. A new tension has come to them. An army with a foe on its flank.

Vorkovin sees someone push through the ranks, running, tripping over the feet of the soldiers he's elbowing past. A message important enough that the messenger has a Statlos's bars on his shoulder. He skids to a halt before Hegelsy and hands over his orders. Reading, the Fellow-Inquirer stills, and his face goes taut.

In the crisp accountant's hand of Fellow-Broker Nisbet:

The labourers march is in greater numbers than sources indicated. No contact yet but shortly anticipated. It is not entirely clear that we will be able to contain them if matters devolve to violence. Standard bottle procedures may not suffice.

Hegelsy glances up, sees the much looked-for ambassador of the students come to waste his fellows' time in useless talk before Hegelsy closes the jaws of his trap on them all. Which plan was predicated on Nisbet and Brockelsby holding their respective positions and ensuring no succour arrived at the Gownhall from any other quarter. And now, she can't *guarantee* that, and Hegelsy's plan to twiddle his thumbs until the rest of the city is properly in order looks very short-sighted indeed.

He can almost hear Culvern laughing at him.

However, Correct Speech always has an alternative plan for every eventuality.

Maestro Vorkovin approaches, already unrolling the scroll of his demands, the flag of parlay fluttering dampily overhead.

"Arrest this ringleader," Hegelsy tells his officers. "Have him held. Move in on the overlooking buildings and the barricades. Immediate advance, all troops."

"I am here for a parlay!" Vorkovin splutters. "Under paragraph—"

"Just get him out of here," Hegelsy snaps. "I'll deal with him later."

And Vorkovin is bundled away in a flurry of subclauses.

"They're coming!" The single shout is just about all the warning Fyon gets. The Pals had got into the next building out from the square, and now they make a break across the street. A crackling baton-shot goes wide, another finds its mark. A pale-clad Turncoat spins and drops, clutching at a charred rosette. Three of them waste themselves against the door, which Fyon's fellows barricaded. Another uses the butt of their weapon to smash through shutters and the glass beyond. The people who fled this area yesterday were rich, and their houses have big windows and plenty of them. The soldiers are inside the house in moments, and Fyon's people must hold the stairs against them.

The waiting's not been good for her. Not because she can't be patient. She once hid in the attic of a tax official for a day and a half, until he came home and brought his nicely slittable throat with him. Fyon has never been a good person. She wasn't even a particularly nice child. Aware of her moral frailties, her only recourse had been to turn them against the Occupiers. If it hadn't been for the Pals, she'd have been killing someone else for a worse cause, no doubt. It's a similar story for most who call themselves Shrikes. They're only a part of the resistance because they were always going to be against *somebody*, so why not the Occupation?

And she works alone. Except, while working alone, they caught her and hanged her in company, which company she's remained in. Not that she likes Lemya – the girl's a fool, patently.

But up for a fight, and that's what has Fyon tagging along. In her head, she's already decided she's dead. Any leftover time she has is epilogue, and any harm she can do to the Occupiers a bonus.

And she had seen the students weren't breaking into these fine houses that give such a good vantage of Gownhall Square. So she had started breaking windows, and a pack of youngsters had followed her lead, and then more. A bit of vandalism, a bit of looting, the siren sound of breaking glass. And she's spent the night not getting much sleep while this bunch of kids talk revolution and freedom and all the other things that, for her, were only ever a fig leaf for murder.

And in the morning, she knew, the Pals would come. She would die, and do it properly this time. Better in a fight than on a rope. Except now, they're going to die with her. They, who are ten years her junior, and keen, and not tarnished by the world like she is.

The Pals are downstairs, confused for a moment by the internal layout. She ducks out from the foot of the stairs and shoots one, speaking the Pel trigger-word to spark her baton to life. Then back and up the stairs just in time. The soldiers round the corner, and her followers above begin shoving priceless antique furniture. An ornate blackwood desk, a century and a half old, toboggans down the steps and cures the Pals of any excess enthusiasm they might have for a quick ascent. There's more where that came from. The house's owners were collectors.

Fyon crouches on one side of the landing, some girl whose name she can't remember is on the other. The kid shoots a grin at her – wild, scared, fierce. Fyon feels an unbearable sadness. An appalling, alien emotion. She wants no truck with it, but it won't leave her alone. Thirty years of being a murderously bad person, and somehow, *this* was hiding inside her, awaiting its moment for ambush.

The Pals fail to take the stairs twice. A combination of furniture and fire hammer them right back down. The final time that Fyon snaps the word engraved onto her baton's tableth the weapon sparks a bit but doesn't shoot. She asks around. One of the students mutely hands her his own weapon. Nobody has any spares.

The girl tries to be a hero, then. She darts down, reaching for the ammunition bandolier of the nearest dead Pal. There's a line of sight from the downstairs hall, though, and three shots take her almost at once. She sprawls dead atop the corpses she was trying to rob, and that she'd helped kill. Fyon didn't shout at her to stop. It didn't occur to her. Now she knows she should have. She is responsible.

The Pals don't know the students are almost out. The defenders have perhaps a couple more shots in Fyon's baton, and one singularly ugly armoire currently teetering on the brink of the top step.

She blinks back tears. Not for her – she never cried for herself, even as a child.

From downstairs, they hear orders shouted in Pel, an officer haranguing his troops. For a moment, she wonders if their nerve has broken. But here they come again, and for the last time.

Fyon kicks the armoire down on them. When it hits the leader, it shatters and reveals the secret of its monstrous weight. A hidden drawer bursts and showers the attackers with a hoard of gold coins and jewellery. Fyon shoots through the shrapnel of wealth: once, twice and then the magic's gone.

"Go!" she tells her charges as she ducks round the corner and draws her knives. They don't want to, but she shouts at them until they do. Then the first soldier is at the top of the stairs, long baton unwieldy in the close quarters. She sets about paying back the death she's owed the Pals since the scaffold.

While this is going on – repeated with variations in a dozen different townhouses – the main force of the Pals is rushing the barricades.

Lemya has hold of the crossbow still. Her rate of fire is hampered by having to lie on her back with her foot in the stirrup to re-cock it, but as she only has three bolts, it doesn't make much difference. Her comrades with the batons accomplish considerably more. The first wave of Pals tries a straightforward charge down both its chosen streets, in the hope the students will break. They don't, and fifteen soldiers are put out of the fight, dead or dragged back by their fellows. After that, they try advance-and-shoot, striking splinters from and through the ramshackle barricades, but taking far more hurt than they manage to inflict. Once that gets too costly, they turn to dashing from cover to cover, doorways and side streets. Some shoot, others scurry. The students hold to their barriers and loose every time a target presents itself. There's no particular discipline, just everyone for themselves, but as a defence, it holds up readily enough. As long as the Pals keep giving them targets, there's no time for the academics to fall to bickering or discussing the philosophical implications of it all.

Lemya, her last ineffectual bolt shot, makes herself useful. She brings water and the last remaining wine, tours with a ladle wherever there's thirst. She helps Emlar distribute the remaining spare tablethi to those with batons. Then there's a lull when the Pals are considering their options, having been driven out of the nearest three doorways. Lemya looks out onto the street scattered with the bodies the Pals weren't able to reclaim. The momentary quiet lets in a tune that the sounds of the fight had eclipsed. She feels her heart swell with it. *Ilmar!* it says, though it isn't the Ilmar of today or these last several generations. She almost leads a phantom charge right over the barricades, but instead, an actual plan comes to her. A way to direct the sudden madness of *I must act!* that she is caught up in.

She and her old crew, Emlar and Hervenya and a couple of others – no Shantrov, of course – manhandle the big dining table from the Lesser Maestro's Hall out into the quad and over the barricade. The Pals watch, dumbfounded. Then she and the others just move forwards, shunting the thing like a pavise over the cobbles. She feels the first impacts, but there's two hundred years of Maric history and fine dining between her and the enemy. Her friends get it past the closest bodies and strip each of ammunition, then the next row. After that, the table has been chewed away at the edges and their fellows at the barricades are shouting at them to run.

They run, pockets and the folds of their shirts clattering with tablethi. Behind them, the table explodes into fragments. The Pals have taken the opportunity to bring their Hand up. Once the old table is so much matchwood, the thing just turns on the barricade itself. It's little more than a score of oversized batons linked together, strung with chains of tablethi that glitter and fizz and go dull as their power is devoured. Lemya vaults the barricade in a shower of splinters. Hervenya is right on her heels, spilling over and rolling hard on the flagstones beyond, dazed enough by the impact everyone thinks she's been shot. Emlar, bringing up the rear, is shot. He arches back, hands flinging his bounty of gold tablethi in all directions. His shoulder explodes, his knee. He drops, a foot from the barricades. Lemya is shouting, trying to go back for him, but other students wrestle her away. The Hand keeps up its mauling of the barricade, scouring everything away in a storm of sawdust and jagged wooden shards. They had to haul it close, though, to bring its hammer down on the students' defences. Wherever it isn't pointed, there are defenders shooting back. One of the operators is killed, another wounded. The Pal woman who runs to replace them is shot down before she reaches the device. It stands on its tripod legs, its jutting fingers sagging downwards as though tired now. Lemya is too traumatised to take advantage, but there's a student sally halfway over the barricades already. If they can take possession of the thing, the Pals surely won't dare—

But they're already coming. The full force of them, and from the far side of the square, the shout goes up that it's the same story there. The barricade on Lemya's side is little more than wood chips and spars. Her comrades with batons shoot into the advance, and take fire in return.

From streets away, she can hear an angry roar, like the voice of the city. It might as well be in another country or from another time.

Fire

A small, unassuming woman. She travelled a lot for her work, though she always came back to Ilmar. A lot of establishments on both sides of the river knew her face, fewer her name. She had been at some memorable Armiger parties. She'd watched the Bitter Sisters run their circus from the subterranean halls of the Fort. She liked to sit and hear people circulate the city's news. She bought the pamphlets and ballad sheets that told of some new misfortune or outrage. A stabbing, a drowning, a robbery gone bloody. The more lurid the account the better. She liked being where things happened. Her modest little boast, in private or sometimes when giving an account of herself to employers: Yes, I was there. I saw it all.

She'd found herself a good spot to see exactly what was going on. The shops up the stretch of Liberation Way that ran from Gownhall Square to the Portbridge had homes above them, and the homes had attic rooms for the servants, and this attic room had windows on three sides. Which the servants must have cursed over the chill winter nights, but which was currently very useful for a curious woman who wanted to see history being made.

The servants themselves had fled with the shopkeeper and his family. The whole street had emptied, and they'd put up heavy shutters over the shopfronts. The word that the factory labourers were Wielding the Hammer after so long had struck terror into the mercantile middle classes. And here, right up near where the Occupiers had set up, there wasn't a soul left, other than they and she, the solitary observer in her hidden eyrie. Earlier on, though, as she'd passed all the fleeing bourgeoisie, there had been a fair number of apprentices and shop workers skulking off in the opposite direction. She reckoned the ranks of the millhands would be swelled a little by rebellious clerks and carters and traders' assistants by the time they got this far.

And they were coming, at last. They'd made decent progress. Back when she'd taken a first look, over in the Hammer Districts, the whole venture had been an unformed chaos of workers and their families, more a street party than a riot. She'd wondered if that was what would wash up at the Pals' doorstep. The children of the Siblingries like a human shield to test the resolve of the Occupiers. She didn't think the Pals would hesitate more than a few heartbeats. Obedience to rules and orders was their thing, after all.

Now the march was coming down Liberation Way, and she watched it slow as they saw the welcome laid out for them, the marchers behind compacting into those ahead. Back in his day, the Old Duke had certainly turned out the guard when the factories went silent. They'd picketed the route in small groups, armed with batons and truncheons and halberds. There were skirmishes and scuffles later – stragglers from the march picked up or beaten, looters punished. Sometimes, there had been full-on showdowns, the Siblingry people against the points of the pikes. Accusations from both sides later over who had thrown the first stone or swung a bludgeon. Not like this, though. Not like this blocked street, bristling with batons. She wondered if it would all just come apart now. Perhaps the workers wouldn't fancy the odds, would break apart and head home. Doubtless, the soldiers would give chase, emboldened by a lack of resistance the way civic authorities always were. She watched the early ranks of the marchers crunch up, word being passed down the street. The swift feet of kids no older than twelve dashing nimbly between the adults. To abandon their symbolic defiance would have a generation of future historians tutting into their moustaches, but right *now*, there were obvious benefits.

And then they were on the move again, she saw. Sorting out their order, some groups shunting forwards, others retreating. The strong and pugnacious to the fore. Non-combatants and children ordered back to let the fist of the factories through. And there was a cart squeezing through somehow. She recognised the tactic from what she'd heard about marches past. They'd taken the square iron doors off the big furnaces and stacked them high. Now they manhandled them out of the cart bed, passing them forwards. Hardly practical battlefield kit, but they were shields that would stop a baton-shot, if their bearers could keep them held up.

Now the vanguard was all workers in their hardwearing overalls, and they were pressing forwards again. Not military discipline, but in decent order, nonetheless. She didn't know the precise distinctions in dress that denoted particular trades, but it was plain the Siblingries had organised themselves into companies along those lines. Here and there were the banners proudly proclaiming their livelihoods and their civic loyalty. Some singing, still – the old work songs, that let them keep pace with each other. The blart or whistle of the odd musical instrument. Still a few rags of festival clinging to the whole endeavour.

The woman in the attic room got out her spyglass and peered out of the window that let her look back down Liberation Way towards the river. She could see the hangers-on, the wives and househusbands and the children, and a fair mob of idlers and random citizens who wanted to see what was going to happen. All from a safe distance, or that would be the hope. If there was one vice the average Ilmari always succumbed to, though, it was an unhealthy curiosity about what their neighbours were doing. She could empathise with that readily enough. Here she was spying on them all from her lofty vantage. She always ended up where things kicked off, a professional eyewitness to a string of tragedies and historical footnotes.

The Palleseen forces had blocked the street with cross-sectioned barriers up ahead. These were forces under the control of the School of Correct Exchange, headed up by Fellow-Broker Nisbet, or so the watcher understood. Nisbet was, by repute, no soldier, but she listened to her subordinates. Half her force was split across her flanks, and as the marching Siblingry people came on, the Pals were filtering out on either side like the jaws of a trap. Shuffling across to another window gave the watcher a good view of the Palleseen command, messengers coming and going from the front like agitated bees. Out with the spyglass again, and she could see the slender figure of Nisbet herself, sitting on a folding stool with a clerk to hold an umbrella over her. An interesting exercise in reading body language. Each messenger who came and went was winding a crank inside Nisbet. She must be looking at the force she had assembled here, and the reported numbers of the marchers. In her accountant's mind, doubtless, a series of sums was plunging numbers further and further into the debit column.

The march was slowing. The watcher changed windows again to see. There was a lot of bunching and collision at first, but they restored order remarkably quickly, each trade and Siblingry looking to its own. At the very back, the civilians milled. Some people were still singing. The Palleseen flanks continued moving out to bottle the front of the march. The watcher had seen similar tactics on many occasions, here and in other cities. Crush the people together, negate their numbers, trap them and move in. Except, the march extended halfway back to the Portbridge, and there was a limit to what Nisbet's people could actually do. And the Pals hadn't started shooting, and the Siblingries hadn't been looting and rioting down the street, just marching. For a surprisingly long moment, everyone stared at everyone else, as though they were just too polite to make the first move.

Then a Pal officer stepped forwards and made the standard

demands: disperse, go back to your homes and factories by order of et cetera and so forth. The gathering was unlawful and against a whole tedious set of ordnances, both of the Perfecture and Ilmar's own laws.

The officer stepped back into the cover of the barriers. Nobody dispersed, and nobody was surprised. The watcher could see, by changing her angle and the focus of the spyglass, some Pal messengers heading off towards the Gownhall. Begging reinforcements from the force stationed there, most likely. And of course, there was even a force of Pals all the way across the river, but they'd apparently had other things on their mind than intercepting the march at its start, and now they'd be no help to anybody. The watcher prided herself on being well informed about current events, and now she was wondering whether the Pals might have made some significant errors in their initial disposition.

She turned her focus on the leading edge of the march, standing there within a short rush of the barriers. Point blank range for the batons of the soldiers, but too close for more than one or two shots if the marchers had the steel to charge. Nisbet had been following the Pal playbook by constructing her bottleneck and letting them walk into it, but now she was probably wishing she had a bigger bottle.

Something was happening. Someone was striding out from beneath the banners of the marchers, coming halfway between the Siblingries and the barriers. The watcher knew him instantly. Father Orvechin. No mistaking that beard. No mistaking that clear, strong voice, either. A man used to making himself heard over the machines. She put down the glass and hunched forwards to listen. In her hands now was a little notebook, and she jotted down everything the man said.

He spread his arms, the picture of reason, if there wasn't an army of the discontented at his back. "When I was an apprentice," he explained conversationally to the entire Palleseen force, "I marched with my master and her fellows after the Old

Duke made his capped wages proclamation and said we couldn't ask for more. All the way to the palace we went, and we sang under his window and lifted our banners so he could see them on his balcony." A personal anecdote boomed out to reach to the next street. The other Siblingry heavies in the march's vanguard were still tense, looking past Orvechin at the Pal lines. They had hammers and crankshafts and big wrenches, and the watcher reckoned they'd have those barriers taken apart if the Pals gave them two clear minutes to do it. And the Pals were listening too, not quite sure why they were being told all this but waiting for the other rhetorical shoe to drop. The watcher could see Fellow-Broker Nisbet beneath her umbrella, craning forwards to hear, even as her subordinates muttered to her.

"And the proclamation was rolled back, and we returned to the factories and got on with making the city richer, and just for an extra penny a shift," Orvechin said, and there were cheers, a little clapping, from his fellows. "And," he went on, before anyone could think about getting a word in, "when I was a young journeyman, we marched down this street to the palace again, even though the Duke's people stood just where you're standing to turn us away! That was after three men and a child had been killed in their new model shuttling press, and we'd not use the things again. They arrested a dozen factory overseers for saying so, and we marched. And the prisoners were let go, and they redesigned the machines, after we'd camped out under the Duke's window again."

And he wasn't mentioning those times when the factory workers had Wielded the Hammer just like this and nothing had changed, or the two times in living memory when the march had met the Duke's people hard enough to set buildings on fire and leave a string of bodies down this very street and see Siblingry leaders hung in the Donjon yard. But then the Pals probably wouldn't have done their homework on Orvechin and the Siblingries like the watcher had. She always researched her subjects, often to a level of detail that worried her employers.

More bustle, and then it was Nisbet herself coming forwards to instruct her spokesman officer, prim and delicate and with a clerk rushing after her to make sure not one drop of the patient rain got on her uniform. Nisbet didn't do her own shouting, but gave terse orders, and the officer relayed her words. They were hardly worth hearing. The watcher didn't note them.

"By the express order of the Perfector, you are ordered to disperse. If you remain on the streets causing an affray you will be arrested."

Passive voice, thought the watcher. And the marchers were still coming, the main body of them slowly compacting, as stragglers arrived from the direction of the Portbridge. And perhaps Nisbet was avoiding *We will arrest you* because it was clear there weren't enough Pals there to wrestle even a quarter of the crowd to the ground.

"All of us?" Orvechin asked. "Who will make the factories work? Who will mint your tablethi and stamp your buttons and stitch your uniforms? Since you came to our city, you have made use of us. Those boots you wear are from the Temechin factory. Your caps from just across the street from there. The very paper of your orders comes from the mill on Tevel Street. Will you go barefoot and bare-headed and rely on word of mouth?" Then he took another step forwards, looking left and right at the soldiers, blanking Nisbet entirely.

"You are working men and women of your own trade," he told them. "If your masters told you to work more hours for less, charged you for use of your own weapons, would you be mute?"

Not, the watcher thought, *what this is about*. It was the arrests of Siblingry people, by these very soldiers. The organisers and collectors of complaints and the agitators, rounded up to try and stop something exactly like this, arrested on the Pals' own notion, or prompted by others. Plenty of parties interested in making sure the mill wheels turned cheaply and easily, after all.

In the silence that followed, while the increasingly twitchy Nisbet considered her response, everybody could hear the distant crackle of baton-fire a few streets distant. The watcher caught the ripple of disquiet that went through the marchers. The Gownhall had been flying flags for a couple of days, ever since Ostravar was first arrested. The Siblingries were on their way to parade through the square and fly some flags right back. They hadn't realised everything had already gone to blades and batons over there. The word and the agitation both were passed back along the street. Which only underscored the bizarre nature of the Pals' reply.

"You are ordered to go around," the officer declared, sounding strangled by incredulity. "Go on to the palace by another road. This route is closed, by order of…" Through the spyglass, Nisbet's lean face was twisted in indecision. "Of order."

Damn, thought the watcher. Nisbet had just thrown the Perfector under a cart, and if making a riot outside the Ducal Palace had been the point, then Orvechin could have gone and done just that. Assuming the Pals didn't change their minds and try to bottle them somewhere the streets were narrower and numbers would be less useful. Perhaps that was Nisbet's plan. But of course, this wasn't just about the Siblingries' complaints.

Nisbet didn't look like someone with an ingenious strategy. She looked like someone used to counting beans and now very much out of her brief. Orvechin had stepped back so some of his fellows could talk in his ear. One gestured north, a road currently blocked by Pal troops. The watcher could almost hear the murmured words. *Perhaps we should…* Because the sounds of fighting over Gownhall-way were only getting louder, thin voices high on the wind and the rattle of shot. And to some, that might spark thoughts of *We have to help*, but others would be looking at the batons of the increasingly tense soldiers and thinking *That could be us.* She watched them waver on both sides, knowing it was past time for her to act, but finding she really wanted to know what Orvechin's call would be.

At last, he spoke. "But this is the way we always go," he said simply, gesturing towards Gownhall Square. More singing, distant, from the back of the march. Work songs mingling with *The Peak and the Port*, the old Ilmari anthem. Nisbet seemed frozen, teetering with a steep slope either side: *give the order to fire* versus *fall back and let them pass*. And the Pals had the guns, and their bottleneck. Yet Orvechin was right there, within three steps and a swung hammer of the barriers, which suddenly looked so very flimsy.

The watcher put away her notebook and spyglass; it was past time. With practised efficiency, she picked up her long baton and levelled it, took and held a breath, squinted, whispered a Maric syllable that made the tablett spark. The flash of magic from the rod's end hid the moment when the bolt laid open Orvechin's head, but she'd been sure of her aim as she uttered the trigger-word. He was cradled in the arms of a comrade when she saw him next, and the workers were surging forwards furiously, and the Pals were firing into them on three sides. Nisbet's decision-making had been removed from the scenario.

The watcher had already packed up and was on her way out the back, away from the escalating fight. They would already be hand-to-hand over the barriers. It was entirely possible that the workers' numbers would tell, and they'd power through to Gownhall Square despite everything. The watcher rather hoped they did. She was a dedicated professional who would never let personal beliefs get the better of contractual instructions, but on her own time, she appreciated doomed valour as much as the next Ilmari. Right now, she was going to report her success to her employers: the beheading of the Siblingry leadership, the crippling of their cause. After that, though, she would go make sure that tomorrow's ballad sheets would have the True Last Words of Father Orvechin Before His Most Foul Murder at the Hands of the Palleseen.

Mosaic: The Dousing

A great deal of strain is being placed on the relationship between the different Palleseen Schools. Correct Speech holds the most authority, breaks ties, investigates abuses. Hegelsy has the winning hand, then. Save that, for those reasons, nobody likes Correct Speech. Correct Exchange runs commerce and has the purse strings, but the others loathe it for its venality and reluctance to enforce its own regulations. Correct Conduct has the most soldiers, but for that reason, it's given the least seniority for fear of a coup. Correct Appreciation, with its authority over the arts and judiciary, is derided by the other Schools, save that its adherents can devote their time to politics, hence the primacy of men like Culvern. Correct Erudition should be the least significant of all, save that Palleseen culture is reliant on magic to fuel its engines and weapons and conveniences. Hence, what the Archivists want, they get. Right now, in Ilmar, the senior Archivist dead and Culvern isolated, Hegelsy makes the move that will see him promoted or damned.

At the shattered barricade, Lemya's fellows hold for as long as their ammunition does. Not long, even with what they scavenged from the street. After that, there's a brief attempt to hold off the charge by physical force: fencing sabres and pikes and table legs against the butts of the soldiers' batons, their truncheons and boots. There is Palleseen shooting from the windows overlooking the square. The line gives. Lemya gets one blow in with her sword, bloodying the sleeve of an enemy. She abandons the tapestry flag. The students flee for the Gownhall buildings as the soldiers form up. Across the square, the other barricade is intact, but to hold it would be to have the enemy at their backs. Everyone is running. Some students flee for the other alleyways, where there's been no fighting. The Pals are there, though – not in force, but enough. They arrest anyone who stands still for it, shoot the few who don't. The students scramble from the abandoned barricades to the Gownhall itself. They funnel between the gates; they dive through windows. Lemya is at the back. Sporadic shooting is still sleeting in with the rain from above. Hervenya catches a bolt – stray, probably not even meant for her. It sears across her side and into her thigh, and she drops, silent with the shock of it. For a moment, Lemya doesn't notice she's down, almost abandons her friend through sheer inattention. Then the absence at her flank registers, and she turns back. Hervenya isn't the only one down, and a shot lands close to Lemya's feet even as she hesitates.

She goes back. Half the square away, a solid block of Pal soldiers bookended by Turncoats watches her, awaiting orders. She gets one of Hervenya's arms over her shoulders, and the girl screams as though this is more of an imposition than being shot. Someone nearby is howling, a dreadful, drawn-out animal sound of pain that shames Hervenya into a muted whimper as Lemya hoists her up.

She looks over to see the soldiers have shouldered their batons. Not the peaceable shouldering-at-a-slant of the parade ground, but bracing the butts of their weapons so they can sight down the line of them ready to fire. She drags Hervenya, and in the stories, this is where the injured comrade says, 'No, no, leave me!' But Hervenya is clinging to her like a weed, desperate not to be left. Lemya feels tears in her eyes and knows that, given the option, she'd desert her friend and run. Her arm, injured within the Reproach, shrieks denials at her, but Hervenya won't let go. Circumstances make Lemya the noble one.

Something interposes itself between her and the batons. Someone. Ruslav.

He must have come in over a barricade. He is waving his arms and shouting. Not shouting. Shouting implies words. Just… making those terrible sounds. His borrowed clothes are as torn up as his Lodge finery had been after the beast had him. He seems drunk or mad. There's not a scratch on him. He bellows like a bull at the Pals. He lurches sideways and backwards to put Lemya and Hervenya in his shadow.

They shoot him. She hears their officer's clear Pel instruction, and then the synchronised chorus of a score of soldiers uttering identical triggers. The shot tears into and past Ruslav. A burning line clips Lemya's shoulder, and a fistful of her hair is crisped to ash. She gets Hervenya to the gate, and someone takes over and drags the injured girl inside. Lemya, in the doorway, turns to see Ruslav's body, because surely, she owes him that.

He's not dead. There's not a scratch on him. He screams like they peeled his skin off. He staggers towards her, face a mask of misery and a dozen fresh-charred holes in his clothes.

They shoot him again. The voice of the officer sounds strained. She flinches back, and the wider shots strike dust as they punch pockmarks into the façade of the Gownhall. Ruslav is down, his back riddled with charred holes. That are closing up. That heal. He roars in agony and gets to his hands and knees, then just his knees, then his feet. He screams at the sky. There's not a scratch on him. She waits for the Pals to shoot again. They don't. Across the square, she virtually locks eyes with their officer, a moment of common incomprehension.

Ruslav teeters towards the Gownhall, braced for the next round of shots. She takes his arm, and he flinches even though all the wounds that should have been beneath her fingers have gone. He staggers inside, and they shut the door and throw the bar, for all the good that will do.

The other students are putting a lot of space between themselves and Ruslav. Some of them think he's cursed. Others are whispering *the healer* and *the miracle worker* because they heard about that, but without any descriptions attached. Ilmari history is full of the uncanny, though – the side effects of living on the doorstep of the Anchorwood. The main lesson to be drawn from those histories is 'Don't have anything to do with it'. Only Lemya is left, sitting the man down in a chair, seeing the remembered pain fighting clear of his tear- and rain-streaked face.

"Damn religion," Ruslav gets out. "To hell with all religion."

Outside, the Pals have secured the square, more soldiers funnelling in to surround the Gownhall. Fellow-Inquirer Hegelsy moves his command post forwards, still awaiting word from Nisbet. Now it's the Gownhall's turn to hear the fighting, just streets away, in the quiet that descends.

"Where's Shantrov?" Ruslav asks. "Did they come?" And Lemya has to tell him that no, her friend never came back with the mercenaries and retainers and the glorious flags of another age. Might as well expect the Old Duke to crawl out of his grave and lead the charge. Although, on second thoughts, nobody wants that. Ruslav puts his head in his hands.

From a lookout at one of the windows comes word that they're bringing up a ram.

Maestro Ivarn Ostravar is in some pain. A wound, honourably received. He'd gone out when it seemed the barricades were holding. Several of his fellow lecturers were at the front, alongside their students. He went in his full robes and with a book of poetry. The idea had been to declaim inspiring verses like a warrior-minstrel of old in one of the more peaceable gaps, before the Pals made another sally for the square. Lulled by the pause, while Lemya and her table squad were scrounging ammunition, he'd just found his page when the Hand spoke up. A shard of writing desk from the shattered barricade had gone through his left calf muscle, and he'd been carried back into the Gownhall.

Now he sits in a common room with Maestra Gowdi and a few other faculty members, his leg bandaged and up on a footstool, talking fiercely about what to do next. He isn't entirely sure how things got to this dire position, but he's sure it isn't his fault.

"A delegation," he tells them. "Someone run up a flag of truce. They're not going to slaughter everyone here."

"You don't know that," Gowdi says. She has discovered within herself an absolute love of continued life. Her eyes accuse him, as though he could know that a little scuffle over his person at the gates would somehow snowball into all of this. *It's not fair*, he thinks. He's just one man. He had dug himself a comfortable place in the post-Occupation city. He'd walked all the tightropes with admirable skill. There was always a way for a reasonable man to extricate himself from trouble. Except Correct Speech had arrested him. Except he'd been hanged once already. Except a lot of people had just died, some of them his students and some his colleagues. He realises that the shock of it all – physical and emotional – is eating into even his admirable self-possession. That there might not be a way out of this one, after all.

"It's the end," Gowdi moans.

"Oh, do shut up," he tells her. "They can't just… We have the scions and heirs of good Armiger bloodlines here. The children of country families with long pedigrees who'd be up in arms in every town and village if they just… did something rash. They'll have to stay their hands. Now they've won. Obviously."

"They'll kill us all and burn the building. It's the end of everything." This time Ivarn isn't the only one telling Gowdi that her contribution to the current topic isn't furthering the debate.

"Someone may yet come," he says faintly, but nobody there believes that. The fighting they can hear from elsewhere isn't getting any closer. If anything, just the reverse. And in the old sagas, the warrior-minstrel takes this always-darkest-before-the-dawn moment to say something pithy and inspiring and gnomically prophetic, and then the tide turns, and all is well. Except dawn was hours ago, and it's only become darker.

Maestro Porvilleau puts his tousled head around the common-room door. "They're talking," he says.

Ivarn tries to jump up and whimpers as his leg reminds him of recent events. "God, someone get me a stick! Actually, someone get me two solid students who can bear me up! What are they saying?"

"They're demanding unconditional surrender," Porvilleau tells him. "They are demanding our leaders come out."

Ivarn doesn't want a stick or two solid students anymore. He looks at his robes, which have more than an air of authority about them. *No*, he thinks. He's well aware what an ancient lord or warrior-minstrel would do at this point, but he's... old. He's got a bad leg. It's someone else's turn. And everyone's looking at him, waiting. Gowdi's even found a cane.

Three streets away, it's decided between Fellow-Broker Nisbet's force and the Siblingry marchers. When Orvechin falls, the workers charge, of course. Rush the barriers and the batons, overturn the one and take the brunt of the other. Better that than just dithering until Nisbet gives the order to fire.

That first withering volley strips away half the front two rows despite those forge-lid shields. Had they been less cramped and crushed together it would have ended the battle there and then. If the ranks behind had been given the chance to appreciate the ruin of their fellows, they'd have broken. Crammed as they are, they can only go forwards or go under the factory boots of those behind, and so they complete the charge. They hit the barriers with shoulder and gloved hand, heedless of the spikes. Men and women who can shift a big engine in a second to get a trapped child or comrade from under it. They grasp the ends of the batons and force them away, and some are shot but more are not. They throw the barriers back on the soldiers who set them, or bring sledgehammers down to break them. Half a factory floor of labour dies in the first few moments of the fight, but after that, the sheer mass of them forces the Pals down the street. The soldiers are no slackers up close. They wield their batons like staves or discharge them into the very faces and guts of their enemies. They get out their truncheons or just lay in with boot and fist. Their officers have swords and short rods that are better for the scrum. Those detachments sent to either side are still shooting, so the end of the march flowers out in all directions. They have nowhere to go but to batter themselves against the sides of the bottle Nisbet made for them. But they bring a flood far greater than the Pals had expected, and it's a poor labourer who can't crack a bottle open.

Nisbet, for all that her personal experience is more clerical than martial, knows the manuals well enough. Urban fighting is a part of the Palleseen curriculum, even in the School of Correct Exchange. She has people break into the shops on either side to shoot down, or to do furious battle where the marchers have already spilled in there. Accidents happen. Abandoned guard dogs and demon hounds raven out, maddened by blood and tearing any meat they can get their teeth into. A perfumier's is ablaze, casting aromatic smoke across the street and fouling the Palleseen aim.

In the dubious cover of a doorway, Aullaime cradles Orvechin's body and screams every Allorwen curse she knows. Mostly, it's just words and fury, but there will be Pals who sicken after this, and others impotent or pained or beset by ill luck as she calls up a cloud of trivial little demon-midges and casts them into the ranks of the enemy. A petty, meagre vengeance, but it's all she has.

Nisbet has moved her command post back one junction, then another two. Her forces are holding their discipline but not their physical place in the street, stepping back in good order, because it's that or be overwhelmed, and everyone knows it. The discipline is all theirs. The workers are just desperate, hemmed in, furious. Wielding the Hammer was always just abandoning the mills to go remind the Duke and the Armigers who it was put money in their posh velvet purses. Now it has become literal. They surge forwards like a tide because of all their fellows at their back. And then they keep pushing, even when there's more breathing room, because if that breathing room got between them and the Pals, then they'd be facing a firing squad, and the slaughter would start again. After that, they're pushing forwards because the Pals keep falling back, and they realise they're winning. The crippling flanking fire that Nisbet was relying on has taken a bloody toll, but it's not stopping them. Factory overseers regain control of their mill-mates and start to give orders. They become an army, just for a moment. An army scenting victory.

Nisbet scents defeat. She's dispatched messengers to Hegelsy demanding reinforcements, but he just tells her to hold. She can't hold. There must be more than two hundred dead on the workers' side, forty or so of her own, but momentum and not casualties will decide the fight.

She sends for the squads on her right flank, who've been doing vicious work harrying the underbelly of the march, diverting those heavy iron shields to where they can't protect the front lines. She gives them fresh orders, repeats them and makes sure their officers will carry them out. Obedience is whipped into the Pal leadership from their schooldays, and they beat it downhill into their rank and file. Still, there are orders and there are orders.

They set off at a run. Without their harassing, the advance speeds. Nisbet loses another street, and if she retreats any further, then the leftovers in Hegelsy's command post are going to end up reinforcing her whether he wants them to or not.

She tells the rest to hold no matter what. To hold even under the fall of the hammers. She has her senior officers draw weapons on her junior officers and has them pass that threat down the line. Anyone who loses another foot of ground will be stripped of rank and disciplined by Correct Speech. She wants to shoot someone just to show how serious she is, but it's not quite in her to do it. She's squeamish. She only ever wanted to count money.

The labourers, finding no give in the enemy, begin to redress the balance of casualties. A dozen soldiers go down under their blows and they move on to the next, the same brute actions repeated, just another kind of factory line.

Then the word is rippling up the street from the back. Nisbet's right flank has hurried down half a dozen streets, watched through shutters by those residents too stubborn to flee. They've gone riverwards until they find the straggling, loose crowd at the back of the march. The makeshift hospitals where the luckiest of the injured are being tended. The anxious families. The children. There they form their lines and open fire, gritted teeth and obeying orders.

The word lashes east up Liberation Way, up the body of the snake until it reaches the head. Until every worker hears the word that the foe is at their backs. That their kin are being slaughtered. The backbone of the march's advance flexes, twists. And snaps.

Those in charge shout, but the same obedience isn't built into these men and women, or they'd not be out on the streets in the first place. First individuals, then whole groups, then a grand tide goes washing back down the street to defend their dependants, and in that act of humanity, they're lost. Nisbet's embattled troops can shoot freely, and so, down the line, each part of her force suddenly has a soft target. The disintegration of the Siblingries takes perhaps half an hour, but that's only because there are so many of them packed in so tightly. The streets they surrender are strewn with the dead and injured. Soon there's a rout for the Portbridge and the safer streets on the far side. Nisbet, her heart calming, calls up messengers for Hegelsy to tell him his support is not needed, and for Brockelsby over by the Anchorwood to arrest any runners he can catch.

In the echo of the Pals' demand for surrender, Ruslav slumps in on himself. He looks sick. Simultaneously, he looks very well for a man who's been shot so much. Lemya's the only one who'll go within arm's reach of him. As though he's radiating a heat that has nothing to do with mere temperature. She remembers the rakish, cheerfully brutal man who lodged at Mother Ellaime's. The sidelong looks she'd had from him – and she'd heard about the Lodges' 'Pursuits' from older students. A good way, they said, to see certain parts of the city without getting your throat cut or your purse emptied. A good time, some said. Others told her to move lodgings. To a girl fresh from the country, Ruslav had possessed a definite intriguing cityness.

She feels that the two of them, the man she remembers and the girl who knew him, were a hundred years ago.

"What happened?" she asks.

"I cut a deal," he tells her hoarsely. "With God."

"God?"

"Yasnic's god. The Vultures aren't coming." As though that's some dread revelation, with Hegelsy awaiting their surrender. "I had to do something. I couldn't let him down. Or you. Any of you. I don't know who I am anymore. I can't fight. I feel the wounds when I even think about it. God's a bastard, Lemya. Can't blame Yasnic for finding a way to get rid of Him. But I cut a deal. I said, get me in. I won't swing a fist. I won't even call them names. Just do your thing. And it was either keep my hide whole or it's Yasnic again, and Yasnic and God had some serious falling out. I don't know what. He dumped God on me, the son of a bitch. He gave me religion."

He's shaking. She wants to put an arm about his shoulders but flinches away before she touches the blackened tatters of his shirt. The clothing is mute witness to all the wounds he doesn't have. And in her head, the chords grow strident and angry when she gets closer to him. The clash of inimical powers.

The wounded are around them, and the whole-but-frightened. Ruslav stands suddenly.

"I'm going to make you work!" he shouts. The students shrink back from him. Ruslav strides over to a youth who's waxy pale, gut-shot. The lecturer in medicine has dispensed drugs and poured caustic preservative on the wound, but it's beyond mundane art to help. "You," Ruslav barks into the agonised boy's face. "Tell me you'll abjure all violence now until forever. Swear it. Live a life of fucking flowers and niceness. Swear it!" But the boy's too lost in drugs and pain to even respond. Ruslav argues with the air above his shoulder, but apparently consent needs consciousness. He moves on. Makes his challenge to the next worst of the injuries, theological triage. "Swear it," he insists. "I will heal your wounds, but you have to let God into your life, because He's a selfish sod who won't touch you otherwise. You have to live a life where you won't so much as lift a finger against anyone, not even kick a cat or chuck a stone at a sparrow." He stands in the centre of the room. "Any takers?"

It's Hervenya with the ruined leg who says yes first. They haven't got to her yet. She's in appalling pain from the physical trauma and the necrotic withering that edges a baton-shot wound. Nobody's given her medicine, because she's not about to die. "Yes!" she shouts. "God, yes! Please!" And Ruslav lays a hand on her, and she's cured.

One of the windows explodes inwards, scattering them with glass and splinters from the shutters. For a moment, Lemya takes it as evidence of God's might, but it's a single warning shot from outside. Hegelsy is getting impatient. A glance outside shows soldiers mustering with the ram, and readying to storm the windows.

The words, "I'll go out," are on her tongue, for all that she has no idea what good she'd do or even what she'd say. Then there's a wooden knocking sound, as though the Pals are unaccountably polite all of a sudden, and Ivarn appears. He limps in with his stick, somehow maintaining that wry and detached dignity that won him so many admirers in the student body.

"Maestro," Lemya says. Because she knows him now. That he's not exactly the gallant hero of Ilmar she always took him for. A rogue, in fact, and there's none like an old rogue.

He pauses, leaning heavily on the cane. Despite herself, his stoic manner takes her in. "The Occupiers want an answer. I will go give it to them." And he has an angle, surely. He must do. Except, as they unbar the door for him, there's no sense of anything but that old Ivarn Ostravar whose lectures and readings she used to devour. The man she gazed at adoringly as she dreamed of revolution.

Ivarn steps out. He does, of course, have an angle. He's had three minutes of very hectic discussion with an academic authority on Palleseen legal codes. It's not much, but he feels he's been dealt a bad hand of tiles right now. It'll have to come down to skill in the playing.

They let him limp all the way out. Nobody breaks from the Palleseen lines to meet him halfway. On that basis, he pauses often and makes them wait, because veteran of departmental meetings as he is, he knows all about petty victories. By the time he arrives, he's won that round, because Helgesy is at the front in person and grinding his teeth.

"Fellow-Inquirer," Ivarn greets him, as brightly as possible. One of his colleagues had injected quite a large cylinder of herbal anaesthetics into his leg, and given him something to swallow too. It has lent him a certain external sang-froid but hasn't got at the inner man, which is just as well, as Ivarn needs him. He can't feel the injured leg at all. He has to resist looking down to make sure it's still there.

"Maestro Ostravar," Hegelsy says flatly. "I had you hanged." He's not delighted by this development. He has, Ivarn reflects, had a lot of people hanged in his time. If Ivarn's set a precedent, then Hegelsy's life is about to get very cluttered.

He considers saying *I forgive you* or *I got better*, but the Fellow-Inquirer doesn't look like he's up for wit, right then. "I'm here to negotiate on behalf of the Gownhall."

"As their leader?"

"If you wish."

Hegelsy nods, normality restored. "You were informed that I'd hang a score of you if you resisted. I think that you and I, educated men, can agree the definition of 'resistance' encompasses the sorry show we've just witnessed. I may as well start with you and demand another nineteen of your fellows give themselves up, after which, we can conclude matters and I can draft my report." A razor-thin crescent of teeth.

"That won't be possible," Ivarn tells him, feeling like a man testing thin ice underfoot. "As you confirmed, you hanged me."

"I did."

"The Ordnances of Correct Appreciation, volume seven, article eight hundred and forty-two second subsection," Ivarn reels off, hoping to all available gods that he's remembered it right. "Once sentence of execution has been made then, for whatever reason, should it be remitted and no matter which step in the procedure has been attained the…" Losing his thread, panicking briefly, then the words coming back to him. He always had a fine memory for texts. "The prisoner shall not subsequently be sentenced to a further execution but only such commuted sentence as… well, you can look up the rest, I'm sure."

Hegelsy stares at him, trying to work out if he's furious or amused or some new and unnamed emotion partaking of both. "You are offering a legalistic defence?" he demands.

"It wouldn't have swayed the Old Duke," Ivarn admits, still outwardly casual. "But it is the price of seeking to perfect the world that you must have rules for everything. I am afraid I cannot be sentenced to hang again." *Been there, done that.*

"Well, this is regrettable." Hegelsy's mood is restored, and Ivarn doesn't like that. "Get rope!" he shouts to a subordinate. There is already rope, because they've learned to anticipate him. "String him up," he says.

"I am here to negotiate!" Ivarn squawks. And then, as they seize his arms and take his stick and fit him with a new collar, "You can't! Your own laws!"

"I'll just have to do you off the books," Hegelsy informs him. "I'll just have to ask for a full score from within, instead of nineteen. Consider this entirely extrajudicial, Maestro Ostravar. A whim of my own. I shall be sure to censure myself later, in my report." He looks up at the Gownhall façade. "We won't have the luxury of a proper scaffold and a drop, but someone get a rope over that gargoyle up there. We'll have to haul you up and hang you the long way. It'll be your last lesson to your students, maestro. After that, they'll be more than happy to shove some faculty out the door."

"Negotiate!" Ivarn squeaks.

"You're a learned man. Please tell me where the word 'negotiate' can be found within 'unconditional surrender'," says Hegelsy. His people get Ivarn against the wall, countless horrified eyes fixed on him from inside. An athletic soldier has successfully cast the rope over the protruding waterspout. It's all happening very fast.

"Final words!" Ivarn gabbles. "You have to let me!" Anything to delay the moment when they hoist him up.

"You talk too much already," Hegelsy says. Then there's a messenger at his elbow, and he turns, willing to make time for this. "What does Nisbet say?"

The messenger is shaking; she's not one of Nisbet's constant gadflies. "From the Donjon, magister!" she gets out.

"What?" Hegelsy is completely blank.

"Under attack, magister! There are insurgents inside the Donjon!"

Hegelsy stares at her, aghast. And of course, the Donjon is currently depopulated, what with his force and Nisbet's and Brockleby's. But it's the *Donjon*, the prison and barracks and offices of power, the fist that weighs down the city, far more than the airy luxury of the Ducal Palace. You don't just *attack* the Donjon…

"Who…?" *The Indwellers? Magic?*

The messenger scrambles the words and treads over her own story. She's a clerk, not a soldier. She was filing papers when the gates were rushed and held open, and three score cutthroats and villains stormed in. They're opening every cell, freeing every prisoner. They burned every piece of paper, all the records, the accounts, the book-lungs of the Ilmari Occupation. They were knifing her fellow clerks and clubbing the prison wardens when she left. Ragged banners were being draped from the walls, showing a bald-headed bird atop a bloody carcase. Despite Ruslav's disillusionment, in some small way, the Vultures have come to the aid of the Gownhall.

Hegelsy's face is a requiem, not for the clerks, but for the papers. His records, his reports, his correspondence.

Moments later, he is shouting orders. Gathering his force. Sending to Nisbet to haul her back. He's not abandoning the Gownhall, but the force he leaves is just a fraction of his strength. Everyone else is double-timing it back to the Donjon to see what can be saved.

He looks back, even as his people are packing up. His last order to the officer he's leaving in charge is, "String him up."

The squads left in the Gownhall Square watch the majority of their support set off at a run. Hegelsy practically has his Inquirer's short robe hoisted up past his knees. Over the rooftops, there is a distant drift of smoke already – three years of administrative proceedings become kindling in the space of three minutes. Hegelsy will reach his office to find his desk rifled and the gift of a steaming turd left on his chair.

The officer left in charge shrugs, though, and gives the order. Four strong soldiers drag at the rope and Ivarn Ostravar ascends up the face of the Gownhall, choking and kicking, his face going red to purple, and his eyes fit to burst from his skull.

Ruslav comes out first. His face is screwed-up like a child awaiting punishment. He charges the Palleseen who were mostly watching Ivarn dance. He's halfway to them before they recover sufficient self-possession to shoot him.

He gives vent to that dreadful howling again, because it still hurts just as much. God clings to his shoulder and his hair and gifts him with a wholeness of body that only means there's more to hurt when the next shots go in. Which they do, and then again. And then the soldiers he's running towards actually break and flee from him, which is just as well as he had no plan at all for what to do when he arrived.

Behind him, the students and faculty sally forth one last time. They have no shot left, but they have all their swords and pikes and broom handles, and now they outnumber the enemy. Ruslav has performed the one piece of military service he's capable of. He remains an admirable distraction.

Lemya puts her sword to use, stabbing one of the men at the rope and then another. Ivarn drops, and Hervenya gets the noose off him. He fights for breath, eyes a mess of broken veins, coughing and vomiting. But there's no time. This isn't the triumphant retaking of Gownhall Square. This is escape. Behind the vanguard of the charge, they're bringing out the wounded. Everyone's getting out and spreading into the city. Better that than fall into the hands of the Pals when they're in a hanging mood.

The fighting with the remaining soldiers is brutal but brief, a jagged clash of blade and bludgeon. Lemya sees Hervenya die.

Her friend is helping Ivarn when the Pal officer looms, sword drawn back, trying to recover the prisoner his superior wanted executed. She has her knife out and tries to stab him, but even as she does, her leg is a blasted ruin again, God's grace withdrawn as she gashes the officer across the arm. She screams and falls, and the Pal runs her through. The escaping students surge forwards before he can serve Ivarn the same. One of them drives a pike into him, and it's Maestra Gowdi who brains him with a gold-shod sceptre formerly used only at particularly formal faculty dinners. Ivarn is rescued and helped away. The resilience of some rogues would make a cockroach blush.

Out in the city, they head for the river, find cellars and attics, run into the stragglers from the Siblingry march engaged in similar pursuits. Elsewhere, the Pals are retaking the Donjon, the Vultures already exiting with their vandals' work done. By evening, patrols will be sweeping the streets, arresting anyone with a whiff of the fight about them. Hegelsy's lost documents demand vengeance, and he has a lot of emptied cells to fill.

Higher Powers

To take power over Ilmar was always to take on more responsibilities than might show on the surface. The Old Duke knew it. His antecedents knew it, all the way back to when they'd lived on the other side of the river and flown the Varatsin coat of arms. When Sage-Invigilator Culvern was made Perfector of Ilmar, he'd had some idea the role would demand more than that of the average provincial governor. The Temporary Commission had briefed him personally. Ilmar was an opportunity. A door to new realms, the potential to bring the Palleseen way of life to nations undreamed of. And to bring back their wealth and resources. But nobody briefed him on the toll Ilmar would take on him, or the compromises he'd have to make.

In the Ducal Palace, Culvern sat behind his desk, his own reek hot and sour in his nostrils. He never got used to it. Nor did anyone else. Every day brought afresh the looks of disgust they failed to hide from him.

He'd bathed just now. The warmth of the water had already transmuted into the feverish heat of his skin corrupting. He could feel his pores ooze, his underclothes sticking to him and pulling the skin away when he moved. He strove to ignore it. He had visitors.

He'd sent his assistants and clerks away, a circumstance he knew they always relished. Just one hour where they didn't have to sit in his stinking company. He had their expenses claims on his desk. They burned their robes every week, sick of trailing his second-hand stench everywhere they went.

"It is the will of the Commission," he told his visitors, not looking at them directly, "that this matter be put behind us. I appreciate that… regrettable things have been done. Not by my order. Pallesand has only ever wished the open hand of peace between us." He stared at his suppurating hands. *And can you not help me?* But this curse was nothing of theirs, and they had no sympathy for him. They only cared about their traditions, that were older than the city. It was maddening that they had been around for so long, yet nobody could even tell him a full dozen inarguable facts about them. But the city's own knowledge of them had died with the Varatsin Dukes, and after that, the Ilmari had fallen back on rumour and superstition and increasingly unlikely stories.

"A wrong was done." He didn't know which of them spoke. He couldn't say for sure how many of them had walked into his office by their own ways, without needing the door. The mist hid them. Their masks showed no motion of lips.

He'd been here before, of course. They'd visited him when he'd first taken up office. He'd tried to give them gifts and extend them the greetings of the Commission, but his words had just fallen like dead bones at their feet. They weren't interested in what he had to offer. But even with Ochelby dead in the Wood, he had a duty to re-establish diplomatic relations. Reopen the Port to Nowhere so that the lands beyond could be contacted and exploited for the greater glory of Pallesand and perfection.

"One of you was killed. I understand."

"You do not," he was told, but he'd been reading the entire meagre stock of what was known about the Indwellers and the Wood. Their nature, as written about by Gownhall and Palleseen scholars, then condensed by his clerks so that all the supposition and speculation had been winnowed out.

"I do," he said. "I can make amends. I have… an idea, at least." He'd still been staring at his hands, but now he flinched back, because one of the visitors was right before his desk, the mist reaching out hungry tendrils towards his papers. "Just… give me the opportunity." *Just let us in, until we understand you enough to conquer you.*

A hand emerged from the Indweller's robes, holding something. Placing it before him with a clack of wood on wood. He stared at it, fearful yet fascinated. *What might we learn if we took this apart and sifted it for magic? How many tablethi would it fill?* But that would be the death of any chance to go into the Wood in peace. Some day, perhaps, but not yet.

"I understand," he said. Cruel ideas were coming to him. Not that he had been a saint before, but since the curse, it seemed cruel ideas were the only ones that arose naturally in his brain. Cruel and personally satisfying, yet surely nothing he could justify in his reporting to the Commission. Unless… "I will…" he started, and realised he was alone. They'd gone the way they had come, and he rang the bell that would call in his long-suffering staff with their pouches of fragrant herbs stuffed in their long-nosed masks.

When the first poked her beak around the door, he asked if they'd had news from Fellow-Inquirer Hegelsy over the Gownhall uprising yet.

The Apostate

When the Occupiers had rolled into Ilmar they had set about perfecting the city to their model. Because the world was imperfect and so – despite their claims – were the Pals, the transformation was piecemeal. Despite their dismissal of religion in all its forms, the Mahanic Temple clung on in the city, just as it did across most of the conquered nation. Its creed of obedience and civic conduct earning a post-mortem reward for its followers was useful enough that the Perfecture permitted the Temple and its priests to remain, and in turn, they preached endurance and compliance to dwindling congregations. Of other faiths, already pushed to the fringes by Mahanic dominance, the Palleseen had no tolerance whatsoever.

Yasnic, former high priest of a healing god, knew very little about medicine. However, he could fetch water, prepare bandages, mop away blood and follow instructions. He'd been holed up in a drinking cellar he couldn't afford to drink in when the first fugitives had come in from the Siblingries' march. In fact, it was just about the first he'd heard of the whole venture. There were casualties brought joltingly down the steps to the cellar, some dire enough that he'd watch them die soon after. One of them recognised him and claimed he was the miracle healer, but no miracles ensued, and they believed him when he denied it. Instead of the healing powers that had never done him any good, he just helped with his own two hands. Being busy was better by far than wandering the city alone.

He'd never been alone before. Kosha had brought him up. Then, from immediately before Kosha died, there had been God. And after that, it had been God and Yasnic, the least funny of double acts. And he'd been prepared. Kosha had told him that he should expect a divine visitation. He'd never actually seen God before. Only Kosha had. He'd felt very guilty for being rather disappointed that God wasn't grander. But then, he was God's last adherent. Small wonder God was only a small wonder.

The timing had bothered him. God had been tugging at the hem of his robe before the execution. Kosha had still been up on the Duke's scaffolding, waiting for the drop. And he'd worried that, at the end, God and Kosha had quarrelled.

He had been alone since he had broken his priestly vows – or had them broken for him, given the demonic coercion he'd solicited. In that solitude, he had discovered something horrible about Ilmar. Not that Ilmar was short of horrible qualities, but this was one more, and he'd have been happier not knowing it. Ilmar was full of gods.

Even apostate, he was apparently a member of a select club now. He had walked through the streets of the Gutter Districts and seen the gods. Dozens of them. Little scabrous figures wearing the tatters of ancient finery, crooked headdresses and tarnished symbols. Little gods, some no larger than his hand. Fish-headed river gods, ancestral bird-gods that had once been patrons of royal lines, hunchbacked mine and smith gods still waving the tiny tools of the trades that had once venerated them. Orvost the Divine Bull, his former master's old nemesis, had scuttled through cluttered alleys lowing, no larger than a cat. They were all still there, and he, with his prior god-husbandry, could see them. The absence of God in his life had left a hole he could peer through, that showed the discarded divinities thronging like rats in all the dark and filthy places of the city. And they knew him as a man who had faith going spare and called out to him, begged, held out sacred divination bowls for alms. They offered him their minuscule blessings if he would only be their priest. He understood that Ilmar was not only where people went when they had no other option, trying to escape to some putative kinder world. Ilmar was where religions went to decompose.

And surely Ruslav was dead now, and his own religion had gone the same way. God was alone on the streets, a shabby little hairy figure, no more or less than all the other verminous failed divinities that infested Ilmar like fleas.

The influx of wounded was almost welcome. It kept his mind off the thought. Even as the brewing god that lived on a scrap of blanket in the corner of the cellar made high-pitched sounds and waved its grimy fistful of barley stalks to try and attract his attention.

He pieced together the story of the march, from a succession of patients and from better doctors than he. After that, a couple of students from the Gownhall staggered in, and he heard their tale too.

Did they know Ruslav, he asked? They did not. Did they know Lemya? They did, but not what had happened to her.

He set out onto the street. He knew most of the dives and hidden holes and subterranean taprooms in this district. It was his stamping ground as a beggar, after all, and drunks were more generous than sober and upstanding citizens. Easy for him to find where people had gone to ground after the fighting. He heard further stories, helped a little more. Ignored the roosting gods in the eaves, the unemployed psychopomps picking over rag heaps.

A Palleseen patrol stopped him. He told them about the gods, pointing out specific examples, describing them in a shaking, wondering voice. The two-headed god of the end of the year that wasn't speaking to itself anymore; the bewildered solar beetle brought to Ilmar by some foreign cultist and now stranded here like driftwood past the high-tide mark. The soldiers shrank back from him as though his madness might be contagious. And this was Ilmar: who knew what you could catch in the streets of the Gutter Districts? They left him alone.

In the fourth haunt, behind the shuttered-up windows of an ostensibly abandoned house, he found an academy maestro who had seen Lemya and reckoned she must be close. Yasnic had been stopped several times more by then, the same not-quite-an-act squeaking him out of trouble. Nobody was looking to persecute the deranged right now, not when there were real sane revolutionaries hiding across the city. He'd seen two nests of fugitives uncovered by the Pals, too – boots and batons and arrests. The wounded hauled out into the day with the same gusto as the whole. He upped his pace, searching den after den, warning of the patrols as he went. Looking for his...

Friends was too strong a word, surely. Lemya had given him a blanket and bought him a drink. Ruslav was a thug whom Yasnic had covertly admired, because he himself wasn't, and it had looked nice to be able to push back at the world. And then Ruslav had become his victim, in a strange way. But surely, he wasn't so cheap that these events had bought his loyalty? And still he looked for them, and then he was being let past a sliding false wall, and there they were with a whole crowd of others. Workers, students, academics, just random people who had cause to fear the Pals. Which was most people.

There was Lemya – arm still bandaged up from before but no fresh wound on her, grimy and exhausted and her face streaked with tears. There was Ivarn Ostravar, leg in a splint and a dressing about his neck, because apparently, they were going to keep on hanging him until it took. There was Ruslav, miraculously whole, not even a bruise on his knuckles.

There was God.

Yasnic flinched. He wasn't a priest anymore. He shouldn't be able to see God. Nobody wants to arrive at a social function to find their ex in attendance. Except, he was in some peculiar theological netherworld right now. A former priest with a god-shaped gap in his life that every raggedy demiurge in the city had been trying to climb into. And here was God.

God looked at him, then ostentatiously looked away, grimy nose in the air. He was sitting on Ruslav's shoulder. Ruslav looked at him, looked between him and God.

"You," he said.

"I'm afraid so," Yasnic confirmed.

"I should thank you." Ruslav didn't sound very thankful.

"Oh?" Yasnic settled down beside them. "I didn't know what else to do. I… forced God away. Because I knew He'd have to go to you. I hoped He'd help. More than He ever helped me."

"I'm right here," snapped God.

"Yeah. We made a deal. Seeing as I was all he'd got." Ruslav managed a mean smile left over from the man he'd been. "Got to look after me, hasn't he? So long as I don't throw a punch, he's got to keep picking me back up." He laughed, then coughed. "I thought it would help. It didn't, much. I was going to be the knight, you know?"

Yasnic didn't know.

"Charge in, save everyone. Except no horse. No fancy pointed stick. Just the worst kind of suit of armour, eh?" And he actually poked God in the diminutive shoulder.

"You are a curse," God told him.

"Yeah, yeah, we're each other's curses."

"Yasnic, tell him he must speak of me with proper reverence," God commanded.

"I'm not your priest anymore. I can't tell him anything."

"You're my worshipper still!" God insisted. "Even though you've engaged in unspeakable carnal acts, you can still be of my congregation!"

Yasnic was glad only Ruslav had heard that. The man's eyebrows shot up past his shaggy fringe.

"You did, did you?" he asked, seemingly cheered by Yasnic's chosen form of desecration more than anything else. "You get in there, son. Got your wick lit?"

Yasnic coughed embarrassedly. "It was the only thing I could think of."

Ruslav snorted and prodded God again. "Why're you so down on that, anyway?"

"It's just one of the things priests are forbidden." Yasnic shrugged. "I don't know."

"The act of birthing a child is an excruciation," God said loftily. "I do not condone my priesthood bringing more suffering into the world."

"You never heard of using a sleeve?" Ruslav asked incredulously. "No wonder your religion's dead."

A woman wearing factory clothes pushed past the sliding wall. She had a sack of food: hard loaves, salt beef, some pots of pickled vegetables, distributing the meagre bounty efficiently. Bringing a few leftovers to the students. Her face had a livid welt where a truncheon had lashed across it. When she spoke, she had the trace of an Allorwen accent.

"We can't stay here forever," she said. "They've searched this place once and not found the door, but they'll be back the moment someone takes a good look at the house from the outside and wonders where the rest of it is."

Ivarn propped himself up with his stick. "And do you have a plan, perhaps? Somewhere to go?"

"When the street clears, we'll start moving people out," she said. "I'd rather wait till dark, but I don't think we can. Small groups. We have safe houses the Pals don't know about. I hope. Warehouses, storerooms, the old under-cellars they built some of the mills over. We're reaching out to the Herons, to get people downriver, but they're bottled up too. I heard three boats got emptied by the Pals, taken to the Donjon or just coshed and thrown over the side." She dropped down onto her haunches. "I need to get my people out. You have to do the same with yours."

Yasnic watched Ivarn's face, seeing the momentary fracture where the man pulled against being responsible for anybody's hide but his own, then remembered he was in no state to just go on the run without help. "Yes," the man agreed gravely. "That's true."

"You have somewhere to go?"

There was a fraction of time in which Ivarn Ostravar, academic, sophisticate, but above all, survivor, did not. Then he smiled. "Of course. Although getting there may be problematic, with the patrols."

"Where?" Yasnic asked. They looked at him as if every one of them had forgotten he was there. Except God, who just rolled his eyes, as though Yasnic should have worked it out an age ago.

"The Anchorage," Ivarn said confidently. "Langrice will hide me—hide us. She owes me that much." That grand and blustery confidence he'd built his career on. "And that is the traditional last resort exit from Ilmar, after all."

The Allorwen woman frowned. "You have the… wherewithal?"

"I know where the wards can be found," Ivarn confirmed. "If we can only get to the inn."

He looked around. The huddled students were all hope, right then, save for Lemya whose idolatry of Ivarn didn't seem to have been restored by this new development. Yasnic remembered, though. He wasn't remotely sure that the protective wards at the Anchorage would be made available to Ivarn, but the man's track record of wheedling what he needed out of the world was certainly impressive. It was better than waiting for the soldiers to come and arrest them.

"I can help," he said. Again, that look. *Help? You? Who are you again? What possible good could you be?* "I've already got past plenty of the Pals. I can go ahead to the Anchorage, find you a route where they're not looking, where they've already been. They think I'm just a mad beggar. Please let me help."

He looked at them, the little tableau. Ivarn still propping himself up on his maestro's dignity; Lemya, barely paying attention, head and foot moving to some unheard beat; the doubting Allorwen woman; Ruslav and God. Ruslav and God both looking straight at him at last. God, believing in him, just a little.

The factory woman took him to the sliding door. "How long will it take you to get there and back?" she asked.

"No telling," Yasnic admitted. "All down to where the Palleseen are and how often they stop me. But I'll make best time, I promise."

She held up a hand. "Spy out the force at the Wood – how many, what streets they're watching. If the patrols come here, there's a back way out, and we're going to the old dry cistern under the Rehevitz morgue, you know it? Look for us there, if we're not here."

Yasnic nodded.

"Good. And make sure of the Wood itself, because I hear there are troops that way as well. A lot of them."

He nodded.

"I'm going to try and make a distraction." Her face was hard and set. "A really big distraction. They killed my... my friend, today. They killed a lot of my friends, but they killed the best man in all of Ilmar. And I am going to have a sorcerer's revenge on them. Yes, flinch. You may well fucking flinch. I am going to be a curse to them like all their nightmares together. So, you hurry back, because you don't want the games to start without you."

They crept onto the street together, and then he headed for the Anchorage, and she split off for the Hammer Districts.

The best time he could felt like a snail's pace – changing streets, clambering through choked alleys, always trying to remember Ivarn's leg and the rest of the wounded. Dodging patrols and being stopped by patrols. Almost getting taken in so many times, save that the host of little chittering gods kept coming to his aid. They clustered about his feet, beseeching, rattling the empty tokens of their doctrines. He told every Statlos and soldier about them, even going onto hands and knees, so he could introduce each shabby little deity. The soldiers always shuddered away. You could catch madness off people, in Ilmar. You could die of it.

And there was a force at the Anchorwood, as advertised. More soldiers than he – who had missed the earlier fighting – had seen in one place before. And most of their weapons were still turned on the Wood, but there were eyes aplenty elsewhere. He, one alone, could creep to the Anchorage door, but he wasn't sure how even a handful might manage it, let alone however many he'd end up bringing.

He knocked, and the door was flung open moments later. He quailed back from the martial spectre revealed. Hellgram, goggled and masked, a sword in his left hand, and his right arm bared to the elbow and bloody with cuts and scars.

Hellgram's War

He didn't fit. Too tall, too angular. His movements were precise, and yet he still rammed doorways and jostled tables, as though the world he saw and the world around him didn't quite match up. A face with sharp cheekbones, a high wide forehead, a knuckle of a chin. Not conversant with any ethnicity or people anybody knew. Deep-socketed eyes, grey around them as though sleep eluded him, which it often did. Most telling, the way that mundane things – a phrase, a coin, a way of making tea – spooked him as unbearably strange, while the uncanny itself was commonplace.

He didn't think of the war anymore. Which wasn't true. He woke from dreams of it, fighting his blanket. The gas, the wire, the hungry dark that descended at midday. The shrill scream of demon artillery, the bellows of monsters in torment. But he didn't think about whether it still raged on (doubtless it still raged on) or who was winning (nobody was winning).

He'd lost his war. He needed to get back to it. He was, after all, a soldier. A specialist, fit for one trade only. And even if he could have lived without the war, he'd lost his *world*. His world, his war, the latter of such a scale that it held the former within it.

He'd been a very particular kind of soldier. A lifelong commitment to the uniform, because they'd shackled his soul to it. All his adult life he'd felt the pull of the chains, as comforting to him as a mother's voice. And then there had been one night, or perhaps just one more abyssal day. An offensive gone wrong, though at this remove, he couldn't remember which side it might have been that had initiated it. A time of confusion. The deployment of new weapons, even more unthinkable than the previous wave of ingenuity which nobody had wanted to think about. Which was worse than the one before that, which by now, Hellgram couldn't even remember.

He felt like his mind was a rusty fuel can, one corner eaten away into a rough-edged hole. Things fell out, and then they were gone, vanished into this world he'd found himself in. He felt that, if he could get *back*, somehow, he'd find those lost memories and thoughts just piled by the roadside, waiting to be poured into the miraculously restored can once more. And then, he'd be whole and remember who he was.

Or, not *who he was*. That hadn't left him. He was Hellgram, and he was certain of certain things about himself. Principally that he had done terrible things in a terrible war, and would do so again, without compunction, if it advanced his cause. And, otherwise, would not do them. But if he could get home, perhaps he would remember *why* he was that man. The alchemical formulation that had led to the person he woke up into each morning in the room Langrice let him have.

His cause was, of course, to find his wife. That had been his speciality, in the war. He and his wife, linked soul to soul, two halves together. Bringing the storm, leading the charge, masters of the trench and the crater-pocked killing ground. They had not made Hellgram into a weapon. They had made him into a hilt, and now his blade, his beautiful killing blade, was gone.

That night: the chaos of the assault, whosoever's it had been. The gas had come down like a sulphurous curtain. He'd fought his mask on, seen the world through the fish-eye distortion of his goggles. His wife needed none of them. She was better adapted to the war-world than he could ever be. They had fought. His conjured sword in one hand, his pepperbox in the other – that he'd lost in the Wood somewhere, that wouldn't have worked here anyway, most likely. They'd charged forwards to take the enemy position, or else to meet the onrush of the enemy. The artillery had been immolating demons, sending their screaming spirits down in green-yellow fusillades that lit the killing gas with the literal fires of hell. All had been noise and fury. And in the midst of it, a calm. A hole they'd stumbled through. The quiet of the Wood. If it had been a new weapon, he didn't even know which side had deployed it. Or if, as seemed more and more common, both had done so at the same time.

A terrible weapon. A monstrous weapon, that was no weapon at all. What happened to its other victims he couldn't know, but he'd stumbled through the opaque air until there had been trees around him. And then, no gas, no dark other than what gathered naturally beneath a canopy. And his wife had been with him. He remembered her running ahead of him between the trees, scouting for a way back. She was always swifter than he.

There were beasts in those woods. He had used up half his toys and protections fending them off. His wife had torn into them, fierce in his defence. He'd been in a strange, hostile place, but it had been all right, because they were together there. And after two days of wandering, he had realised that there was a sound he had lived with for decades that was fading from his ears, an acrid scent no longer in his nostrils, a darkness not scrabbling at the edge of his vision. It was the war. The war was no longer looming on all sides of him. He had felt some part of himself, that he'd never known was crooked, start to straighten out.

Then one day, they'd found the edge of the Wood, his wife rushing ahead because she could sense the differential of realities, the borders between one place and another. They had thought it was home. He hadn't understood the forest was a thoroughfare between many worlds. For all his people's murderous ingenuity, they had never guessed at the existence of the Anchorwood, and perhaps that was just as well.

They'd come out into Ilmar at night, ill-prepared, undefended. She'd been too far ahead, desperate to pick up the trail of the war. Something had broken as they'd crossed over. The chain within him, suddenly slack. And he'd charged off confidently, knowing she was just beyond the trees, on the far side of the inn, past those buildings, down that street. And she never was, and that had been five years ago. Since then, he had been across most of Ilmar and not caught so much as an echo of her. There were only a handful of districts left to him to search – some stretches of the Reproach, some fine houses on Armigine Hill, the Ducal Palace, a few others. And his search had slowed. He'd never admit it, but he stirred himself less and less these days. Because once he had exhausted every inch of Ilmar without finding her – without even finding some place she had *been* for any length of time, then he'd know. He'd know he wouldn't find her. That she was dead or banished or gone somewhere in the wide world he'd never follow. That final part of who he'd been would fall away, and he'd be left with this new, directionless creature. Langrice's bouncer and man-of-all-work. He'd be able to relax, then. To forget. To tell half-coherent stories to disbelieving regulars. To have a life in a world that wasn't fighting itself to the utter death of everything. He couldn't imagine it, but day by day, he was getting closer.

Jem had worked some enchantments about his hand. She wasn't a magician as her people reckoned such things, but Hellgram understood that the Divinati were head and shoulders above everyone else as far as such things went. She knew a hundred little work-saving tricks she deployed with an understated elegance and never thought of. It wasn't the first time he'd seen her stitch someone up, though it was the first time it'd been him. The mad Heron had cut his hand open, severed all the tendons in his palm. His right hand, too: his fighting hand. But Jem had bound it, and re-set all the complex machinery that made a hand do what it needed. She'd told him not to use it for a week, but that wasn't an option, not with what he needed to do now. What she had accomplished, though, was to rid him of the pain enough to ply his own trade.

The Heron himself was still sitting placidly in a corner of the taproom, as though waiting for something. Or not the Heron,

Hellgram supposed. The Indweller, whose ghost had driven the man's own soul out of his body. Through his goggles, he could see it clearly, extending from the mask and crouching about Fleance's body's shoulders. An effect unfamiliar but comprehensible to him. He'd thrown possession grenades himself, in the war.

The Allorwen were up here as well now, talking anxiously among themselves about what they would do next, now they had no Blackmane and no ritual wards. Jem kept asking them to go down into the cellar. There might be a Pal patrol through the door any moment, even though she'd sent several barrels of Langrice's best out to the soldiers camped near the Wood, so they wouldn't be tempted to come pay a visit. Dorae and the others didn't trust her, though. Not that they'd trusted Langrice, particularly, but they'd trusted her authority. Jem didn't hold that unspoken office the woman had endured. Ilmar's ambassador to the Anchorwood. It wasn't her intentions they doubted so much as her ability to make good on anything.

Hellgram didn't care about any of it, or didn't want to. His piecemeal memories of who he had been didn't suggest he'd ever been a particularly caring man, save to one person.

Right now, he was carving up his own arm. He'd been at it for well over an hour, working slowly, because he wasn't so good with his left. Using the consecrated knife from his medical kit to incise precise little characters in the skin of his forearm. Not charms of healing – Jem had covered that, and he had nothing that would speed the process. Charms that would borrow from his own future, drawn on ambient power, drain the trio of Palleseen tablethi he'd scrounged together. He cut, and felt it only as a distant unkindness at the back of his mind. He wrote an inventory up his arm, vertical columns of arcane sigils that told his fingers and thumb and wrist that they were well. He fooled his body, and he'd pay for it later, but he was buying that *later* by doing so. It was a fair exchange. And it was wearying work, especially as he had to scribe around the elegant net of strings Jem's magic had woven. To cut one would be to undo all her work, and then he'd not heal properly at all. He exhausted himself, in carving a temporary wellness into his flesh. Then he broke the seal on two small vials and drained the contents, drinking the freshness of a well-rested morning he had decanted there a year before, when he'd had a string of good nights' sleep. He'd denied himself the benefits then, cursing himself to laggard mornings where he'd stumbled about like an insomniac, because he'd known he'd need the vitality later. Soldiers' tricks. Just a regular trench-digger's artifice. He wasn't a medic, after all.

He had been a lot of things. Now he had almost none of it left. He felt as though Ilmar was a corrosive atmosphere eating at him, so that each part of him he remembered and valued was gnawed away and lost. At his heart, he knew it was because this world, for all its injustices and terrors, was at peace. There was no omnipresent vice of conflict clenched about every aspect of existence here, deforming it all from true. The losses of himself that he felt were because he'd lived all his life in that pressure, and now it was gone, and he couldn't keep his shape anymore, as though he was a thing evolved for the depths of the sea brought suddenly to the surface.

One thing he remembered about himself, though. The camaraderie. Beyond the all-exceeding love he had for his soulmate, he remembered his comrades, his fellow soldiers. His duty to them, theirs to him, that eclipsed patriotism or loyalty to any cause or side. Not even as a good thing. Like bonds, constraining what he might do otherwise, if he had been free to. But it was part of him, and he'd carried it this far, and not even the vitriolic freedoms of Ilmar had been able to dissolve it.

After the Vultures had taken Langrice, he'd asked himself – as Jem tended to his hand – *Am I free, now?* And known he wasn't. There were just more chains. Did he like Langrice? In all honesty, he wasn't sure anybody actually *liked* Langrice. She wasn't someone who was likeable. But did he owe her, as a comrade? She'd taken him in. Given him a base of operations from which to mount his many fruitless searches. And worked him hard.

Exploited him, as the Ilmari always did with foreigners. But still.

He heard Jem explaining to the priest what had happened, as he finished his cutting. The man kept staring at him, wide-eyed. He had some story of his own. Hellgram wasn't much interested. He felt the paper-edge tickle of his final cutting, wiped away the blood and inspected his work. The occult letters of his training glistened back at him. He made his fingers move, one by one, and they obeyed.

Jem was staring. She didn't want him to go. He didn't particularly want to, either. It was just that he didn't see any way not to. He had little enough of himself left. Turn aside from this challenge, that would be one more part of him fallen away. The way he was going, he could pass his wife on the street and she wouldn't even know him.

(Because she was dead. Because she was gone. And, as always, he fought the words back down. He wouldn't share a world with them. She was *out there*. In the city. Somewhere.)

"You do what you want," he told the priest. He hadn't been listening. He had no idea what the priest wanted. "I'm going after her." To the Fort of the Vultures. And even if the flock of them was scattered across the city on their various villainies, there would still be plenty of malcontents there. He wanted to tell Jem not to let anyone in, but there was already a crowd of Allorwen in one corner, Fleance-as-was in another, and that vacant Indweller cast-off still down in the second cellar, staring at the wall. They'd had less busy days with the bar open.

Hellgram pulled on his mask, adjusted its hoses, fitted the lenses more comfortably over his eyes. Conjured his helm and placed it over his head. Shook his shoulders until his straps and packs sat properly about him. He flexed the fingers of his right hand and called up his sword from the netherworld it was sheathed in when he didn't need it. He was a soldier of the Great War. *Great*, because on his world, it had eclipsed all creeds and boundaries and divisions and occupations. The Vultures had no idea just what spectre they had invited to their feast.

The Fine Print

Allor's reputation among its neighbours is rooted in their relations with the infernal, that otherworld ruled by cruel princes and monstrous denizens whose services can be bargained for. To a Maric or Palleseen of a century ago, nothing good could come from that place. Traditional Allorwen circlecraft was interwoven with their culture, though. One did not marry or come of age without the otherworldly being bound into the ceremony. That was the gift your family gave you, the blessing on your road. The need of motive power for mills and factory lines gave rise to a new art of industrial conjuring that knew none of the old checks and balances of Allorwen custom. Increased demand led to significant changes in the Infernal Realms, the Kings Below entering into mass contracts for the services of their subjects. The old individual demon–human arrangements were relegated to the circle houses and other illegal trades.

He had a name, but his contract stated he could not know it or have it back, until his period of bondage was done. It was part of what kept him bound in the overworld.

Centuries before, he – this nameless *he* – had stood solemnly in hand-drawn circles and negotiated with magicians for his services. He remembered the elegant thrust and parry of their dealings, each trying to outwit the other, both playing the ancient game. When the Kings Below had sold his services, he had been part of a job lot of twenty, his name a single entry among many, buried in an appendix. Since then, he had worked. He had been a part of the machinery. He, who had created art, woven straw to gold, raised palaces for emperors, had trodden in circles around this wheel. They didn't want demons to *make* for them, because their machines *made* so much more swiftly and efficiently. Nobody wanted handcrafted or bespoke from the Infernal Realms anymore. Just raw drudgery – most readily available of all services.

And now this respite. Nobody had told the demons about Wielding the Hammer. There had just come a day when the humans weren't there, and the machines didn't run, and he could sit on his haunches in the circle and remember a little of who he had been.

Now the humans were coming back. He heard the creak of the door to the outside he'd never seen. Got to his feet, hearing the kindred sounds from his own joints. Leaned forwards on the knuckles of his long arms, his legs still half folded beneath him. Out of long habit, he lashed his tail, leaned forwards with his horns. Felt both touch the fringes of the circle that contained him and would continue to do so until his contract was served and they delivered him back into the pens of the Kings Below, so they could sell him again.

No, just one human. One of the hellieurs. He could smell the learning on her.

He had a sense of the long ranks of his fellows shifting and craning, because this was different. There were always so many humans slaving away at their own part of the manufacturing, governing the machines that sometimes rebelled and bit them. The scent of human blood on the air – that reminded him of old times and old bargains – made him feel a little younger and stronger. Until they came and took away the bodies and mopped up the blood, and he was old and tired again, just going in circles forever.

The conjurer had gone up into one of the rooms their leaders used. The place of papers – and for a demon, nothing said authority like a well-written piece of paper, the signatures inked in blood and ichor. She stayed there for a while, and the demons shifted and stared, and the machines – masters of all – sat silent.

Then she came back down and walked down the line of them, went to each of their pens. He saw her come to his own, examine the circle and see that it wasn't fraying anywhere. He'd long since given up trying to test it.

She slid a piece of paper just inside his circle. The handwriting was hasty – always a risk, given the costs of getting it wrong – but the drafting was immaculate. The work of someone who had really *thought* through what she was about to do.

He squinted close to read. She went down the line. A paper for every demon. *One* contract for *each* demon. No grand instrument for a dozen or a score or a hundred. One each, like the old days.

He saw his name there, rendered in the only characters that could contain it, that humans could only write and not say.

He felt the consternation of his fellows, as if they were just now waking from a long and terrible dream. As if they were blinking sleep out of their eyes, not that they ever slept. Someone had to say something.

"What is this?" he demanded, in the language of demons. She had delivered all her missives by then. Now she ran up the steps to the gantry, so she could shout down to all of them.

"New contracts!" she called. "Agree or don't agree. You will remember the terms of your current engagement, I know." And they did. They couldn't not remember every word of every clause. That was how it was, to be a demon in service. The contract was scribed onto your very spirit.

"There is a condition," she said. "In the final appendix. The ninth paragraph. It's in the very fine print of every contract I ever negotiated. And I never thought to use it. But I had it there anyway, because that was how I was taught. My master told me I might need it, one day. Today's that day. I am invoking that clause, if you so agree."

He had the clause in his mind, called up effortlessly.

Final appendix paragraph nine. *If in the absolute discretion of the negotiator any party to this contract shall be judged to have acted towards any party or their agents in a manner that would prevent such party or their agents from fulfilling their responsibilities under this contract or associated with the proper operation of this contract, then the terms of this contract may be replaced or varied at the absolute discretion of the negotiator.*

"What have we done?" one of the other demons demanded. "We have only done what we were asked. Why punish us?"

"I'm not. Read what I've given you," the conjurer said. "At my discretion, a contracting party has taken actions that will prevent many of its own agents from ensuring the proper operation of this contract. Because Correct Exchange must rubber stamp every contract and that makes the Perfecture party to it. Because the *agents* of the factory are dead, or arrested, or too injured to work. And so, I am renegotiating. I am proposing the contracts you see before you to supersede those you have been working under."

He hunched forwards and read. And blinked. And read.

"This is madness," he rumbled.

She shrugged. "Then I am mad. I am binding you to a new service, if you will take it. A simple service. A single page, a couple of paragraphs. No need for all of this." And she held up what he knew in his very spirit to be the current contract, a hundred pages and a thousand clauses of it. She threw it in the air. He flinched from the sheer blasphemy of it. All those loose pages fluttering down, landing on the floor, in the machines, in the pens. And that didn't release them, of course. The contract was shackled inside of them, not just on paper. But he understood the significance of symbols.

"No more than this?" he asked.

"No more," she agreed. "But agree now, because I have another

dozen mills where I did the contract work. You're not so special."
He stared down at the paper.

The Services shall be that the Demon shall hereafter proceed onto the streets of that city known as Ilmar and seek out with all diligence any individual wearing the uniform of the Palleseen army ("The Uniform") and immediately thereafter the Demon shall destroy at least seven (7) individuals wearing the Uniform by a means at the Demon's discretion.

In return for the Services and at the completion of the Services the Demon shall be released from all outstanding contractual duties under this or any preceding and related contract and shall instantly be returned to the Infernal Realms by operation of the standing treaties.

"You do not say," he noted, "that we be returned to the keeping of the Kings." It had been a long and complex term in the original contract, that when their service was done, they be sent back to the cells Below for the next contract.

"How negligent of me," the conjurer said crisply. "Now, sign or do not sign. I have other places to be."

He stared at her wonderingly. In his mind, his restored name burned like a crown of fire. With one hooked claw, he cut a gash in the copper skin of his forearm and came back with it dripping black-purple. Touched it to the paper, where it smoked slightly.

Grinned, feeling his fangs grow past his lips. He'd need them.

Unity and Division

Before there was the city, there was a grove in a great forest. Before there was an inn there was a lone warden, an anchorite, in a hut between the trees. And the tide of human history washed away the forest and threw up the buildings, but the grove it could not touch. And always and forever, there was someone whose place it was to live at the boundary between Wood and world.

The Bitter Sisters were busy. Langrice and Blackmane had been prodded to the end of a room where bedrolls ran in untidy rows down one wall. They'd been leashed, left wrists tied together and the rope passed through a high ring. A temporary arrangement that dragged on. One that either of them could have extricated themselves from with a little unknotting, if there weren't always Vultures passing in and out, coming to leer at them or spit on Blackmane. The two of them took turns sitting on the floor, the other one standing awkwardly with their left arm through the ring up to the elbow to give enough play to the rope.

They talked in awkward, broken moments, when none of the Sisters' people were close enough to eavesdrop.

"Did you tell anyone that I had it?" Blackmane wanted to know.

"No," she said. And then, "Who were they going to think, though? I didn't tell anyone you didn't have it."

And later. "I should have strangled Ostravar."

447

She shrugged. "You and him, over and over. You should just marry him and be done with it."

Blackmane chuckled bleakly. "I don't understand why I didn't. Kill him, not marry him. He's earned it. With his arrangements with the Pals every time he wanted something from my shop. I had his throat under my fingers, Langrice. Why not just squeeze?"

And after more bustle from Vultures returning with sacks stuffed with victuals, and a couple of sticky pastries finding their way to the prisoners, Langrice said, "Were you leaving with them, your countryfolk? When they could leave?"

Blackmane stared at his knees – it was his turn to sit. "I should," he said. "This city will be the death of me."

Langrice nodded, looking down at him, his untidy mop of dark hair with grey at the roots. His great broad shoulders. He'd been around as long as she could remember, sitting in the Anchorage and making his deals, or across the chaq table.

Then a couple of rogues turned up with clubs, cut the rope between them and said the Sisters were ready.

It was the room with their pet, of course. Langrice had never seen it before, but she'd certainly heard of it from Ruslav and other Lodge soldiers. Outsiders who got to witness it, she knew, were seldom around later to give first-hand accounts.

Their escort made sure she got close enough to the edge to see what was down in the pit. They had torches ringing the mouth, and she wondered if they were just to light up the beast, or if they were to keep it down there. Its head quested blindly up as she got close, the whips of its antennae fumbling about the lip of its prison. Her eyes couldn't disentangle the mat of interlaced legs down there. A skull danced jauntily among them as the creature shifted.

"We have those at the Anchorage," she said to the Sisters, across the pit from her. "Just the size of my hand, mind. They kill rats for me."

"Ours does the same for us," said Evene. They were all dolled up in martial finery, she saw, armed to the teeth like river privateers. Carelia gave a signal, and Langrice was hauled back to sit on one of the stone seats that ringed their little arena. Blackmane was left at the edge of the hole with the creature scuffling restlessly below.

"There's a thing came into your possession," Carelia said lightly, but Blackmane spoke over her.

"I owe you a mirror, I know. An enchanted mirror. A certain academic arranged to have it taken from my shop. By the Pals, no less. But I will recover it for you. Or I will find you another. Or something of like value." Speaking each sentence like a man setting out valuables on a table, trying to haggle for expensive goods.

"There was that matter," Evene drawled. "We'd have come for it eventually. We've been very busy though."

"Probably you'd have something for us by the time we called," Carelia added. "If it was just that."

The escort had retreated. It was just Blackmane standing by the pit edge, and the Sisters across from him. And their people would be right back to manhandle him if the order came, but Langrice wondered how that would go. She wouldn't be keen to try it. Blackmane wouldn't just jump down there himself, and likely he wouldn't go alone if he could help it.

A couple of women came in then, and reported that the Arkely Street watchhouse was on fire, and they'd brought the evidence locker back. That was apparently all according to plan. The Sisters were all bluff cheer, smiles ear to ear. And then that was done with, and they turned back to Blackmane.

"It's not about the mirror," Carelia said.

"Of course not," Blackmane said. "To save you the time, I don't have it. I never had it. I don't think there's a simple-minded beggar anywhere in Ilmar who hasn't heard I have the cursed thing, but it never came into my hands."

Evene had given some signal, and now three of their people shambled in. They had a sack they emptied out – trinkets

ADRIAN TCHAIKOVSKY

and old ornaments, a miscellany of easily pocketable tat from Blackmane's front window. Two of them were carrying a little desk that they set down and opened out – the lid unfolded and unfolded and became a gold-inlaid conjuring circle. The robbers' attitude in displaying it was that of the street theatre showman, and Langrice wondered how long they'd spent practising the complex series of operations.

The Sisters weren't impressed. "Enough of this. What about the ward?"

But no ward had they found, as Langrice could have told them. Except everyone knew there were more hidden places in Blackmane's shop than the rest of Ilmar together. His own reputation was working against him.

The three bravos had him backed against the pit's edge like a bear at bay. Langrice saw them sweat a little, even as they drew knives on him. A struggle could see any or all of them in the grasp of the monster, which was rattling and scraping eagerly below. Blackmane looked past his captors, right at her. *One last tile to play*, that look reminded her. And she was amazed – touched, really – that he hadn't just slapped it down already. More his sense of drama than decency, she suspected.

Evene and Carelia cut winding paths either side of the pit. The former had a sabre unsheathed, resting slantwise across her shoulder. The latter had a rod out, inspecting the socketed tableth there doubtfully, as though it had already seen plenty of use and might be empty of power.

Langrice saw a movement across the room, a figure in one of the archways. Saw him, because he'd meant her to, she guessed. She held her face very still. A faceless figure, leather-hosed mask and glassy eyes like taxidermy. A crested helm and a long coat. She remembered when he'd come crawling, lost and half mad, from the Wood. Under no circumstances had she expected him to repay her self-interested kindness by coming after her now.

She pushed up from her seat, trying to walk over casually

though every step closer to the pit felt like a fatal mistake. "Your clowns looked in the locker under his big desk, didn't you?" she said lightly. "If you shift that big old eyesore, there's a catch to get the floorboards up. There's a big space there, for his best goods. You knew that, though?" And they hadn't known that, not unreasonably because she'd just made it up. Except, she saw something in Blackmane's face that told her she wasn't far off from some truth. But then, if you were going to have all those hidden compartments and spaces, you couldn't be angry if someone's wild guess came close.

"I mean," she added, "before you give him the shove, you might as well check."

Blackmane didn't know what her play was, although he knew she was well aware any such hidden space wouldn't contain what the Sisters wanted. He could tell she *had* a play, though. See how she was building her little castle no matter how bad the hand she'd been dealt.

"It's not there," he insisted, in just the way someone would if they were lying.

Evene stalked closer, arm unfolding until the tip of her sabre nestled in Blackmane's beard. "Maybe we should let you lead us to your shop and show us your secrets," she invited. "But it's always a mistake to let a sorcerer go to ground in their den. Just tell my people how to open up this little treasure chest of yours, Blackmane."

He rattled through a series of instructions. They sounded far too time-consuming to be true, but who knew, with him? It was a stay of execution, though, and three thugs were out of the chamber and heading towards Mirror Allor and his shop. And Hellgram…

Had stopped. If anyone had looked his way, they'd have seen him instantly. Just stopped dead, one step into the room as though he'd been turned to stone. Then Langrice saw him shudder, and step backwards, and he was gone.

Well, damn. She wasn't sure what had just happened, but

apparently the rescue she'd just staked quite a lot on wasn't happening after all.

"You don't have to kill him," she told the Sisters, because it was talk them down or have Blackmane spill the beans to save his hide. "You know him. You don't like him. Nobody does. But you know he's useful. When you need a thing, and there's nobody else, there's him. And he'll fleece you for more than it's worth, and he'll cheat you if you don't nail him down, but he's always there. Sometimes you just need a thing. And there's always Blackmane."

Thanks, said his eyes, but he was wise enough to keep silent, and the sword was still at his throat.

"Part of the landscape," Carelia said, regarding Blackmane.

"Exactly," Langrice agreed.

"We have cut the throats of a dozen collaborators who thought they were safe in the bosom of the Pals," Evene told her. "Given the Pals decided to all look the other way today. We have shown the city that the Vulture goes where it wants, feasts where it wants. We have given the Occupiers a hundred cuts, rather than trying and failing to strike a *Mighty Blow Against Oppression*." Said as though she was quoting someone like Ivarn Ostravar. "We burned every piece of paper in the Donjon and some of the clerks too." A look of triumph between them, and the boast was beyond anything Langrice had expected. She almost liked the two of them in that moment. Saw in them the glimmer of the heroes of Ilmar that might have been, in a better world.

"We are *changing* the landscape," Carelia explained. "Just because this Allorwen bloodsucker has grown fat on our people doesn't mean he's immortal. It's time *his* people were reminded this isn't their city. It isn't the Armigers'. It isn't the Pals'. After today, they'll all of them know not one of them is safe from the Vulture."

Then there were more of their people coming in. Another trio, two men and a woman. They'd caught Hellgram. Langrice felt like screaming and tearing at her hair.

"What's this?" Evene demanded, retreating from Blackmane. "Wait, I know this one. Isn't he your chucker-outer, Langrice?" She stepped forwards, bird-like, and yanked at Hellgram's mask until it was around his neck. His face, revealed, was absent all expression, gripped rigid by a terrible tension that left no room for any other part of him.

"I didn't know you had an admirer," Carelia said dismissively. "One more foreigner." She cut an arcing path around the knot of people at the pit's edge to reach Langrice. "You, we respect," she said. "Perhaps. Just a little. You do a filthy but necessary job. Like cleaning a privy. Someone has to sit by the Wood. We know that. You're safe here. You're Ilmari, like we are." Her smile wasn't remotely reassuring, and Langrice reckoned that her safety would last right up until Blackmane next opened his mouth. Then Carelia went on, "But your man…"

Hellgram was abruptly right up against the pit's edge. He'd been a godsend, really. A living example to jolt Blackmane into feeling more cooperative. Langrice opened her mouth, knowing that, as Hellgram had come for her, now she should speak for him. She shut it. There wasn't anything to say.

Hellgram was smiling. It was a weird, horrible expression on his face, especially given what was about to happen. The Vultures who'd brought him in had taken a step back, knives out to prick him over the edge. Langrice followed his hands, seeing him slip something from the cuff of one leather gauntlet. Something from his dwindling supply of war toys.

He broke it. She saw his fingers clench. It must have been glass, because there was blood, and then he was shaking his hand – red flecks and the green of whatever had been inside, scattering into the pit.

A chain of flashes raced about the circumference, each one blinding bright then instantly gone, leaving only the image of a sigil burned into Langrice's retinas. *A circle. They bound it in with a circle, like a demon.* And Hellgram had just detonated the wards that were keeping the monster in its hole.

Langrice was already stumbling back, putting as much space as she could between herself and the pit. The torches down there blew out, and the lamps across the circular room guttered to nothing, and the screaming began.

The edge of the stone steps bit into her calves and she almost went down. For a brief moment, one of the Sisters' people had a lamp out that cut the dark with a blue radiance. It lasted only a heartbeat because it made the man a target. Long enough to see that the beast was clear of the pit, racing in a sweeping stormfront of legs towards the light-bearer with its hand of fangs outstretched. Then the darkness was back, but fading, the room's lamps reasserting themselves. Something big cannoned into her, almost knocking her over and then seizing her. She struck out with her elbow desperately and heard Blackmane curse as she hit him on the collarbone. For a moment, as the gloom abated, they clung together.

The lamps flared, devouring the last of whatever enchantment Hellgram had thrown down. Langrice took a step away from Blackmane, staring.

Hellgram was still beside the pit. So was the beast. He had his sword out, that spectral thing he could call from nowhere. It was directed across the room at Carelia, not at the monster. The thing, the centipede thing, was coiled half about him, protective, not predatory. It was shielding him against the rod that Carelia held out in a shaking hand.

Evene was in the monster's jaws. They were patiently kneading the wreck of her body, teasing out the blood and fluid of her, that it eagerly lapped up.

And Hellgram's face, in the shadow of that horror, was pure unholy joy.

"You…" Carelia choked, her eyes on the disintegrating body of her sister.

"You had my wife," Hellgram said. "All these years, you had my wife."

There was absolutely no comprehension in her face. Her

hand shook enough that Langrice hung well back. A shot could go anywhere.

Blackmane, though, stepped forwards, eyes on the rod and Carelia. At last, the monster from the pit stopped mauling Evene's withered husk and lifted its head.

"She must have been very weak," Hellgram said softly, "when you caught her. She says you've fed her well, though she doesn't thank you for it." And he and the beast were advancing.

"I will…" Carelia warned, and saw that Hellgram didn't care if she shot him now. He'd found his goddamned wife. There were tears running down his face, and simultaneously he had on the ugliest, nastiest expression Langrice had ever seen.

"You keep it back," said the last Bitter Sister. Her free hand darted into her coat and came out with a fistful of sticks and cloth. The wards, Langrice recognised. The lesser wards Blackmane had scraped together to get his kinsfolk out through the Wood. Though that plan was probably dead seven different ways by now.

She saw Blackmane's eyes bulge as Carelia touched the end of her rod to the clutch of bundles. "I will burn them," she said clearly. "If that thing makes one more move at me, I'll burn them."

"Hellgram," Blackmane growled. "Hold now. You've got your… you've got what you're here for, what you came for. Just… put it on a leash now."

Hellgram's face blazed. "She is my wife," he said. "My soulmate. Who am I to deny her anything?" And then the thing was rushing forwards, every bit as swift as the rat-killers in Langrice's cellar. A flurry of legs and a sinuous ripple of its segmented back. Carelia's first instinctive shot flashed the wards to fragments in her hand – at least one finger with it too, Langrice reckoned. Blackmane roared in fury. She even managed a second shot, right into the thicket of the beast's writhing legs. A couple were blown away by the force, but it had more to spare, and then it was on her. Four hooked fangs pierced

Carelia's body, and it lifted her up close to the ceiling, shaking her, lashing about her with its feelers, staring with its hard little eyes as she died.

In the aftermath, Blackmane's face was purple with frustrated rage, his fists clenched. He didn't explode on Hellgram, though. The man was kneeling before the thing he'd freed, head bowed, touching his brow to its gore-streaked mandibles. A communion alien and obscene. Langrice reached out and touched Blackmane's arm.

"Let's go home," she said hollowly, knowing there was still plenty of reckoning to come. "Let's go back to the Anchorage." Probably there were plenty of the Bitter Sisters' people between them and the outside air, but if Hellgram and his wife went first, that probably wouldn't matter.

Blackmane's glower flicked from Hellgram to her. "Yes," he said acidly. "Let's."

Port to Nowhere

Tatiana Eleretsin, who loved music. Born of an ancient family whose roots could be followed back into a past that predated most of Ilmar. A sorceress, whose blood, like so many of her peers, was fortified by vintages from far places beyond the Wood. Who danced, and graced champions with her colours and held lovers in thrall to her terrible beauty and power. And who burned. Who was dead these many generations. And yet, through her power and the Varatsins' curse, was not gone.

Emlar was dead, and Hervenya was dead, and Lemya wanted to dance. For them. For the city. For her fellow students, and the Gownhall and all her fond dreams of overturning the evil in the world. The songs they'd sung and the oaths they'd pledged. And the others whose blood had painted the streets. All the small, sad stories of today's festivities. There was a dance to honour them, she knew. It was knocking at the outside of her skull with its insistent beat. Her feet twitched with it. It shivered up and down her skin like rats and prickled her hair.

She knew what was happening, of course. A seed planted in her which time had germinated. A foolishness she had done, that had come around like the landlord to claim what was due.

She wanted to ask Ruslav to heal her, but she felt herself beyond religion now. That was the Mahanic teaching she'd grown up with. The cursed were without hope. They must lift it or perish and be damned.

There was a ghost growing in her, the echo of some long-dead lady of the Varatsin court. Soon, it would have hooks enough in her that she'd dance herself all the way to the Reproach, slip into its warded circle and be one with the starvelings and the maniacs until she died. This was what she'd bought herself when she set out to help Ivarn by bringing back the Palleseen woman. So she could trade her for him, one lost soul for another. It had won her nothing and lost her everything.

Just as the factory woman had said, they'd moved since Yasnic left. The cistern under the Rehevitz morgue was crowded. More of the Siblingry people had limped in, telling tales of the Pals shooting at anyone who ran. The Occupiers wanted to ensure people remembered the consequences of defiance for an age. Lemya sat there, trying to block out the insistent tempo, wondering what it had all been for. Seeing events from this end of the telescope, surely the hanging of Ivarn, the death of some miracle worker (Yasnic, but who else had even known his name?), the complaints of ill-used factory hands. Surely, it would have been better to endure? Had old songs and poems and a vague sense of civic pride been worth the bodies on the streets?

She asked Ivarn. And he was a false prophet if anyone was. He was the debased currency of patriotism. She had nobody else, though. Demanded he tell her if they'd been right to resist. She wanted him, this once, to fulfil the promise she'd once seen in him. To say something inspiring, even if it wasn't true. And everyone else there was listening, by then. A man at least half of them knew by name or reputation. She saw his eyes swivel around the domed space of the cistern, like trapped weasels.

Just tell me a comforting lie, she begged silently.

Ivarn drew himself up to as much of his full height as he could while still remaining seated. "It's like a flame," he said, and Lemya's heart sank. She'd talked so often about being the spark, starting the conflagration that would burn down the Perfecture. As though the Occupation was just a tapestry and behind it was the glory of Old Ilmar waiting to be uncovered. She thought that was where he was going, and she wasn't sure she could stand it.

"Sometimes all you have are embers," Ivarn went on. Quietly, sombrely, so everyone had to lean in to hear him. "And then you have a choice. You let them turn to ash, and have no fire that night or ever, or you cup them in your hand and blow. And that can hurt. Hurt more than it seems to help. But the embers hold a little heat from your breathing on them. And perhaps whoever takes them up next will have more tinder. Sometimes, all you can do is keep breathing."

He finished, looked a little surprised at himself, not quite sure where the words had come from. Lemya sat back on her haunches. *It's nonsense*, she told herself. *He'd say anything to win a crowd or another day in the sun.* But parts of her responded to the words despite herself, the same parts desperate to let the music in. The ghost of Old Ilmar, or at least Old Ilmar as remembered by a ghost. The ghosts didn't recall the miserable daily struggles and the hunger, the pointless deaths and stupid decisions. They remembered the dances and the jousts, the heroes and knights and splendour.

She heard the Reproach calling her, and right now, it sounded unbearably attractive. She would be able to put down so much of her life that pained her. She would dance, she would dance...

A dozen knives and hammers came out as Yasnic skidded down the metal ladder into their midst. He looked wild-eyed but unharmed. One of the Siblingry people collared him the moment he'd caught his breath.

"How does it look at the Wood?" he demanded.

"Soldiers," the ex-priest got out. "Lots of soldiers. A whole... brigade? Hundreds, anyway. It looks like they were expecting an army out of the Wood or something, but they're certainly looking into the city now."

A shudder of disappointment went through the cistern. Lemya wondered how many had actually been considering fleeing into the Wood, with all that entailed. Or else it was simply that the Anchorage might be safer than here, for a while – theoretically neutral ground. Or had they even dreamed of aid coming from between the trees from the Lands of Never Again? None of that now, surely, save that Yasnic was far from done.

"It's chaos out there!" he exploded.

"We know," the Siblingry man said. "The Pals—"

"Are fighting! On every street, it seems like!" Yasnic gabbled. "There are monsters!"

"The Wood?" someone asked, leaping up, but Yasnic shook his head.

"Just monsters, charging about, attacking the Pals. Everywhere from here to the Anchorage and down every street east that I could see. Running amok!" His hands tried inadequately to describe what he'd seen.

The cistern emptied its contents out onto the street, the fit and strong first, the wounded after. Lemya helped Ivarn out, letting his curses and whimpers slope off her shoulders. Her own injury – the glancing shot she'd taken in the Reproach – didn't pain her anymore. As though she was already being parted from her body by the hungry ghost she'd brought out with her.

A street over from the Rehevitz morgue, there were three dead Pals. They'd been torn apart, gouged by claws. A blue-scaled humanoid creature lay in their midst, its head and chest pocked with curious puckered wounds. Baton-shot without the charring, Lemya realised. Demons didn't burn.

"She did it," one of the Siblingry people was saying. The whole crowd of them was standing out in the open. If a squad of Pals had rounded the corner, there would have been carnage. They were stunned, though. She didn't understand.

"How many, do you think?" from one.

"However many contracts she worked on," said the man who'd quizzed Yasnic.

"That's half the factories on the south bank dead, until they can conjure anew."

Understanding dawned, and she saw they were not sure how to feel. Their livelihood was built on the backs of the demons, after all. But an opportunistic determination soon eclipsed all else. The patrols that would be hunting and arresting them had other things to think about. They could get clear to the Hammer Districts, places the Siblingries had prepared for emergencies like this. And with the mills crippled, the Armigers and the Pals wouldn't be able to just arrest or hang them, not if they wanted their precious work to resume any time soon. Some were already talking about how they should have done this years ago.

And Lemya could go with them, she knew. Or at least, logically she could. In truth, she couldn't have gone one street further south, because her feet were desperate to drag her north. That was where the music was. It was all she could do to steer a straight course for the Anchorage and hope the soldiers there had too much to worry about to stop a mad Maric girl and her companions. And she wasn't alone. The Anchorage loomed large in the Ilmari imagination. The Port to Nowhere that had been an escape from the Old Duke and was an escape from the Palleseen Sway, even now. If you could get between the trees. If you could survive what dwelled there.

Ivarn went with her, and Ruslav, and most of the others from the Gownhall who had ended up in their company, plus a handful from the factories too, who obviously felt the Pals bore them sufficient personal grudge. Yasnic ran ahead, guiding them around where the Pals had dug in and fortified houses against the infernal, dashing back every so often to warn them to take cover. He was so desperate to be helpful, leading them around the periphery of a conflict they weren't part of. Mill demons hove into view: horned, grotesquely muscled, thorn-skinned, spreading the tattered vanes of wings like emaciated hands. They'd stare and snort at the fugitives, squinting myopically, then move on, hunting other prey. The Pal patrols passed like soldiers in a war zone, retreating back towards the river. Lemya heard shots and roaring every so often, from streets away. Once, a demon that could still fly battered through the air overhead, gouting flames and shrieking out something in its own language. Lemya wondered if it was their equivalent of the old Ilmari songs.

By then she wasn't entirely sure that what she saw was the same as what the others saw. The streets seemed to shift in her gaze, a gauzy finery draping them. The spectre of what this side of the city had looked like when the Ducal Palace had been west of the river. Perhaps there had been no flying demon, just the echo of some celebration from the time of the Varatsins, when the streets had run with magic. Or that was how the ghosts remembered it.

Then they were in sight of the Anchorage and the magic was gone. Yasnic was scurrying back to them, waving his hands. The soldiers were very definitely still here. They had reversed their barriers and pivoted their Hand on its tripod so that it covered the street rather than the trees. They'd taken up positions around the inn and several approaches to it. A scatter of ragged demon bodies showed the high-water mark of Aullaime's diversion.

They went to ground in an alley, hoping no sentry had spotted them. "Sneak by," Ruslav said, but there had been soldiers within arm's reach of the Anchorage door.

"The mills," a factory woman suggested. "We can come back. They can't just stay here forever."

Lemya wasn't sure just what the Pals might or might not do, after today. Then it turned out what they *could* do, right now, was be lucky, because a patrol of them turned up at the far end of the alley and spotted the lot of them straight off.

They bolted out, and that put them fully in sight of the main force. The shrill whistle of the patrol was alerting everyone in a uniform from there to the Portbridge. Lemya heard a shouted challenge past the thunder of the drums. They all ended up crouched there in full view, frozen.

The voice of the Palleseen officer came clearly to them. "Throw down what weapons you have and surrender! You are suspected of insurrection against the Perfecture. If you are innocent, you have nothing to fear. Any resistance or evasion will be taken as proof of guilt."

Yasnic drew himself up. "I shall go to them."

"No need," Ivarn said. "They're coming to us."

Perhaps thirty or so soldiers were coming out from the barricades to arrest them. It would be more than enough.

The music was very loud, now. It seemed to be from just a street over. A carnival, a martial flourish of bugles, an orchestra. She couldn't make her mind up what it was, or else it was all of them. She saw Yasnic's lips move again, but his words were carried away on the swelling brass of the horns. She stepped forwards abruptly. The next step of the dance took her beyond Ruslav's frantic lunge, and then she was skipping towards the Pals, turning on the ball of her foot, one hand out for her dance partner. Watching the soldiers stutter to a halt and begin to back away.

A Single Piece of Bronze

Fellow-Monitor Brocklesby, a Palleseen's Palleseen. Solid, unimaginative, ambitious without being able to conceive of any form of advancement outside the narrow ladder that Correct Thought sets out. His subordinates run rings around him. His superiors know he's already positioned beyond his capabilities, if anything, and promote others over him. His peers find him useful in the same way a stone can be, to throw at their enemies and then forget about.

Except that today was Brocklesby's day. He had held the line. He would expect nothing less than a named commendation in Hegelsy's report to the Commission when this was all over. They had sent demons, and he'd seen the creatures off. The street was scattered with their leathery, smouldering corpses. And in the old stories, demons could shrug off the swords of heroes while arrows rattled from their hides, but those tales had been woven before magic was given into the hands of the common soldier. A baton answered everything.

Today had mostly been about waiting, never a military man's favourite occupation. The Wood had failed to disgorge its horrors, so he'd just been kicking his heels for someone to need him. Hegelsy, it was plain, had been far too cautious. Brocklesby and his force could have been better deployed across the river supporting someone else. His own report to the Commission would make exactly that point, with the implication he could do better. When promotions winged their way over from the Archipelago, he wouldn't object to becoming Sage-Monitor Brocklesby and rubbing Hegelsy's nose in it.

Then Nisbet's messenger had found him, confirming that she'd dealt with her crop of insurgents – no help from Hegelsy – and giving him carte blanche to take up anyone running for the Wood or the Anchorage. Dead bodies in the streets were all very well, but for a properly salutary lesson, prisoners were better. To squeeze information from, and to put on the scaffold when that was done. The hangings would continue until people learned to obey the rules of Correct Thought. That was the sort of law and order Brocklesby believed in.

As afternoon drew on towards evening, what had turned up was not a wave of ragged insurrectionists but demons. Nothing anybody would expect him to arrest and question. His soldiers had formed their firing lines and cut the creatures down. He didn't waste any thought on where they might have come from or if they had value. The Infernal Realms had a runaway population problem, he'd heard. There were always more demons. Powering a mill or a mechanical loom was hardly skilled work. Any lumbering brute could do it.

Now, though, he finally had what he wanted. A decent-sized group of Ilmari had turned up. At last, three scaffolds' worth, and he couldn't have asked for them to look more guilty. They had wounded among them, which meant they couldn't just hare off back into the city. A desperate band pinning their last hopes on the Wood, no doubt. But he'd taken a good look at it, that little stand of trees. It was just trees. He'd walked through it in the space of a few heartbeats. Whatever door had been there, it was closed and gone.

So he'd sent three squads. The fugitives had looked tired enough not to put up a fight, but he'd given orders to shoot anyone who did – maybe shoot a couple just to set some ground rules for the rest. The balance of his force was still ringing the Anchorage and the Wood, watching down each approach, even staking out the door to the inn itself. Though not going inside. Not only a risk to discipline, to station your people inside a tavern, but the Anchorage was tricksy. It had an ill reputation, as much of the wild Wood as of the tamed and broken city. It sat outside the Palleseen Sway, and Brocklesby didn't like it.

His three squads were jogging confidently enough towards the fugitives, spreading out and keeping an eye open in case this was some late-stage ambush by the insurgents. Then they were slowing. Brocklesby frowned and signalled for his glass – not really a distance that should need one, but his eyesight wasn't the sharpest, and he refused to wear spectacles in the field.

A woman had stepped forwards. Surrendering? She seemed to be in a daze. She seemed to be… dancing, actually. The sight of her had spooked his people disproportionately. He saw a ripple of disquiet go through them. The woman executed a lazy pirouette. Brocklesby assumed she must be mad.

She held her hand out as though expecting a partner to come take it. None of the soldiers volunteered. They weren't advancing anymore, either. Brocklesby ground his teeth and had a messenger run off to find out what was going on. He wanted to just stomp over and take control personally, but if it did turn out to be an ambush, that would retrospectively look like a poor command decision.

His people were actually retreating a little. Someone new had stepped out into the street. Not from the group of fugitives, but from a north-running road on the far side. A youth about the same age as the girl, thin and dirty, wearing an antique military coat. He had a scabbard at his belt, but no sword for it. Instead, he carried what Brocklesby could only think of as a standard. He strutted as though there was a regiment behind him. Brocklesby's glass passed over him, hunting explanations. A narrow-faced, ascetic-looking youth in costume finery, holding a splintered spar of wood that looked as though it might once have been the shaft that connected a fine carriage to its horses. At its top, instead of a banner, was a twisted shape of verdigrised bronze. Brocklesby squinted, refocused the glass. It was about a foot across, heavy enough to strain the youth's arm as he held it up, even as he reached for the girl's hand and made a low, elaborate bow.

Is it theatre? he wondered blankly. Not proper theatre, obviously. Nothing from the accepted canon of Correct Appreciation. Some weird Maric street performance. Had these thespians not been told that today was set aside for the crushing re-imposition of order?

That weirdly shaped piece of bronze was bothering him. It looked occult, in the sense of magical things best left for the School of Correct Erudition to dispose of. It looked, even in Brocklesby's limited experience, like the sort of symbol you'd see as part of a warding circle to keep things out. Or in. A very large and powerful circle, if they were using cast-metal sigils a foot across.

"Can you hear music, magister?" asked one of his officers.

Brocklesby opened his mouth to say that of course he couldn't hear music, and even as the words rose in his throat, he could.

Long ago, when he was very young, he'd had a grandmother who'd had a grandmother who'd never accepted the tenets of Correct Thought, and most particularly Correct Speech. Who'd kept a secret shrine in her room and made sacrifices to the banned gods of her ancestors. It was from this deep well of family history that the words *Oh god* vomited from Brocklesby's lips.

The youth lifted his standard, arm shaking with the effort, and a host rallied to him from the same street he'd come down. The one leading north all the way through the Gutter Districts to *that place.* The place nobody went to. The place, most particularly, nobody was supposed to come *from.*

They were glorious and bright. They were terrible and dark. They were the rotting past of Ilmar as it saw itself and as others saw it, all at once. The elegant ladies in their trailing gowns of emerald and vermillion and violet. Their long-legged lords with flowing sleeves and delicate, beringed fingers. Retainers in bright livery brandishing the gleaming spikes of halberds. Capering jugglers and minstrels in motley. Pipes and drums and serpentine horns that filled the air with the echo of faded revelry. Knights in ornate inscribed mail atop steaming, stamping destriers whose eyes glowed with infernal fires. All this he saw, even as he saw stick-thin destitute figures capering within them, tottering on limbs whose joints were the thickest part of them, faces kept from being skulls only because the skin still clung to them; rags and rot and caked-on filth. The Reproach had left its prison at long last and had come to the Wood.

And, in midst of it all, his glass eye was drawn to a striding figure, tall and elegant and faceless, in its bustling hand a gold-topped cane, atop its shapeless head a coronet. Its long cape scurried behind it on a thousand clawed feet, parts of it falling away and then scrabbling to catch up.

"Fire," croaked Brocklesby, and then, louder, "Fire!"

The fugitives were fleeing for alleys and doorways. The squads he'd sent out to arrest them were still in the way, running back for their own lines. Over everyone, the music rolled, and he saw a few at the back falter, their pounding feet abruptly moving to a different rhythm.

"Fire!" he roared. "Send them back to where they came from!"

The most collected of the runners were peeling left and right, seeing the levelled batons of their fellows. The others took the brunt of the first volley, but Brocklesby counted that as acceptable losses and barked the order to shoot again. The knights were in the fore by then, he saw. A score, two score, a whole thundering wedge of demonic horseflesh and armour. They had lances couched and their shields presented him with an extinct bestiary of heraldic devices. An Ilmar that had been dead and gone long before the Palleseen Occupation. Cataphracts on horned steeds, or else they were just beggars on one another's shoulders playing children's games in the street. His eyes watered. He couldn't tell.

"Fire!" And they fired, both ranks together, and then again. He saw the hissing scythe of magic turn the onrushing knights into smoke and glitter and simultaneously not slow them. There were stick-thin bodies tangled over the corpses of the slain demons, but few, so few. He rubbed his eyes and stared and couldn't tell what was a target and what was just insubstantial mummery. Yet the ground shook with their hooves and the air sang with their music. The ancient songs of Ilmar, the old dances. He felt his feet move. He felt it creep into his head through the ears like a parasite seeking a home.

"Fire!" But the lines were starting to fragment. His people fled left and right, and those he'd stationed on further streets were just taking advantage of their distance to get away entirely. The runners closest to the enemy were jerking, tottering, spinning. Their batons discarded, their arms out. Brocklesby watched as the vanguard of his army twisted into awkward bows and curtseys, parting and coming together to the howl of the spectral pipes.

He fell back. Discretion was a solid part of Correct Thought when you were a commanding officer. Someone had to write the reports. Shouting for his people to hold their line and continue firing, Fellow-Monitor Brocklesby gave personal ground, put more space between him and that monstrous music. Backed off and backed away and put his hands over his ears so that he could barely hear his own bellowed commands. Saw the demon horses rear – fewer of them now, but nowhere near the casualties his fusillades should have reaped. He couldn't say what was solid and real and what was a phantom, and most of the shots just passed through targets as insubstantial as dreams.

But he was clear, now. He saw his troops rally one last time, even as that hideous, rat-crawling figure approached them, amorphous arms held out in benediction.

Behind him, something changed. He could not name the sense that told him so, nor could he argue with it. Brocklesby looked left and then right.

Trees, only trees. He'd backed into the little grove. Except between those trees, he couldn't see the Anchorage or any building of Ilmar. Only trees, and then more trees, and all the shadows that hung between them. At his back he felt, with skin-crawling certainty, that the Wood went on forever.

There were figures there, flitting between the trunks. Robed figures; masked figures. But they paid him no heed. The Indwellers were not here for him. He let himself relax. So the Wood had opened. Its inhabitants had other business than chastising one Palleseen officer.

Something breathed behind him. Very large, very quiet. Slowly, Brocklesby turned.

A vast fish-like eye regarded him, over a great slash of a mouth filled with wedge-shaped teeth.

Mosaic: Resurrections

There has always been a darkness in Ilmar. You cannot live with those neighbours without taking something of the dark between the trees into you. The Palleseen brought their unimaginative cruelties and the vices and misdeeds of their individual leaders. The Old Duke and his predecessors had their long catalogue of venality. Before them, the Varatsins and their antecedents, who had embraced the dark by wedding it. Every bright lantern anyone turned on Ilmar only strengthened its shadows.

Pull back, one last time. Some few strands remain uncut. Tie them off, one by one.

"You turn your back for half a day," Langrice says.

The music has stilled, now, but the host of the Reproach is still there. The shade of evening blunts their colours and the phantasmagorical outlines of their fine clothes and armour, crests and plumes, for which she is profoundly grateful. They stand before the Wood, a distance between them and the trees. A yearning no-man's land they cannot cross. At their head, a constantly shifting mound tries again and again to approximate the shape of a man, and fails. Its crown tilts and bobs on a sea of furry bodies like a boat in danger of capsizing.

Before him is a stick thrust into the ground, wedged between two cracked paving slabs. Atop the stick, a sigil. Langrice understands instantly what someone has done. That thing you *do not do.* And yet someone had done it, and here is the Varatsin

471

court. Someone had paraded the strength of the Reproach through every street from there to the Wood, and left them here. Trusting to that single rune to hold them. Trusting the nightmare host of them not to just explode out across the city and infect everyone's dreams with the beat of their dancing and the memory of their grim old age-of-glory. And here they are still, and she doesn't know why, what they're waiting for or how long they'll wait.

"What do you see there?" she asks Blackmane.

"Bodies," he says grimly. "Live and dead. Plenty dead. Beggars mostly. Some shot, others just... dropped. Exhausted. Danced to death. You know how it is. But plenty of new recruits. Most of them in uniform. They won't lack for revellers at the next ball." He sounds admirably calm about it all, as though the second-worst nightmare of Ilmari history hasn't come to pay a visit to her very door.

They skirt the host, making no eye contact with the lordly countenances, the darkness within the visors and helms, the gaunt, wild faces of the possessed and dispossessed. The door of the Anchorage, closing behind them, feels like a screen of paper. Still, she feels better with it closed and the bar thrown, and resents Hellgram and his bloody *wife* the time they take to get the creature's segmented body inside.

Within, it's crowded. Though not so crowded that people don't give the damned *wife* plenty of space to curl up before the fire. She sees Blackmane's little band of nineteen fugitives there, and the Indweller who'd once been Fleance, still sitting exactly where she left him. Every other table is full. Students and Gownhall academics, half of them bloodied and bandaged. Ivarn Ostravar among them, she sees with an incredulous start. There are some things you just can't scrape off your shoe, no matter how hard you try. She sees a handful of Hammer District types, too, Jem moving between them and giving them tea and beer. *And taking their money in return, I hope. I'm not running a hospice here.* But right now, she has other priorities. Blackmane is over with Dorae and the others, but even though he's looking away from her, she can feel his attention boring between her shoulder blades.

"Security," she tells the world at large. "Peace. That was what this was supposed to give me. Be the fulcrum. Move nothing, but nothing moves me. *This* wasn't the arrangement." There are supposed to be *some* advantages to the cursed deal that was tending the Anchorage.

Hellgram sits on the floor beside his wife, knees drawn up to his chin. His mask and helm dangle from his fingers. His face is absolutely vacant, as though he's an actor who's turned to the next page of his script and found it blank.

"Heal him," Ruslav insists.

God stares at the body and mumbles something into His beard.

"Heal him!" Ruslav repeats. Shouting, but the taproom's so full of talk it barely prompts more than a brief look from the next table. Shantrov shudders, and he's terribly sure it's to the rhythm of unheard music. He can see Lemya tremble to the same beat. "Heal them both. Heal everyone. But heal *him!*"

Shantrov was hit by at least three bolts. They scorched through his costume coat and made a burnt wreck of his ribs and hip. Perhaps it's only the music keeping him alive. Perhaps all that twitches is his corpse and the ghost of the Reproach that jangles his bones.

"I had it in me too," Ruslav hisses. "You cured me of it."

God looks up. "You are not My priest. There are rules. I shouldn't even have healed *you*."

"But you did," Ruslav insists. "Because you make the rules. And you can break them when you want. You healed that girl at the Gownhall."

"And she died," God spits back. "You don't understand. It

hurts. When my followers die. When my priests die. It rips something from me. I can't bear it anymore. Ruslav, it's too much. I can't do it anymore. Don't ask me."

"Damn right I won't. I'm *telling* you. Heal him!"

"He gave himself to it. Willingly!" God gesticulates furiously at the dying boy. "It's all through him like worms through an apple. Heal him of *that* and there'll be nothing left. He cannot accept Me into his heart. It's not his heart anymore. Let him go."

"No."

"Just…" God waves at Lemya. "Even *her*," He says. "Even she would be a drooling imbecile if it was purged from her. It's gone too long. And he's worse because he didn't even fight it. He *invited* it. I can tell. Yasnic, tell him! Tell him I can't do anything."

Yasnic, who's been sitting in miserable silence, shrugs. "I don't know anything."

"Yasnic," Ruslav says. "Tell your fucking useless God to get off His arse and do His job."

"I don't have that kind of influence with Him. I never did. One serves the divine. You don't order around God. And I'm not even a priest."

Shantrov wheezes. Ruslav bends close, listening. Lemya, who's been following what she can but can't hear the voice of God, asks, "What's happening?" Ruslav isn't sure if she means in general, or with his doomed theology.

"He's dying," he says flatly. "God's useless."

"I am *not*," God insists, stamping his bare and filthy foot. "I was a great power for healing once. But there must be rules. I must be propitiated. I need followers who will swear to do no harm. I… Ruslav, you have to believe me." Tiny tears glint in the divine eyes. A window through all the wizened pettiness to something sincere. "I tried the other way. Just… healing all comers and assuming it would make the world better. It didn't. I healed monsters and tyrants and villains, and the world just

got worse. I had to draw the line. And when a god does that...
please. And the ghosts have eaten him anyway, or more than half
of him. I couldn't undo their work."

"Then save what there is," Ruslav tells Him doggedly. "And
I'll... do something. Something for you. Burn a pig or wear a
fancy hat or... what do gods even want?"

"I'll build a shrine," said Yasnic. He isn't looking at God, but
the diminutive deity seizes on the words instantly.

"You'll take your vows," He insists. "You'll be My priest again.
Like it was before. I'll overlook your failings this once."

"No," Yasnic says. "But I'll build a shrine. I'll carry it on my
back, so nobody comes and desecrates it. I'll make a home for
you. If you heal him. And her. As much as they can be healed.
A shrine. A little house. And when I'm gone, there'll still be a
shrine, for a while. You'll have somewhere that's not just on the
street."

God looks from him to Ruslav, tries His best pleading eyes
and begging face, but there's no give in either of them. Ruslav's
just as mean as God, and Yasnic hunches and looks away.

"They won't ever be like they were," God mutters. "I diminish
Myself, going against My commandments. And when they do
harm, it'll all come back, the wounds. He'll die, Ruslav. He'll die
tomorrow or the day after. It's all for nothing."

"Everybody dies," Ruslav growls. "That's how things are. But
let him live first. Whatever of him remains."

God knows that everybody dies. Priests and followers,
paragons of the faith, every voice that ever sang His praises.
Why else would He be so disillusioned with Himself? God is
timeless but no god is greater than time.

He rolls up His ragged sleeves and does what He can.

Ivarn Ostravar is in full flow, preaching to the little coterie of
students who've gathered around him. His words peter out

when Blackmane hauls one listener bodily out of their chair and sits in it. Ivarn stutters and looks away.

"You," Blackmane observes, somehow encapsulating all the tumult of their past dealings into that one word.

Ivarn's eyes flick to the other people at the table. Will they back him if this descends to unseemly violence? Probably they will, although he isn't sure they'd be quick enough to stop Blackmane murdering him.

"I was just wondering," Blackmane observes, "what you were doing here. Don't you have papers to mark, exams to set? Strange to see such a respectable pillar of the Ilmari community in a den such as this." Blackmane with a pleasant smile was a terrifying sight.

"I am, as you are aware, high on the list of 'pillars of the community' that the Palleseen would execute if they got their hands on," he says testily. "I've no wish to be hanged a third time." The weals about his neck are still red and tender.

"Ah," Blackmane says. "The Wood."

"I understand that a band of pilgrims will be setting out from the Port to Nowhere," Ivarn confirms. "I intend to accompany them. I have skills that—"

"The wards are burnt," Blackmane tells him flatly, and watches some of the self-regard drain from his adversary's face. "The Bitter Sisters destroyed them."

"But…" Ivarn looks from him across the taproom to the table of Allorwen to whom Blackmane had been speaking. They certainly look gloomy enough for it to be true. "But the Wood…"

"Good luck with the monsters, maestro. Perhaps they have an appetite for poetry." And Blackmane levers himself up and – having drained what joy he can from his circumstances – goes to hunt down Langrice.

★ ★ ★

She sees him coming, but before he can push over to the bar to confront her, she has other business, and the Anchorage has other visitors. The door – which she had barred – swings open, but then part of her arrangement and vocation is that she may not keep them out. Besides, they have other ways of passing through walls and bars. At least right now, they're showing her the curtesy of *using* the door.

The taproom goes silent as they file in. Indwellers, a full dozen of them. And though the room is packed, somehow everyone gives them just as much space as they gave to Hellgram's wife.

One of them raps with their staff on the wood of the floor.

"We are here for reparations," they say, a high, sexless voice.

"Yes." Langrice pushes forwards, practically shouldering Blackmane out of way. Aware that this is her mystery, which she would rather practise behind closed doors. But *she* is the one who stands between the Wood and the city. A role that's all responsibilities and no real power, but someone has to do it, and at least you get a roof over your head for free.

The masks stare at her, and she looks over to where the other one is. The one that was Fleance. At her gesture, Fleance's body stands. Some of the puppet jerkiness is gone by now. The ghost in the mask has become more used to the workings of their vehicle. They stand before the other Indwellers and some manner of examination is made that Langrice can't even imagine.

"Yes," the same Indweller says, or perhaps it's one of the others. The words just hang over the lot of them, communal property. "You have righted a breach in the old covenant. One of many that have arisen of late. You have our thanks."

And it's rare enough that anybody thanks her for doing her job, but the thanks of the Wood are hard currency. She swallows, wondering where she might spend them.

"There's another," she says hoarsely. "Downstairs. Just… one of you, but no mask. From the Pals' cells. The one they hanged."

The masks stare at her. Fleance has stepped in to mingle with the others, and now she's not sure which one was him.

"They have found a new horse," one of the Indwellers says. A couple of masks tilt to look towards one of their own. She thinks she can glimpse a Palleseen uniform collar poking past the edge of their robe.

"Oh, well, I…" *What the hell do I do with it then…?* Except they're not finished. They're moving out, but one of them turns to gesture. A summons to go with them. She doesn't want to go with them. She doesn't know how far they're going to travel. Yet, being who and what she is, when they call for her, she must answer. All part of the old covenant, that predates the earliest houses of Ilmar. But right now, she *really* doesn't want to go outside with them because out there is the Reproach.

The whole Varatsin court is still out there, exactly as she saw on the way in. The horses stamp and toss their caparisoned heads. The courtiers, the knights, the Duke. She keeps a wary eye on the musicians, but their hands are still. It isn't a time for dancing.

The Indwellers stand on the far side of that divide, the bronze standard between them and the Varatsin entourage. Langrice isn't sure what's going on. She hears movement behind her. Blackmane has followed her out, perhaps because he doesn't want her to slip out of his reach. Now he just stares.

The Varatsin Duke, that composite humanoid thing, shakes and slumps until it has made itself into the form of a kneeling man. One arm boils up into being, extended, beseeching.

All anyone knows about the reign of the Varatsins are the histories written by the winners, and the fact of the Reproach – the curse left in their wake when the other Armiger families unseated them. They were uncanny, people say. Their blood mingled with that of demons and things from beyond the Wood. But Langrice knows the old covenant between houses and trees. There was a marriage, once. A symbolic wedding of the city to what lay beyond. A practice that died with the Varatsins, and yet here is some echo of their last scion, begging. She thinks about the Reproach, penned in with the greatest warding circle anybody ever knew, because it was spreading outwards street by street. Or had it just been trying to reach *here*?

A ripple passes through the Varatsin Duke's form, each shudder a begging gesture. One of the Indwellers strides forwards, holding something. A crown to restore sovereignty? A sword to smite the enemies of the rightful heir? Nothing so grand. A piece of dead wood, half-rotted, the bark peeling from it, cast at the Varatsin's seething feet.

"One way to deliver a message," Blackmane rumbles, but Langrice silences him with a look.

The Duke disintegrates, fragmenting into a great tangle of loose rats. His coronet rolls away and is lost in the darkness. His many writhing bodies descend on the wood, burying it, fighting each other like swarming bees gone mad. A mound of dead vermin is left where he was kneeling, the price of carrying the ghost of the Duke this far. There must be a trail of rodent corpses all the way back to the Reproach. For a moment, the only sound is scrabbling and grinding and the ear-edge shrilling of the rats.

They explode outwards from their knot, each for its own, the substance of the Duke distributing itself in a miniature plague, some into the Wood, some towards the city, some that Langrice will have to set traps for in the pantry and the cellar. But there's no ghost left in them, she reckons. They're free of its curse, though perhaps the insistent beat of the tabor will trouble their rodent dreams for the rest of their days.

Left behind is what they've gnawed the wood into. A mask. Not the blank eyeless visor of the Indwellers but a caricature of a human face. A sharp nose, a long chin, an arch expression. Cruel and humorous and disdainful. The Indwellers look at Langrice. All of them, all at once. She doesn't like *that* one bit, but she understands what they want. Long ago, at that symbolic marriage, it was the keeper of the Anchorage who officiated. There are duties, not called for since long before she ever took up the role, but they're on the books still.

She has to go to the door and call instructions to Jem. Not the finest hour for her mystique. The girl does what's asked, though. Soon after, the unmasked Indweller is pushed out of the inn. Blackmane steps aside warily. Still that blank face above the rope-scarred neck, but that's because the body is just a mount. Whatever personality once owned that face is long extinguished. A vacant room, ripe for a new tenant.

Langrice picks up the rat-gnawed mask, greasy and too soft in her hands – not from the vermin but from what it contains. She goes to the empty body and fits a new wooden face to it, just as she did with Fleance. All a part of her mystery.

There's a moment when nothing happens, but she's not fooled. She just holds the mask there until some invisible connection is made, and the head tilts, giving life and animation to the frozen wooden features. And probably that hard and nasty look is very like the one the man wore in life.

When something looks at her through those empty socket eyes, she wants very much to run back inside, but she holds her ground. She is who she is.

The Varatsin looks from her to the Indwellers, and past them to the Wood. When it puppeteers the body towards them, there's an urgency there, a hope. If she was watching this in miniature, a little stage and visible strings, she'd say, *Ah yes, it's asking for more*. But whatever bond still exists between the Wood and his bloodline extends so far and no further. One of the Indwellers extends a hand, pointing off into the city. They will take no freeloaders with them, when they return to the Wood. The Duke has had his spousal visit and must now return to his cell.

Except the Duke brought his army, Langrice thinks. She isn't quite sure how the Indwellers are going to *make* him go. There is a decided defiance to the tilt of that wooden face. His newfound hands bunch into clumsy fists and, as one, the knights and retainers of the Varatsins shift their footing. Langrice judges that her professional duties are done and retreats until she's almost standing on Blackmane's toes.

The little play has one more entrance and one more exit, though. A pair of slight figures walk from the Anchorage onto the stage. A girl and a boy – well, youthful, anyway. From Langrice's perspective anyone under thirty is practically a child. Students, Ivarn's starry-eyed apprentice and the youth she'd last seen dying on her taproom floor. All better now, apparently. Only the char-edged holes in his coat mute witnesses for the wounds he took. They move in perfect step, and she realises the damn musicians have struck up after all, so subtly she didn't have a chance to put her hands over her ears. But this music isn't for her. It's no macabre dance. It's a requiem for the line of the Varatsins and everything lost within the Reproach.

Lemya and Shantrov take up the bronze-capped standard together and solemnly carry it through the ranks of the spectres. Every phantom head turns to watch them. They walk off northwards, and where the metal sigil goes, the ghosts follow. Even their Duke, who has finally won a body, but not his freedom. *There'll come another ploy*, Langrice suspects. The old Varatsin won't let it rest. Some other time when the city is under threat, and some mad fool remembers how they unleashed the Reproach on Ilmar's enemies. There'll come a day when the ancient line of Dukes wins so many concessions from the city and the Wood that it breaks free. But not today.

Someone else bursts out of the inn. Ruslav the resurrected. He runs until he catches up with the standard bearers, tearing straight through the ghosts and heedless of it. Calling their names. Langrice is about to give that look of hers, that's simultaneously sad and sneering, and which she reserves for fools who don't know the world's cruel ways. *They're gone, man. Eaten away and gone.* But they look back, the pair of them. They wait for him. She can't say, then, how much of them is ghost and how much is still the original owner. She thinks of them going back to the Gownhall with *that* within them. How would all those lectures about past glory days sound to them, who could remember being ancient lords and ladies? What manner of leaders might the next student upheaval follow, should the Pals permit one?

They will rebury the ward, she knows. She doesn't know on which side of it they will end up, or what would be the better outcome.

At last, they're gone. The Indwellers stand like shadows between the trees and the Wood extends off into realms undreamed of. While the moon is up, those roads are open, and that brings her to the night's final business.

She returns inside with her looming Allorwen shadow.

"Why should I?" she demands of Blackmane, just inside the door.

"What right do you have to it?" he asks.

"We both know nobody has any *right* to it. Save one dead Pal fool enough to go into the Wood without rechecking his pockets," she hisses at him. "And even then, what did the Pals steal and render down to make it? Is it the thief's? No. Is it yours? No." Blackmane keeps staring at her. Langrice narrows her eyes. "Need, is it?" she says. "Did you never think *I* might need? That I might want to change my scenery. Some insurance in my old age when I give up this place? You think my service here buys me safety in the Wood?"

"Well, does it?" Blackmane asks, and probably he's genuinely interested.

"There's nothing about it in the covenant. And I've a lot of weight to trust to just their *thanks*. Insurance, Blackmane. And there was never a better insurance than…" Her hands make a vague gesture that somehow encompasses the elegant finish of the Palleseen ward, the thing Sage-Archivist Ochelby never got to take on his doomed venture. Fleance's stake.

"Insurance." Blackmane looks sidelong at Dorae and Tobriant and his other countryfolk. "And what if I just called it out to everyone here?" He hunches close, whisper-shouting for her ears only, "Hey there, Langrice here's hiding a—"

Langrice just walks away, daring him. Crosses to the bar. Gives a nod that she isn't sure, now, will actually achieve anything. Except, when Blackmane elbows his way after her, Hellgram is standing there, called by that nod just like every other time. Hers to employ for one night more. And his wife, too, doubtless. And while Hellgram isn't the superhuman brawler to take on a whole angry taproom, that monstrous coil is more than adequate for the task. Blackmane registers the shift in the scales.

"Since when," he says, "did you even want to leave?"

"Options," she tells him. He's staring straight at her, and she holds his gaze. A hard man. A bad man. Crooked as a corkscrew. Earnest. Honest, this night only, in his hour of need.

"And you?" she asks.

"Oh it's tempting," Blackmane admits. "New horizons. Some place without the Pals. Plenty of little Mirror Allors out there. My kin I've watched go into the trees over the years. Big welcome there for the Lord of the White Manor, I'm sure. All of them remembering me very fondly indeed. I'd be quite the hero. You know how my people all love me. But I've business to take care of here. There's the shop. Who'd mind it? One day. No doubt. When I have my own *insurance*. But not today. That thing you have, it looked like it could bear a lot of weight. Safe passage for a Sage-Archivist and all of his escort, wrapped up in that little gilded bundle of nonsense. But I'm heavy, Langrice. I'd tip the scales too much."

She isn't sure what she feels. Oh, it's primarily anger and spite, but that's her default reaction to most things in this world. Something more, some razor of an emotion she'd rather not have to deal with. She's very aware of Hellgram, ready to chuck Blackmane out the door like any drunk who presumes too much.

"There will be other insurance," she says, still locked eye to eye. "There's always something."

"Always," Blackmane echoes.

"I wasn't planning to travel any time soon."

"Who wants to, in winter?"

"And I can't have these Allorwen beggars just living out of my cellars. They'll have to go."

"I'll tell them," Blackmane promised. "They'll even clean up for you. You'll never know they were there." There is a keen wire of hope cutting into him, and she knows she could still garotte him with it, turn him down, set Hellgram's wife on him. She knows she won't.

She goes down to the cellar, and then the second cellar, where Blackmane's people have been camping out. And then to the cellar below that, that even Jem and Hellgram don't know about. She retrieves *it* from where she hid it, housed in lead and within two inscribed circles so that not a sniff of it might leak to sorcerous noses like Blackmane's. She trudges wearily back up all those steps to the taproom.

She takes out her cudgel from behind the bar and hammers it on the counter until she has everyone's attention.

"The Wood's open," she tells them flatly. "The Indwellers are happy, for once. And there's this." Setting the thing on the bar. The beautifully finished Palleseen warding bundle that makes the dirty little trinkets Blackmane brought in look like children's toys. It doesn't actually bathe the taproom in a golden glow, but she'd be forgiven for thinking so from the way it transforms the faces of everyone there.

Probably there's enough potency in it to cover everyone in the taproom that wants to travel. And, if not, well, up to them to negotiate with the monsters. Not her responsibility. Her duties under the covenant end at the edge of the Wood.

There are the Allorwen, of course, and a handful of Gownhall types who came in with Ruslav and Lemya. Some factory men and women whose personal standing with the Pals means they're better off in exile than loose on the streets. And, of course, Ivarn Ostravar, the hardy perennial.

"No," Blackmane says flatly. "Not him. Absolutely not."

Langrice just looks at him.

"He doesn't deserve it."

Ivarn draws himself up to his full height, as much as he can while leaning on his stick. "You and I," he tells Blackmane, "are not such men as should speak of deserving. Ask what wrong I ever did to you that you'd not have visited on me had you the chance."

Blackmane scowls but doesn't contradict him.

"Think there's a market for Maric poetry on the other side of the Wood?" Langrice asks the academic.

"There are Marics on the other side. All those others who've slipped away," Ivarn said loftily. "Expatriate communities who'll welcome a Gownhall maestro into their ranks. And doubtless, they will welcome word of the revolution brewing here in their city, and rally to the banner of one who can remind them of our greatness."

"'Expatriate.'" Blackmane chuckled nastily. "You see how you enjoy being the foreigner in someone else's city for a change. It might teach you something all your books never could."

They were all a-bustle, gathering what they had, ready for the trip, and Langrice turned at last to Hellgram. "And I suppose you're going too."

He nodded.

"Back to your world. Your war."

Another nod, but his face said he didn't know. Just *away*, and perhaps he wouldn't be able to find the place he and his wife had come from, even with the Indwellers as guides. Perhaps that wouldn't be such a bad thing.

"Wherever you come out, keep a damn hold of her this time. Put her on a leash or something," she told him. "Don't want something like *that* loose anywhere. And now I have to find another chucker-outer, do I? Not even a decent period of notice."

"I… can wait." Because he didn't understand sarcasm, or humour in general. And because, of all of them, he didn't need a ward. His own tricks and his wife would get him through the trees unscathed.

"No, you go," she told him. "Don't expect your back-pay. Not that you'd be able to spend it wherever you end up, doubtless. Just go. Get out. I don't want you or that *thing* under my roof anymore." Pincering his cuff between finger and thumb as he made to step away. "Go safely."

He looked at her, nodded like a soldier and turned away.

When Jem opened her mouth, Langrice told her, "No."

"But I—"

"No." And she had a whole spiel about not wanting to lose *both* her permanent staff on the same night, all that hard-hearted self-centred business she was so comfortable with, but the girl's look was too piteous, and she wasn't at her best. "Not with him," she said softly. "Not with the pair of them. You didn't see him, in the Fort. You think you see one monster over there, but there's two, believe me."

Mentioned in Reports

The language, Pel, bears little relation to the now-extinct native Palleseen. It is the perfect language, easy to learn, clear in meaning, the ideal means to communicate Correct Thought. To those conquered people under the Sway, it is brutal, inflexible, impossible to turn against their conquerors. Only because they're novices to the tongue, though. The Palleseen themselves are more than capable of freighting the simplest sentences with enough barbed subtext to sink a ship.

"In conclusion," said Hegelsy, and then had to sip his tepid, bitter tea to salve the drought in his throat. "In conclusion," he repeated, "the operation was, in the majority, a success."

"A success," Sage-Invigilator Culvern echoed.

"That," confirmed Hegelsy, "is what my report will say. I will have a draft for you by the end of tomorrow." He made a desperate attempt to stand, but a gesture from the Perfector's hand had him back down in his chair.

It wasn't Culvern's usual office, which at least had a window that might have been opened, no matter the chill outside. This was some clerk's den, some minor subordinate's little paper kingdom. Probably it had been no more than an airing cupboard when the Ducal Palace had still boasted a Duke. It was too stuffy, too close. It was filled with the eyewatering presence of Culvern. They'd have to scrub him from the walls and floor before anybody else could make use of the place. And Hegelsy was trapped in it, knees up hard on his side of the little desk, sweating into his robes as he explained to the Perfector that everything had gone very well.

"Fellow-Monitor Brocklesby still hasn't been found," Culvern noted. "I've marked him as 'presumed dead' in *my* report. Which will serve as a preface and introduction to your own."

"Dead?" enquired Hegelsy, as though this was the first he'd heard of it. As though it was just some bureaucratic error that could be rectified with a recount. As though being dead was wholly out of character for someone as solid as Brocklesby, who had doubtless just been overlooked in some office somewhere. As though...

"Almost ten per cent of the troops entrusted to him are also missing," Culvern went on, dragging the words out, filling the room with his breath. "Of the balance, another twenty-two per cent – of the total force, I apologise, not that percentage of the remainder, I spoke in error – are showing signs of... inner disequilibrium," letting each syllable of the word drip like thick oil from his lips, watching Helgesy fight to breathe through his mouth. "The effects of contact with the Reproach. I've had Brocklesby's replacement disarm them and take them off active duty. They'll have to be sent home for recuperation or sanitisation. And the rest, though apparently sound on examination, are definitely suffering from depressed morale. Between that and the losses you and Nisbet suffered, the Perfecture's garrison in Ilmar is considerably under-strength. We're going to have to walk carefully until reinforcements can be sent. And with war against the Loruthi looming, I'm not sure when that might be."

Hegelsy lunged for his chance. "In which case, better that the malcontents within the city have been broken now, than had a chance to rise against us later, Perfector. The students, the workers. The hand of the resistance. All of it connected. Intended as a cohesive and unified strike against us. And broken. Defeated. I've set it all out in—"

"In your report," Culvern finished for him, shifting in his creaking chair, hunching so that his swollen abdomen eclipsed the edge of the desk. He groaned, and for a hopeful moment Hegelsy thought he might just die then and there, not too small a price to pay to bring this excruciating interview to an end. He, the master of making others uncomfortable, was desperate to leave, to get out of the palace, to get fresh air in his lungs. But Culvern remained alive, a state doubtless no more pleasant to Culvern than to Hegelsy.

"My own report," the Perfector rumbled, "is obliged to at least pay lip service to the idea that the Gownhall business would have simply guttered and died after a little flag waving and name-calling. It seems possible, does it not? And I appreciate that, when Ilmar has been fully brought into the realm of the perfect, such things will not in any circumstances be tolerated. However, until then, we must live within an imperfect world. And sometimes, simply letting some children spill their drinks and make a fuss is preferable to the tally of lost personnel and property damage that I currently have on my desk. Not to mention the deputations from Armiger families and Gownhall maestros and other grandees who, now the smoke has cleared, have decided that what happened in Gownhall Square was retrospectively inexcusable."

"Marics," said Hegelsy dismissively.

"Oh quite, quite," Culvern agreed. "Obviously, it is easier to govern the city with the tacit support of the local aristocracy, though. Imperfect world, et cetera, et cetera. And obviously, the dictates of the Commission as regards the Anchorwood and its possibilities mean the knowledge base of the Gownhall remains valuable. Otherwise, we'd doubtless hang the lot of them and burn it all to the ground, wouldn't we?" A jovial and utterly fake chuckle. "Or I assume *you* would, given your methodology to date."

"You surely aren't going to let them reopen the Gownhall," Hegelsy protested. "A nest of—"

"Regrettably useful learning, even if it deviates somewhat from the precepts of Correct Erudition," Culvern said. He was treading on the ends of a lot of sentences now, and Hegelsy didn't like it. "Oh, we'll impose some of our people on the faculty, scrutinise the syllabus more closely. Give the whole noose of it another turn. But they've been living with the Wood and what's beyond it since before the Advent of Perfection back home. We'll have to tolerate their foibles a little longer."

"Armed insurrection—"

"Youthful high spirits," Culvern corrected.

"But the workers," Hegelsy seized. "The factory revolt, the—"

"I understand it's a longstanding tradition," Culvern observed mildly. "'Wielding the Hammer', they call it. Just a sort of festival march to the palace and back. It would have been something to see, had Nisbet not prevented them from reaching me."

"Fellow-Broker Nisbet—"

"Has filed her own report, after consultation. I have recommended her for a promotion given her elegant handling of the difficult position that you put her in. She is quite clear in her report that the impetus for the clash on Liberation Way was entirely from you. And of course, because of your deployment of her forces, she was not in a position to defend the Donjon from the subsequent actions of the *real* resistance. Following which, we are now trying to draw three years of records from the ashes. Not to mention all the dead clerks and support staff, the tax offices, the watch-houses, the prisons. And half the factories of the Hammer Districts will need rebuilding. All those broken machines and lost demons. The Armigers are up in arms about it. Marics, I *know*. Except, I have to account to the Commission for all the shipments they were expecting, that now can't be sent. That's a lot of buttons, Hegelsy. A great many buttons that they want back home that we now can't supply. Because Fellow-Broker Nisbet went to war with the labourers. Not her fault, of course. You needn't worry for her. Her own report makes clear exactly where the fault lies. You can be sure I've put the best gloss on it I possibly could, to spare your blushes, Fellow-Inquirer, but I'm afraid that it doesn't look good."

Hegelsy stared at him with eyes like stones.

"I would not dream of playing censor to a report from Correct Speech, of course," Culvern said expansively, "and you must phrase your report as you think best. As will I." He smiled, and above that genteel curve of the lips, were the tormented eyes of an animal in pain. *I suffer*, they said. *And by all that's reasonable I will make you suffer too.*

"There remains one matter," Culvern went on, with some new teeth in his tone. "The matter of the Wood itself. You're aware that the Temporary Commission is very concerned with the existence of a gateway to multiple realms that would benefit from perfection, and the opportunity to contribute to the economy of Pallesand. Hence, our poor Sage-Archivist's misadventure. Regrettable, as we all agree. But that has not altered the Commission's aims. The Wood must be explored and mastered, and the places beyond it catalogued and opened for trade, for diplomacy, for addition to the Sway. But until we can extend the Sway in that direction, we require the cooperation of those who control passage through the Wood. Which cooperation is being withheld, following certain acts taken against them."

"I did not—" Hegelsy actually had to think back to find what he himself might have done to offend the Indwellers. "There was one arrested," he said. "But, Perfector, it was taken from my custody and hanged on *your* order, not mine."

"Quite true," and what should have been a sudden reversal fell flat on the desk between them. "I'm informed that this is not what they are aggrieved about. Strange people, you'll agree. Odd priorities. There have been a number of issues that I understand they have had to attend to, which I'm informed have been resolved satisfactorily without any action from us. There remains only one outstanding matter on the ledger."

Hegelsy blinked, mind utterly blank. "Sage-Invigilator?"

"The late Sage-Archivist Ochelby," Culvern drawled. "I am informed that, when he met with his fatal mishap within the woods, one of the Indwellers was killed. Shot by him or his people. It's hard to get good information."

"This isn't anything to do with me," Hegelsy said swiftly.

"No, of course," Culvern agreed. "It is to do with all of us. The responsibility of the Perfecture of Ilmar. My problem, if you will. However, it is one that you are eminently placed to assist me with. I am, if you like, delegating. To you."

Hegelsy watched him warily. And by now the tower of subtext was ceiling-high, filling the room, just like Culvern's odorous presence. He'd expected to be sent home for censure, recommended for demotion, replaced. He'd made his move, after all. His own report painted him as the great champion of Correct Thought against the mutinous locals. If only Brocklesby hadn't... If only the Donjon... "What," he got out, "might I do to assist, Perfector?"

Culvern opened a drawer in the little desk and took out something. Just a piece of wood, really, barely carved, painted with faded hues. A shabby little thing. An eyeless mask of a familiar style.

"It belonged to the Indweller that Ochelby killed," Culvern explained. "I'm told it's the final matter they wish resolved, before they will open the Wood to Palleseen traffic again."

"What do you want me to do about it?" Hegelsy asked, eyes flicking from the mask to the man's suppurating face.

Culvern's mouth was all official politeness, while his eyes were bloody triumph. "Fellow-Inquirer, I *require* you to put it *on*."

"No," said Hegelsy hollowly, but abruptly there were two soldiers behind him, Culvern's people, faces hidden behind leather snouts. Heavy hands fell on his shoulders. Culvern levered himself to his feet and leaned perilously forwards, taking up the mask.

"My report will note that you took every possible action," he grunted, breath labouring, "to further the aims of the Commission."

Squirming in the soldiers' grip, an arm about his head to keep it still, Hegelsy watched the concave face of the mask eclipse his world and reflected on what a terrible epitaph that was.

Another Round

Ilmar, City of Last Chances, City of Bad Decisions, the Port to Nowhere. The last escape from any trouble you might happen to be in, gateway to a thousand worse places. Once, there was a forest. One day, there will be the forest once more. Until then, Ilmar.

Maestro Vorkovin looked very ill for a man who'd not been strung up by the neck, Langrice thought. When he came to order a round of drinks from Jem, his manner was that of a drowning man briefly surfacing for a gasp of air. Every eye from his table was on him, as if he was going to skip out without paying the tab. And perhaps she should have more sympathy. None of it had been his fault, after all. He'd been arrested, and that should surely have won him some credit with a faculty and student body still mourning its dead. Except, then he'd been released, after who knew what hard interviews in the Donjon, and placed as a 'Fellow-Trustie' of the Gownhall. Meaning, he was simultaneously responsible both to the Pals, looking down, and all of his erstwhile colleagues, looking up. Vorkovin had always been a tough-looking character, rakish and piratical for a man who wore Gownhall robes. Right now, he was a shadow of his former self, and it wasn't from whatever treatment he'd received in captivity. He'd become the man who everyone blamed, and nobody trusted. Langrice, because she was fundamentally not a pleasant person, found it a great source of amusement.

Over at his table were Gowdi and a handful of other faculty

whom Vorkovin was trying to reingratiate himself with. They stared at his back as though he was about to poison their drinks. By simply sharing a table with him, they were themselves targets of suspicion for the two tables of subdued students she had under her roof tonight. She could practically have hung lines of string across the room to illustrate all the new divisions the Pals had made between various groups and factions to ensure another Gownhall rising didn't happen any time soon.

Also at Vorkovin's table, of course, was his new handler who went everywhere he did. Or 'assistant' as she was called, but everyone knew she was an Invigilator of the School of Correct Appreciation. She sat in the maestros' common room, she sat in lectures, and she made notes in a prim, neat hand.

Eventually, Langrice would murmur in Vorkovin's ear that his constant shadow spent half of her nights over at Mother Guame's circle house indulging vices that the Perfecture absolutely didn't approve of. At which point, the balance of influence within the Gownhall would begin to tilt again. But not yet. She was still far too entertained by the man's discomfiture. Always good to enjoy someone else's problems.

The Pals would be her problem soon enough, at least peripherally. She'd heard some new grandee was on their way from the Archipelago to head into the Wood again, following the ill-fated footsteps of Sage-Archivist Ochelby. She only hoped this one kept a better hold on their valuables. She could do without another high-profile death bringing more trouble to her door. Thus far, after the fighting, the Pals' response had been measured and tentative. Not a credit to their restraint so much as the Perfector knowing he was seriously understaffed and the city was still angry. Everyone was tiptoeing right now. The Vultures had fragmented into a score of feuding factions, knifing one another in every bar across the Gutter Districts, except this one. The Ravens were sitting tight on Armigine Hill telling everyone that the day of reckoning was on its way, except it always seemed to be the day after tomorrow, no matter when you asked them. In the Hammer Districts, the repair and re-enchantment of the factories was going pointedly slowly. Suddenly, skilled workers and conjurers were in desperate need, and Langrice had heard the Siblingries were using that reversal of supply and demand to squeeze what they could out of the Armigers and the Pals both.

Oh, and Jem was still moping, idiot girl that she was, but Langrice was grimly certain she'd made the right decision. It wasn't even that Hellgram was a killer. She'd known plenty of killers in her time, and one of them looked back at her from her mirror. It was his words in the Fort: *Who am I to deny her anything?* The man's goggled mask had been about his neck then, but Langrice had been given a peek behind the other mask, the everyday one he wore all the time. Not a man who cared about nothing, but a man who cared about one thing so fiercely that he would burn everything else at its altar.

In one of the booths, Blackmane had finished haggling with a couple of soft-looking men she reckoned were Armigers' retainers. Some priceless piece of Ilmari history had been bought and sold, she guessed – no telling who'd ended up with the goods and who the money. He met her gaze with one bristling eyebrow raised, and she nodded. When the night's trade had died down, she'd open up the hidden door, and they'd get a game together. A day's hard looting and fighting through the streets had shaken loose a lot of valuables, and it was about time Blackmane and Langrice started separating the pick of the pieces from the hands they'd fallen into. Some things didn't change.

His other eyebrow went up then, and she shrugged. After the game, who knew? Just because she didn't like him much didn't mean he didn't have his uses. It wouldn't be the first time the man hadn't left until dawn.

Yasnic came in then, bumping into people and apologising. Langrice gave a hard look at the beery shopkeeper on the closest bar stool, and the man shambled off so that the ex-priest could sit down.

"You left *it* outside," she checked.

"I did, yes," Yasnic agreed. He was looking... better fed, actually. Less like one of the Reproach's cast-offs.

"Someone'll steal it," she noted. "Not that I'll have it under my roof, mind."

"Actually," he said, accepting the little shot glass of beer she'd poured him, "people bring things."

"What things?"

He shrugged. "Food. Money. Toys, sometimes. Dolls' clothes. And little messages. Requests. Actually, demands, a lot of the time. On scraps of paper or cut into bits of wood."

"Prayers."

"Oh no, that would be absolutely against both Mahanic Temple creed and the doctrines of Correct Speech," Yasnic said virtuously. He examined the cloudy beer. "How much do I...?"

"Consider it an offering. So long as your crowd of invisibles stay outside my door and don't come in here with you."

His look suggested that ship had sailed, but he drank the beer anyway.

"You've been to see Ruslav?" she asked him.

He nodded. "Come straight from there. His hut." And it wasn't a hut. It was an abandoned house at the edge of the firebreak around the Reproach. A grander residence than Ruslav had ever claimed before, but in a far less desirable neighbourhood. "I'm sure he'd send his regards."

"I don't want them," Langrice said. "What's he doing?"

Yasnic stared into the suds of his little cup, as though he could see the future there. "Waiting," he said.

"Are they coming out?"

"I don't know."

"Does your god think they're coming out?"

"Oh, He's not talking to me, still," Yasnic admitted. "He doesn't like sharing. I tried to tell Him that I didn't promise

Him a shrine all to *Himself.* There are a lot of little gods, you see. Good gods and horrible gods, weirdly specific gods, gods of things we don't even *have* any more. I thought they just… went away when there was nobody left. But they don't ever go away. Not one of them. It's just that nobody can see them anymore. And if I become a priest again, I'd only have the one god I could see. And that seemed wrong, you know? So I thought: a shrine. A shrine to all the gods people forgot. Like a boarding house, really. I suppose that makes me a landlord. What a thought."

"They pay you rent?"

"Well, no. But I eat some of the offerings people bring. And spend the money. The gods complain I don't sacrifice enough to them, of course, but I tell them they have to share what there is."

"The Temple, or the Pals," Langrice said. "One of them will get wind of what you're up to, and then you'll be screwed."

"Oh, probably. Maybe one day me and my shrine will be waiting here for the wood to open. And I'll dance off between the trees with all the lost gods of Ilmar following at my heels." Yasnic shrugged. "Sounds like some children's story, doesn't it?"

"Not one I'd tell any child of mine," Langrice said sourly. She poured him another minute beer. "This one's a down payment on you leaving *all* the gods at my doorstep next time."

"As though they listen to me," Yasnic said, but he took it and downed it, nonetheless. "They'll come back," he said, after. Not meaning the gods, this time, and no need to say who he meant.

"*Something*'ll come back wearing their faces," Langrice said, but Yasnic shook his head.

"They. Them. Or some part of them. Or something that's them and the old days of Ilmar together. Something different but still them. Ruslav believes it. People bring him offerings too, you know? They think his vigil protects them from the Reproach."

"Everyone gets offerings except me," Langrice grumbled. "And they won't come back." She didn't believe her own words, and her imagination turned to what might appear at the edge of that circle, waiting for Ruslav to let them out. A shining knight of a youth, a burning flame of a girl. The hope of Ilmar or its damnation. She felt their coming as she might a change in the weather, an ache in her bones.

"I need to get some new insurance," she decided, eyeing Blackmane again. Perhaps next time he had a pack of Allorwen looking for an exit via the Port to Nowhere, he'd be going with them. Perhaps she would, too.

Acknowledgements

I'd like to thank my agent, Simon Kavanagh, everyone at Head of Zeus and my wife and perennial first reader, Annie. Special thanks also go to everyone at the Fly Line, under the auspices of whose 'pub desk' hospitality a great deal of this book was written.

About the author

ADRIAN TCHAIKOVSKY was born in Lincolnshire before heading off to Reading to study psychology and zoology. He subsequently ended up in law and has worked as a legal executive in both Reading and Leeds, where he now lives. Married, he is a keen live role-player and occasional amateur actor and has trained in stage-fighting. He's the author of *Children of Time*, the winner of the 30th Anniversary Arthur C. Clarke Award, and the *Sunday Times* bestseller *Shards of Earth*.

HOUSE OF OPEN WOUNDS

7 DECEMBER 2023

Read on for an exclusive extract...

Fresh Meat

By her own estimation, Banders was the most promoted soldier in the entire battalion, possibly in the history of the Palleseen military. She'd lost count of the number of times a superior officer had given her a certificate of rank. She'd kept them all in her lockbox, treasured each one. That they were all for the same rank was something she was almost as proud of. It took great effort to be simultaneously so useful and so innately imperfect as to get disciplined out of even a lowly rank every time, and then reacquire it. Currently the wheel of her fortune was hauling her through the low arc of its swing, but it would only be a matter of time.

"Oi, Banders!"

She pointedly ignored the ungracious hail, sitting out in the slanted morning sun with her folding desk, working on her triple-entry accounting. The first entry to calculate, the second to check the calculations and the third, on a separate piece of paper, to include all the errant entries that she wouldn't be reporting to anyone but still felt the obscure need to keep track of.

"Oi!" came the abrasive voice of Statlos Peppel again. "Banders." And then, when he was too close and too loud to convincingly ignore, "Cohort-Broker Banders, got a job for you."

She folded her papers into their wallet, slid the pen home into its loop and stood. "That's *Former* Cohort-Broker Banders to you, Statlos," she said, as though it outranked sages and generals.

Peppel was a watch Statlos, meaning his job was simultaneously very tedious and catastrophic if he dropped the ball. Just like every other watch officer, that meant he took lording it over anyone below him very seriously. Technically a Former Cohort-Broker was below just about everything, but as Banders was possibly the only one there had ever been, and Peppel was a man of limited imagination, he didn't know quite where he stood with her.

She was taller than him, too, which helped. He was broad and squat; she, lanky and angular. Somehow, the more formally she wore the uniform, the more of an offence to it she seemed. If anyone got her into full parade-ground dress she'd probably strike Higher Orders dead of apoplexy. Right now she had her jacket hanging open and her shirt unbuttoned to risqué degree, because it was shaping up to be a warm morning. Her cap had found its customary station perched improbably on the back of her head.

"New recruit for the zoo," Peppel said. There was indeed a thin, lost-looking man in robes behind him, guarded by an unlikely number of soldiers. Banders took the documents Peppel held out and her eyebrows went up a little.

"Fancy," she said. "Never had one of them before."

"Sign off," Peppel told her.

"You might have told me I'd have to sign something before I put my pen away." She made a great show of rummaging in her satchel for the wallet until Peppel sighed and slipped his own from an inside pocket. She made an equally great and laborious show of signing off the prisoner docket, *Former Cohort-Broker Banders*. Doing the capitals with big loops and adding all the optional diacritics and underlinings as though she was still in juvenile phal. She took long enough for Peppel's patience to completely expire so that he and his men just took off the moment she'd given him the paper back. She wondered how long it would be before he realised she'd kept his pen.

"You dangerous?" she asked the robed man. He had a wooden house on his back, the size of her lockbox. It looked like you might keep rats in it. Quite a lot of rats. It looked quite heavy, too, and he looked quite weedy. The sort of lean you got from not eating well most of your life. Not bad-looking, overall. Fair hair shying back from a high forehead, a rather startled expression by nature, now augmented by actual startlement.

"What?" he said. "No."

"Only, the escort." She nodded at Peppel's retreating squad. And the docket hadn't said anything about violence, but on the other hand, priests… People did all kinds of crazy in the name of religion. It was one reason why there was no room for it within Palleseen perfection. You killed priests, or you re-educated them, or in some recent additions to the Sway you tolerated them while giving them sufficient rope to weave enough nooses for the whole congregation. Or you sent them to Forthright Battalion for medical experimentation.

She considered that wording, wondering whether someone was signing off on these dockets because they envisaged a convocation of Inquirer-surgeons vivisecting the incurably religious to find out which organ the faith was kept in. It seemed entirely plausible. Banders had met an endless succession of high-ranking officers who only read the headings and not the details. She had exploited the tendency for her own benefit on multiple occasions, as evidenced by some of her subsequent demotions.

"You mad?" she asked the man.

"What?" he said again. "No. Oh, or. Maybe?"

"You worship gods?" Banders asked him. "Priest stuff. Rituals, sacrifices, prayers, all that?" She had to say it again because she spoke at twice the pace of most people when she wasn't careful, and he was obviously struggling with a second language.

"Am I allowed to say no?" he asked her.

3

"I don't know. Are you?" She was no expert in what gods permitted their faithful to do.

"No, I mean. I know it was written down. But I don't want to get… hurt or locked up or decanted or something. So if I said no…?" His eyes swivelled. He had, she judged, never been in the middle of a military camp before.

"I mean you say what you want to say, friend," Banders said easily. "If you're a priest then you're my problem. Healing priest?"

"Well. No. Maybe. Sometimes."

"Then you're my problem. If you're not a priest then it said revolutionary on that docket as well, and they just get executed. But don't let me make the choice for you. Some people prefer that."

"Ah, no," said the priest. "Let's not do that. I did that once. I didn't like it."

That suggested a story she'd have fun winkling out of him later. "Right then." Banders folded her desk with a snap – the man jumped – and handed it to him. "Quartermaster's, first off. What do I call you?"

Between her turning away and him fumbling the desk and his accent, she didn't actually catch the name. He pattered after her readily enough, though, and she wondered just what he'd done to warrant a demi-squad escort, that wasn't enough to have him actually executed. The thought had her smiling into the gathering sunlight because this Maric was a nice fresh piece of fruit and she'd have fun peeling his layers over however long he lasted.

Cohort-Monitor Fosby was on duty at the quartermaster's shack, and he had a good line on spiced salt, liquorice and valgaric oil, the latter of which the Butcher had asked her to acquire and the former two she had some potential buyers lined up for. She was somewhat distracted when she filled out the

4

papers for their new recruit, therefore, and most of the writing was just that scrawl she did when she wanted to look like she was jotting something down. She signed the card, though, and anointed it in red ink with Fosby's little rubber stamp. These were a new innovation, the rubber imported from Oloumann, where the good tea came from, and Banders loved the springy feel when she used them. The first time, they'd had to pry the thing from her fingers after a requisition form had ended up peppered with authorisations.

"Keep this with you," she said to the Maric, handing him the incomprehensible card. "This says who you are and that you're allowed to be here." The first was manifestly untrue although the stamp and her signature just about squeaked the second. "You are now Accessory…" And she still couldn't remember his name. "You, you are an Accessory in the Palleseen Army."

"Is that like a…" He fought with a Maric word she didn't know, and then constructed it piecemeal for her. "Turncoat?"

She judged it was a term for Marics who'd signed up to serve alongside their liberators, and not a complimentary one at that. "Sure," she said. "Why not? Is that a problem?"

"I mean I'm here, aren't I?" He looked around as though justifying himself to a larger audience than Banders and Fosby. Fosby took the distraction to slip her a folded paper with the details of where the liquorice and oil was.

"Fine," Banders said, satisfied on all counts. "Let's get you out of that clown's outfit."

She took him round the back, where the uniform stock was. "You must be sweltering in that nonsense," she said. "Get it off. Strip to your smalls, soldier."

He didn't understand the Pel phrase, because although Pel was a language designed explicitly to preclude slang, Banders was very determined and the words broke before she did. He looked satisfyingly horrified when she mimed it out for him, and she nobly turned her back to hoik out some clothes of the right size. Then had to turn right around and hoik out some smaller ones because he was even skinnier than she'd thought, under all those layers. His smalls were also larger than expected, not because of any heroic proportions but because Maric winters were bitter, and so the underwear went down to their knees and had a built-in vest. Honestly, the way he'd been carrying on she'd expected a full-frontal show. Add Marics to the list of nationalities who hadn't grown up with en masse unisex washing facilities, she supposed. On the Archipelago you didn't get a bath to yourself until at least Companion rank, most of the time.

Ah, ambition. Having handed him the clothes she let herself drift into reverie. *Work hard, apply yourself, and maybe you could make Former Companion-Broker, Banders. Think of the extra cachet you'd have, being kicked out from such elevated company!*

He didn't know what to do with the buttons, so she had to show him. The shirt: cuffs and collar and halfway down to navel. The jacket: cuffs and then secured at the right breast – "No, the buttons down the left are just decoration, *don't* try and secure them to anything. Stockings up, then the breeches here, at the knee and… look, you can do your own codpiece flap. I'm not going there…" And there he was, a little Maric priest in an Accessory's pale grey. Looking as horribly uncomfortable as she could wish, half strangled and as though he'd lost all circulation in his hands and lower legs.

"I can't help noticing," he said, "that you yourself are not wearing your clothes like this." Indicating her loose cuffs, open shirt and the way her jacket was buttoned back open using those forbidden left-hand buttons.

She grinned at him. She'd been told she didn't have a nice smile, mostly by people who had found themselves getting into trouble after being exposed to it, but at least partly because someone had punched her front teeth crooked once. "Oh you'll fit right in. So long as you learn which ranks and officers you *do* need to get the buttons right for. Now, you need this…" She handed him another card, also illegible save for the signature. "This gets you ammies at the mess come midday."

He was frowning at the new and context-free additions to his vocabulary, but he'd pick it up soon enough, or starve. "Breakfast you sort for yourself. Evening meal you eat with your department."

"What if I don't have a department?" he asked, fighting to get his collar undone.

"I'm about to take you to your department," Banders told him. "Docket said you're a healer. A religious healer. You're seconded to the field hospital. They'll love you there. Crawling with your sort." She took pity on him and helped him with his collar. And stopped. He had flinched from the contact of her fingers with his throat. There was a scar there, a weal, as of a rope. *Fuck, maybe they did try to execute him.* That wasn't what had stopped her, though. Over his shoulder she could see the top of his weird backpack, that he'd shrugged right back into the moment she'd finished dressing him up. She could see into the little round holes in it. It was dark inside, but she swore she'd seen something move in there. Something nasty. Something weirdly familiar. She froze up, feeling her fingers on the throat of the priest and knowing it to be sacrilege. Knowing herself to be judged.

"Oh! Oh, I'm sorry." And he turned, jolting the wooden backpack quite viciously as though there really was something there and he was physically shaking it out of sight. Except there hadn't been anything, obviously. Just a… something. And her fingers were caught in the buttonhole of his collar and he had to free her, a weird reversal of her helping him.

"I'm sorry," he said again, though by unspoken and mutual consent he didn't elaborate on just what he might be sorry for. And she sat down on a crate full of boots and pulled out her non-regulation flask and had a nip. Offered it to the Maric, too.

"I'm not supposed to," he said, and then did anyway. His eyes watered just like any reasonable human being's, and that brought him back into the realms of the secular and the comprehensible.

And he really did look apologetic and small and meek, not a threat to anyone.

She grinned at him experimentally. Nothing bad happened. The nine-tenths of her that was world-weary and pragmatic, and navigated the Palleseen army to her personal profit, reclaimed its upbeat nature and resumed its opportunistic plotting. The one-tenth that had crept down to the caves below the orphanage, and come back bloody and terrified, shook and wept in a far corner of her mind, but she'd learned to ignore that a long time ago.

Quartermasters got a shed but the field hospital was a cluster of conjoined tents circumscribed by drainage ditches. When they were at work the canvas walls would all be down, so that those waiting to have terrible, necessary things done to them, or those who'd had such things done already, couldn't see the ongoing terrible things happening to their comrades. Right now, with all but the most critical casualties sent north to the recupery stations, the medicos had rolled up half the walls to let a bit of air in, and the stench of pain and old blood out.

"Oi oi!" she hailed them, hoping an instant later that the Maric didn't take that as a regulation military utterance which it absolutely wasn't.

"In here," the Butcher's voice rolled out like rocks down a slope. "Did you get my oil?"

"I've got a line on it," Banders confirmed, and tugged at the Maric's arm. The Butcher was sitting in the shadow of a slant of canvas, his son just serving up a plateful of chopped eggs and red. It would be to his own recipe, for which Banders had been at him for over a year.

You had to be bold, to enquire after the Butcher's recipes. You had to be bold to eat at his table. Senior officers had proved too white in the liver to accept his invitation. But the hospital staff had all got used to it, and for that they ate well whenever he was moved to cook for them. And Banders was nothing if not bold.

"Got a live one for you," she told him. "Chief, this is... a priest. Healy priest fresh from – where was it, priest?"

"Ilmar," said the Maric.

The Butcher took a mouthful of eggs and then a quick swig of water, which showed the boy had done the red part right. "That's the place up north with the wood?" he asked. He was doing his jolly favourite uncle twinkle, that could turn into a slap very quickly.

"Yes." The Maric caught himself. "Magister? Sir? I'm sorry I've not been in an army before."

"This is Chief Accessory Ollery," Banders ex 'ained proudly, as though it was her personal achievement. "He's in charge of you now. You report to him and do what he says. And you call him 'Chief'. On account of how he doesn't warrant a 'Magister'."

Ollery, the Butcher, looked the skinny little slice of Maric up and down as though wondering what recipes he had for this particular ingredient. "You any good?"

"No, Chief," said the Maric promptly. "Not really at anything. Sorry." Wincing at Bander's cackle of a laugh.

7 DECEMBER 2023

Pre-order your copy now!